"I think your brother's the father of my daughter."

At Brooke's mention of Max's identical twin, all traces of his amusement had vanished. He went absolutely still. His sapphire eyes glazed over as if they were shielded by a protective screen.

She'd just told him he was an uncle, and she'd prepared for denial, laughter, questions. She got nothing but piercing silence. For a moment in the fading sun she thought his swarthy skin had paled.

She waited for him to say something. Anything. But he loomed silent and still. Yet, if the throbbing vein at his neck was any indication, beneath the cool exterior he seethed. With rage or disbelief—she couldn't say which, didn't know him well enough to guess. She only knew she had the overwhelming urge to talk fast, explain, spit out the story and her suspicions.

That would be a mistake. Now that she had his full attention, she intended to keep it. At least until he told her what she wanted to know.

ABOUT THE AUTHOR

Susan Kearney likes suspense-packed romance with unforgettable twists. This is her third Intrigue novel, and she was so fond of the hero, Max Braddack, in *Lullaby Deception*, she had to write the compelling story of his identical twin, Ford. Watch for *Sweet Deception*, coming in July.

Books by Susan Kearney

HARLEQUIN INTRIGUE
340—TARA'S CHILD
378—A BABY TO LOVE

Lullaby Deception
Susan Kearney

Harlequin Books

TORONTO • NEW YORK • LONDON
AMSTERDAM • PARIS • SYDNEY • HAMBURG
STOCKHOLM • ATHENS • TOKYO • MILAN
MADRID • WARSAW • BUDAPEST • AUCKLAND

This one is for my husband, Barry—who knows why.

Special thanks to Charlotte, Julie, Judith, Genie and Margaret for getting me through this one. Couldn't have done it without you.

ISBN 0-373-22410-9

LULLABY DECEPTION

Copyright © 1997 by Susan Kearney

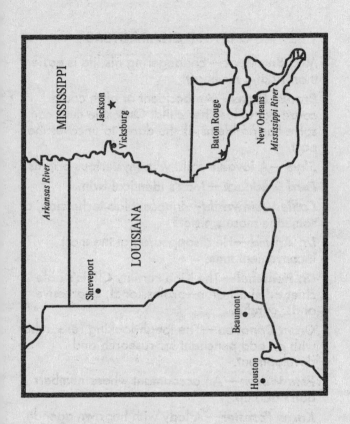

CAST OF CHARACTERS

Max Braddack—Endangering his life is easier than risking his heart.

Brooke Evans—An accident at birth could cause her to lose her child. Only one man can solve her problems, if she dares to uncover the past.

Skye—A lovable child with mysterious origins.

Ford Braddack—Max's identical twin.

Callie Wainwright—Innocent lab technician, or someone more sinister?

Dr. Arnold—He disappeared at the most inconvenient time.

Dr. Henschel—The Kine Fertility Clinic's able chief administrator—professional, aggressive and...careful.

Grant Donovan—The tough-looking researcher with an odd penchant for research and development.

Pete Wilson—An accountant whose numbers don't add up.

Karen Forester—A lady with her own agenda.

Chapter One

The pediatrician returned to the examining room with an anguished look in his usually composed eyes. "Brooke, I need to speak with you in my office."

Not like to, but need *to speak with you.*

At the doctor's soft words, a cool shiver slid down her spine. Something was wrong. Never before had Skye's pediatrician suggested they speak in private.

What could be so terrible that Dr. O'Brian couldn't speak in front of Skye? The thought of losing another family member had panic pounding behind her eyes and at the base of her skull. After Brooke's sister died six years ago, love for Skye had drawn her out of her grief. Now her precious little girl was the last remaining link with family. Any family.

Brooke took a deep breath and glanced at her daughter. In five years, Skye had rarely been sick. The child glowed with health.

The doctor opened the door wider. "Skye can stay with my receptionist while we talk."

Her daughter gazed at Brooke, her cherubic face shining with curiosity. "I want to stay with you."

Brooke stooped until she was at eye level with the little girl and forced casual words through a mouth dry with tension. "It's okay, sweetie."

"Don't let the doctor change your mind," Skye said. Always perceptive, her daughter had clued in on Brooke's anxiety. "You promised I'm going to camp like a big kid. I'm old enough. I'll be starting school soon."

"I'm just going to talk to the doctor about your paperwork," Brooke reassured her.

Skye threw her arms around her neck for a quick hug, and as Brooke scooped her daughter into her arms and carried her from the examining room, she breathed in the scent of shampoo and chocolate chip cookies. She wanted to hang on tight and never let go. Skye was really too old to be carried, but she couldn't resist one all-too-short embrace before setting Skye on her feet. Brooke handed her a book from her purse and steered her daughter toward the receptionist. "Be a good girl. I'll be back in a few minutes."

While Skye settled happily in the front office, Brooke followed Dr. O'Brian down the hall. The minute his office door shut behind her, she spun around on shaky legs. "What's wrong? Is Skye sick?"

"She's a healthy little girl. I'm sorry to have alarmed you, but during my examination, something else came up."

The knotting in her stomach eased but her eyes must have mirrored her confusion. "I don't under—"

"Please, let's sit where we can be more comfortable." Creases of compassion and puzzlement deepened in his weather-lined face.

Brooke had never been in his office with its dark paneling and lush emerald carpet. Instead of seating himself behind his mahogany desk, he led her to a leather sofa.

Her words came out in a rush before she sat. "What is it?"

"Until you brought Skye here for her summer camp physical, I've never typed her blood."

Brooke crossed one leg over the other. She leaned forward, her bouncing foot betraying her nervousness. "And?"

"We triple checked the blood test."

"And?"

"There's no mistake."

"Tell me," she demanded.

"Skye isn't your daughter."

THE SETTING LOUISIANA sun cast shadows through the overhead branches along the dusty road as if taunting Brooke's resolve. The decision she'd made during this past week to search for Skye's biological family hadn't been an easy one. Wrestling with her conscience had taken its toll in restless nights and a tension that had grabbed her stomach and wouldn't let go.

Now that she was close to her destination, Brooke hesitated. Despite the closed windows of her air-conditioned car, a film of dust that tasted of ashes and shattered dreams coated her mouth, stifled her breathing. Perhaps she shouldn't have come to the marina. She could still hang a U-turn, go home to her daughter, mind her own business and forget what she'd learned from her investigations.

Any sensible woman would do just that.

But she had to think of Skye's future first—no matter how much pain it might cause Brooke. Stepping on the gas, she turned down the dilapidated lane overhung with century-old oaks draped with Spanish moss. Doing her best to avoid potholes around a bend, she cornered too fast. The rear tires slid. She braked hard. The car skidded to a halt, launching clouds of dust so thick she was tempted to turn on her windshield wipers.

Instead she waited for the grime to settle in the sultry air, chagrined to discover her clumsy entrance into the boatyard had drawn attention. Standing on a stepladder behind a cigarette boat, a man wearing stained mechanic's coveralls worked on an engine, his arms covered in oil up to his elbows.

The mechanic squinted at her through a haze of swirling dirt. Head up, dark eyes staring arrogantly and broad shoulders squared, he scowled. Her gaze wandered to the broad chest peeking through the open vee of his uniform. Grabbing a rag, he descended the ladder in one graceful leap and approached her car, wiping oil from his hands as he advanced.

Sweat mixed with dust trickled down the sculpted planes of his cheekbones in grimy rivulets. Sapphire eyes framed by jet lashes locked with hers. Hard eyes that saw everything and gave away nothing.

He walked closer, and his inscrutable expression made her think twice about unlocking the car door. Good shoulders, flat stomach, long legs—altogether a chiseled body, albeit ten degrees too dirty for her taste. A five o'clock shadow outlined a broad jaw. As he made a futile attempt to clean his hands, the corded muscles of his tanned neck tensed.

She should have waited until Saturday. The marina would have been busier then. The place was deserted, except for several seagulls cawing overhead. A glance toward the docks showed them as empty of humanity as the patch of dirt used for a parking lot.

She hadn't cut the engine. She could still drive away. But since she'd been unable to reach Ford Braddack, the man she'd learned might be Skye's father, Brooke would settle for speaking to another family member. While Ford was currently unreachable, she'd lucked out when she'd found Max Braddack's address in the phone book. After leaving Skye with a baby-sitter, she'd driven here determined to discover the truth. If she chickened out now, she might not find the courage to come back again. As her sister Nicole used to say, it was too late for should-haves and could-haves.

Still, if it weren't for the challenging smile curling the man's bottom lip, she couldn't have found the nerve to silence the engine and exit the car. Then he was close, too close. She craned her head back to look him in the eye.

Her breath caught in her throat. She couldn't stop her stare. The resemblance hit her with the force of a tornado. This man's coloring, tanned to a deeper hue, mirrored her daughter's. The shape of his eyes, the angle of the brows and the thickness of his lashes were Skye's features staring back at her. Even the way he tilted his head in amusement reminded her of Skye. The only difference was in the color of the eyes, his a deep blue, her daughter's a few shades lighter.

"Sorry about the dust," she said breezily in an effort to hide her nervousness. "I'm looking for Max Braddack."

One oily finger pushed the car door shut, keeping out the dirt, but also preventing a quick escape. "Lady—"

"The name's Brooke Evans."

"You just clogged my carburetor with dust, not to mention what you've done to me, and all you can say is 'sorry'?"

Her stomach danced a quick jig. But sensing no violence in the stranger's Southern drawl and guessing that he simply wanted to toy with her, she raked her gaze from dark, slicked-back hair to the tips of his dingy sneakers. "It's not like you didn't need a shower anyway."

He grinned at her gibe, radiating a confident but easygoing vitality under the last rays of the setting sun. "I clean up just fine, thank you. However, I'll be flushing the dust from that open engine for—"

"You're Max Braddack, aren't you?"

"Why do you want to know?" His smile, which made him look five years younger than her original estimate of thirty-five, took the sting out of his evasive answer.

Her eyes narrowed. "You're Max Braddack? Brother of Ford Braddack—'Wonder Boy of Wall Street'? Can you help me find your brother?"

He folded his arms across his chest and cocked his

head at a wry angle. "I should have guessed you didn't drive out here for a boat mechanic. You know my brother?"

"I've been trying to reach him. His private number's unlisted. His secretary keeps putting me off—she won't even convey a message unless I tell her why I'm calling."

One cavalier brow arched. "So tell her."

"It's personal."

He studied her thoughtfully for a moment. "How personal?"

Very personal. And coming from his lips, "personal" took on the most intimate of meanings. The last thing she wanted was to explain her predicament to this all-too-perceptive man. But he wasn't giving her much choice.

At her first remark about his identical twin, all traces of his amusement had vanished. Was he being protective of his brother? Or perhaps this was a case of sibling rivalry. After all, Ford was wealthy, famous, respected. Max didn't seem any of the above. Yet she didn't sense jealousy from Max but wariness, like a just-fed tiger, not hungry but ever ready to strike. With pulse-skittering certainty, she knew he wouldn't send her to his brother until she'd satisfied his curiosity.

At least he was part of the Braddack family. She took a deep breath, held his gaze and blurted the pent-up secret she'd kept all week.

"I think your brother's the father of my daughter."

He went absolutely still. His sapphire eyes glazed over as if shielded by a protective screen.

She'd just told him he was an uncle, and she'd prepared for denial, laughter, questions. She got nothing but piercing silence. For a moment in the fading sun she thought his swarthy skin had paled, but it must have simply been a trick of the light.

She waited for him to say something. Anything. But he loomed silent and still in the marina parking lot. Yet if the throbbing vein at his neck was any indication, beneath the cool exterior, he seethed. With rage or disbelief—she couldn't say, didn't know him well enough to guess. She only knew she had the overwhelming urge to talk fast, explain, spit out the story and her suspicions.

That would be a mistake. Now that she'd shaken him out of his amusement and had his full attention, she intended to keep it. At least until he told her what she wanted to know.

As coolly as she could manage, she stared back at him, determined to outwait him. A flag flapped in the breeze. Boat riggings clanged as their hulls rocked. The air between them crackled. Her feet itched to take a step back in the Louisiana dirt, but she didn't retreat.

Grudging respect flickered across Max's face and disappeared in a heartbeat. "I'll finish and clean up, then we'll talk."

With an economy of motion, he climbed back to his engine and used an air hose to blow away the dust. He looked so much like her daughter that she wanted to cry. But this past week, alone in her room as she'd thought of losing Skye, she'd cried so many tears, she had none left.

Quick, efficient actions of his hands and the easy grace of his motions as he folded the ladder and stored it with his tools in a shed, drew her from her thoughts. He reappeared from the building with a clean towel, a bar of soap, and a bottle of shampoo. Obviously he intended to bathe—perhaps in the Gulf?

After tossing a towel over a waist-high fence, he pulled his arms out of his coveralls to reveal a broad, tanned chest slick with sweat. As if sensing her gaze on him, he gestured past the shed. Next to the dilapidated building and beside the towel he'd tossed over the fence was a shower, really little more than a hose hooked to a spigot.

"I'm too filthy to rinse at home." He spoke easily as if unaware of her interest in him.

When he peeled the coveralls past his waist, she turned and looked out to sea. He might not give a fig about modesty, but she'd been brought up with more restraint and found his actions unnerving.

"Don't worry." His words carried to her, threaded with laughter. "I'm wearing running shorts."

At his reassurance that he'd maintained his decency, she turned back to catch him striding into the shower behind the waist-high fence. Although the fence hid him from waist to knees, when he kicked off the running shorts, she swallowed hard. As water sluiced down, she studied his calves—muscular, lean, and powerful but in familiar proportions.

"If you see something you like—" his tone mocked her "—you're welcome to share the water."

Heat rose to her face. She *had* been staring. "Sorry." Why did she always seem to be apologizing to this man? "You reminded me of Skye."

Determined to regroup from confronting an adult

male version of her daughter, Brooke strolled to the docks and watched the splendid colors wash across the sky. The sun had set, leaving a trail of lavender and pink clouds hovering under darker thunderheads in the distance.

Had she done the right thing in coming here? The decision had been a difficult one—the most pain-racking of her life. After Dr. O'Brian dropped his bombshell, she'd returned to the Kine Fertility Clinic where Skye's life had begun. Brooke had been unable to discover the identity of Skye's biological parents until a kind research assistant, Karen Forester, had whispered the name Ford Braddack. The nervous researcher had refused to say more at the lab, but the name gave Brooke her starting point. Now that she'd seen Ford's identical twin, she knew she'd found Skye's family. Her scheduled meeting with Karen for tomorrow was unnecessary. Except for one thing. *How* did this happen?

She'd tried to talk to Ford Braddack to find out what he knew. When she couldn't reach him, she'd come here to speak to his brother. She had to be insane, risking the loss of her child to strangers. Yet if Ford and Rhonda Braddack were Skye's genetic parents, and this man Skye's uncle, her daughter had a right to meet them. Didn't she?

With Ford unreachable and Max clearly suspicious, Brooke was glad she'd left Skye with a baby-sitter. Until she was sure of her daughter's welcome, Brooke wouldn't disturb Skye's happy world.

Even now, doubts troubled her. Perhaps Skye would be better off not knowing. But suppose something happened to Brooke? Skye would be totally alone and could find herself in the same foster care system that Brooke and her sister had hated. Fiercely, Brooke strengthened her resolve. Hiding from the truth was not a solution. Besides, Brooke had known the loss of growing up without any family except one sister, and she couldn't deprive her daughter of relatives.

Brooke took a seat on a wooden bench, pulled her feet up and hugged her knees. She'd gone over the same thoughts a thousand times. Each time she came to the same conclusion: Skye had a right to the truth. The right to an extended family.

Once Brooke had made her decision, she hadn't expected contacting Ford Braddack would prove so difficult. Apparently, the man had almost-star status. If to get to Ford she had to go through every member of the family, she'd do so. Ford's parents were next on her list. But she'd prefer to explain the difficult situation only once.

Convincing Max wouldn't be easy. On first acquaintance, Ford's brother had appeared playful, prideful, and imbued with stubborn confidence. So why hadn't he bombarded her with questions?

His seeming disinterest had thrown her off balance, and her thoughts raced. She hadn't expected Ford Braddack's brother to be a mechanic—not that she'd thought much about it beforehand.

Footsteps interrupted her musings. Max joined her on the dock, smelling of soap and shampoo. His dark hair glistened and his lashes were spiked with water droplets. He wore ratty but clean jeans and a sweatshirt with the sleeves cut out. Max hadn't only taken time to clean up and change, his previously casual demeanor had turned more serious. She sensed a tautness in him that hadn't been there before. He offered her a beer—as what, a peace offering? More likely a way to get her to let down her guard.

"No, thanks. I'm driving."

"Suit yourself. After that shower of dust, I'm thirsty."

Leaving plenty of room to avoid rubbing elbows, Max sat next to her, stretched out his long legs and tipped his beer to his mouth. His unreadable eyes stared across the lake. Sensing he wasn't going to start a conversation but would leave that to her, she braced herself for a difficult discussion. "Will you help me talk to Ford?"

"That depends."

"On what?"

"Your story."

Damn, he could be frustrating—just like Skye. Maybe stubbornness ran in the family. She'd learned from newspaper articles that Max and Ford were identical twins, sharing the same genetic makeup. It was likely Skye had inherited those genes. When her daughter made up her mind, it was set in concrete. Orders, cajoling, even outright bribery, failed to change her opinion. Only one thing could do that—a logical argument that had no loopholes.

Resigned to telling him the entire story, Brooke's hands shook with the fresh attack of nerves scrambling through her. She made herself lift her chin. "Skye needed a physical to start summer camp. Last week her pediatrician did a blood test."

"So?"

"She can't be mine." Brooke choked over the words. Held back tears. She would not break down in front of him.

"It's usually the fathers who don't know when a kid is theirs," he said dryly.

"My sister Nicole couldn't have kids, so I donated an egg."

Max stiffened. "Donated an egg?"

"The Kine Fertility Clinic specializes in helping women get pregnant. My egg should have been fertilized in a test tube with my brother-in-law's sperm, then implanted in my sister. At least, that's the way it was supposed to happen."

An odd look crossed Max's face, but then he swigged some beer and hid his thoughts behind downcast lids. When he didn't comment, she forced words past a throat dry as sand. "Two months after my sister bore Skye, Nicole and her husband John died in a car accident. At the time, I was baby-sitting Skye."

"You kept the baby, thinking she was yours?" His face was unreadable and she had no idea what he was thinking.

"I would have kept Skye whether she was Nicole's or mine. She's the only family I have left."

"Now you think Skye is my niece. Why?" His drawl softened to an ominous murmur, a direct contrast to the nonchalance of a moment before.

His lightning mood change confused her, but she tried to ignore it. "After I spoke to Skye's pediatrician, I thought maybe Skye could have been mixed up with another child at City Hospital. But while she wasn't the only delivery that morning, she was the only girl. My sister went home the day after Skye was born.''

"Go on.''

"Once I learned a hospital mix-up was unlikely, I went back to the Kine Clinic. If I'm not Skye's mother, I need to find out who her parents are. I'd also like to learn what the clinic did with the egg I donated.''

"You didn't find any answers, did you?''

She flinched at the skepticism in his tone. In the nightmare she'd been living every day since she'd heard Dr. O'Brian's news, she'd expected to face wariness. But she hadn't thought explaining could be so difficult. He was staring at her intently and she shifted her gaze back to the water. "Dr. Clifford Arnold, my sister's doctor, wasn't available. His secretary refused to give me any information.''

Out of the corner of her eye, she saw him lean back and sip the last of his beer, a thoughtful expression on his face. "Not surprising. The legal implications could force them into bankruptcy. But there is a lot more at stake here than legal ramifications.''

Brooke's throat tightened. She could lose Skye, and she would never have another child, but she had to speak past the lump in her throat. She owed it to the daughter she loved to find her family.

"A researcher...'' She paused, unsure how to tell him the rest. Discovering that Skye wasn't her child had scared her to the bone. She still hadn't recovered from the shock of learning that Skye's father might be an international businessman who could—besides offering a two-parent family—give Skye advantages she couldn't.

Max perused her face, a hint of impatience in his eyes. "What?"

Just say it. She had to tell him. Obviously he wouldn't believe her unless she did. She spoke in a rush. "Karen Forester keeps track of equipment and supplies at the Kine Clinic. She told me about six years ago she had overheard that your brother and sister-in-law's embryo was implanted in my sister."

"What else did she tell you?" He balled his fingers into a fist, belying his casual words. "Did she offer proof? Who was responsible? Did she think the mix-up was an accident or deliberate?"

She should have known he'd leave no statement unchallenged. Brooke sighed. "Karen wouldn't say more. I have an appointment to meet her tomorrow. But whether or not she has proof doesn't matter except to find out how and why the mistake happened."

"And just why are you so sure Skye is Ford's daughter?"

"Because she looks just like you. And you and your brother are identical twins."

"Looks can be deceiving. My brother won't believe he's a father unless the researcher provides us with more information. I hate to get his hopes up. Ford and Rhonda have wanted a child for a long time."

Scientific tests would do the proving for her—but first she had to talk to Ford, find out if he was willing, and what his intentions would be. To do that, she had to go through his stubborn brother. She struggled to keep her tone even. "A genetic test will prove the truth."

"If you're right, then what?" His tone was soft but woven with steel. "Will you give your daughter to my brother?"

"No!" Anger layered over her fear and she stiffened, barely containing her fury. "I have no intention of giving my daughter away. But if Ford and Rhonda *are* her parents, they have a right to know. So does Skye."

He lowered his voice to a menacing whisper. "You want money, don't you?"

Her hand itched to slap his arrogant face. Instead she reiterated her reason in as calm a tone as she could manage. "Skye should know her parents."

All his intensity focused on her. "The thought of the Braddack millions never crossed your mind?"

Although it was likely some people were after Ford for his money, she resented Max's assumption that she was no different. She fought to hold steady under his scowl. "Something very wrong happened at the most prestigious fertility clinic in the country. I want to find out what happened and why. The idea that Skye isn't my daughter is tearing me apart, and I have her best interests in my heart. Why else would I be searching for her genetic parents?"

"For Ford's money."

"Wrong."

Clearly, he didn't believe her. An icy knot coiled in her stomach. How dare he accuse her of ulterior motives when all she cared about was Skye's welfare?

She twisted on the bench to face him, her eyes burning with pride. "I'm here for Skye."

"Sure, lady."

Cut deep by his sarcasm, she refused to bleed in front of him. Taking a quick, sharp breath, she stood, back straight, refusing to crumple at his condemnation. "If your brother knew about his daughter, surely he would want the best for her, wouldn't he?"

SHE HAD A POINT. One he didn't wish to concede until he decided if the indignation in her tone and the fury in her shimmering eyes were due to his insults, or because he'd seen through her plan so quickly.

She was bold, this schemer. Usually women sank their hooks into him before making demands. Especially the pretty ones. Like her. He'd always been a sucker for redheads with attitude, and Brooke Evans had it in spades. From the sassy tilt of her head, he read her ambition while her soft pouty lips suggested greed.

Of course Brooke was the first attractive woman who hadn't thrown herself at him in a coon's age. But then he'd been too busy to notice women much lately. With readying the *Sea Mist* for the race, his socializing had suffered. Now that he'd finally come up for air, she'd stolen the wind right out of his mainsail.

Why did she have to be slender yet curvy in all the right places? Her incredibly long legs encased in blue jeans distracted him as did the ribbed T-shirt that molded her breasts. Round breasts of the variety a man could worship, and right now, they heaved with each furious breath she drew.

As much as she appealed to him on a physical level, Brooke Evans wasn't for him. Even without the complications of her daughter and his brother and wife, there was so much more at stake here than she knew.

He debated his next step, wishing he could dump Brooke Evans in Ford's lap. But even if Ford and Rhonda weren't out of the country on vacation, Max wouldn't go to Ford with Brooke's story without substantiating facts. Ford and Rhonda had wanted a child for too long for him not to consider the ramifications of carelessly divulging such information.

Rhonda had suffered through numerous miscarriages and disappointments. His brother adored his wife and he wouldn't appreciate Max raising Rhonda's hopes that Skye might be their daughter, only later to possibly find out otherwise. Before Max informed Ford of the situation, he needed to check out Brooke's story.

Yet he didn't want to spend much time in her company. Max had a habit of picking the wrong type of woman—a habit he was determined to break. So as the clouds moved in over the marina, casting shadows across the lake's curling crests, he resisted his attraction to the leggy redhead.

"Ford and Rhonda have wanted a child for a very long time," he admitted.

Her eyes flashed. "Then I think it's time you put me in touch with them."

"Not just yet."

The air charged with the electricity of a storm about to break was temperate compared to the bottled pressures inside the woman in front of him. She stood, the wind whipping her T-shirt and hair, her chin angled defiantly. Seemingly too young to be a mother, too scared to be scheming, she revealed a vulnerability that appealed to him on a level he didn't care to acknowledge. Damn!

He had one thing in his favor. She didn't want him, didn't like him. He should be safe from any flirtation on her part. Now if only he could curb his own desires and concentrate on the child.

A Braddack granddaughter. His mother would be ecstatic. She'd gladly cancel all her social engagements to spend time with a grandchild. Dad would enjoy sitting a kid on his lap as he drove his golf cart over the green... But first Max had to make sure little-miss-ambitious-for-her-daughter's-sake wasn't fabricating her story.

"What will you do if my brother decides to take Skye from you?"

"He won't."

Pain laced her words, and yet he couldn't stop himself from wounding her further. "Do you have the kind of money it would take to fight him?"

She swallowed hard. "Not on a secretary's salary."

He suspected she was close to tears, but she stood proudly on the dock, as if courage and determination made her invincible.

Fear wouldn't make her back down, and he didn't understand why. Surely she knew the forces his brother could bring to bear on her, his influence in the judicial system, the clout of the best attorneys. She couldn't be so ignorant that she thought to fight and win.

Was it possible to share a child? Turning off his roiling emotions in what he saw as a painful situation for everyone, Max finally asked the question he couldn't hold back, unsure he wanted to hear her answer. "Suppose you lose your daughter?"

She squared her shoulders, meeting his gaze straight-on and without flinching. "I hope your brother and his wife won't be so heartless. I'm doing what is right. I can't give her two parents. I owe it to her to find out the truth."

"On a mere hope, about people you've never met, you risked your future?"

"Skye's future," she insisted, "is what is most important. To keep father and mother and daughter apart is wrong."

No one could possibly be that selfless. Rhonda was a wonderful, giving woman and Ford worshiped her, but Brooke had no way of knowing that no matter how badly Rhonda wanted a child, she was not the kind of person who would take Skye away from the only mother the child had ever known.

Max looked at Brooke, really looked at her, past the pretty facade to the pouty lips trembling with stress, to the ruler-straight back held so stiffly she seemed ready to snap. And reconsidered. Her spirited eyes flashed with an iron will she appeared to impose over welling panic. Perhaps she was telling the truth.

The thought startled him into testing her resolve. "Go. Leave here. What my brother doesn't know won't hurt him. We'll forget this conversation happened."

While he had no intention of forgetting what she'd

told him, he saw no reason he couldn't do a little investigating on his own. He'd keep his inquiry quiet.

But when every curve in her body blazed defiance, he got the distinct impression she wasn't about to drop her mission. She snapped her fingers. "Just like that you make the decision for your brother, his wife, and my daughter. Just who the hell do you think you are, mister?"

A pushover—with a tendency to allow redheads to wrap him around their little fingers—that's who. A habit he'd hoped he'd broken.

If she was telling the truth, she hadn't deserved what he'd put her through. Guilt pricked at him. On the other hand, he couldn't allow himself to announce the possibility of a Braddack child just yet—not before he did some investigating of his own.

He eased to his feet and towered over her. "I think it's time I met Skye."

Chapter Two

Brooke's eyes widened in outrage. "Why? Why do you want to see her?"

Max took her arm and led her toward her car. The sun had set and as they walked though the dusty boat-yard amid the chirps of crickets and croaks of tree frogs, mosquitos buzzed their heads. But Brooke's re-action to his suggestion was sharper than any mosquito bite.

In spite of the fact she had no reason to trust him, that he'd deliberately goaded her, he'd foolishly hoped she wouldn't hold his skepticism against him. But clearly she didn't want him anywhere near her daughter.

Too damned bad.

"My brother will want to know what Skye looks like, where she lives, how she's been treated—"

Brooke yanked her arm from his grasp and her eyes flared with anger. "Skye's been treated just fine. She's a healthy and happy five-year-old child. I won't let you upset her just to satisfy your curiosity."

When he spoke, he kept his voice flat. "You're the

one who wants to bring her back to her family. But if it will put your mind at ease, I have no intention of discussing her parentage with her.''

Brooke looked deep into his eyes, swallowed hard and nodded, acceding to his request.

As he followed Brooke in his pickup truck southward from Lake Pontchartrain and its massive levees, Max debated what he would say to the child. He was no closer to an answer as he passed through the Vieux Carré, the old French Quarter with its streetfront Creole houses, iron balconies and sizzling nightlife. When he finally left the city and drove past the Superdome, he was glad she lived in the suburbs. He imagined it was a better atmosphere in which to raise a child. Not that he was any expert.

He'd always liked children and had planned to spoil Ford and Rhonda's kids rotten. Unfortunately, the couple had had difficulty conceiving and not even the renowned Kine Fertility Clinic had helped.

Panic gnawed his stomach. He supposed people gradually became used to babies and learned how to talk to them as they grew. The idea of meeting the five-year-old while Brooke watched curiously had him almost squirming in his pickup seat.

Much too soon for his liking, she pulled off the broad avenue into a parking lot. They passed a swimming pool and a playground in a brick apartment complex before he'd begun to set his edgy thoughts in order. He rolled his shoulders to loosen them and, resigned, wiped his sweaty palms on his jeans before exiting his truck.

Get a grip. Skye's just a kid.

But she wasn't just *any* kid. Would Skye look like his mother, Eva? Would she possess his father, Red's, calm determination? Or would she have Rhonda's easy personality?

When he joined Brooke on the sidewalk, she already had keys in her hand. A slight jiggle of the metal revealed he wasn't the only nervous person here. A need to get this over with suddenly overwhelmed him.

As if sensing his unease, she shot him a warning look from eyes clouded with worry. "Remember, Skye knows nothing about this. Don't scare her. Right now I'm the only family she has."

He had the strangest urge to take her into his arms and kiss her—not a passionate kiss, but a gentle show of affection on the forehead to reassure her. The front door flung open, interrupting his thoughts. A little girl in pink overalls flew over the threshold and made a beeline for Brooke.

"Mommy, Mommy. Look what I made."

Max barely glanced at the pot holder in the child's hand or the baby-sitter following close behind. The parking lot lights revealed a dark-haired child with glossy curls framing her rounded face. She looked up at Brooke with deep-set blue eyes the exact same shape as his and Ford's.

Skye was a miniature—an almost exact feminine version—of him and Ford.

Stunned, he rocked back on his heels and stared in marvelous fascination. Her pixieish lips split into a wide grin, revealing gleaming white teeth beneath a button nose. She spoke in animated torrents, her sunny face bursting with pride. "I'll already know how to weave pot holders when I go to camp."

At the sight of her daughter, Brooke's face brightened. "Max, I'd like you to meet my daughter, Skye. Skye, this is Max, a friend of mine."

Skye glanced at him, seeming not the least bit shy. "Hi. Do you know how to make pot holders?"

She certainly was a friendly kid and he was grateful she'd given him an opening. "Think you could teach me?"

Skye looked to her mother. "Can I teach him? Can I?"

Brooke nodded at her daughter, then nailed him with an I-told-you-she-was-a-Braddack expression in her eyes. "Sure, sweetie. Take him inside."

Brooke paid the baby-sitter while Skye took his hand. "Come on. We can make a red and white design. You do like red, don't you? It's my favorite color. Mom says I can take my red sleeping bag and pajamas when I go to camp. 'Course I won't be sleeping over until the special weekend."

Max grinned at Skye's contagious enthusiasm. He could see he needn't have worried about what to say. Skye could chatter on like a magpie, and he wondered who she got that from. Her hand felt tiny in his and surprisingly strong.

As she tugged him into the apartment, she looked up at him with those big blue eyes that branded his heart. It wasn't fair that Ford and Rhonda and his parents had missed watching her grow up. He'd bet she'd been a beautiful baby. While Brooke had taken care of her, the Braddacks had all missed Skye's first tooth, her first word, her first steps. Now more than ever he understood the sacrifice it had taken for Brooke to contact him.

He glanced around the apartment. Although not large, the place was clean and comfortable, consisting of a combination kitchen and den with the bedrooms down a short hall. Evidence of Skye was everywhere. Her crayoned pictures stuck to the refrigerator with cartoon magnets. A child-sized red tent with a matching sleeping bag unrolled inside stood beside the coffee table scattered with children's books, and the couch had a doll propped in a corner.

Skye led him to the kitchen table where a plastic frame with colorful cloth loops awaited. Instead of letting go of him, she turned over his hand and examined it. "Your fingers may be too big for the frame. This may be hard for you. But my mom says we can do hard things if we try."

"Your mom is a smart lady."

He sat next to Skye who busily explained pot holder making as Brooke entered the apartment and puttered around the kitchen. Over the phone hung a framed black-and-white photo of two girls with their arms around one another. In the background was an old Victorian farmhouse with peeling paint on dilapidated shutters.

Brooke must have picked up on his interest as she wiped down the kitchen counter. "That's Nicole and me in front of the foster home where we grew up."

"In New Orleans?"

Brooke shook her head. "We were originally from Baton Rouge, but when the oil business went flat, the family ended up in Bayou Goula. The people who ran the foster home said our parents were there looking for work when they both succumbed to swamp fever.''

"Nobody dies of the swamp sickness anymore," Skye piped in. "They have medicine now."

"So how did you end up in New Orleans?" Max asked, steering the subject away from losing one's parents.

Brooke dried her hands on a towel. "Nicole fell in love with John when she met him at Tulane University. Nicole was the only family I had—"

"Till me," Skye interrupted.

"Yes, till you, sweetie." Brooke ruffled her hair. "And now it's time for bed."

"But, Mom. I haven't finished showing Max how to make the pot holder. You always say I should finish what I start."

Brooke shook her head with a grin. "Nothing like having your own words used against you. You can finish tomorrow. It's bedtime. Say good-night to Max and don't forget to wash your hands and face and brush your teeth. I'll leave the pot holder right here. It'll be waiting for you in the morning."

"But I want Max to have one."

"I could stop by tomorrow," he offered, the words out of his mouth before he stopped to think. The homey atmosphere was more enticing than he'd expected. He liked the easy mother-daughter relationship between Brooke and Skye, the way Brooke valued family—a trait he found in so few people. They clearly cared for one another the same way his family did. When Brooke's head jerked at his suggestion, he wheedled an invitation. "Your mother has an appointment tomorrow. I thought I'd go with her."

"Goodie." Skye slipped off the chair and hugged Brooke. She turned to him next and with an impish grin, blew him a kiss, and skipped off down the hall. "Night-night."

"Don't let the bedbugs bite," he responded with a sheepish grin, drawing on childhood memories long buried.

"You did well with her." Brooke complimented him, clearly aware of his previous nervousness.

"Thanks. She made it easy."

Brooke placed the last plates in the dishwasher, poured soap and set the timer. "After I tuck her in, I'll be right back."

"What time are you leaving for your meeting with Karen Forester?" he asked as she followed Skye down the hall.

"Nine o'clock," she told him over her shoulder.

"I'll see you tomorrow then." He slipped out the door, acknowledging the cowardly action for what it was. She watched him leave, her eyes narrowed in frustration. Tomorrow she'd probably give him hell for his rude behavior. But he couldn't face talking with her about Skye—not until he settled his feelings.

Ah, Skye. The child had captivated him the moment he'd seen her. Her dark, curly hair framed a round face, but it was the shape of her eyes beneath arched brows that made a genetic test superfluous. The girl was pure Braddack, tempered with his sister-in-law's sweetness but with a practicality that had to come from Brooke.

He couldn't deny Brooke had done a terrific job raising Skye. And as a single parent, struggling to make a living, raising a child couldn't be easy.

Skye's presence had spun him for a loop. He drove back to the marina knowing one thing for sure. Skye was going to be welcomed into his family. He hadn't really believed Brooke until he'd seen Skye. Now he felt as if he'd been flattened by a ten-ton truck. He should have been happy, yet heartache awaited both families. To take Skye from Brooke would be cruel. She loved the child and had taken great pride in raising her. His brother and his wife would face unimaginable pain. They could never regain the years they might have had with Skye. And what kind of relationship with their daughter could they hope for in the future?

Back at the garage apartment over the marina's shop, he glanced at the phone. He should probably call Ford, but his brother would want to know who was behind the mix-up at the Kine Clinic and how it could have happened. And Max wouldn't have more information until tomorrow, after he spoke with Karen Forester.

Tomorrow he'd see Brooke and Skye again. As he lay in bed, for the first time in a long time, he was eager for a new day.

BROOKE DIDN'T SLEEP well. She'd tossed and turned after Max's abrupt departure. She'd finally fallen asleep only to have the alarm blast her awake. A few hours of sleep hadn't relieved her anxiety from the night before. Why hadn't Max waited to leave until after she'd put Skye to bed and they'd had a chance to talk? He'd raced out the door as if the apartment had been on fire.

She'd kept glancing at Max and Skye as she'd straightened the kitchen, but she hadn't been able to read him. Had he recognized his own features in Skye? Or had he refused to see the evidence right before his eyes?

The pressure had her on edge, and she hoped he would put her in touch with his brother today. Waiting was nerve-racking. Even if Ford and Rhonda agreed to the genetic test that could prove Skye was their biological daughter, it would take two weeks for the results to come in.

But Brooke didn't need scientific proof. In her heart she knew. Skye was Rhonda and Ford's child, and her throat tightened.

For once, oblivious to Brooke's feelings, Skye ate quickly so she could work on her pot holder. The sitter and Max arrived at the same time and again, Brooke had to wait until she got him alone.

He showed up in a faded shirt and frayed jeans and sauntered through the front door whistling "Dixie." Freshly shaven and with his hair still damp, he had an appealing bright-eyed quality that made her notice him more than she would have liked. "Morning. You ladies ready?"

Skye looked up from the table, saw the baby-sitter, and turned to her mother. "I want to go with you."

"Not this time."

Skye's lower lip trembled. "But you said you would take me on an adventure today."

"How about when we get back, we'll take you on a streetcar ride?" Max suggested.

Brooke didn't appreciate him offering a treat without first clearing the idea privately with her. If she said no, she'd be the bad guy. But she supposed Max didn't know better so she forgave him. Besides, it was difficult to stay angry at a man who was trying to make her daughter happy.

At Max's suggestion, Skye immediately brightened. "Can we go? Please, Mom."

"As long as it doesn't rain. Now give me a kiss and a hug."

While Brooke issued instructions to the baby-sitter, Skye insisted Max help her brush her teeth. He pretended horror Skye brushed after every meal, and she giggled in amusement at his silliness.

Finally Brooke and Max were ready to go. As he opened the door for her and she stepped outside into the crisp morning air, she hoped it would stay sunny. The radio had predicted rain later, but she wouldn't mind a trolley ride herself.

"I'm sorry," Max said as he headed for his truck. "I should have cleared the outing with you first. It won't happen again."

"Thanks."

Damn, he could be charming and intuitive when he wanted, and he looked even better than she remembered. The dark hair framing his piercing blue eyes both unnerved and interested her. But then how could she not find him appealing when she'd fallen in love with his features, Skye's features, years ago?

Still, she wasn't about to allow him to charm her

out of her annoyance with his disappearing act last night. She let him open his truck door for her, then she fastened her seat belt and waited for him to pull out of the parking lot before she asked the questions that burned in her mind.

"Did you call Ford?"

"Not until we talk to Karen. Do you have directions?"

"Karen lives in an apartment in the Old Quarter." She shifted so she could watch him. His body language clearly said he was loose, eager and ready to go. He kept his gaze on the road, checking the rearview mirror every thirty seconds or so. At first appearance he seemed relaxed, but then she noted how he avoided her gaze, and reconsidered. Perhaps he wasn't finding this as easy as she'd thought.

She tempered the sharpness in her tone. "What do you think of Skye?"

"She's inquisitive, intelligent and damned cute."

"And?" she pressed.

He raised a brow. "And she looks just like me. Is that what you wanted to hear?"

No, she wanted to scream at him. That's not what she wanted to hear. She wanted Skye to be hers in every way. But she tried to remain calm and keep her voice even. "Then there's no reason to avoid calling Ford and Rhonda."

"Fine. We'll call after this meeting."

At his sudden capitulation, relief flooded her, but as his words sank in, wariness overtook her once more. "Can't I talk to them in person?"

"Ford and Rhonda are skiing in Switzerland. A phone call will have to do for now."

While she absorbed the surprise that the Braddacks were out of the country, Ford switched on the radio and jazz engulfed them. Fifteen minutes later he parked in front of a three-story building that borrowed from both French and Spanish designs. They walked on uneven pavement through wrought-iron gates into a courtyard with dogwoods, magnolias and azaleas.

"That's Karen's apartment." Brooke pointed. "Number twelve."

Max rapped on the door. A curtain in the window moved. The door opened about three inches and the Kine Clinic researcher, Karen Forester, peeked through the opening left by a latched chain. "I'm sorry, I can't talk to you."

She closed the door in their faces. The latch snicked shut.

Puzzled and frustrated, Brooke spun to look at Max. He furrowed his forehead and shrugged.

Unwilling to give up, she knocked on the door again. "Karen. Karen, it's Brooke. Brooke Evans. We met yesterday. We have an appointment."

The door remained closed. The curtain didn't move.

Karen had been willing to talk to her yesterday. What had happened since then to change her mind?

When no one answered, Brooke's shoulders slumped. Without verbal confirmation, Max might not call his brother. She'd be right back where she'd started.

"Let's get out of here." Max took her elbow and ushered her away. "She's not going to answer."

"I don't understand. Do you think she has a guest?" Brooke asked as they walked back to the truck, disappointed with Karen's refusal and all too aware of Max's fingers on her elbow.

"It's possible. But I think someone got to her."

"What do you mean?"

"This smells like a cover-up."

"I don't understand."

"Someone scared her into keeping her mouth shut."

She jerked up her head. "But how? Why?"

"How is the easy part." Max started the truck and headed to Brooke's place. "She could have been told that if she talked to us, she'd lose her job."

"But no one knew I spoke with her."

"They didn't have to see you. You were at the clinic asking a lot of questions. Word must have got around."

Max stopped in the traffic as the cars waited for an old mule-drawn carriage to clip-clop by. Brooke shook her head at the mule decked in ribbons, flowers and a hat, glad she didn't have to drive. Her head pounded and the sunshine hurt her eyes. "Why would someone threaten Karen with losing her job for talking to us? Isn't that illegal? She could just go to the police."

"Not necessarily. Medical records are confidential. Someone in authority at the clinic would be within their rights to tell her if she talked out of turn, she'd be fired or sued."

"But why did she tell me anything in the first place?"

"Look, the best-case scenario is someone accidentally screwed up in the clinic when Skye was implanted in your sister. The clinic could be sued for millions. If a doctor is found negligent, he could lose his livelihood—not only be sued and fired, he could lose his medical license.''

She sighed. ''We need to talk to Dr. Arnold, but he won't return my calls.''

Max weaved through the heavy traffic with expertise. ''Ford is on the board of directors of the Kine Clinic. His name ought to get us in to see the chief administrator.''

''Ford's on the board of directors? I didn't know. You'd have thought he'd have gotten primo treatment.''

Max frowned. ''Yeah. You'd think so, wouldn't you? There's a phone book by your feet. Look up the number of the clinic, please.''

He used his cell phone to make an appointment with the administrator, turned his pickup around and headed into the city. Driving straight to the Kine Clinic, they had parked and entered the building in less than fifteen minutes. They took the elevator to an upper floor of the facility. A strawberry-blond secretary escorted Brooke and Max around a saltwater aquarium into a corner office with a magnificent view. Glass windows provided a panorama of an elbow of the muddy Mississippi and the Greater New Orleans Bridge.

Dr. Edward Henschel, a short, balding man with a baby-smooth face sat behind a massive desk covered with papers. ''Max. It's good to see you again. What can I do for you?'' He stood and held out his hand. ''Is Ford enjoying his vacation?''

Max introduced Brooke and gestured for her to take the chair beside him. "I haven't heard from Ford. That probably means he's having a great time."

Brooke stared at the framed diplomas over the desk, unable to read specifics from her position. Before she'd always taken for granted the integrity of a physician. Now she realized doctors were people and, just like in any other profession, they sometimes made mistakes.

To find out if an honest mistake or an accident had caused the mix-up would be tricky. When faced with trouble, doctors usually closed ranks, but Karen's whispered words about overhearing a conversation and naming Ford Braddack as Skye's father, indicated that someone might be hiding beneath the Kine Clinic's spotless reputation.

Brooke would have preferred to speak with Dr. Arnold, the physician who had culled her egg for Nicole. He'd always seemed pleasant and professional. She had no wish to malign Dr. Arnold and wondered why he hadn't returned her calls. That he hadn't sent suspicion prickling at her nape.

Dr. Henschel moved a few papers out of the way, adding them to a stack, and then placed his forearms on the desk. "How can I help you?"

Brooke fidgeted in her seat. "I—we were hoping to speak with Dr. Arnold."

"I'm afraid that's going to be difficult."

"Why?" Max asked. "He still works here, doesn't he?"

Dr. Henschel sighed. "He's on his sailboat for a

few weeks. He prefers to take vacation time in late spring.''

Max leaned back in his chair and peered at the doctor. ''Does he have a radio?''

''Oh, yes. But don't get your hopes up. He never turns it on. Arnold says if we could reach him, he'd never have any time off. And he's right. There's always some kind of medical crisis in a facility the size of this one.''

Upset that Dr. Arnold was unreachable, Brooke's thoughts raced. Arnold had been in charge of the fertilization and implantation stages, but there must be records on file.

''Could we look at my sister's file?''

Dr. Henschel focused a genial smile on Max. ''Patient files are confidential.''

She glanced at Max, sprawled in his chair, hands clasped behind his head. He tilted his chair onto its rear legs with an unruffled poise and confidence that surprised her.

She turned to the doctor. ''Six years ago, through the efforts of the Kine Clinic my sister had a baby girl, Skye. I donated the egg. Last week after a blood test, her pediatrician told me the child cannot be mine—nor was she Nicole's.''

Dr. Henschel removed his glasses and pinched the bridge of his nose. ''Dr. Arnold works directly with patients. My talents run toward administration. I'm afraid I can't be much help. Is the child healthy?''

''The point is that Skye's blood proves she couldn't be my daughter or my sister's.''

Dr. Henschel replaced his glasses. "Dr. O'Brian, your pediatrician, called me last week."

While Henschel spoke, Max leaned forward and reached down to tie his shoe. Out of the corner of her eye, she watched him pick up a piece of paper that had missed the trash can. When he straightened, he thrust the paper into his pocket.

Dr. Henschel didn't seem to notice. He continued to speak nonstop. "But with everyone working extra shifts to cover my colleague's patients, I didn't take the call. Since your sister wasn't my patient, I'm unfamiliar with the particulars of her case. I'll check our records, talk to our attorney. Why don't you stop by tonight around seven, and I'll see if I can give you some answers?"

Max nodded appreciatively. "That would be very helpful."

"But why consult an attorney?" Brooke asked impatiently. "Right now, all we want is evidence the mistake was made. My sister is no longer alive. I assure you, I'm only here to learn the truth." It seemed such a simple thing for Dr. Henschel to check the files and give them the information they sought. She had no plans to sue, or even to expose the mistake because of the publicity it would bring on Skye. Max didn't look any more pleased by the delay than she did, yet he seemed to be taking the news more in stride.

"It's our policy—uh…Ford's and the board of directors'—to have our attorney deal with these matters." Henschel's tone indicated he disagreed with this practice, but what was a poor doctor to do except follow the rules?

Max stood. "We understand. Thank you for your help and your time, Doctor. I'll see you this evening."

When Brooke and Max left Dr. Henschel's office, the secretary was nowhere to be found. Frustrated by Dr. Henschel's delay, Brooke gazed with longing at the unattended file cabinets behind the reception desk. They might hold some answers, but with the door still open to Henschel's office, she dared not attempt to peek in his files.

They strode past Dr. Arnold's office. Max looked up and down the empty hall. Then his hand snaked to the doorknob while her heart leapt into her throat. What would happen if someone caught them trying to get into Arnold's office?

Max shook his head. "It's locked."

As he held the elevator door open for her, she didn't know whether she was disappointed or relieved they hadn't stolen inside. The doors swished shut, and simultaneously they pushed the elevator buttons. Max for the lab, Brooke for the ground floor.

"Let's find Arnold's lab assistant and ask a few questions," he suggested, his stance relaxed, but she didn't miss the hint of determination in his eyes.

How did he stay so calm and composed? Perhaps she'd been mistaken about the seething emotion she sensed deep beneath his surface. Her perception might be way off, especially when she was so worried about the possibility of losing Skye.

"What did you take from Henschel's office?" she asked curiously.

Max smoothed the crumpled paper while the elevator descended. "It's a note from the company accountant. He says he needs to talk to Dr. Henschel about overbilling.''

"That could mean the clinic is being overcharged. Perhaps someone is taking kickbacks," she suggested.

"Or it could mean the clinic is overcharging for its services.''

For all of Max's laid-back ways, she couldn't criticize his resourcefulness. She took in the strength of his shoulders and followed the clean lines of his shirt down to his hard flanks. She couldn't help but admire his persistence in looking at every possibility—and the way his clothes fit.

Stop it.

Annoyed by her lapse, she redirected her thoughts from the sensual strut of his walk to the cunning, patience and intelligence he'd displayed during their quest for information. She needed to follow his example and keep her mind on business.

Max stuck the paper into his back pocket. "I'll ask Ford about this when I call him.''

They exited the elevator and approached the brightly lit entrance to the lab. From the locked metal doors barring their entrance, she guessed they had new problems to solve.

A security guard stood in front of the laboratory, his arms crossed over his chest. "This area is off-limits.''

"We just want to speak to Dr. Arnold's assistant.'' Brooke smiled, hoping the man would allow them by. He didn't.

"Sorry. Without permission from Dr. Henschel, no one goes in there.''

Max's hand squeezed her elbow, a silent signal to

let him try. "Could you ask Dr. Arnold's lab assistant to come out here?"

"Sorry. I'm forbidden to go inside."

Max gestured to the phone on the wall. "What about calling?"

"Sorry. That's only for emergencies."

With each refusal, Brooke's annoyance grew. Her blood pressure skyrocketed. As they returned to the elevator, she barely contained her temper.

Once the doors closed, Max chuckled. "Do you think he begins every sentence with 'sorry'?"

His laughter aggravated her exasperation. "This isn't funny. This place is locked up tighter than the Pentagon."

Max faced her and his serene blue eyes drilled her with innocence. "Hey, I'm on your side."

"Then act like it."

"What do you want from me? Would putting my fist through that guard's face have made you feel better?"

"How perceptive of you to notice my annoyance," she snapped, realizing she did indeed wish to goad him into a reaction, although not one so violent.

His forehead creased. "Why are you so angry?"

"When you don't show the same frustration I'm feeling, it seems as if you don't care."

He raked a hand through his hair. "Nothing could be further from the truth. Would you feel better if I cursed, started a fight, got myself arrested?"

She almost smiled at the image. Yesterday, in the boatyard, she'd have believed him capable of violence, but now she was thankful for his self-control.

Still, she refused to allow his statement to go un-challenged. "There's detachment in your calmness."

"It works for me," he admitted. "If I acted other-wise to make you happy, I'd be living a lie." The doors opened and he switched topics. "Why don't we try the research department?"

"I shouldn't have taken out my frustration on you, but we've wasted half the morning and haven't found anything useful. I want to know how this happened. And I want to know what became of the egg I donated to my sister."

Max winked. "Patience."

She wanted to choke him. "Something obviously went wrong in this clinic."

"Agreed." He shoved his hands into his pockets. "And somehow I don't see the clinic's attorney giving us information. Whatever happened took place six years ago. There's been plenty of time for someone to cover their tracks. All documentation would have been destroyed long ago."

Brooke moved past him and through a door into a fifth-floor windowless office. A brass plate on the door told them the researcher's name. Grant Donovan had the build of an NFL linebacker and his huge frame looked ridiculous cramped behind a desk. His meaty fingers lumbered over the keyboard, his face fixed in concentration.

"Excuse us," Brooke interrupted. "We thought you might help us solve a problem."

"Problem-solving isn't exactly my department." He'd stopped typing and looked up, his lips twisted in a parody of a smile.

"Look, all we want to know is how the Kine Clinic mistakenly placed his brother's embryo," she pointed to Max, "in my sister. We know from the blood tests someone in the clinic made a mistake. We want to see the records."

Grant shrugged and returned to his typing. "Sorry, lady, I can't help you."

"I want to know what happened to my egg," Brooke insisted, hoping a different tack might sway the man.

Grant cracked his knuckles. "Look, I'd like to help you, but I could lose my job."

Brooke didn't blame the man. Still her thoughts whirled in frustration as she and Max exited the office and, finally, the facility. "We aren't getting anywhere," Brooke complained as they made their way to the pickup. "Surely there must be a record of Rhonda and Ford's blood type somewhere?"

"Since we're identical twins, Ford's blood is exactly the same as mine."

"Then there's no need to return to the lab. If you'll consent to a tissue scraping of the inside of your cheek, a genetic test will prove within a week or two whether Skye is Ford's daughter."

"After seeing Skye, I'm convinced she's a Braddack," he said, opening her door. "Do you think the mix-up could have been deliberate?"

The idea worried her. "I can't help wondering how a distinguished institution, renowned for ethical and compassionate treatment of fertility problems, could treat us as if they are a fly-by-night facility."

"We should consider all the possibilities. What

would be the motive? Tonight if we get a chance to look around, maybe we'll pick up a few clues. If there are records to be found, no lawyer worth his pay will let us within a hundred miles of them.''

Her stomach lurched. The idea of skulking around in the dark had her nerves jumping. "But suppose we're caught?''

He winked at her. "We'll tell them Ford gave us permission.''

Chapter Three

The afternoon rain held off while Max treated Skye and Brooke to the hour and a half trolley ride down St. Charles Avenue. After they boarded on Canal Street, Skye sat happily by the open window in the seat in front of the one Max and Brooke shared.

Max was good with Skye, Brooke thought. She bit back a smile at the memory of him helping Skye brush her teeth that morning. He hadn't complained at the delay.

When they'd returned to her apartment, Max had even tried to call Ford. But he hadn't been in his room. She still hoped Ford would use his influence to get the records. But until Max talked to him, that's all it was—hope.

As they rode along St. Charles past a statue on a white granite pedestal in Lafayette Square and Galier Hall's Greek Revival architecture across the street, Brooke's thoughts veered again from the familiar New Orleans' landscape to more pressing problems. Max's suggestion about a deliberate act of sabotage at the Kine Clinic unnerved her. Why would anyone do something so cruel? She wasn't out to make millions in a lawsuit, but she certainly didn't want this to happen to anyone else. And for her own peace of mind, she needed to find out what had happened to her egg.

She'd been thinking all along that an accident at the clinic had caused the mistake. The possibility that someone *deliberately* switched genetic material had never crossed her mind.

"Max, why would anyone want to—"

He raised his finger to her lips, the pad teasing an intimate response, and she gasped, then jerked back at his unexpected gesture. "Shh. Keep your voice down," he whispered, softening his words of caution with a grin of satisfaction at her reaction to his touch. "People from the clinic or a neighbor, or family or friend might be on this trolley. We're going right through the Garden District. I know Dr. Arnold and Dr. Henschel live there. We don't want anyone to overhear our speculations."

At his simple touch, her pulse accelerated, but she hid her reaction as she looked around. The trolley was about three-quarters full and no one appeared to pay them the slightest attention. Still, she lowered her voice. "What do we know?"

"The right questions to ask." His mouth curved into a wry grin as if he guessed the effect he was having on her. "First we need to figure out who at the clinic had the opportunity to swap genetic materials. Then we need to find a motive for doing so." As he spoke, he ticked each point off on a finger, and each time he did, she recalled his finger touching her lip.

As they stopped by Lee Circle, she drummed her

fingers on the purse in her lap, trying to ignore his hard thigh pressed against hers. "Motive usually comes down to money. Although I can't imagine how anyone could make money mixing up embryos."

"Look, Mom." Skye pointed to the huge statue of Robert E. Lee.

"He's facing north so his back will never be to his enemies," Max told her.

Skye's eyes rounded. "What enemies?"

He chuckled. "It was a war fought a long time ago. It's over, and the enemies are now our friends."

Brooke enjoyed watching Max talk to Skye. He'd immediately realized he'd frightened her, and he'd reassured her with simple truths Skye could understand. If only he could find Brooke such simple answers to what happened at the clinic.

She couldn't let go of the mystery. Recalling Max's warning, she kept her voice low. "Dr. Arnold has to be at the top of our list. He was in charge of the entire procedure."

"And he's on vacation. Convenient." His eyes, narrowed in calculation, burned with fierce intensity. For the first time she understood just how formidable an enemy Max Braddack could be. Her initial instincts about him had been correct. He was dangerous.

It had been so long since a man had been a part of her life, she'd forgotten the raw animal power they exuded, concealing their predatory instincts behind more civilized manners. Reminding herself not to cross Max without good reason, she forced herself to continue the conversation. "There's Dr. Henschel, the head of the clinic, his medical assistants, and secretary.

I suppose we'll have to include the entire impregnating team. We can scratch anyone off the list unless they worked there six years ago."

The trolley stopped again and several people got on. A young man with a backpack took a seat beside Skye.

"How about former employees that have since found new jobs?" Max rubbed his square jaw, drawing attention to a small indentation in his chin. "Then there're the lab techs and research assistants. For all we know, the cleaning lady could have mixed up a test tube."

The trolley lurched forward, pressing her closer to Max. She edged away, but not before a tingle spiraled through her. "You're right. We can't discount a simple mishap."

"I'm betting the records we need are in the lab."

She lowered her voice to the merest whisper. "So how're we going to sneak past that guard?"

He grinned, a pure macho grin. "I'm betting the guard won't be there tonight."

But what if he was? A student exited in front of Loyola University across from Audubon Park. Skye, her expression wistful, eyed the live old oaks and the lagoon. "Can we get off here for a while?"

Max looked to Brooke, leaving the decision to her. "Sure, why not?"

Skye skipped ahead of them through the park, taking a winding path beneath evergreens with spreading limbs that turned the walkway into a covered alley. They ambled past gazebos, playground areas, and shelters toward the pavilion on the riverbank of the Mississippi.

While Skye played on a swing set, Max and Brooke watched steamboats full of tourists ply the river, tugboats pushing enormous barges, and ocean-going ships heading out into the Gulf of Mexico. From a vendor Max bought them all *beignets,* square, French donuts heaped with powdered sugar. While she and Max drank strong chicory-laced coffee with hot milk, Skye raced back to play, sugar still coating her lips.

Max grinned. "She has a lot of energy."

"Keeping up with her can be a full-time job. But she's a great kid."

"It must be tough raising her alone. You've done a good job."

And she wanted to go on doing a good job. She gazed into her coffee, then back into Max's blue eyes. "Skye means everything to me."

His voice softened. "I can understand why."

Brooke glanced to the playground. Skye no longer played on the swing. She moved her gaze to the slide, then the teeter-totter. But she wasn't there, either.

Her heart fisted in her chest and she leapt to her feet. "Skye!"

"She was on the swing just a minute ago." Although Max's words were meant to comfort her, his jaw knotted and a hint of panic entered his tone. "She can't have gone far."

Brooke raced toward the playground, fear feathering down her spine. "She never runs off."

They rounded a grouping of trees. Skye was bent over a cardboard box, a stranger beside her. As they approached, the man hurried away.

"Skye!" Brooke swept the child into her arms and

buried her face in her baby-soft neck. "You know better than to wander off."

Skye pulled back. "I didn't wander. This is still the playground. The man said so."

"The man who just left?" Max asked, an odd expression on his face.

Skye pointed to the box. "He said I could have a free kitty if I want one."

One tiny gray and white kitten curled in a corner and meowed.

Brooke eased Skye down, realizing she'd overreacted. The man had probably hurried off so they would keep the abandoned kitten. And Skye was still on the playground, she'd just been out of their view. While she didn't like the stranger's tactics, she couldn't resist picking up the cat, which immediately licked her hand.

"She's hungry. Can we keep Fraidy-cat?" Skye pleaded.

Max chuckled. "Fraidy-cat—now there's a fine name."

Brooke handed Skye the kitten. Max knelt down and showed her how to hold it. "The coffee vendor sells milk. Why don't we pour some onto a paper plate and see if she'll eat?"

On the streetcar ride home, Skye slept in Max's lap with the kitten curled in her arms. Brooke would have given anything for a camera. But then she remembered there would be many moments like this in the future, memories with Skye sleeping in her uncle's arms.

When they got back, Max was going to call Ford.

THEY STOPPED at a fast-food restaurant on the way home. Skye, tired from the long afternoon, never woke as Max carried her from his truck to her bed while Brooke hunted for a place to keep the kitten. She found a shoe box and lined it with newspaper. "This will do until tomorrow."

In the kitchen, the light on her answering machine was blinking. Brooke retrieved the message. "This is Dr. Henschel's secretary calling to cancel the meeting tonight. The doctor was unable to get in touch with our attorney. He'll call you back next week."

Brooke sighed in frustration. "I guess I should cancel the sitter."

"Don't." Max's eyes twinkled with mischief as he straddled a chair.

"Why not?"

"Suppose we hadn't returned and heard that message."

"But—"

"We could have spent the day at the park, eaten out and gone straight to the clinic. Let's show up for the meeting."

She cocked her head. "But what's the point? Dr. Henschel won't be there."

He grinned. "Exactly! We'll be free to look around."

Her stomach twisted into knots. She couldn't decide if she was more anxious over their upcoming foray into the clinic, the way her heart stuttered when he looked at her with that gleam in his eye, or the phone call he was about to make.

As if reading her thoughts, Max stood and removed a slip of paper with Ford's number from his wallet.

He used his credit card to call Switzerland, while she sat at the table, staring at her hands, wondering if Ford would believe his brother.

"Ford Braddack, please."

Brooke couldn't seem to draw enough air into her lungs. She'd thought about this moment all week, couldn't wait for it to arrive. Now the moment had come too soon. How should she begin?

"This is his brother."

Brooke's stomach lurched with anticipation. Finally she would speak with Ford Braddack, and she still hadn't decided what to say. That would depend on what Max told him. She turned and listened more carefully.

Suddenly Max's shoulders slumped and his eyes lost their teasing glint. Disbelief and grief deepened his tone. "What? Are you sure?" He listened some more. "I see." Finally, his face bleak, he hung up without mentioning one word about Skye.

She forced herself to breathe. "What is it?"

"My brother and Rhonda were heli-skiing in the Alps. An avalanche swept down the mountain yesterday. Rhonda's dead."

"Oh, no!" Brooke went to him and wrapped her arms around him. "Max, I'm so sorry."

She'd agonized all week over the decision to come forward. If only she'd called sooner, the Braddacks might have ended the trip, might be back here now safe.

Max's tone deepened with grief. "They're holding back the news from the press until all the bodies are identified and the families notified. They just found my sister-in-law's body. Ford was seriously injured and has lapsed into a coma.''

She didn't want to imagine how he felt. When she'd lost her sister, she'd fallen apart. Only caring for Skye had pulled her together. And Ford was his identical twin. His only sibling—they had to be especially close.

His hard body shuddered and she held him tighter.

Tilting her head back, she looked up to see tears flowing down his face. He didn't appear the least bit ashamed of his tears as he pulled her tighter into his arms.

She had no idea what to say. Nothing could make this better. She stood there with a lump in her throat, holding him, letting him hold her, the two of them swaying on their feet.

"You should tell your parents.''

"I will. Give me a few minutes.'' He put his hands on her shoulders and gently leaned away from the hug so he could look at her face. "The desk clerk told me one more thing.''

"What?''

Max's eyes darkened with pain. "Before Ford passed out, he gave the ski patrol that brought him down a message for me. He said, "not an accident.''

She took a napkin from the counter and gently dabbed the tears from his cheeks. "He must have been delirious.''

Max pivoted and slammed a fist on the counter in frustration. "I don't think so. It's too much of a co-incidence that you discovered Skye isn't yours the same week her biological mother is killed and Ford is barely hanging on. And I'm not so sure that man in the park was innocent.''

She recognized blazing fury in his eyes. "But he didn't do anything."

"Because we stopped him."

"This is crazy. You think he meant to hurt Skye?"

He clamped his jaw and paced, obviously too wired to sit. "I don't know. Maybe I'm half out of my mind with grief. But Skye is living proof of the mix-up at the clinic. With Ford and Rhonda out of the picture and Skye gone, what evidence would you have?"

"You're scaring me. Maybe we should go to the police?"

"They won't do anything without solid documentation. We've got to go to the clinic. I want to see Dr. Arnold's files. But first, I'm going home to tell my parents about Ford and Rhonda."

THE KINE CLINIC, with its black glass windows, was eerily silent at night. As a malevolent gust coughed across the Mississippi, wheezed over the empty pavement and whistled around the lofty building's corners, Brooke was glad Skye was safe at home with the sitter. She was also glad Max had returned from his parents' house to drive. He'd claimed navigating through the bad weather would help take his mind off the news that had devastated his parents.

As if death loomed around them, overhead, storm clouds, choked with dark moisture, obliterated the moon. On the horizon, magenta heat lightning fizzled across the sky. Moments later thunder rolled, an ominous precursor of the impending storm.

The tiny hairs on the back of Brooke's neck stood on end as she climbed out of the pickup. Telling herself her reaction was simply due to the static electricity in the air didn't stop her hands from shaking as she glanced at her watch. It seemed too dark for seven o'clock.

The wind blustered around her. Fat drops of rain splattered, and she debated whether the downpour would hold off until she and Max came out. Not likely.

Leaning against the wall of the clinic, finding what shelter she could, she tapped her foot with impatience. The front door was locked. When no one answered Max's knock, he pounded, the loud thumps barely audible over the thunder.

Finally, the door opened a crack. "Who is it?"

"We have an appointment with Dr. Henschel."

The woman, Callie Wainwright, according to the name tag clipped to her lab coat, opened the door. Her eyes widened at the sight of Max.

Uh-oh. Had the woman recognized Max from their previous visit? Or had Dr. Henschel warned her against letting them in?

"Ford?" Callie opened the door and gestured them into a brightly lit waiting room, a wide smile breaking through her obvious shock.

"No. It's Max. I'm Ford's twin."

Her face dimmed a bit but she recovered fast. "Sorry, Max. Do you have an appointment?"

"With Dr. Henschel," Max replied.

"Is he working late again?" She relocked the door behind them. "No one tells me anything around here."

Glad that Callie had let them inside, but annoyed by her too eager smile at Max, Brooke followed him, feeling like a drowned rat compared to the perky technician. Water dribbled from her hair into her eyes and down her collar. As Callie led them through the empty waiting room and down a hall, drops of water sprinkled around Brooke's feet.

Max smiled at Callie. "Are you the only one in the lab tonight?"

"Yes. Except for security."

Brooke noted he'd never smiled at her like that—open, warm, charming. So what? It's not as if she wanted Max Braddack for herself. He was too laid-back, too uncommitted for her taste. Conveniently ignoring her former impression of him, she put her annoyance down to his unnecessary chitchat, impatient when he didn't ask a few more important questions.

Callie led them to the elevator. "You remember the way to his office? I've got work in the lab I should return to."

"Don't let us keep you."

Unnerved by the quiet building, Brooke couldn't wait to search the place and leave. When the elevator door closed behind the lab tech, she asked, "Now what?"

He moved close to her, close enough for her to appreciate the fragrance of soap and rain mixed with his masculine scent. He spoke softly, his tone low and husky, making it difficult for her to forget what they were supposed to be doing. "I'd like to check Dr. Arnold's office first, then Henschel's."

"I thought we were going to the lab."

"We will. Maybe Callie will be through by then. But I'll bet some of the important paperwork is kept upstairs."

"Let's go." She stepped toward the elevator door, uncomfortable with his nearness.

"Wait a sec."

"Why?"

He held the elevator door open. "Let's listen for a moment."

With his damp shirt emphasizing the muscles of his virile chest and revealing too much golden skin, his closeness had her nerves jumping. Although he didn't appear the least concerned by the darkness or their proximity, heat rose to her cheeks. She had to quit thinking about him in a way she shouldn't.

Her hormones had picked one hell of a time to act up. The elevator doors closed and they ascended. Ever since they'd met, she'd had that tingly alive feeling she hadn't felt in years. It was a great feeling—but not when attributed to Max Braddack. No way. In the past, her choices in men might not have been too terrific, but a relationship with Max Braddack could never happen.

Not a chance.

Reining in her emotions, she followed him out of the elevator to Dr. Arnold's office. He'd come prepared. Using his penlight, he picked the lock with a tiny screwdriver. She entered Dr. Arnold's office with a shiver of anticipation that quickly died. The walls stood bare of the framed pictures of his family and the numerous medical degrees that she vaguely recalled from her first visit.

Max shone the penlight on the desk. "It's empty."

"All his personal effects have been cleaned out, as if he doesn't expect to return."

Except for the nameplate still on the door, nothing indicated a vital man had once worked in this office. Meticulously, Max inspected every drawer of the desk, searched the back of the closet. Brooke checked the fax and copy machines but found only blank paper.

They spent a long time searching until anxious to move on, she opened the door into the hallway. "Come on."

They tiptoed to Dr. Henschel's office across the hall. Brooke glanced at her watch. "What are we looking for?"

Max shrugged.

He didn't have a plan. But after the bad news he'd received, it was a wonder he could focus at all.

Where Dr. Arnold's office had been vacant, Brooke couldn't even see the surface of Dr. Henschel's desk for the stacks of medical journals, patient files, and pharmaceutical brochures. Walking over to the file cabinet, she tugged on a drawer and found it locked.

Max shone the penlight on the lock. "I can open that—but I can't relock it."

"Let's see what else we can find first." With a frown of distaste, she sorted through papers on the cluttered desk. "What should I look for?"

"I don't know."

She glared at Max, suddenly furious.

He returned her gaze with a scowl. "What? What did I do?"

Her gaze dropped from his perplexed frown to a

stack of books on the floor. Tax documentation. Kneeling, she sorted through brochures on oil fields, global bonds, and commodities.

Max aimed his light so she could read. "This place must be making a fortune."

"They're supposed to be very successful. That's why my sister came here." She held up a brochure of a Mississippi riverfront mansion. "But would the doctors be this rich?"

Max turned away, losing interest. "Maybe Henschel sold his private practice before coming to work here. Or he might have inherited his wealth, or have a rich wife."

Suddenly Brooke wished she could put her hands on the corporate financial statements, especially the expense reports. She wanted to see if the company was overbilling. As she restacked the papers and slipped a few loose financial papers into her pocket, a niggling suspicion that something was not right pricked her mind.

The elevator doors suddenly clanged open. Footsteps echoed down the hall. Her mouth went dry. Max turned off his penlight and dragged her beneath the desk.

Her back pressed against a lumpy briefcase. Her heart hammered so hard—she assumed—the guard couldn't miss the thumping. With her shoulder tucked into Max's side, her hip pressed to his hard thigh, he must feel her trembling. Calm and composed, Max squeezed her icy hand. As the footsteps slowly faded, she released her pent-up breath, but the tension would not recede.

With every nerve stretched taut, she yearned to bury her face in his chest and have him tell her they'd be fine. Of course, she did nothing of the sort.

Down the hall, the elevator doors shut.

He released her hand, shoved up from behind the desk and reached down to her. Pretending not to see his outstretched fingers in the dark, she ignored his offer of help. The spot where he'd touched her still pulsed iron-hot. The less touching, the better.

Brooke bent to retrieve the briefcase from beneath the desk. She fumbled with the clasp and jerked it open. "Max, I need some light."

She extracted papers and her hands trembled with excitement. "These are Nicole's and John's medical files. And these are Ford's and Rhonda's."

"Henschel must have pulled them for the attorney."

Max flicked on the copy machine. It warmed up with a loud hum. "I'll keep watch. Put everything back like you found it."

With copies bulging in her pocket, they exited the office and hurried down the hall. Max twisted the knob on the door marked Billing and Records. "It's locked."

He took out his penlight and examined the lock. "Picking this is beyond my abilities."

"Then let's go." She headed toward the elevator.

"I don't think we should take the elevator again," Max whispered. "That might be why someone came up here."

In silence they walked down five flights of stairs. Brooke expected the lab to be locked, but the metal doors stood open wide. Her instinct screamed a warning not to enter.

Max boldly stepped inside the laboratory. "Callie. Callie, you in here?"

Brooke's gaze swept the lab, and she recognized a microscope, a centrifuge and not much else in the sophisticated array of equipment. Science had never been her strong suit.

They rounded a counter, and she took in the rest of the room. "Maybe Callie took a break."

"A permanent one, I'm afraid." Max had jerked back to avoid stepping on the lab technician who lay on the floor, her face twisted in agony, her eyes wide and sightless.

Chapter Four

Certain she would be sick, Brooke spun around to spy the security guard from the afternoon shift, his gun drawn and pointed at them.

His gun didn't waver. "Sorry to interrupt your little party."

Max straightened.

"Stay right there." The guard's free hand fumbled for a red button and a siren wailed. "The police are on the way."

The blood drained from Brooke's face. With the guard aiming the gun in their direction, she was sure the killer must be behind her. She edged closer to Max and glanced back to see empty aisles between counters laden with lab equipment. No one else was there.

The gun was aimed at them. The security guard thought she and Max had murdered that poor woman. "Y-you don't u-understand," she stammered. "We didn't—"

"Save your story for the police." The guard sidled toward a phone on the wall but kept the gun pointed at them.

The evidence against them flashed through her mind creating havoc with her trembling nerves. They'd entered the building under false pretenses. She had financial papers from Dr. Henschel's office stuffed in her jacket pocket. Damn it! They'd been found standing over a dead body. She and Max would be accused of murder.

At the thought of spending the rest of her life in jail, her palms went clammy and her mouth turned so dry she couldn't swallow. My God! What had she done? Who would take care of Skye?

Paralyzed with fright, she thought she'd be sick. Her feet rooted to the spot.

Max gripped her fingers. From the corner of her eye, she saw his free hand whip out and flip the light switch, plunging the lab into darkness. Understanding sliced through her with the sharp pain of a razor.

Oh, God! He meant to escape.

He jerked her toward the hallway. She stumbled, careened into a table, and scrambled for balance.

In the blackness, a shot fired. The gun flash seared her vision, the noise loud enough to leave her ears ringing. Her heart battered her ribs. Glass shattered, liquid splashed onto the floor, and the sharp odor of chemicals mixed with the stink of gunpowder. All the while Max yanked her through the darkness. She tripped after him blindly, hoping he could lead them to safety.

It seemed like hours of racing through the blackness, but it must have been mere seconds until they reeled into the hallway. The absolute inky dark of the lab softened into the murky gray of tenuous shadows.

An Exit sign over the far door cast the minimum red glow necessary to sprint down the hall.

"Run," Max ordered, his voice low and urgent.

He needn't tell her twice. Unquestioningly, she sprinted toward the exit, racing several steps before realizing Max had remained behind to close the lab doors to delay the armed guard. By the time she reached the exit, his long strides had made up the distance between them. He shoved open the metal door and they climbed a staircase to ground level.

Stumbling into the downpour, disoriented, she gasped for breath and looked right, then left. Rain pelted her face. Over the crack of thunder, police sirens wailed, but she didn't yet see blue flashing lights in the darkness. They still might get away.

At the thought she was a fugitive on the run from the police, her knees almost buckled. They should have stayed and tried to explain. Doubt slowed her.

Max grabbed her arm and almost dragged her around to the west side entrance. The building had seemed to turn around and she'd lost her bearings in the rain. Still running, they splashed through puddles, and she dragged air into her lungs in an attempt to calm her rising panic.

The siren closed in on them as they sprinted around the building. Max dug into his pocket for the keys and dropped them.

"Keep going. I'll get them." Max scooped up the keys from the pavement with barely a pause.

She darted to his truck, the only vehicle in the lot, a prime target. Max caught up with her and unlocked the doors. She jumped in and before she had shut the door, he peeled out of the lot, tires squealing. Fumbling for the safety harness, she jammed the clip in the buckle. Soaked and shivering, she turned up the heat. The windows steamed and she notched the toggle to defrost. As they lurched over a curb, Max found the wipers.

Getting away would do them no good if they crashed into a telephone pole. She braced against the dash. "Take it easy."

"I haven't even floored her. Yet."

She braced her hands against the dash and wondered if she'd live long enough to hold Skye again.

They hadn't driven two blocks before blue lights flashed ahead of them. Just when she wanted him to press the pedal to the floorboard, Max slowed to a normal speed and turned left as two police cars screamed by.

Images of being handcuffed and dragged off to jail flashed through her mind. That she who had never had even a speeding ticket could be accused of murder had her senses reeling.

Although she'd turned up the heat, she couldn't stop shivering, couldn't stop the hysteria rising in her. Rubbing her palms across her thighs, Brooke fought to keep her thoughts from pummeling out of control. Max had been right to slow down and appear like an ordinary driver instead of a criminal fleeing a crime scene. His instincts and luck had led them this far, yet she worried whether she could rely on his judgment. "That was close."

"We're not out of the woods yet. After the guard

gives them a description, they might remember us driving by and be able to ID us.''

''But how?''

''Cops see things other people don't. They're trained to be observant. In this weather, how many pickups do you think they passed on the way here?''

''You aren't making me feel better.''

''Sorry.'' He turned left and crossed under the interstate. ''I figure we've got an hour—maybe two—before there's an A.P.B. out on us.''

Her stomach lurched. '' 'A.P.B.'?''

''All Points Bulletin. Maybe the investigation at the clinic will buy us an extra hour or two. We can't count on it.''

Everything had happened so quickly. As she thought it over, her stomach roiled with nausea. It wouldn't be hard for the cops to match the guard's description of them with Dr. Henschel's or Grant Donovan's.

She blinked back tears. ''Perhaps we should turn ourselves in.''

''Not until we make sure Skye is safe.''

A skittering sense of panic welled in her chest. ''You think she's in danger?''

''Yes. First Rhonda is killed and Ford is injured. Then we go to the clinic and are caught standing over a dead body. The connection has got to be Skye.'' A streetlight flickered through the sheets of rain on the window and reflected off his harsh cheekbones. ''The cops got here too fast. We were set up.''

Had they walked into a trap? An icy chill scrambled

down her spine. "How? No one knew we were coming."

"Perhaps we're being watched. That guard wasn't toting a weapon this afternoon. And isn't it odd how Dr. Arnold's office was cleaned out when Henschel implied he was on vacation?"

She sighed. "We have no proof."

"If our butts are parked in jail, we won't find answers."

He sounded more annoyed than frightened. In fact, since the entire disaster began, he hadn't once raised his voice or panicked. He'd reacted in a calm, unemotional manner, as if he evaded cops for a living. Either he had nerves of steel or he didn't know enough to be afraid.

Suspiciously, she faced him, unable to hide her tone of accusation. "You sound like you know about this kind of thing from experience."

"I wasted more than a few years of my misspent youth around a courthouse."

He'd been a juvenile delinquent. As if her innocence wasn't already hard enough to believe, now she was hanging out with a habitual offender. That would add to her credibility. Yeah, right. Unable to contain a shudder, she wondered just what kind of man she'd hooked up with.

She slumped in the front seat, grateful for the darkness that hid the mixture of distaste, fear and horror rumbling inside her. Yesterday, Brooke had been a normal single parent. Today she'd stumbled over a dead body. Tomorrow her face might be plastered across Wanted posters on bulletin boards throughout Louisiana. And what would become of Skye?

Max's low voice, soft but alarming, broke into her thoughts. "If we don't want to risk the cops pulling us over before we reach Skye, we need to ditch the truck. Soon."

"But—"

Reflected in the headlights of an oncoming vehicle, Max's expression stilled and grew serious. "We need to leave Skye somewhere safe until we work this out."

Leave her daughter? A bitter taste soured in her mouth. He sounded as if he expected her to go on the run with him like some kind of modern day Bonnie and Clyde. "I'm not leaving. I can't uproot my daughter. Besides I have a job—"

"You have no choice."

Brooke shuddered. She was tired of his cool and calm demeanor in the face of what they'd been through. For a moment the horror of her situation overwhelmed her. Refusing to burst into tears, she straightened in her seat and spoke with a confidence she was far from feeling. "What's your plan?"

"We'll leave the truck in Ford's garage and borrow his car. Then we'll pick up Skye and stash her with my parents."

Didn't he have feelings? No matter how well he planned, she wouldn't refer to her sweet little girl as an object. "Skye is my daughter, and I'm not *stashing* her anywhere. She stays with me."

"Fine. Okay. Whatever you say," he agreed, while his tone mocked her. "If you think it's safe to leave her with a baby-sitter to protect her from harm."

"She stays with me."

"By tomorrow our faces will be plastered on the front page of every Louisiana paper. Depending upon current state and national disasters, we may be the headline on television news. We're going to be questioned, maybe arrested. We need to be prepared. And Skye needs to be someplace safe."

"What are you suggesting?"

"We'll leave her with my parents. I'll talk to my attorney, then we'll make our statement to the police."

Before she could answer, Max, alert and wary, veered off the highway, turned down several streets past manicured lawns, and finally drove between the wrought-iron gates of a three-story house with a wrap-around porch. Max parked beside the three-car garage.

"After I back Ford's car out, park the truck inside. Maybe we can keep the cops and anyone else off our trail."

A quick switch into Ford's four-door Mercedes sedan, and they were once again on the road. The idea of leaving Skye while she went to jail continued to horrify Brooke. Unless her missing egg had also been mistakenly implanted in another woman, Skye was the only child she would ever have. If this kept her holding on to Skye too tightly, she couldn't help herself. They'd never been apart. "Your parents won't mind taking in a stranger's child?"

"Nope."

"Your lengthy explanations are so reassuring," she muttered. When he remained silent, checking the rear-view mirror every few seconds, she asked, "With Ford hurt, won't your parents want to be with him?"

"The housekeeper can look after Skye. She used to watch Ford and me."

She didn't want strangers watching her daughter. The woman might be ancient. "Oh, I feel much better now, seeing how you turned out." She couldn't keep the sarcasm from tumbling out.

"Skye isn't just a stranger. She's Eva and Red's granddaughter." Max paused, glanced at her, then continued. "I wasn't going to tell you this until after I'd cleared it with Ford. There's something else you should know."

"What?"

"During one of the few times Ford and I were separated as children, he caught the mumps." If not for the catch in his almost too casual tone, she wouldn't have guessed how much Max cared about his brother. He'd obviously been caught up in Ford's problems. "The disease left my brother sterile."

"Sterile?"

"His sperm count is so low that by the clinic's standards, he's considered sterile."

Then Skye wasn't Ford's child, either. Brooke's thoughts raced. A suspicion niggled at the back of her mind, something didn't fit. She struggled to understand why the Kine Clinic would attempt to fertilize an egg with "Ford's" sperm if the man was sterile. What would be the point, unless they were just taking his money? And he was on the board of directors, so that didn't make sense.

She gasped. How convenient that Ford had an identical twin who could provide healthy sperm. "You donated the sperm? You're Skye's father?"

"Yes." For a moment he studied her intently. A light flickered in his eyes. Then the mask descended once again, and she couldn't read him. "I would have told you sooner but I wanted to clear it with Ford. You have to understand, it wasn't my brother who cared whether people knew he's sterile. Rhonda was determined that their child should always consider Ford the father. But apparently their problem wasn't only due to his childhood illness. Rhonda couldn't carry a child. She suffered one miscarriage after another until Ford forbid her to try again. Ford loved her so much, he didn't want to risk losing her."

Brooke's laboring heart battered her ribs, but she forced herself to speak in a casual tone. "You and Rhonda are Skye's parents."

"It's horribly ironic and sad you turned up with Skye just before Rhonda's death. She died without knowing the daughter she'd wanted so badly really existed."

"I'm sorry Skye will never meet her biological mother. Rhonda sounded like a wonderful woman. But I don't understand how you pulled off the switch with your brother."

"I just walked into the clinic and pretended I was Ford. Acquaintances often can't tell us apart."

"How many people are aware you donated sperm?"

"As far as I know, only Rhonda and Ford."

Her mind spun in shock. Skye's biological mother was dead. Max—not his twin—was Skye's father. Max had been willing to let his brother and his wife raise his child. But that wasn't the same thing as allowing her—a complete stranger—to raise Skye. Would Max try to take Skye from her?

He'd certainly been playing his cards close to the vest. And while she understood his reasons for keeping the information from her, anger at his deception clouded her thoughts. In her eyes, Skye had to come first and he shouldn't have kept his fatherhood a secret.

"So how do you feel about being a father?"

"Frankly, I'm scared to death. I'm a bachelor, a man without a home to call my own." He winced. "I'm not exactly prime father material."

"I see."

He spoke quietly, as if realizing she was shocked by his admission. "My parents have plenty of room. The grounds are fenced. There's a state-of-the-art alarm system, too. Skye will be well cared for and safe there."

Her fists clenched in her lap until her nails dug into her flesh. No matter what he said, she wouldn't leave Skye with his parents unless Brooke and Skye felt comfortable with them. With that settled, she considered the immediate future. Nervously she straightened her fingers and wiped damp palms on her thighs. She had to think ahead. Tomorrow they would turn themselves in.

With her meager savings, money was going to be a problem. Her sister and husband had spent their life savings at the clinic and what few assets had been left, Brooke had sold long ago. Since then, she and Skye managed to live on her salary. But she never saved much.

Now, she might need to make bail. Frustrated by her lack of money, she knew her problems had only just begun. What would her boss think when she failed to show up for work and if the police started asking questions? Before her hands started shaking again, she told herself grimly that if she couldn't clear her name, she wouldn't need a job—not if she landed in jail.

And it might be months until a trial. A lump formed in her throat over the possibility of being separated from Skye. If convicted, she could lose custody. She blinked back tears. "How long do you think your parents can watch Skye?"

"Don't worry. My parents will take care of her forever if necessary."

"Forever! You're scaring me. And when we turn ourselves in, I won't have enough money to make bail."

A hint of huskiness edged his velvet tone. "You can owe me."

She stiffened at the amusement beneath the surface of his words. What could he possibly find funny in their situation? That she was broke? He didn't seem much better off.

But it was kind of him to offer, and she had no choice but to accept. "I don't know when I can pay you back."

His eyes glinted with a hint of unspoken promises that set her senses on alert. "Rest easy. You can be sure I'll collect—with interest."

She almost protested aloud at his insinuation, then bit her lip, wishing she didn't have to depend on a stranger. She didn't like owing people, especially a handsome man like Max.

The fact she had no real choice filled her with apprehension. Ignoring his innuendo might be the best way to defuse the situation. "I always pay my debts."

PACKING FOR SKYE and herself while she tried to stay calm had been a nightmare. At every sound, Brooke expected a hand to clamp on her shoulder and a cop to haul her off to jail. Max called the Swiss hospital to check on his brother, but there was no change in Ford's condition. He also left a message on his attorney's voice mail.

Skye didn't awaken as Max carried her to the front seat, gently placing her into the car seat, and tucking the kitten into her hands. He seemed casual enough about holding his daughter, but she'd caught him staring tenderly at Skye. His lips softened, and he hugged her daughter closer. A moment later he caught Brooke staring, and his face gave away nothing.

They drove into the Garden District, an area of beautifully landscaped gardens surrounding elegant antebellum homes. Brooke flinched at every passing car, fearing the police would pull them over before Skye was safe.

About ten minutes later, Max pulled through wrought-iron gates onto a pecan-shaded drive. A Victorian-style mansion with the gingerbread look of steeply pitched gables and even a tower dominated the grounds. Their headlights flashed on geraniums blooming in flower boxes under arched windows and a charming wraparound porch with delicate wicker furniture.

The moment they drove through the gate, an upstairs light came on. What would Max's parents be like? Knowing she might have to depend upon strangers, blood relatives or not, to look after her child made Brooke's stomach knot. Unstrapping Skye from her car seat, Brook pulled her daughter closer as Max got out of the car. Brooke dipped her head and kissed Skye's tender neck.

Skye snuggled against her shoulder. Even as the front door slammed shut, she didn't wake. Brooke looked up to catch sight of a couple hurrying toward them. Although not as tall as Max, the man, who wore his salt-and-pepper hair short, possessed the same calm intensity as his son, and the family resemblance was striking. With his harsh cheekbones and piercing grief-stricken blue eyes, he looked an older version of Max. The haunting sorrow in his eyes reminded her how inappropriate their timing was. While she and Max might be accused of murder, the Braddacks' daughter-in-law was dead and their son in the hospital.

Max's mother raced down the steps, uncaring of the misting rain soaking her designer dress. His father wore a golf shirt and shorts, as if he'd come in and heard about Ford, then hadn't bothered to change for an elegant party that his wife had been dressed for. Concern marred Eva's thin face as she hurried past the porch light. Her short brown hair helmeted a thin face and huge eyes puffy from crying. She hugged Max with a fierce passion that left no doubt of her love for her son. "Have you more news of Ford?"

Max pulled back to look the woman in the face. "There's been no change in his condition."

"Something else is wrong, isn't there?" Eva asked perceptively as Max moved from her arms to his dad's, hugging him as he'd embraced his mom.

"Mom, we'll all be staying the night."

No wonder Skye was so affectionate. Hugging and caring about one another seemed to come naturally in this family.

Skye had begun to awaken when Max shut off the engine. She straightened as Max's mother came around to Brooke's side of the car. "I'm Eva Braddack. And that's my husband, Red."

Brooke helped Skye from the front seat of the car. "This is my daughter, Skye. I'm Brooke Evans."

Skye held up her kitten. "And this is Fraidy-cat."

Eva squinted curiously at Skye in the dark. Up close, Brooke could see that Eva's mascara had run, probably from tears over her son and daughter-in-law. "Please, come inside. I'm not thinking straight, and being rude keeping you all out here in the rain."

Obviously wanting a few private words with his dad, Max gestured for her to go with his mother. "I'll meet you inside."

Feeling abandoned, Brooke and Skye, clutching Fraidy-cat to her chest, followed Eva into the house. The foyer boasted a chandelier that shone on a staircase that ascended to a gallery on the second story. Nineteenth-century art was framed on plastered walls. And Persian rugs protected the gleaming polished oak floors from scuff marks.

Eva bustled around her visitors, a tight expression

of worry on her face. Brooke could see the woman was bursting with questions. Max's mother must be fretting over Ford, and now Brooke and Skye had caused more problems. With all that Eva had on her mind, the last thing she needed was guests.

Still, as if reading Brooke's mind, Eva sought to reassure Brooke as she led them upstairs. "The distraction of having guests will help take my mind off Ford and..." She paused. "The guest room is on the right with a double bed for Skye. There's a connecting bath to your room. The bed's made up. Would you like to rest?"

Brooke glanced into the bedroom and saw a canopied wrought-iron double bed with a quilted spread. Lacy curtains hung over the windows and another carpet decorated the wood flooring. Brooke looked from the welcoming room to Skye. "Oh, this is such a nice room. Do you want to stay with me or go back to sleep?"

Skye's eyes were rounded in curiosity at the elegant surroundings. She was wide awake. "I want to stay with you."

"That's fine, honey." With shaking hands, Brooke ruffled Skye's curls. How was she going to explain to a five-year-old that her mother might be wanted for murder? That the only parent she knew may have to leave her with strangers?

Eva took one good look at Skye in the full light of the upper hallway and gasped. Her face whitened and then her lips split into a wide, welcoming grin. Her gaze flew to Brooke as if seeking silent confirmation that Skye was her granddaughter. Brooke simply held the woman's stare, and let Eva draw her own conclusions.

Max's mother seemed to take only a moment to regain her composure before she took charge of Skye. "Your mom brought you to visit us. Would you like to help me make a pie?"

Had Brooke heard right? Eva Braddack was going to bake a pie, wearing a designer dress? At 9:00 p.m. at night?

Eva's suggestion lit up Skye's eyes. "Can I, Mom?"

"Sure, pumpkin. Let's leave Fraidy-cat here and I'll come, too. We can all get to know one another better."

As Brooke followed her daughter and Eva downstairs and into an oak-floored kitchen with all the modern conveniences, she wondered where to begin. Should she explain the mix-up at the clinic? How could she when she didn't know if Max had told his parents he'd donated his sperm. Eva and Red might not be aware that Ford and his wife had tried to have a baby with the help of a fertility clinic. Even if Eva had guessed some of the truth, with one look at Skye, she must be curious. Brooke was grateful Eva didn't say anything in front of her daughter.

Where was Max? It wasn't Brooke's place to make the explanations.

As if her thoughts had summoned him, the back door opened. Max and his father walked inside, the older man's arm curved over his son's shoulders, affection for one another on their faces. The two men showed their feelings so easily that Brooke felt better about leaving Skye here. Clearly there was a lot of love in this home. As much as she didn't want to leave her daughter, the child would be well looked after and safe.

Eva shook out an apron. When she tied the apron around Skye's waist with no care for her own gown, she won over Brooke's heart. As grandmother and granddaughter poured flour into measuring cups on the otherwise spotless granite-topped counter, Brooke caught Max's parents exchanging glances over her daughter's head. Eva nodded and Red lost his grief-stricken expression for a moment. Clearly they'd both guessed Skye was their granddaughter.

Brooke couldn't tell what Max was thinking from his expression. Did he realize his parents had guessed the truth? Did he think of Skye as his? She couldn't forget the way he'd lovingly cradled Skye in his arms as if he'd always known her. She would have given a lot to have known his thoughts at that moment. Was Max thinking this was the first time he'd been together with both his daughter and his parents?

Brooke should have felt triumphant that she'd finally found Skye's family, but a sense of loss was already seeping in. Within minutes his parents appeared to have accepted Skye. In the coming days they'd probably come to love her. They might not want to give her back—especially to a mother who didn't share Skye's blood, a mother wanted by the police.

Her stomach clenched. No matter how painful a separation would be for her to bear, she wanted Skye to have a family, relatives, and love. So why did Brooke hurt so badly that a lump formed in her throat and she had to hold back tears? Her feelings had nothing to do with the fact that she could never have another child. Skye's world was opening and hers was threatening to close.

As if sensing her fears for Skye, Max stepped to her side and eased her into a kitchen chair. "She's going to be fine."

Brooke licked dry lips. He couldn't understand what she felt. He didn't know Skye's good fortune was ripping her insides out. Brooke still had to explain to her daughter she was leaving and didn't know when she'd be back.

The phone rang. Brooke jumped and glanced at her watch—9:30 p.m.

"I'll get it." Eva wiped her hands on her apron and picked up the phone. "Hello?"

Eva blanched. "It's your attorney." She held out the phone to Max. "He says it's an emergency. He needs to talk to you right now."

Chapter Five

While Eva and Skye put the pies in the oven, Max took his attorney's phone call in his father's den. Before he returned to the kitchen, Brooke had taken Skye upstairs to put her to bed. Max chose this time to explain to his parents about Ford and Rhonda's involvement with Skye and Brooke Evans. He also told Eva and Red about the police wanting to question Brooke and him concerning the murder of a lab technician at the Kine Clinic.

When Brooke returned downstairs, his mother assured her she was happy to have Skye to fuss over. Clearly his parents were overjoyed with their granddaughter and as Brooke and Max readied to leave, Brooke seemed confident they would take good care of Skye.

As Max drove toward the police station where they would meet his attorney, he glanced at the woman beside him. Even in the dark, whenever they passed a streetlight, he could see her face was pale. Dark circles curved under eyes, wide and unfocused, that stared ahead. In her lap, her fingers repeatedly rubbed her thighs.

Even worried and nervous about Skye, Brooke had an inner beauty that shone through. Although she was a strong woman, he suspected it had been difficult for her to leave Skye, probably more difficult than he could imagine. He'd only known his daughter a short time, yet he'd had to tear himself away, too. He'd already missed so much of Skye's life, each minute seemed precious. But he and Brooke would return soon.

He tried to reassure her. "My folks already adore Skye."

"I could see that. Do you think..."

"Think what?" he prodded.

Brooke spoke hesitantly as if trying on the idea for size. "Do you think we'll be arrested?"

She looked so fragile and sad in the seat beside him, he reached over and rubbed the back of her neck. "We're not going to jail. At least not for long."

"Max, are you sure we should turn ourselves in?"

"My attorney says that if we cooperate, our actions will go a long way with the police. We should make bail. And it's possible we won't even be arrested. Besides, if we run, we'll be too busy hiding to get to the bottom of who is behind our problems."

"I suppose." She fidgeted in her seat. "But the idea of running away is more appealing than a waiting jail cell."

"You'd have to leave Skye behind," he said gently.

"I know. That's why I'm here with you." She didn't protest his touch, but sighed and closed her eyes. "Are we going to play this by ear? Or do you have a plan?"

He continued to massage the tense muscles of her shoulders with one hand while he steered with the other. "First we'll talk to my attorney, Akins. He'll advise us which questions to answer and which to refuse. And he'll be right there with you during the police interrogation."

"Then what?"

Hearing the slight tremor in her tone, he tried to reassure her. "We're going to find Dr. Arnold and learn what he knows about the mix-up at the clinic. He's on a sailboat. By law, it has to be registered. We'll check around with his neighbors and at his marina. Someone will know where he sails on vacation, then we'll go find him."

Her eyes flew open, shining with hope. "You really think the police will let us go?"

He winked, glad he'd lightened her mood just a bit. "Akins seems to think so."

She turned to face him, her lips set with determination. "Suppose Dr. Arnold won't talk to us?"

"Don't worry. I can be very persuasive."

And so could Akins. He was the best attorney money could buy. But Max kept Akin's high fees to himself. He had no wish to add money worries to all her other problems. With the charges they might be up against and their freedom at stake, he wasn't about to quibble over attorney fees. He had confidence in Akins.

His confidence was well placed. Five hours later, he and Brooke walked out of the police station. Although the detective had told them not to leave town because they were part of an ongoing investigation, he had seemed to believe Max. Since both he and Brooke lacked a motive to kill someone they didn't know, and the police had no physical evidence against them, there wasn't anything to hold them on.

When the detective pointed out that Callie had fallen near the alarm and suggested Max and Brooke shot her to prevent her from sounding the buzzer, Akins had told the police they were stretching reality. When asked why they'd run from the guard after Callie had been shot, Max said they ran to take Skye somewhere safe. Besides, he'd had no way of knowing if the guard was about to shoot them, too.

Without a motive or a weapon, the circumstantial evidence against them wouldn't convince a grand jury, much less hold up at a trial.

But the possibility they could be blamed for Callie's murder weighed heavily on Max. The police hadn't found the murder weapon. Yet he mentioned none of this to Brooke on the way back to his parents' home.

He couldn't make up his mind about Brooke. He glanced at her in the seat beside him, and she sent him a weary smile that sped his pulse. Normally the additional responsibility of having her with him would have annoyed him. Instead, he wanted her close, and refused to delve into why. The laboratory may have accidentally given his daughter to Brooke to raise, but fate couldn't have chosen a better mother.

At first he'd suspected Brooke had tracked him down to extract money from Ford. But after she'd learned that he, not his twin, was most likely Skye's father, Brooke didn't seem disappointed. She had told him the truth from the beginning. Skye's welfare was her primary concern.

He made a left turn and smothered a yawn. "My parents are arranging for Ford to be flown here and admitted to a private hospital. When Ford doesn't show at Rhonda's funeral, there's going to be lots of questions. The official version will be that he's still in Switzerland and too grief-stricken to return."

She turned her head but still leaned against the seat. "Why the lie?"

His tone hardened. "If someone is trying to kill my brother, we don't want them to know he's lying in a coma, helpless to fight back."

She nodded. "If anyone asks, I'll remember what to say."

He appreciated her cooperation, and he was learning he could count on her to hold up her end. Much like Eva, she was stronger than she looked.

It was almost dawn when they pulled into the driveway. But as he knew they would be, the house lights were still on. Max walked around the car and opened her door.

Brooke stood, blinking her eyes sleepily, close enough for him to take in the lingering scent of her lemon-scented shampoo.

"It's great the way your family pulls together. Nicole and I only had one another. That's why I wanted Skye to have more than just me to count on."

He put an arm across her shoulders and it felt like the most natural movement in the world. He drew her closer to his side until her hip brushed his. "I think Skye's lucky to have you for a mother."

She fought the urge to lean against his chest. "I don't know how I would have handled this by myself. I'll pay you back the attorney's fees when I can."

He considered telling her the truth about his financial status to put her mind at ease. But it had been a long night, she was exhausted, and he still had to fill in his parents about their legal situation. And he was anxious to find out if Ford's condition had improved.

Vowing to come clean tomorrow about his means of support, he squeezed her arm. "Don't worry about money. Consider it part of the back child support I owe you for taking care of Skye for all these years."

At the front door, she stopped and faced him. "I don't want your—"

In the dark intimacy of the front porch, he raised his hands and cupped her chin, surprised to find her skin as silky as Skye's. "Hey, your daughter isn't the only one that has a new family. You're her mother, so you belong, too. And we take care of one another. Now, no more arguments. Go to bed before you fall asleep on your feet."

"But—"

Without thinking, he dipped his head, ending her protest with a kiss. She gasped, her lips parting. But he didn't take the opportunity she offered, instead he nibbled her lips, reveling in her softness as he gathered her into his arms.

She felt good against his chest. Too good. His jeans were tight with his arousal. He fought the urge to

lower his hands from her waist to her bottom and press
their hips together, sensing the action would shock her.

She wound her arms around his neck, hesitantly,
sleepily. He held her tenderly, sensing this wasn't just
a kiss, but an emotional barrier they'd crossed. She
was vulnerable, her feelings close to the surface with
what she'd been through these past few days.

No matter how much he wanted her, his sense of
fair play wouldn't let him take advantage while she
was exhausted. He wanted her awake, her pulse on
fire when he kissed her.

Tomorrow was another day.

AFTER SLEEPING IN late, Brooke and Max returned to
Ford's home in hopes of finding information that
might illuminate what Ford had meant about "not an
accident." Skye stayed behind with the Braddack
housekeeper but either Red or Eva would soon return.

Max had a key and the code to his brother's alarm
system so they had no trouble entering the impressive
three-story house. Yesterday, Brooke had been so concerned over reaching Skye and spiriting her to safety
that she hadn't noticed the opulence. But today in daylight, she couldn't help but notice this house was three
times the size of his parents' mansion.

Max led her through an impressive plant-lined car-
riageway that led to a fountained courtyard. Most of
the second-floor rooms had balconies that faced the
courtyard and each room they passed was different in
size and decor, and furnished with French, English and
Louisianan antiques. The floors, polished hardwoods,

were covered with Oriental rugs. Brooke craned her neck looking at the luxurious rooms.

She especially liked one bedroom with its crocheted lace canopied twin beds, exposed brick walls, charming fireplace and an eighteenth-century armoire. Max led her past an elevator that, she assumed, led to the third floor.

"This is some house."

"Ford collects houses the way some people collect stamps. He has homes in more countries than I've been to. Luckily for us, when it comes to business, my brother is the most organized man on planet Earth. His office in his house is a duplicate of the one at Norton Industries."

She matched his easy stride, losing interest in the house. "Let me get this straight. The Kine Clinic is a subsidiary of Norton Industries, where your brother is a major shareholder."

"That's right. I'm hoping we might find something indicating why that avalanche was no accident. I seem to recall Ford mentioning a power struggle." He frowned. "I was otherwise occupied at the time."

She arched a brow.

"It was game point at Ping-Pong. I wasn't paying attention to Ford and his business deals."

The pleasant way his mouth curled at the memory caused her to picture Max playing while his brother talked about balance sheets. She had no right to feel impatient with Max that he played while his brother worked. After last night's kiss, she had to admit she liked the way Max played. Besides, she had no claim on him. To keep him from guessing at her thoughts, she stared at a sculpture that looked like it belonged in a museum.

They'd walked down so many hallways and past so many rooms she'd lost count. While the house was most impressive, she couldn't picture living here. How would she ever find Skye amid so many rooms? "Where is his office?"

Max chuckled. "The place is a little overwhelming. We're almost there."

Just a *little* overwhelming. Her entire apartment could fit in the front hall.

Max stopped in front of a massive mahogany door. His lips curled in amusement but his eyes watched her warily. The man was so in control, just once she'd like to see him lose his cool. All that unleashed passion would be magnificent. Dangerous.

"This house just doesn't seem to fit you. I thought identical twins would be more similar in nature."

"Ford likes to blaze new trails. If he thwarts a few less hardy souls in the process, he can live with it." She thought he meant to evade her question, but he surprised her by continuing. "I prefer to take the path of least resistance."

"Why?" she asked, hoping to provoke an honest response and find out what seethed beneath his surface. Maybe then she wouldn't find him so fascinating.

"Why not?" he answered flippantly.

She should have known getting to him wouldn't be easy. He was a master at putting up walls. "Why is it so hard for you to tell me what you do for a living? Somehow I don't think you're a boat mechanic."

His eyes pierced her. "And why is that?"

"Between your pictures that Eva has framed on the walls and the huge trophies in the closet, I'm assuming you do more than work on boat engines. You own that boat, don't you?"

"I race on the World Cup circuit. It's just a hobby."

"An expensive one."

He chuckled. "You know what they say about men and their toys—the older the man, the more expensive the toys."

"Fine." She threw her hands into the air. "Keep your secrets. I just thought it might be nice to have an answer when Skye asks me what you do for a living."

"I'm an inventor," he told her as he opened the door into Ford's office.

She preceded him inside, paying little attention to the magnificent furnishings. She was much more interested in Max. "What do you invent?"

"I had a dream about a more fuel-efficient carburetor."

She should have known. Remembering their first meeting and how he'd treated his boat engine with the deft and delicate touch of a lover, she bit back a grin. Him and his precious engine. He even dreamed about it. Odd how she found the trait so typical of him and at the same time, endearing. "Did you make it?"

"Only one, a prototype."

"It worked?"

"Yup."

Dragging information from him was harder than making Skye brush her teeth. But clearly he was more comfortable inventing than speaking, so she made the extra effort to get him to explain.

"What happened?"

"I sold the idea and moved on to more interesting projects."

Like fixing boat engines? She held the words back, and as he settled in the leather chair behind Ford's massive desk, her thoughts dwelled on Max. Who was she to question what he did for a living? She figured the money from his invention must not have lasted long since he lived at the marina. So what?

How could she be falling for a man who probably had no savings account, who had no interest in a savings account, who lived from day-to-day, avoiding responsibility?

She didn't consider money the be-all and end-all of life. Yet she wanted a roof over her head in a decent neighborhood. She wanted Skye to take dance and piano lessons. She wanted to drive to work in a car that wouldn't break down once a week, and she intended to save to send her daughter to college.

What Brooke wanted as much as her own independence was the chance to graduate from college and win the marketing promotion that would start a career. It was important, this dream of hers. So she had no business thinking of Max as anyone more than Skye's father.

Max fired up Ford's computer, a smile of satisfaction on his face that made her heart skip. Even after the talking-to she'd just given herself, her pulse soared.

She peered over his shoulder at the computer screen. "Do you know the password?"

"In a manner of speaking. My brother and I share

our love of gadgets. Ford had this system installed with retina imaging. All I have to do is look at the screen and the computer will think I'm Ford."

"Okay, you're in. Now what?"

"I don't know. I've never done this before. Do you have any suggestions?"

"We need a connection between Ford's accident, the Kine Clinic and Skye. See if he has a file on the Kine Clinic."

Max shot her a thumbs-up. "Bingo."

"Now check the subdirectories for personnel files. Maybe we can find something useful on Dr. Arnold, the doctor in charge of Nicole's embryo." Her eyes widened as Max brought up the data. Each employee's file was complete with addresses, phone numbers and education. "How'd he get all this information?"

"These are copies of the clinic's personnel files. As a member of the board, Ford has full access to these records. But why did he bother to bring a copy home?" Max swiveled, grabbed a pad of paper and a pen and handed it to her. "Take down Dr. Arnold's address and phone number."

She scribbled happily. She'd tried to get that number but it had been unlisted.

He moved the cursor, skimming. "I don't see anything else useful in his file. Any other suggestions?"

"We should check for memos about internal problems at the clinic, too."

Max switched to a calendar and perused his brother's notes during the last financial quarter. "Ford strongly encouraged Dr. Henschel to replace Karen Forester with Pete Wilson."

"Wilson is an accountant."

"My brother has a reminder to check research and development but doesn't say about what. Could be about advertising, public relations, or ordering high-tech equipment."

She looked at the screen while chewing on the pencil tip. "Does Ford have background information on everyone at the Kine Clinic?"

"Looks like it."

"Can you print the entire file?"

"It'll be thick as a book."

"I'd like to see what comes up on Callie Wainwright, Dr. Henschel, Karen Forester and Grant Donovan. Oh, and the accountant, too. That crumpled memo you found on overbilling bothers me."

Max craned his neck to look at her. "What could the financial status of the company have to do with Skye?"

"I'm not sure. That's what we need to find—a connection."

After sending a command to the printer, Max leaned back in the chair. The printer started but she barely noticed the hum over her focused concentration. Brooke tapped the pencil on the desk. "When I was researching your brother, I read that the Kine Clinic is traded on the stock exchange."

Max raised his arms and laced his hands behind his head. "So what? I still don't see what this has to do with Skye or Ford."

"I'm no expert, but I do know if the scandal of an embryo switch in the clinic hit the papers, the price of the stock would plummet."

Max groaned.

"What?" Expecting him to poke holes in her theory, she braced for an argument.

"My brother sees to it that every employee owns a piece of the company. So *everyone* at the clinic would lose if news of Skye got out. That leaves a lot of people with good reason to cover up the switch."

She let her shoulders relax. Max's groan had been one of agreement of her point. Why was she so defensive around him? Or was it that she didn't want to disappoint him? "Competitors would be eager for a scandal. I'd hate to think our investigations could hurt your brother's company."

"Ford isn't hung up on money. Business is more a challenge with him. He'd give everything he owned to have Rhonda back alive. And he won't care if we bankrupt the company if we find out who was behind Skye's embryo being placed in your sister's womb."

"Let's search his desk." Brooke opened a side drawer, leaving the top middle drawer for Max. Her drawer was full of hanging folders and she skimmed through the numerous corporations filed in alphabetical order. Spotting the Kine Clinic folder, she pulled out and opened the file. She flipped though pages of financial documents until a familiar date on a report caught her eye.

Her voice rose with excitement. "This is the same quarterly report we found in Henschel's office."

"And?"

"The numbers are different. I'm sure of it! The research and development costs are much lower on this statement."

"So maybe the accountant adjusted them. Maybe the first statement was a mistake."

"Maybe." But she didn't think so.

He shook his head and a lock of hair fell across his forehead. Her fingers itched to smooth it back. To distract herself, she flipped through the rest of the papers.

"There are several interesting memos in here. This one's from the researcher, Grant. He's claiming they have a virus in the computer system. He's taking the system off-line for a few days to fix the problem." She stood and paced excitedly. "Max, suppose the Kine Clinic isn't being overbilled. Suppose the clinic is overbilling patients. The computer records would have to be altered regularly to conceal improprieties."

"What are you saying?"

"If a scandal breaks *now,* there would be an intense investigation. They may need time to doctor the books and cover their tracks."

"Those are some gargantuan assumptions from a note about overbilling, two financial statements that don't match, and a computer virus."

"Grant could be taking the computer off-line to hide the overbilling. He may be stealing."

He shook his head. "Or maybe the computer really is down, the accountant made an error in the first financial statement and corrected it. And the overbilling refers to ordering too much paper for a copy machine or an overcharge on cleaning supplies."

Her theory did sound crazy—even if the pieces all fit. "You're right. We need proof."

She thought Max would drop the idea. But he surprised her. "Let's go with your idea for a moment. As a stockholder, any employee might want to cover up the mix-up with Skye. If we can find out who actually switched the embryos, maybe we can resolve the reason behind the cover-up and whether it has any connection to Ford's accident. The way I see it, we still have to find Dr. Arnold."

A PHONE CALL to Dr. Arnold's housekeeper gave Max the name of the Lake Pontchartrain marina Arnold had sailed from. They'd left Ford's Mercedes in his garage, and now, back in Max's truck, swung by his parents' house. Eva had left them a note, informing them that Ford would arrive later that day and would be transferred to a private facility. Rhonda's body would go straight to the funeral home.

Skye sat listlessly in a chair in front of the television, her cat in her lap. She perked up when Brooke told her they were all going on a boat ride on Lake Pontchartrain. While Brooke and she scampered upstairs for swimsuits and towels, Max queried the housekeeper. "Skye's not settling in, is she?"

The older woman frowned. "She wants to go to camp. And she misses her mother. I'm afraid she feels cooped up in the house. I gather Brooke normally takes her on a daily outing—to the park or the library. I've kept her busy coloring, but she's restless. And she won't put the kitten down."

Max vowed to make the day pleasant for Skye. He wanted her first impressions of him to be good ones. And he didn't want her thinking he was taking her mother away from her, either. Unfortunately, with the funeral tomorrow, Skye would be stuck with the housekeeper again. So today he'd do his best to entertain her with lots of fresh air and sunshine while they searched for Dr. Arnold's boat.

Brooke came downstairs wearing a sunflowered short-sleeved shirt and navy pants. A wide belt with a sunflower buckle cinched her narrow waist, and a yellow jacket completed the outfit. He finally admitted to himself that Brooke would look good in anything she wore, but he'd really prefer her in nothing at all.

Thoughts like that would get him into trouble. Brooke wasn't the kind of woman to indulge in one-night stands. He wasn't the kind of man to offer more. Keeping his randy thoughts to himself, he turned his gaze on his daughter.

Skye looked adorable in red overalls and a white T-shirt. "You think Fraidy-cat will miss me?" After Brooke convinced Skye the kitten would live up to its name and be afraid of the boat, Skye had agreed to leave her pet at the house.

"Of course," Brooke told her. "She'll probably curl up and go to sleep."

Max had changed into khaki slacks and an ivory shirt he'd found in a closet. He wore soft leather boat shoes—no socks—and suddenly felt outclassed by the two ladies. Startled at the direction of his thoughts, he wondered what was happening to him. Never before had he much cared how he looked.

They left a note for his parents, said goodbye to the housekeeper, piled into the pickup and set off for Lake Pontchartrain where he would put the *Sea Mist* into the water.

In the afternoon light, the soft reds in Brooke's hair

took on copper highlights. She'd been a terrific help in Ford's office and amazingly creative about piecing together a theory from the few clues they had. As if feeling his gaze on her, she looked at him over Skye's head in the front seat of the truck and smiled.

He was getting to like that smile. He was getting to know her lips. And he wanted to know them better. Pushing the sensation of what she would taste like from his mind, Max kept his gaze on the road. Still, whenever he forgot his resolve, he found his eyes returning to catch glimpses of Brooke.

Even as he opened the garage, and hooked his boat trailer to his truck, his thoughts were on Brooke and Skye. He hoped they'd enjoy the outing. Yet he couldn't shake the feeling they shouldn't be exposing themselves on the open water. Grimly, he reminded himself he couldn't keep Skye behind alarm systems and high walls forever, and there had been no further sign of trouble since the man in the park. While they sought the key piece in the puzzle—and right now Dr. Arnold held it—Max wanted this to be a pleasant outing for Skye.

He returned from the garage with hats for Skye and Brooke. "I'm going to need both your help."

Skye's eyes sparkled from beneath the brim of her hat. "Mine, too?"

"What do you want us to do?" Brooke asked.

Max shifted the truck into gear and headed for the boat ramp, ignoring the dust he kicked up. Luckily the place was empty and so was the parking lot. With Brooke's help and Skye on "lookout" to make sure he backed straight, he soon had the *Sea Mist* in the water and tied to the dock.

"First things first. Let's put a life preserver on Skye."

"But I know how to swim." Skye's chest puffed with indignation.

Max grinned. "On my boat, everyone wears a life vest. Even grown-ups."

"Mommy, too?"

He nodded, snapping her into the yellow jacket, then lifting her onto the front seat. Brooke hopped into the boat with a show of a slim ankle and an agility he couldn't help but appreciate. "Now what?"

He handed her a life jacket. "We won't use helmets, but after you put that jacket on, I'd like you and Skye to strap in. The lake is some forty miles long and twenty-five miles wide. Our best bet is to drive down to the Southern Yacht Club and ask which part of the lake Dr. Arnold likes to sail."

"Sounds good."

The racing boat had only three seats. He'd placed Skye in the middle one and Brooke took the other. He made sure each was strapped in before donning his own harness. She rubbed her thighs, a sure sign something was worrying her. Finally she looked up at him. "How fast does this boat go?"

He should have figured she'd be concerned for Skye's safety. "Don't worry. I have no intention of opening her up."

"Opening who up?" Skye asked.

He chuckled. "The boat is a her. And 'opening her

up' means to go full speed. But this isn't a race. And besides, two engines are down.''

Skye looked at the deck. ''Down where?''

''That's boating talk. Two engines aren't working.''

''Is boating talk like French?''

Max grinned and shook his head at her curiosity. Brooke laughed outright, but even when she laughed, shadows haunted her eyes. While Brooke explained, he steered for the old, white coast guard lighthouse, omitting the fact that even with two engines out, this boat could go more than a hundred miles an hour. They passed parks, several yacht clubs, a marina and a few restaurants before he turned into the Southern Yacht Club and docked.

Getting a mechanic to tell him Arnold liked to sail the north side of the lake proved easy. And a friendly kid in the office marina looked up the boat's registration number for him. But after hours of searching, only Skye's bright smile and the fixed determination in Brooke's eyes kept him from suggesting they suspend their search for Arnold until tomorrow.

After they'd checked out countless marinas and anchorages, Brooke untied her hat and tossed it under the bow. ''It seems hopeless. I never knew so many marinas existed on one lake. Almost everyone here has a boat.''

Skye frowned. ''Why do we need to find a doctor? Are you sick?''

''I'm fine, sweetie. We just need to ask the man a few questions.''

Max kept his tone confident. ''We'll find him. Not many doctors live on their boats for weeks at a time.''

"He may not tell anyone he's a doctor."

At each marina, Max had stopped and asked if anyone knew of a doctor living aboard a boat at anchorage or in a nearby slip. "It's possible," he conceded. "But men who earn their medical degrees are often too proud to go back to being called plain mister."

Sunlight glistened off the ripples in the choppy water. They drove by shrimpers, trawlers, yachts and ferries, spotting many sailboats but none with registration numbers that matched Dr. Arnold's.

In spite of Brooke's doubts, she didn't give up or suggest they turn back. And Skye seemed to be enjoying herself—especially when Max held her in his lap and let her steer.

Max sped into a bay with a lone sailboat at an odd angle. The boat wasn't facing into the wind and suspicion prickled his neck. As Brooke held the binoculars to her eyes and read off the registration numbers, he sensed their search had ended.

Brooke's voice trembled with hope. "That's Arnold's boat. We've found him."

"I knew Max could do it." Skye looked at him as if he were some kind of hero.

Max ruffled her hair. "Thanks for the vote of confidence, sweetie."

He looked forward to a long, enlightening conversation with the doctor. As Max slowed his boat and entered the shallow area, he frowned, wondering if he should have brought Brooke and Skye with him after all. He wouldn't voluntarily bring either of them into danger. And from the way the boat tilted, he suspected something was wrong. "What does Dr. Arnold look like?"

"Six years ago, he was in his mid-fifties, with surprisingly dark hair going gray at the temples. About medium height, he had a slight paunch at the stomach."

"You'd recognize him if you saw him?"

"I think so."

The three-masted sailboat didn't bob like a boat at anchor. Nor did the hull swing into the wind. An eerie misgiving feathered down Max's spine.

"Do you see an anchor line?"

Brooke raised the binoculars again. "No, why?"

"I think the boat's aground. I don't want us to end up stuck in the mud, too. I'm going to anchor you and swim over." He handed her a cell phone. "Stay here until I signal. The coast guard number is taped to the back of the phone."

Worry darkened her eyes, but she didn't ask questions. She kept glancing at the sailboat, spookily silent.

It didn't take Max long to secure his boat or change into swim trunks in the tiny cabin. When he exited the cabin, Brooke had taken their swimsuits out of a bag to change.

"Be careful." She looked as if she would like to say more.

He gave her hand a quick squeeze, then lowered himself over the side. The water was too shallow to swim. He ended up wading to the other boat.

As he neared, he saw that the boat's chrome, polished to a high shine, had the look of a well-loved craft. Homey curtains of bright blue in the portholes prevented him from seeing into the cabin. A flag flapped and the halyards clanged against the mast.

"Anyone home?" Max called as he drew closer, his gut tight.

When no one answered, he climbed aboard and looked inside the cabin.

The boat was empty. Arnold was gone.

Chapter Six

Max ducked into the cabin and did a quick walk-through to make sure there would be no nasty surprises. The letter on the table was ominous enough. The boat had no damage. There were no signs of a struggle. Except for the note, it was as if Dr. Arnold had left for a swim.

He climbed back into the cockpit, gave Brooke the thumbs-up signal and prepared to return to help her with Skye. But she splashed over the side and took Skye into her arms, clearly not needing his help.

He leaned over to lift Skye into the cockpit, then lent Brooke a hand. "The boat is empty."

He turned to Skye. "Somebody lost his boat and the police may need to search for fingerprints. Can you stay right here and be lookout while your mom helps me read a letter?"

Skye sat cross-legged. "Okay."

Brooke followed him into the cabin. Her gaze went to the letter. "What does it say?" she asked softly.

"A suicide note."

She leaned over the table and read the short note.

"'I have no wish to live. To whoever finds this boat, she's yours. Take good care of her, she's a good boat.' And it's signed, Clifford Arnold, M.D.''

Brooke's shoulders sagged and she slumped. "He must have gone overboard in the middle of the lake and his boat drifted into this cove. How long do you think the boat's been here?''

"A few days, not more than a week.''

Brooke began opening and closing drawers, sifting through charts, radio instructions and the silverware drawer, careful not to leave her own fingerprints. She frequently glanced up into the cockpit to check on Skye.

"What are you looking for?''

"I don't know. This boat is immaculate. Would a man about to kill himself leave it so spotless?''

"Maybe. We should call the coast guard.''

Brooke leaned over the chart table and her brows furrowed. "I think I've found something.''

"What?''

She lifted a clipboard from a hook. "This is the same pad of paper the suicide note came from.''

"So?''

"Look.'' She held up the pad. On the top page were indentations from a previous page. "It's a grocery list.''

Comprehension kicked in, and he realized how smart she was. "You think he wrote the suicide note and tore it off the pad. Then he wrote a grocery list?''

"Tell me, Max. Why would a man about to kill himself write a grocery list after he writes a suicide note? I don't think he's dead.''

"Dead or not, Arnold's the key to the puzzle. He was your sister's doctor. He was Rhonda's doctor. And when you started asking questions, he suddenly disappeared."

BROOKE AND MAX went to Arnold's house and found it empty. They questioned his neighbors but no one had seen him. If Arnold had faked his suicide, he'd vanished without a trace.

Later, at Max's parents' house, while Max visited Ford in the hospital that evening, Brooke thought about what they'd found on the boat. Had Arnold killed himself? Or had he killed Callie and set them up for the murder and, when his plan hadn't worked, decided to disappear rather than risk being caught?

Brooke came to no conclusions. They simply didn't have enough information.

She fed and bathed Skye, then read her a bedtime story. Her daughter clung to her in a babylike fashion she hadn't exhibited in years. Brooke hated to leave her with the housekeeper during the funeral tomorrow, but she didn't have much choice.

At least she didn't have to worry about her work. When she'd called her boss and told him she wouldn't be in for the rest of the week, he told her he'd call a temporary service for a substitute until she returned.

After Skye was in bed, Brooke went through the files they'd printed from Ford's computer. She must have fallen asleep in the den because when she woke up, Max was watching her.

"How's Ford?"

Max shook his head, his eyes filled with pain. "His

condition hasn't changed. He could wake up tomorrow or stay in a coma for the rest of his life. We have two guards in the room with him and one in the hall at all times. Mother and the nurses read to him to stimulate his brain's activity. There's nothing else that can be done."

He must have talked to his brother for a long time. His voice was hoarse.

Max took a seat next to her on the couch and she sensed his need for comfort. He'd dimmed the lights. "My folks went to see Rhonda's parents."

Suddenly nervous at being alone with him, she reached for the printout. "I was going over these files—"

"Anything that can't wait?" His tone turned ever huskier, resonating down her spine until she yearned with anticipation.

Heat in his eyes burned into hers. She read his intention in his eyes. He was going to kiss her. And she wanted him to.

Leaning over slowly, he cupped her chin and let his lips brush hers. He tasted of his own wonderful brand of masculinity. Her heart lurched and she wound her arms around his neck, aching to draw him closer.

He tugged her onto his lap, and she snuggled against him. Her bottom curved against his thighs. Her shoulder nestled snugly under his arm, and it required absolutely no straining to hold their kiss, as if they were made to fit.

He rubbed his hands over her back, wound his fingers into her hair, and inhaled as if he wanted to learn her by scent. Beneath her, his jeans grew tight with his need. She tried and failed to smother a groan.

Wrenching away, he inhaled a ragged breath. "Unless you're prepared for me to remove every stitch of your clothing and make love, we'd better stop."

Surprised by the harsh adamancy of his words, her eyes widened. Heat flushed her face. "I—I..." she stammered, shaken as much by the intensity of her emotions as the ferocity of his need.

Tossing her hair out of her face, she pulled herself together and stared him straight in the eyes. "If all you're offering is a roll in bed, I'll pass."

She held her breath, waiting to see what he'd say.

"What if I offer more?"

Her heart skipped. Before she could respond, the lights went out. The alarm's siren shrieked.

"Mommy!"

Brooke leapt off Max's lap and stumbled for the stairway in the dark. Was someone in the house? Could they have broken into Skye's room?

Max pounded up the stairs ahead of her. From the sound of his footsteps, his long legs were taking the stairs three at a time. Streetlights shone through the upstairs windows, casting light beams into Skye's room. Max had already scooped Skye into his arms, blanket, kitten and all, when she arrived.

"She's fine. The siren scared her." Max handed Skye to her. "Stay here. I'll go downstairs and check out the house."

"Max?"

He paused, his silhouette outlined in the moonlight. "Yes?"

"Doesn't the alarm call the police?"

"Yup."

While she couldn't fault him for how fast he'd raced to Skye, he was so composed now, she wondered if he was concerned in the slightest.

"Why don't you stay here with us and let the cops check the place?"

"It's probably nothing. An electric surge or a squirrel could set it off." Nevertheless, he returned to the bed and put his arm around both of them. "But if it'll make you feel better, we'll wait together."

Skye sucked her thumb, and she hadn't done that since her second birthday. "I want to go home. And I want to go to camp."

"You will, sweetie. Didn't you like the boat ride today?"

"I want to go home." Skye sobbed in her arms while Max punched in the code to silence the alarm. Within a few minutes, Skye fell asleep. Brooke smoothed the tears from her daughter's face.

Although she hadn't explained much to Skye, her daughter obviously felt the tension. Her life had been turned upside down. Brooke ached over Skye's unhappiness, but her daughter's safety was paramount. Especially after tonight.

The police arrived and searched the premises but found nothing, except one footprint in a flower bed—directly below Skye's second-story window.

THE DAY OF Rhonda's funeral, gray clouds hung over the skies until the horizon was lost in a sullen foglike mist. Max had bought Skye a Disney video and, planted happily in front of the TV, she hadn't seemed upset with their departure. While Brooke hated leaving Skye, the sooner she and Max figured out what had happened, the sooner Brooke and Skye could return to their normal lives.

Hour by hour the cloud deck lowered, thicker and darker. By the time Brooke and Max arrived at the cemetery and parked, the air was moist with clinging humidity.

Brooke strode beside Max past the outer walls of the cemetery where rows of vaults, called "ovens," held the remains of the city's poor. Inside, the cemetery grew more elaborate. To overcome the high-water table, aboveground tombs were constructed out of brick walls. For the wealthy, the entrances to the plastered, whitewashed tombs were closed with marble tablets and enclosed within iron fences.

Max led Brooke down a narrow path to the family vault that had a rounded roof and tiny eaves. A tent had been set up for the service with chairs reserved at the front for the immediate family. The size of the crowd who had left the dry and warm church to accompany the family to the graveside service surprised her. Rhonda must have had a lot of friends for them to venture out in this weather to pay their last respects.

Max leaned over and whispered in her ear. "Many of Ford's business associates are here. And Rhonda chaired several large charities in the area."

As the service began, the skies opened and rain sluiced down. Those not covered by the tent opened umbrellas. No one left, but the minister wisely kept the service short.

Max sat beside her, his face calm, but anger radiating off him in waves. She took his hand and held tight, knowing he was thinking of Ford.

Beside him, Red and Eva clung to one another. Not only had they lost a daughter-in-law, they might lose a son if Ford didn't surface from his coma. If Ford didn't recover, they'd have the comfort of Max, but Ford's twin would always be a visible reminder of what they lost. She issued a silent prayer for Ford's recovery.

Brooke glanced at Rhonda's parents who sat drawn and white-lipped in front of the rose-draped casket as if they were in shock. How horrible to lose a child. From Ford's files she had learned Rhonda had endured six embryo implantations, and with each progressive attempt, her chances of having a baby diminished. Dr. Arnold had finally recommended adoption. After struggling so long and hard for a baby, how sad that Rhonda had died before she'd known Skye. Ice clenched around Brooke's heart at the thought of ever losing Skye.

She'd never met Rhonda, and even though Skye looked nothing like the pictures Eva had of Ford's wife, Brooke wished she could have talked with her and observed her temperament and demeanor. Rhonda's personality might have held clues to what kind of woman Skye would become.

From everything Brooke had heard about Rhonda, she was sweet, kind and gentle. Tears rolled down her cheeks for the woman who'd wanted a child so badly and had died never knowing her beautiful daughter.

More tears followed for Skye, who'd never know the special person her biological mother had been.

Rest in peace, Rhonda. You were an angel on Earth. Look down now and be a guardian angel for Skye.

The service concluded and people came forward to offer condolences to both families. Time and again Max explained that his brother was still in Europe, grieving over his wife and not yet ready to face coming home alone.

Brooke noticed one young woman whose eyes were puffy and red from crying. "Who is she?"

"I think her name is Denise. She's a cousin of Rhonda's and was very close to her."

Karen Forester broke from the crowd and laid a red rose on Rhonda's coffin. After the way the Kine Clinic researcher had avoided them at her apartment, Brooke was shocked when she joined them.

Karen's face was shadowed by a wide-brimmed hat. "Rhonda helped me find a job at the clinic. I didn't know her well, but she was a nice woman."

Knowing the question inappropriate but thinking she might not get another chance, Brooke spoke in a low voice. "Why did you change your mind about talking to me?"

"I'm sorry. Dr. Arnold told me not to violate company policy."

"When did you speak to Dr. Arnold?" Max squeezed Brooke's hand tightly but from his tone she'd have never guessed how interested he was in Karen's statement.

"Let's see. I left a message on his voice mail last week. He returned my call on Friday. Why?"

Brooke watched Karen's face closely for any indication that Arnold might still be alive. "His sailboat was found empty. He left a suicide note. It'll probably make the evening news."

"Oh, God! No."

Karen's face turned white and her pupils dilated. Max reached out to steady her, but Karen turned and stumbled off into the rain.

Max frowned. "Do you think she and Arnold were close?"

"I don't know." She couldn't say more because Grant Donovan had approached them and she wondered what he was doing here. But then many of the Kine Clinic's employees had come to pay their respects.

Grant shook Max's hand, cleared his throat and looked at the ground, clearly not knowing what to say. "How is your brother?" he finally asked.

"As well as can be expected under the circumstances. He's shocked and grieving," Max lied smoothly.

Grant moved on, but his appearance reminded her of what she'd learned from Ford's files, and she filled Max in. "Several years ago, at about the time Rhonda started making appointments at the fertility clinic, Grant was accepted to medical school. Apparently he didn't have the funds for tuition and couldn't secure a loan. Ford made an endowment to the school and was put on the screening committee for loans. When Grant wasn't chosen, he blamed Ford."

Max followed her line of reasoning. "So Grant had

a reason to dislike Ford, plus he knows the computer system."

"And why is he here if he disliked Ford?"

"Good question. We need to find out if Grant has access to the embryos."

"Why don't we ask Dr. Henschel?" She tugged on Max's hand. "I saw him at the back of the tent."

They wound their way through groups of people talking in low voices beneath the pattering of the rain on the canvas.

Dr. Henschel broke away from a group when he spotted them, peering through glasses foggy from the humidity. He nodded a greeting to Brooke and shook Max's hand. "I'm sorry this happened. How's Ford holding up?"

"He's going to be okay. It'll take some time though. Since Ford isn't here, I thought maybe you could help me out by answering a few questions."

Brooke carefully watched Henschel's face. He didn't reveal his emotions easily, yet she caught a hint of impatience in his eyes.

"Sure. What can I do?"

"Does Grant have access to the laboratory and the embryos?"

Henschel took off his glasses and pinched the bridge of his nose. "I shouldn't be telling you this, but it's not a secret. I know all about Grant's old grudge toward your brother over the medical school loan, but even if Grant had wanted to switch the embryos, he doesn't have access to the patients' lab. Research and Development has their own facility."

"Thanks. I appreciate the information. I assume

you've heard about Dr. Arnold?'' Max asked before Henschel could escape. Brooke admired his quick thinking.

"The police contacted me last night. What a shame to lose such a talented man. But I'm not totally surprised. The man's been overworked and on edge for years. Still, replacing him won't be easy."

The wind picked up, driving a drenching rain through the tent. The remaining mourners quickly scattered.

Max opened an umbrella and they walked to his truck, huddling beneath it. Behind them, workers slid Rhonda's coffin into the vault and Brooke shuddered. "It's horrible Rhonda died so young."

"There are no guarantees. Her life was short, but she made the most of it."

Brooke's thoughts turned to Skye. "If anything happens to me, promise me you'll take care of Skye."

He guided her around a puddle. "Nothing's going to happen."

"You just said there are no guarantees." She chewed her lip. "One of the reasons I searched for Skye's family was because I didn't want her to end up in foster care if anything happens to me."

Max wound his fingers between hers. The gesture was oddly familiar, as if he'd touched her so comfortingly a thousand times before. "Skye's part of the family now."

Brooke's spinning thoughts broke away from Max and focused on her daughter. Nicole hadn't planned to die. Neither had Rhonda. If a similar fate befell Brooke, what would happen to Skye?

She spoke past the tightness in her throat, spurred by grief and unchecked emotions to press Max for an answer. "Will you promise to raise Skye if something happens to me?"

"Sure," he agreed with an ease that surprised her. "I promise she'll have a good home."

A good home? What did that mean? After their mother had died, the state had sent Nicole and Brooke to one foster home after another. The sisters had food on the table and a roof over their heads, but few of the foster parents had cared if they brushed their teeth or made good grades in school. No one had cared what they did or thought as long as they stayed out of trouble. But at least the sisters had had each other to share their dreams. Skye would be all alone.

No. A good home wasn't sufficient. She wanted Skye to have the love and security of family that she hadn't had.

"Promise me, you'll be there for Skye."

She didn't think he was going to answer. Although he gripped her hand tightly, he remained silent. Behind her someone swore softly as the wind turned their umbrella inside out. Her insides churned. "You can't do it, can you, Max?"

"Do what?"

"Commit yourself. Not even to a little girl."

"Hey, I'm here right next to you. We're seeing this through together. Both of us."

"But what if something happens to me?"

His steady blue eyes looked at her as if she was worried for no reason. But his calm grated on Brooke's nerves. Not exhibiting some emotion was unnatural. She wondered if Max didn't worry about death because he wouldn't miss anything in life. Or did he care so much he only pretended indifference?

Even after his sister-in-law had died, proving how easily life could be snuffed out, he found making a commitment difficult. He'd been silent so long, she jumped when he spoke.

"I'll be there for Skye."

He'd spoken the words so softly, she almost hadn't heard him over the patter of rain. Stunned, she thought for a moment she'd imagined the words, since she'd wanted so badly to hear them. As she turned and saw resolve flaring brightly in his eyes, she knew that he'd irrevocably acknowledged responsibility for his daughter. The comforting rightness almost over-whelmed her.

"Thank you. It means a lot to know Skye has some-one else to count on." They walked along the side-walk, his large frame shielding her from much of the rain, cocooned in their own little intimate bubble. His hand still gripped hers and she wasn't the least sur-prised. He seemed to need the comfort as much as she. The past two days had brimmed with tragic tension. For a moment, Brooke wondered how it could be pos-sible that they'd once been strangers.

When they reached his vehicle, Max released her hand, raised the keys to the lock and stopped. His hand shook and only a deep breath that lifted his whole chest stilled it.

"Max?" Brooke laid her hand softly over his.

His blue eyes pierced her. "You're worried about Skye, aren't you?"

"I've been leaving her too much. She's not happy staying at the house without me."

He held her hand tightly. "It's the safest place for her. The alarm going off and that strange encounter in the park were probably both harmless incidents—but I'd rather not take any chances."

"Isn't there somewhere safe we could take her? I want to spend a day with her outside, if it stops raining."

"I may know just the place. Let me talk to the folks when we get home and I'll see what we can do."

Brooke should have been relieved and happy at his words. Instead of making light of her concerns he'd agreed and actually volunteered to help. An outing would cheer Skye.

But thunder clapped and lightning zapped a tree less than a block away. A bad omen. A premonition of doom. She tried to shake off the odd prickles diving down her back. The storm and the funeral had her imagining things.

Chapter Seven

The next morning, Skye was happy to go with Red and Eva, especially once they had asked her to call them Grandma and Grandpa. They hadn't explained the situation in detail, simply telling Skye they didn't have any grandchildren and would like it if she called them by nicknames. Skye loved the idea and hadn't minded being left with her "grandparents," especially after Brooke and Max promised to meet them at Indian Lake for a picnic after they visited Ford at the hospital.

Max steered through the traffic with ease, but his fingers tensed on the wheel as he thought about how much he'd wanted Brooke last night. Once, many years ago, Max thought he'd found what he'd been looking for—a love special enough to last a lifetime. Then his life had careened out of control until he'd thought he'd never get over his past. He had. Now he protected himself by never allowing anyone to come too close, by moving on before his feelings deepened.

He'd stopped looking, deciding what he needed didn't exist. Then he'd convinced himself he no longer had those needs. He'd thought he'd damn well learned to live without them.

But Brooke Evans with her emerald eyes flashing a challenge when he'd accused her of interest in Ford's wealth had intrigued him from the first. Her selfless honesty and love for Skye had almost convinced him that perhaps, with the right woman, he might find a balm to the restlessness that churned in him. She was a wonderful mother, giving, kind, loving. And she'd faced up to Skye's biological origins with a maturity and selflessness that amazed him.

Last night, the need to go to her had been almost unbearable. Oh, how he'd ached from wanting her. He'd wanted to take her into his arms and kiss her again, taste her until he had his fill. He'd wanted to indulge in her womanly scent and feel the warmth of her silky flesh under his palms in a celebration of life. He'd wanted to fill his hands with her breasts. He wanted to delve inside her and drive her wild until she moaned and screamed his name in release.

But he couldn't touch her. Not when the permanency and responsibilities required of fatherhood shook him to the core. He loved Skye. If things didn't work out between him and Brooke, suppose she took his daughter away?

Keeping his hands off her delectable body would have been much more difficult if he hadn't been so drained from the funeral. Still the recollection of her silky skin beneath his fingers as he'd cupped her chin during their kiss had him twisting and turning. Luckily, fatigue took over and at last he'd fallen asleep.

He'd awakened this morning with the same problem—wondering if she was awake, wondering what she'd worn to sleep, wondering what she'd do if he carried her into his bed. Not even a cold shower had stopped his fantasizing.

He'd stepped into the icy spray, reminding himself to stay sharp. And now, as a car followed them through one right and then three left turns, he reminded himself again. He suspected someone had arranged to kill Rhonda and Ford in Europe while simultaneously framing Max and Brooke at the Kine Clinic in Louisiana. Chances were they were up against more than one individual. Or had their foes tried to fix it so both Max and Ford looked guilty of 'crimes? Why? What was the connection to Skye, the clinic and the avalanche?

No matter how unlikely, he was stretching the possibilities, trying to come up with a motive that made sense. There had to be a connection to Skye, but he just couldn't see one.

As the car that had followed them for a short time veered onto the interstate, Max relaxed. He was beginning to see danger around every corner, even where none existed. Today, after this visit to Ford, he intended to kick back and clear his head and enjoy Skye.

WHEN THEY'D REACHED the hospital, Brooke opted out of the visit to Ford's room, preferring to wait in the lobby. Max had been quiet on the way over, and the tension between them hummed. She didn't know what she wanted to do about it, and she needed time to think.

As Max exited the hospital elevator, striding in her

direction, her heart raced a little, just knowing he was coming for her. Controlling her response to him was getting old. She wasn't sure how long she could maintain the constant vigilance over her own reactions to him, but she wanted him to make an emotional commitment to her first. And to Skye.

With his brother's condition unchanged yet stable, Max had kept the visit short. He helped her into the truck and quickly merged with the traffic. "Are you ready to head into Cajun country?"

"I haven't been back here in years." She relaxed as he drove through a countryside dotted with tiny towns and villages where antique seekers could poke around in bliss. Centuries' old oaks covered with Spanish moss formed canopies over bottle-green bayous. The rural road Max took followed the contortions of the Teche, the state's largest bayou, meandering through ancient Arcadian villages of cypress cabins that rose out of the water on stilts. Moored fishing boats and pirogues barely rocked on the still waters.

Max drove the speed limit; Brooke kept an eye out for alligators or wild boars that might dart across the road. The only wildlife she spotted was a snow-white egret.

They took a curve in the road and ahead a small town nestled in the crook of the bayou. A school bus pulled out into the road, cutting them off. Max jammed on the brakes. Their speed didn't slow. The pickup kept traveling on collision course—straight toward the bus. Max swore, shifted into low gear and steadily applied pressure with the hand brake. The rear wheels screeched across pavement. As they skidded off the road, gravel battered the fenders.

Oh, God. They were going to die.

Brooke's heart jammed like a fist in her throat. Bone-scared, she braced her hands against the dash.

The truck spun.

She lost sight of the bus.

She squeezed her eyes tight, held her breath, waiting for the crash, breaking glass and twisted metal.

It didn't come.

She opened her eyes, her nostrils flaring at the stench of burned rubber. They sat partway off the road, facing away from the school bus, the pickup engine dead. Miraculously, Max had managed to stop the truck by pulling a one hundred and eighty degree turn.

"Are you all right?" He released the hand brake, restarted the engine, and eased the pickup fully off the road as if he'd pulled that stunt a hundred times.

Nausea churned her stomach. "I think I'm going to be sick."

Max cut the engine and came around to her side of the truck. He opened the door and gently pushed her head down to her knees. "Take several deep breaths. That's it. Breathe in through your nose and out through your mouth."

She did as he instructed and the nausea eased. She straightened at the sound of footsteps pounding the pavement.

A mechanic ran over from the corner garage. "You folks all right?"

Max nodded. "The brakes went out."

"That was some mighty fine driving, mister. If you

hadn't stopped, it would have been a sorry accident with that busload of kids.''

"Could you take a look at the brakes?"

"Sure enough. Drive her over and we'll put her up in the rack.''

Brooke preferred to walk on unsteady legs the half block to the garage rather than ride in the truck. The fresh air cleared the last vestiges of dizziness. She caught up with the men as they inspected a dripping hose.

Max's expression didn't change, but the muscle in his jaw was so tight he had to be gnashing his teeth. He rammed his hands into his pockets in a gesture so violent, a shiver rippled down her back.

"What's wrong?"

"Looks like someone cut the brake line, ma'am."

It took a moment for the implication to sink in. This was no accident. Someone had tried to kill them. And only because they'd changed plans at the last moment, Skye hadn't been with them.

"Someone's after us," she whispered as Max walked her into the air-conditioned waiting area.

"They must have sliced the brake line while we visited Ford. This isn't pressure to back off our investigation. These people are serious.''

She sank onto a cracked vinyl couch. "I think we should give it up. It's not worth risking our lives to find out what happened.''

Max's eyes darkened. His voice was grim. "We no longer have a choice. If we don't find out who is behind this and stop them, they'll try again until they kill us.''

How could he be so calm when she was shaking inside like a leaf in a summer storm? "But why is anyone after us?"

"We must be close to finding out what's going on at the clinic."

"Let's talk to the police."

Max folded his arms across his chest and leaned against a wall. "What do you expect the police to do?"

"Investigate. Protect us."

He shook his head, dashing her hopes of an easy way out. "We don't have any legal proof until a genetic test confirms our suspicions. Besides, the police don't have the manpower to guard us twenty-four hours a day. There's nothing they can do to help us."

"Then what's the answer? I refuse to do nothing but wait until someone tries to kill us again."

"My sentiments exactly." He paced the tiny office. "We have to solve this fast. Before someone takes another shot at us."

Goose bumps raised on her flesh. "Do you still think my theory is crazy? Something fishy is going on at the clinic with the money—and somehow it's connected to Skye. Maybe the accountant can provide the connection. We should talk to him."

"I agree. But for Skye's sake, let's try to put what happened aside and enjoy the rest of the day. I don't want to upset her any more than we absolutely have to."

Before long the mechanic had the hose and the brake fluid replaced. Max checked the engine thoroughly to make sure nothing else had been tampered with before they continued their trip.

They swung south from the two-lane highway to a dirt road. He monitored the rearview mirror with a vigilance that reminded her of their narrow escape.

"How much longer?"

"About twenty minutes once we go through those cow pastures. We should arrive in time for lunch."

Max halted at the pasture, opened the barbed-wire gate and motioned her to drive through. He closed the gate behind them and slid back into the pickup. "My parents own this place. We should be safe here."

She wondered if she'd ever feel safe again, but didn't say so, not wanting anything to spoil these hours with Skye. Perhaps his parents would have some suggestions on how to proceed. Always in the back of her mind, she hoped the police would catch Callie's killer so they would be without-a-doubt in the clear, and hopefully, the danger would end.

They drove through several cow pastures separated by fences. In the distance lay a blue-green lake in a valley between two rolling hills. Max opened his window and let in the scent of fresh air and campfire smoke. "We vacationed here when we were kids. There was plenty to eat and not much trouble to be found. Dad hunted and fished. Mom barbecued. Ford and I ran wild."

"It sounds wonderful." His free and easy childhood sounded like a scene from a movie. She couldn't imagine growing up in such a normal environment. Instead she remembered struggling to keep warm in a thread-bare coat during a brisk Louisiana winter while she walked to school in hand-me-down shoes with thin soles. Most of all, she remembered struggling to keep her grades up so she could someday go to college—a dream she still intended to fulfill.

She wanted a better life for Skye and wondered how her daughter would like the country. As she sensed her daughter's nearness, anticipation washed away Brooke's weariness. Today, for Skye's sake, she'd try to put aside her fears and pretend nothing was wrong.

Max pulled around a bend. In the distance was a comfortable-looking farmhouse. Ahead, two canopies had been pitched overlooking the lake to provide shade, and a blue tent stood nearby. Red fished from a canoe. Eva and Skye sat on a blanket by the lake bank and waved.

When the car rolled to a stop, Brooke opened the door and ran toward her daughter. "Skye!"

"Mom!"

Her daughter, in a swimsuit Brooke didn't remember buying, let out a whoop, clambered to her feet and raced to Brooke. She swept the giggling child into her arms, wishing she'd never have to let her go. "I missed you, sweetie."

"Missed you, too." Skye planted a sloppy kiss on her cheek, and Brooke had never felt anything so wonderful. No matter whose blood ran through the child's veins, Skye was hers.

Ever impatient, Skye wriggled from her arms, grabbed her hand, and tugged her toward Eva. "Mom, we're having a tea party in the mud. Come on."

Brooke grinned at Skye's exaggeration. Eva had spread towels along the lake bank, and she needed to muddy only her feet to join the party. As Skye tugged her toward the lake, Brooke glanced over her shoulder to see Max wave her on.

Free to turn her full attention back to Skye, she rumpled the little girl's black curls. Like yesterday's gloomy weather, her worries faded. "Are you having a good time?"

"We baked bread and I have some for you." Her hand went to her mouth, spreading mud onto her cheeks. "Oops. That was supposed to be your surprise."

Eva laughed from her seat on the blanket, doing her best to keep the atmosphere light. "It's okay. We won't tell your mother what kind of bread we baked."

"Hi." Brooke joined Eva and surveyed the peaceful setting. Several gulls swept over the lake. A turtle sunned on a broken log by the bank. Still, she couldn't shake the premonition of disaster that had kept her awake half the night.

"I appreciate your looking after Skye this morning. I hope she wasn't any trouble."

"Mom, I'm a good girl. I even made my bed."

Brooke raised a brow. "Really." Over Skye's head she smiled at Eva. "You'll have to tell me how you managed that."

Max strolled down to the lake, took off his shirt in the sultry air, and plopped into the water in front of them, creating widening ripples that soaked the mud pies. Max looked as if he hadn't slept well, either. New worry lines crinkled the edges of his eyes. "Mom's a whiz with kids. After twin boys, I'd imagine Skye is a piece of cake."

Skye picked up a mud pie and threw it at Max. "Am not a piece of cake."

Brooke gasped. Eva chuckled.

The mud spatted Max's forehead and slid down his cheek. Skye broke into a fit of giggles. She didn't seem the slightest bit alarmed when Max said, "You think that's funny, do you?"

Max lunged from the water, scooped a happily shrieking Skye into his arms and spun her in the air. "Does she know how to swim?"

Brooke nodded, a warm feeling going through her at the sight of the two of them playing together. It was great to feel normal for a change. She realized just how tense she'd been. "Skye's a regular fish."

"Nooo!" Skye screamed as her eyes widened, but the grin stayed on her lips when Max dunked her. The little tease was daring him, and Brooke's heart melted as Max rose to the challenge.

Despite Brooke's assurance that Skye could swim, Max hovered over the spot where she'd disappeared until she surfaced. She surfaced, a mischievous gleam in her eyes, a scream on her lips, and splashed Max full in the face.

He roared, pretended blindness, and played at catching her. Sunning on the bank, Brooke was content to watch them. This was how life was supposed to be— full of laughter and sunshine and innocence.

Eva rinsed the mud from her hands and dried them on a towel. "If I know my son, he won't leave you out of their play for long. If you want to change before he throws you in, I brought an extra swimsuit. It's in the tent."

Brooke rinsed her hands in the water and stood. Eva's planning and thoughtfulness amazed her. If their circumstances were reversed and she was the one with a son in a coma while the other might soon be charged with murder, she doubted she could remain so calm or considerate. "Thanks."

Ten minutes later, she reclined on the bank to let the sun warm her before taking a dip in the lake. After sitting in the truck, stretching out her arms and legs felt delicious. She wanted to enjoy the sun heating her, savor the scent of fresh air and clean grass and wash away the sadness left over from Rhonda's funeral, the terror of their near accident. Most of all, she wanted to watch Skye laugh with her father.

But the minute Max spotted her, his gaze raked the skimpy one-piece maillot, inflaming her with his wolfish grin. He yelled to Skye. "Let's go get Mommy."

"Okay." Skye squealed in delight, paddling to keep up with Max's long strokes.

Despite his hurry, he didn't leave Skye's side, carefully watching until she reached a place where she could stand. Red had moved his canoe to the far side of the lake—no doubt all the commotion had frightened away the fish.

Eva left towels on the bank and wandered toward a hammock strung in the shade of two granddaddy oaks. "I think I'll nap before lunch."

Max rose out of the water, his bronzed chest gleaming, his dark hair slicked back to reveal a high forehead, emphasizing his sharp cheekbones. As he stalked her, a wicked glint in his eyes, she sucked in her breath, thinking how much she wanted him to catch her, so she could run her fingers over his muscled and bared flesh.

Firmly putting aside her worries, she pretended to make a game of it. Skye joined in the fun, grabbing her free wrist, and together the three of them splashed into the lake up to Brooke's knees. The sand-bottomed water was cooler than she expected. "It's cold."

"Baby!" Skye splashed her, her dimples deepening in a delighted smile.

"Yes, she is a baby." In one swift movement Max bent with a playful grin, placed one arm beneath Brooke's knees, the other around her waist, and scooped her into his powerful arms. Flinging her hands around his neck, she threw back her head and laughed.

The tension had left Max's face, and his eyes, a deep blue, reflected the lake's sunlight-sparkled surface and radiated a new kind of intensity. Suddenly she wanted to grab all life had to offer. She wanted to live only in this moment. She wanted to play with Skye and Max and forget her troubles.

He carried her deeper into the lake, and she took the opportunity to run her hands down the cords of his neck, over his shoulders and pecs to the sleek muscles of his chest.

With a teasing grin, she shook her hair, tilted up her chin and gave him a provocative smile. "Sure you want to drop me?"

Leading the way, Skye chanted. "Throw her in. Throw her in."

"Hmm." His tone turned husky, but although Skye was in front and couldn't see them, he never appeared to forget her daughter was in listening range. "I think you're one hot lady. And what I want…is to get you wet."

He dropped her, but she was ready. Instead of popping back to the surface, she swam down, found his ankles and yanked, toppling him. Before he could recover and retaliate, she took off after Skye with swift strokes.

Brooke caught her daughter, stood, and lifted the wriggling child by her waist until she held her aloft. "So you thought your mother deserved a dunking?"

Skye giggled and kicked her legs. "It was Max's idea."

Brooke threw her toward Max, who scooped her out of the water and tossed her back. Skye screamed with joy. The three of them frolicked without noting the passing time until Eva called them to lunch.

"Race ya." Skye scampered out, an endless bundle of happy energy.

Breathless, Brooke followed, a pleasant weariness in her muscles. Max curled his arm across her shoulder, clearly not embarrassed at showing affection in front of his parents.

She draped a towel around her neck before walking to the picnic table. Eva had large plastic cups filled with crushed ice and tea waiting. Platters of cold cuts and a bowl of fruit salad beckoned. "Dig in."

Skye snuggled against Brooke and spied her plate already filled with a sandwich. "Goody. Peanut butter and jelly."

Eva already knew her granddaughter's favorite sandwich. Grateful that Skye was being so well cared for, Brooke swished the child's hair back so it wouldn't drip into her sandwich. "What do you say?"

"Thank you, and could I have some juice, please?"

As if anticipating the request, Eva plucked a carton of juice and its attached straw from the ice chest and handed it to Skye. "There you go."

Eva had laid out a veritable feast. The fruit salad full of fresh strawberries and pineapple accompanied by French bread set Brooke's mouth watering. While she and Max filled their plates, Red joined them.

Max took a seat beside Skye but spoke to his dad. "Catch anything?"

Red winked at Brooke, his eyes reminding her of Max when he was up to devilment. "Nothing as good as you did."

Brooke fought the heat rising to her cheeks, thankful when Skye piped in, "Max wasn't fishing. The only thing he caught was a mud pie in the face."

Brooke admonished Skye with a grin. "That'll be enough sass, young lady. Eat."

She turned her plate upside down. "All done. Can I go feed the fish?"

"Already?" Brooke noted the half-eaten sandwich in Skye's lap but didn't have the heart to scold her when she was finally having a good time.

Eva handed her a brown paper bag filled with bread-crumbs. "Here you go. Stay where you can see us."

As much as Brooke hated to let Skye leave, she sensed that Eva and Red wished to speak with them in private. Picking up a strawberry, she bit off the end and let the sweet juice trickle down her throat.

Max helped himself to a second turkey sandwich.

"Someone cut our brake line while we were at the hospital."

Red's eyes narrowed. "Was anyone hurt?"

"Not even a scratch," Max assured his parents.

Eva twirled her glass of tea as if the condensation could wash her hands of the truth. "Max, I didn't worry about you this much during all the years you lived away from home."

Red shook his head. "MIT and Harvard Law aren't exactly dangerous hotbeds."

Shocked by his father's revelation, Brooke's mouth fell open, seemingly of its own accord. Max had never told her about his degrees. He'd let her believe he was a mechanic and dilettante inventor. She speculated over why he'd misled her. No wonder he knew so much about business—he was a lawyer. Forcing her mouth closed, she swallowed her protests, deciding to talk to Max in private.

Over the rest of lunch, which she couldn't eat but which Max had no trouble devouring, he and Red discussed strategy and tactics. They decided Max and Brooke would talk to the accountant, Pete Wilson, and then try Grant again next. With their plans settled, Brooke spent another hour with Skye. The time flew, and all too soon she kissed her daughter goodbye. Knowing Skye would have a better time on the horse ride Eva and Red had promised her rather than listening to Max and Brooke question the accountant made watching her drive away with her grandparents only a little easier.

Brooke consoled herself by keeping in mind how contented Skye seemed with Max's parents. But knowing how easily she could be replaced only made her feel worse. At least Skye had snapped out of her depression. Yet the playful time with Skye also made Brooke all too aware of how much she had to lose. If she lost Skye, she'd have no one.

Walking along the lakeshore, she stooped to pick up a flat stone and skipped it across the water. In searching out a family for Skye, would she lose the only child she would ever have? She had no biological claim on Skye—Skye was Rhonda's and Max's, and Brooke couldn't forget that.

Max joined her at the lake and, as if sensing her worry, gathered her into his arms. She rested her head against his chest and let the thump of his heartbeat against her ear give her strength.

"She means everything to me."

He smoothed the hair off her forehead in a comforting gesture. "It's going to be all right. My parents will take good care of her until we figure this out."

"Suppose Skye doesn't want to live with me when she learns I'm not her mother?"

"You're the only mother she's ever known. Years of love can't be eliminated by the genetic truth. Besides, there's no need to tell Skye the details until she's older and can fully understand what happened. By then, she'll probably have brothers and sisters and be so wrapped up in a family that the thought of leaving would break her heart."

Max meant well, but he'd unknowingly caused a lump to rise in her throat. She blinked away tears. Even if Max, or Red and Eva, decided not to contest custody, there would never be sisters and brothers for Skye.

Max led her to a log, and they sat side by side to watch the sun slip below the horizon. "What's wrong?"

She might as well tell him. Lying to herself about her feelings for Max served no purpose. She had to stop denying how much she wanted him. If their relationship was to go further, he had a right to know.

"After I donated the eggs, I acquired a massive infection. I can't have children unless I find out what happened to the eggs I donated." She raised her head to meet his gaze and saw her pain reflected in his eyes. "Now you know why Skye means so much to me. She's all I have. All I'll ever have."

There was nothing he could say, and he knew better than to try. Instead he gathered her closer, his arms slipping from her shoulder to her back, his fingers lightly caressing her.

He kissed her forehead with a tenderness she'd never felt before, and it plucked a chord of desire in her. She nipped his neck, her lips grazing a path to his. When he boldly claimed her lips, her willful heart kindled a craving too strong to refuse.

She arched against his chest, her palms running over his bared biceps, along his muscled shoulders and into his thick hair. His skin was smooth, slick with the thinnest layer of perspiration, hot enough to melt into.

His scent, all male, pierced her with a need all its own. She could have him. His parents and Skye were long gone. There were only the wispy clouds overhead, the droning crickets, and the one tent—almost as if he'd planned the scene for seduction.

As she drew in a breath between kisses, she realized Max was so good at making the most of opportunities. Through the steamy smoke of his kisses, something pricked her sense of well-being. She thought back to this afternoon's conversation and recalled that he'd misled her. She wasn't about to make love with a man who couldn't tell her basic truths about his past.

With a jagged catch in her chest, she pulled back. Max pursued until she placed her palms flat on his chest. "Wait."

He nuzzled her ear and whispered. "What's wrong? Tell me and I'll make it better."

If he thought she protested his kissing techniques, he obviously couldn't tell he had her head spinning. Yet she wasn't about to give herself to a man who couldn't be truthful. "You deliberately misled me about MIT and Harvard."

He reached with his palm to caress her arm. "I may have left out a few facts."

"You don't trust me."

So how could she trust him with her feelings or her body? She pulled away, crossed her arms and looked him straight in the eyes. Keeping her tone soft, but firm, she let him know she needed answers. "Why, Max?"

He jerked to his feet as if snake bit and raked a hand through his hair. "You've picked one hell of a time to ask about my past."

"I don't make love to strangers." She said the words primly, but with heartfelt emotion. He might not be her first man, but she didn't take making love lightly. For that, she needed the degree of trust that was missing.

Bitterness entered his tone. "Is that who I am, a stranger?"

"That's the point, isn't it? Are you going to make a career out of inventing things? Do you work every day?"

"Sometimes."

Obtaining a straight story from him was harder than unscrambling an egg. "And the other times?"

"I take time off whenever I like. I work when motivated." He spun to face her, his lips pressed in a grim line, the words torn from a throat tight with huskiness. "Does it matter what I do for a living when I hold you in my arms? Does it matter that when I kiss you, I can think of nothing else but being inside you?"

"It matters that you lied to me." He still hadn't answered her, but deflected her query with one of his own. Well, it wouldn't work. Not this time. "I can't help wondering what else you haven't told me."

"I'm rich, probably as rich as Ford. I stopped counting my money and competing with my brother a long time ago. We used to vie for Red's approval. Striving to win Dad's attention probably drove both of us to financial success. But I never liked stress. So, unlike my brother who collects assets, I travel light, without excess baggage. Are you happy now?"

"Why didn't you tell me sooner?"

He shrugged. "I'd made up my mind to tell you, but before I did, you started asking questions that made me change my mind."

She would have been happier if she'd never started this conversation, never learned how much he distrusted her. With a sigh, she pulled her knees to her chest and wrapped her arms around them. "When we met, you thought I was after the Braddack money."

He propped a foot on the log, rested his forearms on his bent knee and spoke in a silky soft tone. "I was wrong."

"But you wouldn't listen. You should know better by now. You're still not listening."

His lips turned in a wry grimace, but his eyes were haunted by a vulnerability she'd never seen before. "I assure you, you have my full attention."

Her feelings were already so out of control, she didn't want to deepen them by making love, not if he intended to leave like her parents and Nicole had, like every person she'd loved. He'd never claimed to be more than a love-'em-and-leave-'em guy. "Perhaps we should nix going further until you're sure what you want for us."

He glanced at her before focusing on the road ahead. "What about you? Are you sure what you want?"

"I'm not the one whose life is as loose and fancy free as an eagle's." She had a daughter to raise and couldn't run off with him on a whim.

"Sometimes the freedom is lonely," he admitted. Satisfaction zinged through her. Sternly she reminded herself his acknowledgment was a long way from a three-bedroom house with a white picket fence and a two-car garage.

She stood and wiped her hands on the towel slung

around her neck. "You don't trust me because you don't trust yourself. I'm not about to make love to a man with so little faith in me." Now that he'd stirred her up, the words poured out to douse him with the truth. "I don't just want your body and your wealth, Max. I want something harder for you to give. I want your heart. And I want your soul."

Chapter Eight

Brooke's words cooled Max's passion more thoroughly than a dozen icy showers. He was usually long gone before a relationship became complicated, but this time he didn't want to run. Compared to the honest way she faced life, fleeing seemed cowardly. Her inner strength called to him on a level he preferred not to acknowledge, but she refused to let him coast.

He faced her then. "What makes you brave enough to risk losing Skye?"

She answered him simply and without evasion. "When you love someone, you do what's best for them, no matter how much pain it may cause you."

Brooke thought it best for Skye to know her real family, so she'd put her own feelings aside. She expected him to put Skye's welfare foremost. Only he didn't know if he was capable of such selflessness.

He'd had his share of women, and he hadn't minded spending money on them. What he'd objected to was being unable to distinguish whether they wanted him or his money. He'd blamed the women for being shallow.

But now it struck him like a thunderbolt; the fault was his.

He hadn't opened himself up enough for them to know him. He hadn't shared his hopes, his dreams, his needs—so all they saw was a hunk with money—and that wasn't enough to love. By shutting everyone out, he'd kept his emotional distance, ruining his chance at finding love.

Always before, he'd been treated exactly how he'd expected. Until now.

Brooke offered him a chance for something different, something more, something better. He'd have to be a coward to refuse, and yet his stomach plummeted as if he was stepping out of an airplane without a parachute.

He bit his bottom lip, reached for her hand and brought it to his lips. "I don't know if I can give you what you want."

"All I ask is that you try."

"Okay. I'll promise to try. Now what? Do we start over?"

"Absolutely." She pulled her hand away and her lips turned up in a mischievous smile. "If you want me, you have to catch me."

Before he guessed her intention, she raced away, her nimble feet splashing the water along the lake and throwing sand up in her wake. Her laughter rippled across the water.

Letting out a whoop he dashed after her.

He caught her, and they shared a kiss and a swim before life caught up with them again. All too soon, it was time to start searching for answers.

MAX WISHED they could have spent more time at the lake, but with someone from the clinic after them, they couldn't delay. They'd have to work out their feelings later. In the meantime, Brooke seemed willing to give him another chance—but then, she didn't give up on people.

From beside him in the front seat of the truck, Brooke pulled out the printout of the Kine Clinic employees' files. "We have pictures, names, addresses and bios on almost everyone who ever worked there." Max headed back into New Orleans. "Let's start with Pete Wilson, the accountant."

Brooke nodded. "Money is usually a good indicator of what's what in a company. And when the cops investigate a murder, they follow the money trail—at least on television they do."

She found the accountant's picture, stared at it, then angled it so Max could see. Pete Wilson was short, heavyset, with a stiff smile plastered across his otherwise bland face. Brooke smoothed the picture under the paper clip, reattaching the picture to the file.

"There's not much on him in the file. He graduated from L.S.U. with honors, earned his C.P.A., and did the books for a grocery chain before the clinic's board of directors hired him four months ago. He lives in a modest home and is a widower with three kids. That must be tough, raising kids alone."

"How'd his wife die?"

"It doesn't say." She fingered the picture again. "He looks even-tempered enough. You think he'll talk to us?"

Max nodded. "I hope so—especially after we gave up the afternoon at the lake."

"Your parents are taking turns watching Skye while the other one visits Ford so we can work."

"My parents are watching Skye because there's nothing they'd rather do. Having her helps take their mind off Ford."

"I'm glad. The arrangement suits all of us. But I can't hide forever and even if you don't have to work, I do. My boss can't hold my job for me much more than a week. And I'm missing my night classes at the university. If I fall too far behind, it'll be tough to catch up. What about you?"

"Huh?" He had no idea what she was asking.

"Haven't you had to rearrange your life to deal with all this?"

"I don't like to make plans."

"You just get out of bed in the morning and decide what you'll do that day?" she asked, her tone incredulous.

He barely contained a grin. "Unless the woman I'm with decides otherwise."

"Do you know you're impossible?" Brooke shook her head but her lips turned up in a grin. She looked down at the file and returned to business. "With Callie murdered and Arnold's reported suicide, the accountant is bound to be nervous. Perhaps you should let me—"

"No." At her suggestion, he clenched the wheel tightly. "Let's get one thing straight." No way would he allow her to question anyone from the clinic without him there to protect her. "We're doing this together. I'm not letting you out of sight."

Some women might have been rattled by his vehemence, so when she turned to him with a pleased smile curling her bottom lip, she almost knocked the wind out of him. "Do you think I'm incompetent?"

"Hell, no."

"Then you're afraid of losing me?"

"Damn straight." The words slipped off his tongue so easily, he jerked upright in the seat. A man should stop and think before making an admission like that. About to explain, he risked a glance at her and promptly snapped his jaws together. Her eyes sparkled with happiness, and he didn't want to utter one word to dim her pleasure.

If speaking the truth rewarded him with one of her sunny smiles, he'd have to try it more often. Her smile made him happy and he wasn't sure why. He ought to qualify his statement, but his throat closed tight as a vise until he forcibly made himself relax.

They rode in silence into the city. Back in New Orleans, the odds of being recognized by whoever had tried to kill them would increase.

Unfortunately, they had no choice but to go where they might be recognized—back into town. Max parked across the street from the Kine Clinic. As they debated the best way to get Pete Wilson to come out of the building, Brooke pointed. "There he is. The guy in the dark green shirt carrying a brown bag and a rolled paper stuck under his arm. He must be taking a late lunch."

They'd lucked out that Pete Wilson wasn't eating

at his desk and that he was alone. They followed him along the sidewalk bustling with shops, keeping the accountant in sight, but mixing with the busy crowds.

Max took her hand, not wanting to be separated, enjoying the idea of being part of a couple. "If he's having lunch in the park, that will make it easier for us."

Brooke walked beside him, her forehead creased in concern. "What are we going to say?"

"We'll tell him the truth. Just be yourself."

She shot him a wry grin. "I should be able to remember that."

They entered a park busy with mothers taking a shopping break, office workers on their lunch hour, and tourists enjoying the scenery. The scent of roasting almonds coated in sugar and cooking hot dogs permeated the air. A sidewalk vendor kept a dancing monkey tied to a leash to attract customers.

Pete Wilson settled by himself on a bench beside a fountain. After removing his sandwich from the paper sack, he flipped open his newspaper and scanned the front page. Brooke took a seat on one side of him, and Max hemmed him in from the other.

Max leaned forward and kept his voice low. "Hi, Pete. I'm Max Braddack, Ford's brother. And this is Brooke Evans."

When Pete looked up and spied Max, he put down his sandwich and held out his hand. "I'm sorry about your brother's wife."

Max shook his hand. "Thanks."

"I couldn't make Rhonda's funeral because I couldn't find a baby-sitter."

"Could you answer a few questions, Mr. Wilson?" Brooke asked.

He swiveled to look at her and then stared hard at Max. "I'm not supposed to reveal company information. I really need this job."

Brooke's lip quivered but she kept her tone even. "Mr. Wilson, six years ago, embryos were switched at the Kine Clinic. I just recently discovered the child I've been raising isn't mine."

His brown eyes widened in sympathy. "That's terrible. But it's really not my department. I'm a C.P.A. I only do the books."

"We've been asking a lot of questions," Max said, "and this morning someone cut the brake line in my truck. We'd go to the police, but we have no idea who did it."

Pete shifted uneasily in his seat. "Look, I'd like to help you. Your brother hired me when I really needed a break. But I don't go into the lab."

Max applied a little pressure. "I think the same people who are after us caused Rhonda's and Callie's deaths."

Brooke pulled out two financial quarterly statements and handed one to Pete. "We found this is Dr. Henschel's office." She pointed to the second one. "And this in Ford's."

Pete peered at the paperwork. "My predecessor either made some errors or was working from inaccurate information. I had to redo her work. That's why the statements are different. I never did understand where the data came from. It was as if she made the numbers up." Pete handed Brooke back the papers. He glanced at Max, then down at the ground as if debating whether to speak or not.

"We'd appreciate anything you could tell us," Max said to encourage him.

"All right. But I'm only telling you this because I'm grateful to your brother."

Max nodded, noting a gleam of interest light Brooke's eyes.

Pete wet his lips. "I think someone is skimming profits from the clinic. But I can't prove it. Either my predecessor pulled those numbers out of thin air or she'd seen them somewhere."

"I don't understand," Brooke muttered. "You're the C.P.A., how could anyone hide profits from you?"

Pete sighed. "There are always ways to cheat. I work from a computer system. Someone could keep two sets of books right within the computer system."

Brooke stiffened. "But if this was going on, wouldn't you know it?"

"Not if I don't have access to that part of the computer. Not if the computer records are altered and the money transferred within the company. Amounts drawn daily or weekly would be easiest to hide and could then be siphoned off in a variety of ways."

"Kickbacks?" Max asked.

"It's a possibility. I've also noticed research and development costs are high at the clinic."

"So who has access to the computer?" Brooke asked.

"Me." Pete waited for a couple of kids to roller-blade by before continuing. "And Dr. Henschel, Dr.

Arnold, Callie Wainwright, Grant Donovan, my predecessor…''

"Who had the job before you?" Max asked.

"Karen Forester. But she hated it. She's much better at keeping track of equipment and supplies."

Brooke's voice rose in excitement. "Could someone be overbilling, collecting the funds, then siphoning the money to research and development and stealing the illegal profits?"

"I haven't been able to prove it. Whoever is doing this must be wiping their tracks in the computer almost daily."

"Wouldn't customers notice if they were billed too much?" Brooke asked.

"Probably not. Most medical cases are complicated. When a doctor orders a series of tests, most patients won't notice an additional one tacked onto the bill. And if a patient's unconscious during a procedure, who would know if they were billed for an extra pint of blood?"

Max scratched his head. "Why would the thief care about an embryo switch?"

Pete grimaced. "The thief might not. Then again, a thief might fear any investigation could blow his lucrative scheme. But mind you, I have yet to prove anyone is stealing."

"But you have suspicions."

Pete nodded. "A few days ago, Callie asked me about investing a large sum of money. I asked her if she'd inherited the money because I was concerned over estate taxes."

Brooke looked as if she was holding her breath. "And what did Callie answer?"

"We were interrupted. She said she'd get back to me. The next day she was dead." Pete looked at Max with sad, round eyes. "I'm a single parent with three kids. Please don't mix me up in this."

"You have my word. And you've been extremely helpful, Mr. Wilson. We appreciate it."

Realizing Pete had told them all he could, Max took Brooke's arm and led her through the park. "Every damn time we learn a new fact, it leads to more questions. I think we need to wait on Grant for the moment and investigate Callie and where her money came from next."

"But she's dead."

"She must have had friends and family. Let's start with where she lived."

Twenty minutes later they parked in front of a modest apartment building. Brooke hoped they'd discover something helpful. After Max locked the car, he took her hand, outwardly calm while every muscle in her hummed with tension. The thought of going through a dead person's things seemed improper, and yet, how else would they find answers?

While she steeled herself for the unpleasant task, they headed for the office of the three-story stuccoed building. Max knocked once on the manager's door, then entered.

A young woman with dark, soulful eyes and skin the color of caramel looked up from her books. "Can I help you?"

"We'd like to look at Apartment 3-D, please," Max said.

The woman placed a pen between the pages to mark her place and closed her book. "Are you reporters? The police said not to let anyone in."

Max smiled engagingly at the young woman, and Brooke wondered why he never looked at her that openly. "We're not reporters. We're trying to find out who killed Callie. It's possible the same person who murdered her tried to kill us this morning."

The woman hesitated, assessing them with fear and doubt in her eyes. Brooke stepped forward, her hand outstretched. "He's telling you the truth. We buried Max's sister-in-law yesterday, his brother is still recovering from a severe *accident* and someone cut the brake line on his truck this morning. Please, we need your help. I've a little girl waiting for me at home. I'd like to sleep at night without worrying if someone is trying to break in."

The woman stared at her, then shrugged. "Call me crazy for believing you, but I do. I'm Leila Gagnet." They shook hands, and the manager nodded at Max, then led them to the apartment.

Callie's one-bedroom quarters certainly didn't have the look of a wealthy woman. If she'd been stealing from the clinic, would she have lived like this? An afghan tossed over a couch hid a color so faded Brooke couldn't guess at the original. Milk crates stacked along the wall served to hold CD's, books, and several healthy plants.

Leila filled a beaker with water at the kitchen sink.

"I've been watering these as if Callie's going to return."

"Were you close?" Brooke asked.

"When Callie didn't have a date, we went out for pizza on Friday nights."

Brooke motioned with her chin for Max to go to the bedroom so she could ask who Callie had been seeing. He took her hint, and she smiled inside at how well they worked together before turning back to Leila. "Was Callie dating anyone special?"

"For a while, she dated a man from the clinic. Grant Donovan." Leila glanced toward Max. When she didn't see him, she confided, "Callie was waiting for Grant to tire of his wife. I told her to quit pining, tell the loser to get lost and find a man who appreciated her. She'd form this secret little smile of hers and say, 'He's the one, Leila, the one I've been waiting for.'" Leila sighed. "Callie isn't ever going to have him now, is she?"

"How long did their relationship last?"

"A year or two." Leila rolled her eyes before she turned the plants toward the sunlight shining through the window. "Lately they hadn't been getting along so well. Callie was depressed, and then all of a sudden she…"

Brooke lowered her voice to a whisper. "Leila, tell me, please."

Leila sighed. "She came in one night last week, all excited, saying she was about to strike it rich and get out of this dump."

"What happened?"

"Nothing for a day or two. The night before she died, she came in smiling this huge grin, her eyes all bright and pretty, waving a wad of money. She took me out for crawfish *étouffée*, sausage gumbo and at the end of the meal we drank *café brûlor*. The waiter brought it to the table in this special dish and lit it on fire right at our table. I'm telling you, it was something—''

"Callie and you had never gone out like this before?"

"She never had that kind of money before. Afterward, we went gambling on a riverboat. When she won, she smiled and said the rich just kept getting richer."

"Do you know where the windfall came from?" Brooke asked. "Did she inherit it?"

"She didn't say. And I didn't ask. But I don't think anyone died—she was too happy, if you know what I mean."

"Did she mention Grant that night?"

"Nope. I figured she finally had him out of her system."

"Is there anything else?"

"I told the police, the night she died, the apartment was tossed. Nothing was missing—except the money, and I know we didn't spend it all."

As if knowing the conversation had come to an end, Max exited the bedroom. "Did Callie leave any letters or notes in her desk?"

"You won't find anything interesting," Leila told them with a quiet dignity. "The police already took her papers—not that she had much."

Ten minutes later they were back in the car, heading south. "Grant doesn't have a wife, does he?"

Despite the hushed tones they'd spoken in, Max had heard the conversation through the thin walls, so she didn't need to fill him in. "If she didn't inherit that money, where did it come from?"

"I don't know." Brooke thumbed through the files. "Grant lied to Callie. He's not married."

"That doesn't make him the culprit. Men lie about their marital status all the time."

Brooke tossed the files onto the seat. "Pete Wilson thinks the financial statements might be off, too. How much research and development can they possibly be doing?"

"That's a good question. One we'll have to get Grant or Henschel to answer. Those two have to be next on our list."

"Where are we going now?"

"To see Grant Donovan." He read the address off the top sheet on the file and headed west, pulled down the visor as he drove into the late afternoon sun and merged with the traffic flowing out of town.

Brooke glanced at him, and a shiver chilled her through to her soul. His hair, raked back from his face, revealed an expression carved of burnished stone. His eyes, the pupils a sapphire-hard spark of blue behind the soft gray tint of his sunglasses, narrowed to slits as he squinted into the glare with a determination that emanated from him in solid icy sheets.

The easygoing man she'd come to know had turned into someone she barely recognized. For one nanosecond, she could see past the laid-back calm to all the inner expectancy he normally kept banked. Energy poured off him, as if he was readying himself for battle.

Her heart zigzagged into her throat. She blinked.

The hard side of Max disappeared so quickly she would have thought her imagination had played tricks on her—except the revelation confirmed what she already knew to be true. Max had more passion humming in his pinky than most men had in their whole body. Right now he was directing his energy toward their foe. She could almost pity them their fate. Almost.

Chapter Nine

Max's determination didn't make Brooke feel better. The idea of confronting Grant or Henschel was fraying every nerve in her body until she could barely keep her voice sounding reasonable. "Do you think it's safe to risk a face-to-face with Callie's murderer?"

"We shouldn't be in danger. Neither Grant nor Henschel will be expecting us. If you like, you can wait in the truck. If there's trouble, you can go for help." He shot her a smile warm enough to thaw a block of ice.

She wasn't about to let him distract her—not with their lives at stake. "So I'll be running away while you face the killer?"

He arched a brow, then turned at the corner. "Grant may be innocent. Once I have a better idea of what we're facing, we can adjust the plan."

Icy fear slid down her neck and back and curled around her heart. Dread sharpened her tone. "You're going to confront Grant with what? You don't even have a gun."

From the beginning, they'd assumed they'd been set

up—that someone wanted it to appear as if they'd killed Callie. But discovering the relationship between Grant and Callie had put a whole new slant on things for Brooke.

She wanted to see if Max agreed. "Callie's murder might have been a lover's quarrel and have had nothing to do with us. We may have simply walked into the clinic at the wrong time."

"Exactly. That's why we need to talk to Grant."

She sagged in her seat, knowing he was right. They didn't have much choice but an eerie premonition grabbed her and wouldn't let go. "A lot can go wrong if we anger the wrong person."

"I'll be careful." His eyes flashed a look that scorched Brooke to her toes and simmered through her veins. "Worried about me?"

Yes. The answer stuck in her throat but seared her mind before she could stop it. *Yes, I'm worried about you.* The thought rushed like a river raging over Niagara Falls. *Yes, I care about you.* She crossed her arms over her chest, unwilling to yield to the emotion suddenly pumping through her.

When she remained silent, he took her hand and tugged her nearer. "Do you always worry so much?"

She couldn't resist brushing a finger down the taut muscle of his forearm. The hot feel of him made her eager for another kiss.

"I'm trying to cover every contingency," she replied, pleased her voice sounded reasonable.

He wasn't impervious to her touch—a muscle tightened in his jaw. His flesh was warm and hard, yet surprisingly smooth. She wanted to lean into him. Her gaze roamed over his broad shoulders and she remembered the heat of his flesh beneath her palms when they'd kissed. She admired the smooth coordination of muscles contracting and releasing in a mesmerizing ebb and flow as he turned the steering wheel.

"Covering every contingency is impossible," he said, and she heard a biting frustration in his tone that she'd never noticed before.

Somewhere in the deep recesses of her mind, she buried her fears, freeing her to consider him with speed and clarity. Unusually alert to the changes in him, the rigid muscles of his neck, the stiff tilt of his head, the broad shoulders that didn't relax against the seat, she concluded Max was more concerned than he was letting on.

"What is it?" Her hand brushed the light hairs and the tense muscle of his forearm.

She couldn't quite believe she was allowing thoughts of him distract her. Somehow, she'd scooted over until she'd ended up snuggled beneath his arm. Blood rushed to her face.

He kept driving, but glanced at her, his eyes dancing with amusement as if guessing her thoughts. "You going to sit there ogling my body, or are you going to help me find Grant's home?"

"I think I'll ogle," she said, unable to suppress the unguarded hunger in her tone.

He chuckled with a wolfish growl that fired her nerves to overcharge. His hot breath stirred the wisps of hair at her temple. "We might get there sooner if you take out a map."

"Is that so?"

"But we could delay our visit."

At the hope in his voice, she cast a glance at him. "Why?"

"Because you want me."

Her heart sputtered. "And just how do you know that?"

"Instinct. My instincts are telling me, I should park the truck in those trees up ahead, take off your clothes, right here, right now. Ever so slowly. My instincts tell me I'd enjoy watching you quiver in expectant anticipation. My instincts say you would be hot. Receptive."

She mustered every force of will she could gather. "Do your instincts say whether you intend to stick around when this is over?"

"Are you holding out for marriage?"

She wanted him to tell her he cared for her. She wanted him to make a stab at commitment—even if that meant staying in one place for the next few months. The words lodged in her throat. She couldn't bear for him to say the words without meaning them— and that meant they had to come from his heart, not at her suggestion.

She ducked out from under his arm and slid toward the window, proud she hadn't given in to what her body so obviously craved. "I'm holding out for more than you're willing to give me. Or yourself."

At her words, he stiffened. His lips thinned and his expression blazed thunderclouds. Then, like turning off a switch, he regained his air of insouciance. "In that case, we'd best pay Grant Donovan a visit."

How did he bottle up his roiling passion as if it

didn't exist? Knowing better than to ask, she leaned back, closed her eyes and tried to rid herself of tension. But even with her eyes shut, she envisioned Max, the passion uncorked, his face inches from hers, a wanton love effervescing in his eyes.

She suspected when he made love, he kept his emotions behind the wall he'd built. Ah, but she longed to free that passion, longed for him to take her because he could do nothing less. Max out of control and crazy in love was the dream she pictured in vivid color. She wanted steaming, sizzling, red.

Right now, she didn't trust herself to be idle around Max. Better they spent the evening working. Concentrating on solving their more immediate problems would prevent her from torturing herself with intimate thoughts of him.

GRANT DONOVAN LIVED in a modest trailer park. They pulled into his driveway after dark to the sound of country music blasting out the open windows of his double-wide. A Jaguar and a shiny red Cadillac sat in the driveway.

Max whistled. "Expensive wheels for a computer researcher."

"Maybe he has company." Brooke wondered if the Kine Clinic researcher would even speak to them. She recalled Grant's overbearing size and immense fists but stiffened her back with resolve. During the drive she'd regained her courage. No way would she sit in the car while Max took all the risks. They were in this together.

Max opened his door. "Let's hope he's in a talkative mood."

When she followed Max to the door, he raised a brow and his lips twitched as if he'd expected her to change her mind and come with him despite her misgivings. How had he come to know her so well?

To be heard over the music, Max pounded on the door while she waited below on the metal steps. When no one answered, he tried the knob.

As he entered the trailer, her breath lodged in her throat. "Grant? Anybody home?"

Grant was hunched over a table that looked like a restaurant booth. He didn't look up and apparently hadn't heard them come in. His gaze riveted on a computerized chess set, his meaty hand fondled a can of beer.

The trailer was surprisingly neat and clean, with carpets recently vacuumed. A four-tiered, top-of-the-line sound system with blinking red lights and huge speakers blared at them. A sleek laptop computer rested on the counter beside a leather briefcase. One bedroom wall had been knocked out to make room for a big-screen television. However the place lacked a woman's touch. Actually it lacked a personal touch. She didn't see any pictures, letters, magazines or even a book.

Max angled forward toward the sound system and flipped off the power. In the sudden silence, Grant raised his huge head like a lumbering bear, his beady eyes blearily focusing on them.

"Braddack!" Even drunk, he recognized Max, and he reached for the phone.

Unhampered by alcohol, Max snaked out his arm and ripped the phone cord from the wall. Before Grant could work up a protest, Max slid into the booth, crowding the larger man. "How well did you know Callie Wainwright?"

Grant's eyes drifted back to the chess set, avoiding Max's piercing stare. "Who?"

With a sweep of his arm, Max knocked the chess pieces onto the floor. "The murdered woman at the Kine Clinic."

"Oh, her. Never met her." A crafty look entered Grant's beady eyes. "Different department, you know."

Max's voice softened dangerously. "Cut the crap. You spent the night at her place. Often."

"So, what of it?"

"Tell me about the research and development money," Brooke said, attacking from a different angle. "Why are the costs so high?"

"How should I know? Ask Pete Wilson, he's the accountant."

Max pounded the table with his fist. "You are in charge of research. What the hell do you spend all that money on?"

Grant cracked his knuckles. "Can't say."

"Can't?" she asked. "Or won't?"

Grant slouched in his seat, pretending he hadn't heard her. Lifting the beer can, he chugged.

Max jumped in with another question, obviously hoping if they kept switching topics, Grant would spill something they could use. "Have you altered the financial data?"

Grant's face turned smug. "That's part of my job."

"It's not your job to keep two sets of books," Brooke muttered.

"Who said it was?" Grant turned suddenly sharp eyes on her.

"Did Dr. Arnold order you to alter the books? What about Dr. Henschel, does he know what you're doing? Did Ford know what you're doing?"

"I don't know what you're talking about."

Max grabbed the man by his shirt collar, yanking it tight around the neck. "You're lying!"

"So sue me."

Max shook him, then let go. "We'll find out what's going on whether you cooperate or not."

Grant lifted the beer and when he found the can empty, gazed longingly toward the fridge. Brooke didn't think Grant was drunk, but pretending. His eyes were a bit glassy, but not red. While Max asked questions, she examined the kitchen trash can and found only one other empty beer can.

Behind her, Grant hiccuped. "Henschel knows exactly what's going on. Ask him. Ask the board. Ask your brother. Just leave me the hell alone."

Whether Grant was ignorant or loyal to his boss, Brooke couldn't discern. Clearly, he wasn't going to help them.

"There's just this little problem." Max paused, and Grant lifted his eyes. "The board relies on your data. And Ford's unavailable."

The researcher didn't even fake surprise. In fact, a satisfied smile pursed his lips. "Well, you don't expect me to keep track of Ford Braddack, do you?"

While she snooped in the kitchen, Brooke noticed a bank deposit receipt amid a stack of bills. Shielding her movement with her body, she slipped it into her pocket and signaled she was ready to go.

Max nodded and gripped Grant's shirt once more. "If I find out you had anything to do with what happened to my brother and his wife, I'll break every bone in your body."

As they sped away in his truck, Max let out a frustrated snort. "That was a waste of time."

"Maybe not." Brooke removed the receipt from her pocket and flattened it.

"What is it?"

"It's a bank deposit, dated two days after Callie's murder, for one hundred thousand dollars." Excitement raced through her in an energizing hum. "Why would Grant have that kind of money? Did you notice the expensive electronic equipment in that trailer?"

Max flexed his fingers as if wishing he could tighten them around Grant's throat. "Maybe he inherited the money."

"Like Callie?"

"Could be a coincidence."

"I don't think so, and neither do you. There has to be a connection."

"Maybe." The red from a traffic light at the intersection lit his inscrutable features. He couldn't seem to take his gaze from her trembling lips, and she couldn't keep her eyes from drifting to the fascinating flicker of the pulse at his temple.

"Do you want to look for Henschel?" he asked.

She couldn't answer, her gaze glued to the way his

shirt molded to his chest, leaving a sexy vee of bronzed skin at the neck. Energy seemed to bubble off his skin, enveloping her like a rare champagne.

"Or are you ready to go home for the night?" he pressed, leaving the decision to her.

At the mention of sleep, her stomach clenched. Sleeping in the same house—even if it was the size of a small hotel—was out of the question. No way would she sleep. Apparently she hadn't lost her earlier tension. Nor did she wish to confront it. "Let's find Henschel now. I'm too worked up to sleep."

After the light turned green, Max tore his gaze from her mouth. He easily found Dr. Henschel's home among the palatial houses in the Garden District. The white brick Colonial with imposing two-story columns was set back on a manicured lawn.

Every light in the house was out. Clearly, Henschel was asleep or not at home. Max knocked on the front door, but no one answered. He climbed into the truck and headed home.

Now she was going to confront the tension between them whether she wanted to or not.

MAX PULLED THROUGH the wrought-iron gates of his parents' home and parked in the garage. He led her through a private courtyard scented with blooming bougainvillea and magnolias to the east wing, which had its own side entrance. The high walls cast dark shadows across a moss-covered fountain that trickled water into a goldfish pond. Ivy climbed the walls, lending an Old World ambience to the garden. Birds fed at a feeder, their dark wings flapping in a blur of soft moonlight.

While Brooke appreciated the luxuriant grounds, she couldn't ignore the nervousness that gripped her. Max led her past columns that flanked an arched entrance and into a foyer of darkly paneled walls. The pine floor was polished to a deep shine. A crystal chandelier warmed the dark edges of the hall.

Brooke presumed Max would lead her to her room, but he whisked her across the antique Persian carpet. Beside her, hands deep in his pockets, Max didn't appear to have a care in the world. In the burnished gold reflection of the hallway mirror, she caught a spark of amusement in his eyes and a slight tilting at the corner of his mouth. What was he up to?

"Aren't you taking me to Skye?"

"There's the phone." He gestured to a table and chair in a corner nook. "Why don't you call?"

Her forehead creased in confusion. "You want me to call your parents from inside their own home?"

"Why not? They don't have to know where we are. While you check on Skye, I have a few arrangements to make of my own."

He avoided her gaze and unlocked a door. She glimpsed what looked like a laboratory before he swept inside and shut the door behind him.

Skye was sound asleep, Eva assured her. She'd had a wonderful time riding her pony and had talked them into a fast-food dinner. Eva suggested if Brooke and Max wanted to catch a late dinner, she and Red intended to stay in and would be happy to watch Skye.

Brooke hung up the phone, wondering if Eva was

matchmaking. Before she could decide, Max returned with a secretive smile.

"What?" she asked, curious.

"I've ordered a special dinner. Would you like to see my rooms?"

She walked inside the living room of his apartment and gasped. The scent of jasmine drew her like a bee to pollen. An extravagant bouquet of orchids and baby's breath sat on a marble stand by the fireplace. A magnificent sunflower and fern combination rested in a silver urn on a coffee table. Carnations, daisies, and bougainvillea in cut crystal occupied almost every flat table, counter or cupboard.

She turned to face Max in confusion and found him staring at her, a satisfied glint in his eyes. She placed her hands on her hips, her mouth trembling as his eyes focused on her mouth. "How did you arrange this?"

"Ever since you moved into my parents' home, I've been hoping to lure you over here."

Her brows rose. "You brought in fresh flowers every day?"

He cocked his slim hip and rested his thumbs in his belt loops. One long lazy glance spun out and shimmered with tenderness. "Do you like it?"

"Oh, yes." A frightening weakness weighted her limbs as she circled the room, as if embraced in one giant, velvet hug. To distract herself from the sudden urge to fling herself into his arms, she paced, barely noting the antique furniture, plush carpets, and rich draperies that merged in one swirl of luxuriant golden ambiance. "I love it. But this must cost a fortune."

She secretly hoped the reference to his wealth

would cause him to draw back. She couldn't fight this seductive setting much longer—not when she wanted him so much.

He chuckled, his tone low, deep and husky. "I can afford it. Maybe I've finally found a good use for my money."

At his words, a rush of satisfaction flooded her. His expression implied his feelings for her were stronger than she'd dared to hope. The pulsing muscle in his neck, the hard wildness in his eyes, the tense set of his shoulders indicated emotions that had to be close to love.

At that realization, her blood hummed through her veins, spiking her with anticipation of tonight, tomorrow—and the day after that. Hope surged with the possibility he might come to love her enough to change his rootless life-style. In an oddly heightened state of awareness, lost opportunities and regret filtered through her mind and filled her with bittersweet sadness.

She could have made love with him at the lake or in the truck. She'd wanted to. Desperately.

Her damn principles had held her back.

Now her past foolishness haunted her. Life was too priceless to waste, and she'd squandered precious moments that could never be relived. Besides, protecting herself from the possible pain of leaving Max before she knew how well suited they really were for each other seemed cowardly. But past mistakes could be remedied.

And she didn't intend to waste another moment.

A bowl of fresh fruit, almost hidden by the flowers,

sat on the counter. Brooke plucked a grape and playfully placed one between Max's lips. "Good?"

"Find out for yourself." A spark kindled and the sapphire in his eyes smoked with a mixture of turbulent emotions. Lust or love? She guessed a combination of the two. Knowing she belonged with him, whether or not he would admit it, she leaned toward him and let his fierce embrace enfold her.

She burned for him. And when he kissed her, taking absolute possession, she knew by the tremble in his lips, he burned, too. Her breasts crushed against his muscular chest, and she wound her hands around his neck, pulling him closer, her fingers resting on the turgid pulse at his throat. Her heart stuttered and desire swept her in spiraling sensation.

She breathed in his pleasant male scent mixed with the sweetness of jasmine. Her fingers trailed over his neck and shoulders before curling into the silky thick smoothness of his hair.

Giving herself over to his ravishing mouth, she enjoyed the eagerness of his lips on hers, the warmth of his chest against her breasts, his hips tight to hers, leaving no doubt of his passion. He wrapped his arms around her back, one hand tenderly supporting her neck.

Pulling back just inches, he whispered while staring directly into her eyes, "I want you. If you don't feel the same—"

"I want you." She might die if he didn't kiss her again. It was frightening how much she wanted him. There was honesty in that. And a dangerous flash of heat that caused her head to fall back limply as he nuzzled her throat. Blood hummed through her veins, and suddenly she couldn't stand the clothing that separated her from his flesh. Aching to explore his every contour and hollow, she tugged his shirt out of his jeans and helped him pull it over his head.

Standing face-to-face, she reached up and ran her fingers over his rugged brows, sculpted cheekbones and square chin, down his neck and over the ridge of his collar bone. Beneath her touch he quivered, but remained still enough for her to explore at her own pace.

His flesh was both warmer and smoother than she'd expected. The hairs on his chest tickled her palms, the muscles firmer, but somehow softer than she remembered.

She trailed her fingers over his flat stomach to his jeans. Undoing the top button, she looked into passionate eyes that brought a raging flush to her face, but slowly she unbuttoned the rest. His eyes flared with a heat that shot a flame straight to her core. Her fingers shook, but she pushed his jeans down, pleased she wouldn't have to bother with underwear. He wasn't wearing any.

As she lowered her eyes and took in his male beauty, his lack of boxer shorts wasn't all that pleased her. Without a shred of embarrassment, and brimming with confident male pride, he stepped out of the jeans. She ran her fingers lightly over his lean hips and muscular buttocks.

There could be no denying his wanting her, and the power at her own femininity escalated her need to a fervent pitch. She wanted to make him lose his control.

She wanted his passion. She wanted his heat. All of it.

Boldly she reached for him.

"Not yet," he whispered, his voice laden with sensuality.

He kissed her again, tiny, teasing, taunting kisses. While finding it powerfully erotic to stand fully clothed while a naked man embraced her, she wanted her clothes off. Her hand rose to remove her shirt.

"Let me do that." He nipped kisses across her cheek and toward her ear, his hand staying hers in a gesture tender, yet commanding.

He teased her lips with his fingers while his mouth placed a necklace of kisses along the sensitive flesh of her throat. Finally his hands dipped toward the edge of her shirt and pulled it over her head.

Cool air rippled along her heated flesh, exciting rather than soothing. Her breasts swelled from just his glance at her bra. She started to unhook it.

Gently he pushed her hands away. "That's my job."

She should have known he wouldn't be hurried or denied any pleasure or lose one iota of control. One glance at his face reflected his enjoyment and anticipation of each slow touch, each slower brush of the lips that took aeons. With a sigh, she waited, the trembling need keeping her dizzy.

Without haste, he unhooked the front snap of her bra, leaving the lacy silk to dangle while his fingers traced the arch of flesh now revealed. Her breasts trembled, more aroused than if he'd bared her completely.

He played with the straps of her bra, slowly, sensuously, letting them fall to her shoulders. He slid the cups aside—but not enough. He'd left the edges just covering her taut nipples that were aching for his touch. As if he had forever to explore, he ran a finger from her chin, between her breasts to her jeans.

"Don't move," he half pleaded, half ordered, until her nerves, strung tight, seemed ready to burst.

He removed her jeans and left her standing in panties, her bra unclasped while he gathered her hair and lifted it behind her shoulders. He feathered the tip of his finger over her neck, the hollow of her shoulder and toward her inflamed breasts.

"Touch me," she demanded in a voice so filled with need she barely recognized it as her own.

"I am." He parted her bra. When he looked at her, he sucked in his breath and his pupils dilated, shooting a wanton heat straight to her groin. "You're beautiful. Gorgeous. Do you know what part of you I like best?"

"What?"

"The sexy gray matter between your ears."

His answer both surprised and pleased her, giving her reason to hope he loved her. But as his finger circled her exposed breast, thinking became more and more difficult. She was the one losing control.

Trying to regain mastery of her spinning thoughts, she murmured. "You like the way I think?"

"Yup."

"I think you should hurry."

"Is that so?"

Lazily, with just a finger, he continued to circle one breast then the other and the heat of him made her ache for the caress of his palms. When she didn't think she could stand another moment, he bent his head and took the tip of her nipple into his mouth, shooting tiny zaps of pleasure straight to her heart. He gave equal treatment to her other nipple and her legs almost buckled.

She grabbed his shoulders for balance. "I can't take much more of this."

He chuckled knowingly. "How about a shower?"

"What?"

"I'll wash your back." Ignoring her groan and without waiting for her answer, he led her into the largest bath she'd ever seen. Along the way, she rid herself of bra and panties, oddly unselfconscious. Before she could take in more than the lighted mirrors above a marble counter, he'd hauled her into the two-spigot shower.

Stepping into the water, she closed her eyes and tipped her face to the spray. He came up behind her, the rich vanilla scent of shampoo giving him away. Then his hands were washing her hair, his fingers massaging her scalp. Nothing had ever felt this good.

She tilted her head back. "Mmm. If this is the reward, I should get dirty more often."

"You're thinking dirty thoughts?" Amusement colored his words.

"Oh, yes." She lifted her clean hair off her neck. "My back, please."

He worked the soap into a lather and used his hands on her shoulders and waist, his fingers slippery and slick. As he moved lower over her buttocks, the exquisite sensation almost unbearable, she trembled in anticipation. By now she understood he intended to keep his control, prolong their anticipation—but the waiting was so hard.

Her skin, exquisitely sensitive, flared in response to his slightest touch, increasing the ache deep in her belly. When his soapy hands slid over her breasts, she couldn't contain a soft moan.

He nipped her neck. "I could do this for hours."

"No, you can't."

His fingers tweaked her nipples. "Why is that?"

"Because." She attempted to turn away. The fiery pleasure was about to surge out of her control, set her on fire.

His fingers playing with her nipples kept her right where he wanted her. "Because? That's no reason."

Her mind whirled in confusion, but amid her burning senses, one tantalizing thought focused. Two could play this game. If she wanted to drive him wild, she'd have to be bold. After lathering her hands, she reached behind her hips. His sex was easy to find, and when she grasped him, he let out a muffled snort.

His breathing grew ragged. "You can't—"

"Oh, yes, I can." That she could drive him out of control and over the edge heightened her own arousal. Only she could no longer stand the waiting. She wanted him inside her.

Leaning to the side, she let the water wash off the soap, fully intending to guide him into her. He foiled her plan by flicking off the water and wrapping her in a thick terry-cloth towel.

He had her stand in front of him on a thick rug. Making a game of it, he dried her slowly, caressing her breasts, her belly, lower—until every inch of her burned. Kneeling on the fluffy rug at her feet, he urged her thighs apart. His mouth found her. Pleasure rippled through her, and she climaxed hard.

She dug her fingers into his hair, expecting him to stop. He didn't.

No longer a thinking being, but only a creature of sensation, she marveled that the first climax had been only a teaser. What was bubbling inside her now was like a shaken bottle of champagne ready to froth over the top. The sensations gathered, building, burning, bursting. If his strong hands hadn't supported her buttocks, she might have slumped to the floor.

Whimpering sounds—hers—filled her ears. Of their own volition, her hips gyrated, but he did not release her until the caldron of fizzing bubbles in her veins turned her frantic with frenzy.

He stopped, and she let out a cry of protest. "Max! I need you."

"No more than I need you," he rasped.

He lifted her and carried her to a king-size bed strewn with rose petals. Reaching into a drawer by the bed, he pulled out a silver packet. She took it from him, tried to put the condom on him, but her hands trembled so badly he had to finish for her.

He lay on his side and fondled her breasts, but she could no longer stand the sensations cascading through her. Kissing him deeply, she rolled him onto his back, reached down and slipped him inside her. His fullness alone almost made her climax again.

With every ounce of will, she tamped down the sensation. Her hips rocked and she looked directly into his eyes. He was burning with her, rocking under her, wild with need. The fierce passion in his expression, combined with his magic fingers between her parted thighs, was her undoing.

''Come with me, Max. Give me everything you've got.''

At her words, his hips pounded upward, and he filled her completely. With his intensity as out of control as an erupting volcano, she climaxed again. He spasmed inside her before she collapsed atop his chest, a quivering mass of satiated flesh.

Her heartbeat slowed, and she'd never felt so complete. Toward the end, the cool and collected Max Braddack had lost his famous control. He may not have said the words, but the fiery possessiveness in his eyes hadn't lied.

He pulled the covers over her, cradling her atop his chest, clearly unwilling to release her. She hoped he wanted to hold her forever. Whether or not he would admit it, they belonged together, she and Max Braddack. She wanted a future with him. She wanted to spend the rest of her life with him.

With her head on his shoulder, she catnapped, averse to questioning the joy she'd found in his arms, just knowing it was right. Surely he had to know that, too.

A knock on the front door awakened her. Still half asleep beside Max, she woke up frightened that something was wrong with Skye. But that was silly. She took a moment to get her bearings and recalled Max's words about ordering dinner. At the sound of another knock, she climbed from the bed and slipped into Max's fluffy robe.

Padding across the thick carpet to the side entrance, she wondered what the servants would think of her answering the door at this time of night in her robe. She shouldn't have worried. A van with a local restaurant's logo on the side was heading down the road. The delivery person had left a rolling cart laden with silver trays.

Max had thrown on jeans and joined her in rolling the cart, steaming with mouth-watering scents, to the dining table.

"Gourmet take-out?" she asked.

He grinned, sounding eminently pleased with himself. "Only in New Orleans could dinner be delivered at this hour."

Beneath the cart were all the accoutrements with the name of a superb restaurant discreetly embroidered in the corners of the fine linens. While he removed the bouquet of flowers, Brooke floated a lace tablecloth over the table. Together they set out linen napkins, silverware, china, and crystal, then carried the gleaming sterling platters of food with their matching covers to the table.

Brooke pointed to a large manila envelope propped against the coffeepot. "What's that?"

"Dessert?"

"I thought I'd have you for dessert." She laughed, comfortable with her sudden boldness.

"Greedy woman. You can have two desserts."

Only her grumbling stomach prevented her from having him for dessert first. Max poured them each a flute of champagne. He touched his glass to hers in a toast while looking deep into her eyes. "To us."

"To us," she repeated, wondering exactly what he meant by that.

They started with a cup of tasty bouillabaisse seasoned with saffron, and crusty French bread drizzled with garlic butter. The main dish, lobster and crayfish over wild rice, was complemented by a light Caesar salad.

While Max ate his last bites, she poured them coffee, her gaze lingering on the envelope. With her hunger sated, she sat back and sipped, wishing Max wasn't so good at arousing her curiosity.

Finally, he handed her the sealed envelope, which she now noted was from a prominent, highly respected medical research laboratory in New Orleans. "Don't open it yet. There's something I want to tell you first." He sounded so serious, his tone rang a warning bell.

"I'm listening."

"No matter what the results of that test, I will never take Skye away from you." He planted his elbows on the table and rested his chin on a closed fist.

The rich food suddenly curdled in her stomach. "I don't understand. How did this—"

"I swabbed the inside of my cheek and Skye's, then mailed the sample to the research center."

"When?"

"The day we all rode the streetcar. I helped her brush her teeth and did it then."

"Why didn't you tell me?"

"I'm telling you now."

That he seemed to trust her at last calmed her stomach. Her eyes darted to the envelope and back to him, sensing he wasn't finished talking.

"We could rip it up," he suggested, again sounding serious with just a hint of mischievousness in his eyes.

"What?" She hugged the envelope to her chest.

He leaned forward and took her hand. "I'm prepared to take care of Skye physically, financially and emotionally whether she's my daughter or not."

At his words, her heart swelled with love, but her head issued caution. "Why?"

A sheepish grin and a slight flush crossed his features, revealing how difficult this conversation must be for him. Impatiently, she awaited his answer.

He cleared his throat. "I don't want you to think that what's happened between us—the way I feel about you—has anything to do with the possibility that Skye might be my daughter."

That had never occurred to her. She tapped the envelope with her nails. How *did* he feel about her? Max had never said—not with words. Yet she sensed he was saying all he could right now and even this much was hard for him.

"Max, I'm sure she is yours. But if she's not, I'll have to keep searching for her parents."

His eyes held steady, boring into her. "It's your decision."

She ripped open the envelope. "Skye has a right to know her medical history. She needs to know who her biological parents are."

Brooke pulled out three loose pages and scanned the cover letter. Her reading stopped. Relief and happiness flooded her. "She's yours Max. The chance of error is infinitesimal. She's yours."

"I knew it in my heart the moment I saw her. It just took a while to get accustomed to the idea. Now I find it amazing. I'm a father, and you're the only mother she'll ever know."

"Ford might contest—"

He shook his head. "Since Rhonda's gone, I don't think my brother will object to our raising her—not under the circumstances."

"*Our* raising her?"

"I'd like to be there, too."

She wanted him to be there—so much her heart raced with joy. Was that a proposal? Her mouth went dry and she vowed to ask just as soon as she swallowed a sip of champagne.

A pounding on the door ruined her chance. Her pulse raced, and she prayed Ford's condition hadn't taken a turn for the worse.

"Max! It's Eva. Is Brooke with you?"

Max stood and unselfconsciously opened the door. Brooke couldn't be so nonchalant. She was wearing Max's robe, in his room, late at night. She might as well have a sign painted on her forehead that said she'd slept with Max. Heat blazed in her cheeks.

Max frowned. "Brooke's right here. What's wrong?"

Eva ignored the intimate dinner setting and Brooke's state of undress. His mother stalked into the room, her eyes darting wildly back and forth. "Is Skye here, too?"

Chapter Ten

Despite a light sweat on Max's skin, a chill of foreboding scissored down his spine, chopping his nerves into pulsating pieces. One glance at Brooke told him she was as shocked as he. Stepping to her side, he wrapped an arm across her shoulder and vowed whatever they faced, they would face it together.

Brooke's skin was as white as the terry robe that swallowed her. Her voice shook. "You said Skye was in bed."

"She was." Eva covered her face with her hands. "I thought I heard a noise and went to check on her. She wasn't in her room. She's not in our end of the house. I thought it unlikely, but hoped she might be here with you."

Even through the thick terry-cloth robe, he could feel Brooke trembling. Forcing words past the lining of his mouth turned dry with fear, he sought to comfort her. "We'll find her. We'll bring her back home."

Red sprinted down the hall and skidded to a stop. Before he had a chance to speak, Eva shook her head, answering his unasked question about Skye.

Had Max found his daughter only to lose her? He hadn't had time to learn to take her hugs and smiles for granted. He recalled the sound of her sweet voice, her ready smile, and the quick curiosity in her eyes, and swallowed a lump in his throat.

Skye. He could close his eyes and see her face. Hell, he saw her face every moment. And right now he saw her frightened tears.

As he thought how terrified Skye would be without her mother, pain knifed through him. Fear for her safety shuddered down his spine. She was the innocent here, but one who might be forced to pay for adult mistakes. If anyone hurt one strand of hair on his daughter's head, he'd spend the rest of his life hunting down the kidnapper.

Damn it to hell! He'd promised Brooke she and Skye would be safe here. Why hadn't he hired a full-time nanny and round-the-clock security guards? Why had he assumed he alone could protect her?

His parents looked as if they'd aged a decade within the last week. Eva's eyes were red and puffy with tears. She must have been crying as she'd searched for Skye.

"What about the alarm system?" Max asked, trying to think logically despite the shock that had jolted him numb.

Red's face was drawn, his mouth grim, yet he spoke with a calming strength. "The back door was forced open. Someone must have tampered with the alarm."

Brooke sagged against him. Her voice, filled with terror, helplessness and shattering pain, rose an octave. "They've taken my baby!"

"Skye's been kidnapped?" Eva sank into a chair, confusion clouding her eyes.

Max cursed at the agony his parents were going through. First, Rhonda had died. Ford lay in a coma. Now their only grandchild was missing.

He glanced at Brooke and the horror on her face mirrored his own. She probably felt just as guilty as he did for leaving Skye alone. Brooke's eyes riveted on the coffee table. She stiffened and lunged toward the phone. "We should call the police."

In the space of a gasp, the phone's shrill ring jerked her to a halt. She rounded on him with a silent plea to do something.

Inhaling a deep breath, he steeled himself against her searing pain so he could function. Yet he couldn't shake the apprehension that spiked in unexpected intensity.

He strode to the phone and picked up the receiver. "Hello?"

"If you want to see Skye, don't call the police," threatened a gravelly whisper that shot adrenaline through his veins.

"Agreed. No police." He motioned Brooke over and tilted the receiver so she could hear.

With his free hand he held her close to his side. So close he shared her trembling, weariness and sense of defeat.

"Don't talk—just listen," the voice continued in a noxious hush. "You and the kid's mother meet me out on the lake in your boat in thirty minutes. Head north three miles from the marina and cut your engines. I'll find you. Oh, and don't forget to bring the ransom."

He'd give anything he owned to save his daughter, his bank account, his stocks, his patent. Clenching the phone so tightly he had to ease his grip before the plastic cracked, he smothered his fury behind a cool tone. "What do you want?"

"The diamond necklace your mother wore to the charity ball last Christmas Eve."

The caller must have seen his mother's picture in the paper's society pages. Obviously the kidnapper didn't know their family well or he would have asked for a great deal more.

Something wasn't right, something darker and infinitely more sinister assailed him fleetingly, but he couldn't think past his acute need to know his daughter was all right. He ached to hear her voice. "Let me talk to Skye."

"Don't be late."

The phone clicked. Anger clenched his jaw.

Brooke swayed. "Oh, God! I'll never see my baby again."

"Yes, you will," Max insisted fiercely. "Now go dress. We haven't much time." He gently shoved Brooke toward the bedroom and her clothes, then turned to his father before doubts engulfed him. "He wants some diamond necklace Mom wore last Christmas."

Eva spun on her heels, her soulful blue eyes luminous with tears. "I'll get it."

After both women left the room, Red shook his head, anger in the sharply drawn lines of his mouth. "That necklace isn't much of a ransom."

Exactly. With his family's wealth, the kidnapper

could have asked for much more. While the necklace was expensive, it wasn't close to the fortune he could have demanded. Was the kidnapper ignorant? Or in a rush? Why not give them time to withdraw cash from the bank?

Max locked stares with Red. "There's only one reason the ransom is so low. The kidnapper doesn't intend to release Skye."

Red nodded, his eyes narrowed. "Most likely, he intends to draw out you and Brooke."

Max had to give Red credit. His father didn't even try to talk him out of going, didn't try to remind him with Ford still in a coma, Max was their only remaining son. Red understood no matter how much Max loved his parents, he could never abandon the daughter who had so recently come into his life and won a piece of his heart.

His father clapped him on the shoulder and squeezed. "What can I do to help?"

At his offer, Max had never loved his father more. "We have only a few spare minutes. I could use weapons, a flare and—"

The hurried beat of approaching footsteps injected a shred of caution into his words. His mother rushed back into his rooms. At the same time Brooke, still tucking her shirt into her jeans, joined them from the other direction.

"Whatever else you think might be helpful," Max finished smoothly, unwilling to alarm Eva any more than necessary.

As Brooke watched his mother casually toss Max

the sparkling necklace, Brooke's eyes brimmed with thanks. "I'll pay you back, somehow."

Eva took Brooke into her arms. "They are only rocks, dear. Skye is flesh and blood and infinitely more precious. You bring her back safe. You all come back safe."

Then his mother was hugging him, making no attempt to hide her tears. She felt frail in his arms, but then she stiffened her spine, reminding him of her backbone of steel.

"I love you, Mom."

"I love you, too." Reluctantly, she released him and wiped her eyes. "You'd better go."

Red met them in the drive and Max shoved aside the uneasy thought he might never see his parents again. While Brooke slid into the passenger seat of the truck, Red handed him a Swiss army knife, which Max slipped into his jeans' pocket, and a handgun, which he tucked into his belt.

"There're extra clips and a loaded shotgun behind the seat. I couldn't find a flare but threw in binoculars." Red handed him a tiny penknife. "Hide this in your shoe."

He didn't think to argue with his father's unexpected vehemence. Max knelt and tucked the tiny weapon away, hugged his father, banking his stirring emotions, then hurried behind the wheel. He started the motor and shifted into reverse, doing his best to ignore the dark despair clawing at him. "Got your seat belt fastened?"

From his rough tone, Brooke must have surmised he had no intention of obeying the speed limit. She braced a hand against the dash. "Just remember we can't help Skye if we don't arrive in one piece."

He sped to the lake, silently cursing the weather. The wind beat the windshield like a fist against a face, while the air was heavy with the promise of rain. Ragged edges of dark clouds scudded across the crescent moon smudging the dim light. The lake would be rough and though the *Sea Mist* could handle choppy seas, fear bolted through him at the thought of Skye out on the lake in the stormy blackness.

Brooke tensed in the front seat, her palms rubbing her thighs, the resolve on her face never wavering. With her lips pressed firmly together and her nostrils flaring slightly, she looked ready to battle dragons. Clearly she was terrified, but she wouldn't give in to the fear.

He reached over and squeezed her icy hand, offering the gesture in support and unity. "We'll find her and bring her home."

Conviction frosted her voice. "I'm holding on to that thought."

She was no coward. No matter whom or what they faced, no matter how frightened she was, his lady was determined to see this through for her daughter.

His lady.

The words had a compelling appeal to them, but he had to concentrate on driving, corner his whirring emotions and shut the door on them so he could protect them both. And yet he couldn't help thinking how much she meant to him. He didn't want to lose her. An impulse to force her to stay behind gripped him.

Enough.

They had no choice. The kidnapper had demanded both of them come and she could no more refuse a chance to free their child than he could. His heart swelled with pride at her courage. Yet, no matter how much a part of him Brooke had become, he had to put those kinds of thoughts out of his mind. Their lives might depend on it.

BROOKE SHIFTED in the front seat of the truck at the marina and peered anxiously through the condensation on the window, awaiting Max. Before he'd left, he'd leaned over and kissed her, his lips hard and greedy, his actions saying what he'd never put into words. Max had kissed her before, but never had he jolted every inch of her flesh until she felt courage surging back into her with a power that defeated her despair. A scalding charge zipped along her skin, spurring her determination to function despite her fears for Skye.

As she'd dug her fingers into the muscles of his shoulders and back, she'd clung to the thought that Max wanted Skye back as much as she did. The kiss lasted the briefest of seconds but gave her the strength she needed. All too soon, he'd slipped from her arms, out of the truck and into the garage.

He'd left her parked under a stand of oaks while he unlocked the boat. She glanced at her watch. What was taking him so long? They had to get out on the lake. She shuddered to think what could happen if they missed the deadline.

She tried to stay calm, but it was impossible when she might never see Skye again. Wishing away the weighty feeling of dread that pressed on her chest and had her inhaling in short, raspy breaths wasn't the answer.

She needed to stop fretting over her daughter and concentrate on helping Max. Yet how could she not worry about Skye? Her daughter must be terribly frightened. Why hadn't the kidnapper let them speak to her? Could the worst have already happened?

Don't think it. Get hold of yourself.

Brooke glanced at her watch again. The minute hand was approaching 1:00 a.m.

Her palms went clammy. She fidgeted in the seat, rolled down the window. Something had to be wrong. The last time they'd taken out the boat, the hookup hadn't taken this long.

The humid air entered the truck in hot, heavy puffs and tendrils of dank oxygen snaked into her lungs. The tree branches in the woods around the marina clicked and clattered but she barely noticed over the sound of her own heartbeat roaring in her ears. In contrast, the boats rocked in the rough waters, straining their docking lines, sailboat halyards clanging against their masts in discordant bursts.

She'd give Max another minute. If he didn't show, she'd go looking for him.

Sweat beaded her forehead, her upper lip, and between her breasts. Shoving her hair from her damp face, she searched the building for movement and listened hard. Realizing she'd been holding her breath, she exhaled and then drew air into her starving lungs. Even the crickets seemed to be hiding from the rush of the storm.

When a shadow stepped from behind the garage,

she let out a tiny gasp. A tall man lumbered toward her, his long legs closing the distance between them with menacing quickness.

It wasn't Max.

Frustration layered on fear until her stomach curled into a twisted knot. The silhouette wasn't tall enough and moved too heavily to be Max. Tension knotted her shoulders. Brooke leaned on the horn to let Max know something was wrong. But when the stranger emerged from the shadow, her adrenaline surged.

She knew that face, those beady eyes, the sneering lips.

"Grant?"

"Get out of the truck. Slowly."

She spied the gun he aimed at her chest and her knees turned rubbery. "Where's Skye?"

"Turn around," he ordered. Without waiting for her to comply, he grabbed her shoulder, spinning and slamming her against the truck.

Where was Max? She had to signal she was in trouble, warn him of the danger without betraying his presence. "Help!"

"Shut up, fool woman. Your brat's not here. My partner has her. And as for Max, he ain't going to save you when he's all trussed up like a chicken."

Hope of rescue plummeted. Grant had found Max, too.

That's why Max had taken so long in the garage. He might have been struggling while she'd just sat in the truck and done nothing to help. A shiver of bleak despair snaked down her spine as she realized they'd walked right into a trap. Grant had no intention of releasing Skye.

Grant wrenched her wrists behind her back. At the sound of shredding tape, she jammed an elbow into his stomach and stamped his foot.

When he didn't release her, she realized she hadn't the strength to hurt him. Tears of frustration ran down her face as he taped her wrists tightly. Where was Skye? Would she ever see her again?

Grant yanked her away from the truck. She gasped as agonizing pain shot to the sockets.

Preferring to remain upright rather than letting him drag her, she forced her rubbery feet to walk and focused the power of her attention on Grant.

He hurried her toward the garage, muttering all the while. "You didn't have to die tonight. You could have minded your own business. But, no. You couldn't leave the clinic alone. You had to go poking your nose where it didn't belong until we had to do something about you."

"Let us go and we'll never return to the clinic."

With a growl, he shook his head, a hard, set look to his features. "It's too late. You've caused too much trouble. My partner said if we left you alone, you'd give up and go away. But not you."

Frantic, she twisted, struggling with all her weight, but she couldn't break his grip. He jerked her toward the garage. She had no choice but to stumble along.

"What is it with you females?" Grant snarled. "I figured it was only a matter of time before you started blackmailing us."

"This is all a mistake. You're wrong. Let me explain. I would never blackmail you. I—"

"That's what Callie said." He grabbed her chin and jaw in one hand and yanked her around to face him. "She lied and you are lying, too. Rather clever of me to have you stumble over her body. That was your first warning—but you ignored it. You ignored all my warnings, so now you're going to pay."

"No. I—"

He jerked her arm and shoved her forward again.

Brooke's heart vaulted into her tight throat. Her heart hammered her ribs. Callie must have found out Grant was stealing from the clinic. When she'd blackmailed him, he'd killed her. And now he was going to kill her, too.

Grant snapped her to a stop by the stern of Max's boat. He chuckled grimly. "Up you go."

He forced her to climb into the boat, which still sat on the trailer. She stalled for time. "If you kill me, it'll look suspicious. The clinic will come under investigation."

He shook his head, a twisted grin drawing the cheekbones tight on his face. "I'm going to take you out onto the lake. You're going to drown. The boat will sink. It'll look like an accident and have nothing to do with the clinic."

And where was Skye? Was she alive? The thought of her daughter alone out in the storm had her crazy with fear.

Grant ripped off another piece of tape and placed it over her mouth, cutting off questions. While she concentrated on dragging enough air through her nose to breathe, he led her around a partially inflated dinghy and stuffed her into the forward cabin.

She tumbled onto a body and would have screamed if her mouth wasn't covered. Then she realized she'd fallen on Max. His hands and feet were tied, his mouth taped. Before she could recover, Grant taped her ankles and shut the cabin door, leaving them in the dark.

Max rolled her off him. In the dark, she felt him struggling, heard the rustle of his clothes catching on the hull. An elbow dug into her side, a knee kicked her shin. What the hell was he doing?

She couldn't see him, but sensed he'd turned his body so his feet pointed at her head. His feet rested on her shoulder and she moved away to give him more room.

"Uh-uh."

He put his feet back on her shoulder. What did he want? What was he trying to tell her?

The truck's motor started and boat and trailer shifted. As Grant backed the trailer into the water, Max's feet fell from her shoulder. The two of them rolled helplessly, abrading their skin on rough fiberglass.

Within moments, water lapped against a hull turned cold and clammy. As soon as the boat settled, Max again put his feet on her shoulder. The heel of his sneaker scraped her skin. Excitement zipped through her as she realized he wanted to take off his sneakers.

Although she had no idea *why* he was so determined to remove his shoes, helping was preferable to contemplating the terrifying prospect of drowning or wondering what would become of Skye. She did what she could to help. Rolling to her side so that her back was to Max's feet, she inched up until her fingers reached his shoes. Immediately understanding her movements, Max scooted the other way. Finally her finger caught on the shoe leather and yanked.

The shoe didn't budge. Forcing patience, she felt for the laces. Grant jumped into the boat with a thud and revved the engines. As the boat peeled into choppy waves, untying Max's laces while the bow rose up and slammed down became more difficult. Too often his feet jammed her outstretched fingers, but she didn't give up, although she silently swore curses she didn't think she knew.

Finally, she untied one lace and pulled off the shoe. By his insistent motion, he needed the other one off, too. Either he needed both shoes off, or she'd removed the wrong one. It took precious minutes until she succeeded and earned a rest. She lay panting while Max flipped himself over until they were head to head. He wriggled, as if feeling for something on the deck.

She rolled to her side, scooted into him and grunted to catch his attention. His face bumped her backside. He wriggled until her fingers reached the tape and tore it free of his mouth.

"There was a penknife in my shoe," he whispered.

So that's what he was scrambling for. It seemed to take aeons, but it was probably only minutes before her hands closed on the knife. She grunted, wishing her mouth was free of the tape and she could tell him Grant's plans.

"Find it?" he asked.

"Mmm-hmm."

She opened the blade and tried to cut the tape at her own wrists. Bending her hands backward and maintaining a constant pressure proved futile. Maneuvering until they lay on their sides, back to back, she sawed at his wrists, praying she didn't open a vein as the boat slammed into wave after wave.

Her arms trembled with fatigue and sweat beaded her brow, but finally she cut him free. Within moments Max ripped the tape off her mouth, and freed her ankles and wrists. Last, he liberated his feet and, unfettered, donned his shoes.

Finally free to tell him what Grant had said, she wasted no time. "Grant doesn't have Skye. His partner does. This was a trap."

"I'm sorry. He took me by surprise in the garage, and confiscated the knife in my pocket. I didn't expect him to show until we were out on the lake. Dumb mistake."

"There was no way you could have known. He's going to kill us."

"How?"

"He said he would drown us, sink the boat and make it look like an accident so our deaths wouldn't be connected to the clinic."

"How's he getting away?"

"There's a rubber dinghy in the back."

Max gave her a quick hug. "You did great getting that out of him. Now, it's time to turn the tables."

Her heart quickened with hope at his words. "How? We're free, but he still has a gun."

"Yeah, but this is *my* boat." Max pulled away from her and edged toward the hull.

"Where are you going?"

"To pull a spark plug and cut a gas line. Don't worry. The boat won't blow until I flip a switch on the dash to turn on the number three engine."

She tugged on his pant leg. "Wait! Even if you don't kill us, we can't kill Grant. If he dies, we'll never find Skye."

"We won't be on board when the boat explodes. I won't set the final switch until I'm sure we'll be safe. Grant might survive the explosion. But we have no choice. We can't find Skye if we're dead."

Without staying to argue further, Max squeezed through the narrow passageway along the hull that led to the engines. She had no way of knowing how long he would be gone, but the wait seemed interminable. She had too much time to think what could go wrong. If Grant reached their destination before Max returned, their plan would fail. Once Grant saw they were free of their bonds, he might tie them up again before throwing them over to drown. She pictured him waiting for them to go under, then ghoulishly removing their bindings so their deaths would appear accidental.

Suddenly, she scrambled about the cabin, searching for the discarded tape. They would have to make it appear as if they were still tied up. By the time Max returned, smelling of bilge water and gas, she'd collected the pieces of tape.

"Put this back on." She slapped the tape into his hands. "If Grant sees we're free, he may retie us."

"Good thinking."

Brooke had just wound the tape around her wrists and placed her hands behind her back when Grant killed the engine. He shoved open the cabin door, letting in a cool gust of wind and dim light. "Well, did you all have a nice bumpy ride?"

He held the gun in one hand while he yanked her from the cabin. Before she realized what was happening, he'd picked her up, tossed her, and she was flying through the air. Instinct made her hold her breath and close her eyes. She landed in the chilly water with a smack. After several harsh jerks, she removed the tape at her wrists and her ankles.

Something large pitched into the water beside her. Max!

Had he had time to flip the switch on the dash? Kicking over to him, she surfaced, blinked the water out of her eyes and searched for the *Sea Mist*. Convinced they were helpless, Grant hadn't even driven away. He stood in the stern, pumping air into the dinghy.

"Can Grant see us?" she whispered.

"Maybe. Hopefully, we're just a dark blob in a large black lake."

"Now what?"

"Swim fast," Max ordered in a whisper. "The boat's going to blow."

A wave knocked her sideways. Her clothes weighed her down. She kicked off her shoes and swam after Max, wondering how long she could stay afloat in the lake. No way could she swim to shore, but she refused to give in to despair. Perhaps they could float and tread water through the night. A boat might spot them in the morning light.

"Hurry," Max urged, and she redoubled her efforts, kicking for all she was worth until her lungs burned.

Looking over her shoulder at the boat, she saw Grant, a purple-black silhouette against a murky sky, wrestle then slide the dinghy overboard and attach a line from the bow to a cleat at the stern of the *Sea Mist*.

Without sparing a glance in their direction, Grant moved forward toward the throttle.

Brooke held her breath. He turned a key and the engine sputtered. Grant cursed.

Suddenly the engines roared to life. Grant turned the boat directly toward them. He meant to run them over!

The boat exploded, blinding her with red, orange and yellow fingers grasping the stormy sky. The blast rang in her ears. Bits of fiberglass sparked, hissing as they landed in the bubbling cauldron of water around the boat. Even from this distance, the flames heated her face.

She didn't wait for her heart rate to dip back to normal before swimming to Max and touching his shoulder. The flames cast a hellish light in his pupils. His cheekbones looked gaunt, his lips grim. She knew he had loved that boat.

"I'm sorry about the *Sea Mist*."

"The boat is replaceable. I'm waiting for the fire to die to see whether Grant or the dinghy survived the blast."

His dire reminder that they could drown had her squinting into the flames. When the brightness dimmed, she spotted neither Grant nor a dinghy. Her heart sank. Already her limbs grew heavy with fatigue. As the fire died, they swam closer to the wreckage, avoiding patches of burning gas, hoping to find something large enough to use for flotation.

They had only one other hope. That another boat had spotted the explosion and would come to investigate. But as the wind howled and the lake water churned, she wearily realized any chance of rescue was slim to none. Any sane person would stay ashore, safe and dry on a night like this.

Grant's intended end for them might have been more humane. At least it would have been quick. But with both of them dead, what would happen to Skye?

Just when she thought their situation could get no worse, lightning lit up the sky and thunder roared. She took in a mouthful of water and coughed.

"Over there!" Max shouted, his excitement giving her renewed energy. With long, sure strokes he swam toward a dark object partly submerged in the water and she followed a bit more slowly.

The dinghy had survived. Sort of. A small motor attached to a wooden bracket was the only part of the boat completely above sea level.

Max heaved himself into the floating morass of rubber. "These inflatables have separate compartments. If we can pump her up, then bail, she may float us."

Max inflated one section at a time with a foot pump. Several sections held air. A few he patched with the standardized emergency repair kit taped to the underside of the seat. As the boat rose out of the lake, Brooke climbed aboard. She had nothing to bail with, but plucked a scooped piece of fiberglass from the debris scattered around them. For the first time that evening, her hopes rose with the thought they might survive and find her daughter.

After the water level in the dinghy was down to their ankles, Max fiddled with the motor. While the air hissed out of the leaky boat, she kept pumping air into the different compartments.

"You think the engine will run?" she asked between chattering teeth.

"She will if the engine didn't submerge. The air held best in the stern by the engine since it was farthest from the blast. Let's hope the gas line is intact."

She didn't dare ask if the dinghy would explode if the gas leaked. She didn't want to know.

Max stood, yanked on a cord. The engine sputtered. And died. He adjusted the choke, tried again. This time the motor revved and settled to a steady purr.

Max grinned and turned them away from the center of the wreckage. Something large floated on a wave in front of them, and Max steered around a flat piece of decking.

At the sight of a body floating in the water, her stomach lurched. She pointed a shaking finger. "There's Grant."

But was he alive? They needed him conscious and talking to help them locate Skye. Grant could identify his partner.

She stared at the body, wondering if his movements were by design or simply the waves causing his hands to mimic lifelike action.

Max steered over to the body cautiously. She envisioned Grant rearing out of the water, gun in hand, to threaten them again. But up close, they could see Grant floated facedown. He was dead.

Damn Grant to hell. He wasn't supposed to die. He should have lived and told them what he'd done with Skye. Now all they had for their efforts was another dead body for the police to blame on them. And they couldn't afford the time for police questions. They had to find Skye.

Max held on to Grant by his shirt and steered the dinghy back to the large piece of deck that still floated. With a grunt, he heaved Grant onto the fiberglass.

"This dinghy can't support his weight. The coast guard can claim the body tomorrow."

She closed her eyes and shivered, rubbing her arms with her hands, hoping Skye wasn't out in this weather and that her daughter was safe and warm. She couldn't muster any sorrow over Grant's death, callous as that seemed. Her only emotions were for Skye. They had to find her soon. They had to.

Max sensed her dismay. "We'll find Skye."

"We don't even know where to look."

"We can start with Grant's trailer."

"I suppose. But he said his partner had Skye."

She didn't sound as if she believed his reassurances anymore, but at least she opened her eyes and made an effort to shove the hair out of her face. Even dripping wet, without makeup and clearly exhausted, she looked better to Max than any woman he'd ever known. No plunge into a lake could wash away the inner strength he found so attractive.

The urge to take her into his arms was strong, but

he didn't dare risk upsetting the boat's precarious balance. The best he could do was distract her from her worry over Skye. "When we get ashore, I'll call my folks and ask them to report that the *Sea Mist* has been stolen."

"The detectives will check out their story. If we get lucky, maybe Grant will have left some clues to the identity of his partner."

"And if he didn't?"

Chapter Eleven

During their trip to shore the wind had picked up, and in the high waves, the dinghy's pace had been slow. Chilled through to the bone, Brooke had shivered and shaken.

When they finally reached the marina, Max phoned his parents and asked them to call the police. He instructed them to say his boat had been stolen and was probably out on the lake as they spoke. Hoping the call would buy them enough time to avoid the inevitable police questions, he drove straight to Grant's trailer.

And they found nothing.

Not one sign of Skye. Not one sign of Grant's partner.

Even now, with the truck's heater on high, Brooke's teeth chattered as they drove toward his parents' home, once again filled with disappointment and heartache. When they reached the house, Max insisted Brooke take a hot shower before changing into dry clothes.

Still towel drying her hair, she met Max, Eva and Red in the living room. Max looked up as she entered.

He, too, had changed into jeans and a dry shirt. "We may not have much time. A tugboat captain found Grant's body soon after we left. His wallet was still in his pocket. The police want to question us."

"They'll ask questions for hours." Panic gripped her. She had to find her daughter. To do that, they had to find out what Henschel knew about Dr. Arnold. They couldn't afford to delay. Skye's life depended on their moving quickly.

"That's why we need to get out of here," Max said.

A brash knock on the door interrupted her reply. Her pulse raced. How could they escape if the police had already arrived?

Max checked the peephole, his brows arched in surprise as he opened the door. "Come in."

She steeled herself for the inevitable delay, the explanations. Instead a man with bloodshot eyes and a haggard face followed Max into the den. "Max Braddack? Brooke Evans? I'd like to make a deal."

The man looked vaguely familiar but she couldn't place him. He must have read her puzzled expression.

"Don't you recognize me? I'm Clifford Arnold."

The skin on her scalp tightened and Brooke staggered backward. Max put a steadying hand on her shoulder. The man was medium height and his dark hair, now grayer at the temples than she remembered, reminded her of Arnold's. He'd lost his paunch but still had the same fatherly expression that had won her misplaced trust.

"Dr. Arnold!" Brooke tried to steady her racing pulse. "We thought you were dead. Where is Skye?"

He frowned. "Who?"

"My daughter's been kidnapped. And I want her back. Tell us where she is," Brooke half pleaded, half demanded.

"I'm sorry, I don't know where she is. I was on my boat when Grant murdered Callie. I expected him to come after me next. That's why I faked my suicide. I've been hiding."

Red and Eva remained silent, clearly puzzled by the turn of events but allowing Max to handle the questions. Max loomed over Arnold, his face fierce, his eyes glimmering with restrained anger. "Why are you coming out of hiding now?"

"I heard on the news that Grant is dead."

Max glowered. "I don't understand. What kind of deal are you after?"

"You're a powerful man. If you protect me, I'll tell you everything I know."

Max shook his head. "I need to hear you out first."

What shreds of control Brooke had left, began to crumble. "We don't have time for this. We need to find Skye."

Max lowered his voice. "We don't know what really happened or who has Skye. If he tells what he knows, we may get some answers."

When he spoke with such utter conviction, she had to believe him. But remaining here was hard when she wanted to search for her baby.

Max turned back to Arnold. "You'd best make your story quick."

Max guided Brooke toward a brocade chair while gesturing for Arnold to take a seat. She eased into the chair at first appreciative she no longer needed to support her shaking legs. But then nerves took over and she stood and paced.

Would Arnold tell the truth? Was he afraid for his life? Or had he kidnapped Skye and come to gloat over the anguished parents in some macabre scheme?

"When I heard about Grant's death, I risked coming here to find you."

"So you said. Why?" Max asked.

Arnold glanced at the well-stocked bar and licked his lip. "Could I have a drink?"

Nobody answered his question.

Max's gaze darted to Brooke, conveying a mixture of frustration and apology at the delay. But obviously he thought what Arnold had to say was too important to rush off without hearing it. She could only pray he was right. If Arnold had lied about taking her daughter, perhaps he would slip up and they could take advantage of his mistake. And if he was telling the truth, he must have his suspicions about Skye's kidnapper. Despite her impatience, she vowed to listen carefully to his story.

Arnold rested his elbows on the arms of his chair. "Scotch on the rocks, please."

While Max fixed drinks, Red and Eva settled quietly on the sofa, their faces lined with worry, their hands locked together. Brooke paced.

Arnold leaned forward and caught her hand. "I'm sorry you've had to go through this."

She jerked back and brushed her damp hair out of her eyes. "Please get to the point. Every minute counts."

Frustration and fear for Skye made it difficult to

restrain her impatience. Arnold knew how Skye had ended up in her sister's womb. He might even know what had happened to the egg he'd culled from Brooke that had been meant for her sister. But most important, he might tell them where to find Skye.

Dr. Arnold accepted the drink from Max. "I'm not sure where to start."

Brooke, knowing she needed the sugar charge, sipped the soft drink Max pressed into her trembling hand. "Start at the beginning, please. We need every clue to find my daughter."

Red and Eva refused drinks and Max pulled up a chair and folded his arms over his chest. "How did the Braddack embryo end up in Brooke's sister?"

Wincing at Max's hard tone, Arnold set his glass down on the side table and stared into the liquor. "I mixed up the codes on the test tube labels."

"Why?"

There could be no mistaking the sorrow in Dr. Arnold's eyes. "It was an accident. We were extremely busy and working long hours. Everyone was tired, and it was a combination of errors."

Max's look remained harsh, the living room light sculpting the planes on his face into one dangerous expression. "When did you discover your mistake?"

"I knew nothing until..." Dr. Arnold covered his face with his hands. "God forgive me." He looked up, tears running down his face. "A few months after the birth, Nicole called me with suspicions—"

"What caused her doubts?" Brooke reeled with surprise that her sister had suspected something was wrong.

"Skye didn't look like anyone on either side of the family. I told her characteristics could pop up from the genes of ancestors three generations back, but she insisted I check Skye out."

A lump formed in Brooke's throat. "She never said a word to me."

"She and her husband brought Skye to me," Arnold said. "I ran the tests and asked them to return the next day to receive the results in person and discuss what we should do."

"That never happened, did it?" Brooke asked.

"I had every intention of telling your sister about the mix-up. In the meantime I told Henschel about the error. He said not to worry, he'd handle it." Arnold paused. "I assumed he'd have our attorney and insurance company quietly take care of the matter. Then Nicole and her husband died in a car accident before our appointment."

"How convenient for you," Max snapped. "So what did Henschel do next?"

"He instructed Grant to alter the computer files so no one would discover the deception. Karen Forester overheard Henschel's order to Grant, but Henschel said I needn't worry about her loyalty to the clinic."

Max stood and clasped his hands behind his back. "You decided to keep silent when you realized that with Skye's parents dead, you could keep your error a secret."

Arnold flushed a deep red at Max's accusation. "Henschel ordered me to consider the matter closed. He convinced me the clinic wouldn't survive a scandal."

"Or a lawsuit," Brooke added bitterly.

Max's eyes narrowed. "Your reputation would have been in shreds."

"That, too," Arnold admitted. "But if the clinic closed, hundreds of couples we might have helped would remain childless."

"What of *my* brother and his wife?" Max asked. "You didn't think Rhonda should know about the child she wanted so badly?"

"Henschel insisted Ford and Rhonda would have other children, but I needed convincing."

"Why did he have to convince you?"

Arnold sighed. "Every time Rhonda became pregnant, she miscarried. I had doubts she'd ever carry a child to term. With each attempt to impregnate, the chance of success goes down."

Max pounded the table and Arnold jumped. "And you would have lost your medical license if this embryo screw-up had come to light. Isn't that right?"

"I'm sorry." Arnold hung his head. "Most of the time, I'm proud of what I do. Henschel insisted on sweeping the mistake away."

"Then what happened?" Max asked, and Brooke realized what a brilliant trial attorney he would make. Nothing laid-back about him now, he sliced straight for the carotid artery.

"For six years, nothing."

"When I called after all those years," Brooke guessed, "you must have panicked."

"When my secretary told me you'd called, I knew you'd discovered what had happened. But I was packing the boat and leaving on vacation. Henschel sug-

gested I disappear for a while and let him take care of
things. I thought he'd make a settlement, keep the incident private—especially since Ford was on the board
and wouldn't want the Kine Clinic's reputation
harmed. I thought we could work something out. But
then I heard about Ford and Rhonda's accident and
Callie's death and I got scared. With almost everyone
connected with the embryo switch dead, I feared I
might be next."

Brooke felt ripped in two. Part of her yearned to
search for her daughter, to take some kind of action,
while her more rational side insisted what Arnold had
to say would be vital in locating Skye. "But why was
Henschel so anxious to cover up *your* mistake?"

"At first I thought he didn't want a scandal attached
to the clinic. But later I learned he, with Grant's help,
was skimming profits. Any outside investigation into
the clinic from a scandal would reveal his stealing."

This was the connection they'd been looking for.
Max shot her a significant look. "What skimming?"

"I discovered the fraud almost by accident. A patient complained she'd been billed too much."

"And?" Max prodded information out of the doctor
while Brooke paced. Having their suspicions confirmed was all well and good, but they still were no
nearer to finding Skye.

"The patient had been overcharged, but only by a
few dollars. I checked the billing on my other patients
and found the same overcharges. I took the problem
to Henschel."

"What did he say?" Max asked.

"To drop the whole matter or he'd reveal the embryo switch, blame it all on me, and pull my license."

"So you kept quiet," Brooke said with disgust.

Arnold nodded. "And Henschel amassed a fortune. Overbilling can add up to a modest fortune when totaled in every patient's bill and each laboratory invoice. If someone noticed an error, there wouldn't be a big stink since most of the clinic's income is not billed to insurance companies. The money was siphoned into Research and Development."

The pieces were starting to come together in Brooke's mind. Once Arnold had agreed to remain quiet about the embryo deception, he couldn't turn his colleague in for theft. The billing fraud also explained Grant's expensive electronic equipment.

"That's where Grant obtained his money," Brooke said. "Then Callie found out about his skimming and blackmailed him."

Max nodded and held her gaze. "When Grant killed Callie and we stumbled over her body, he probably thought he was solving two problems at once by implicating us in her murder."

"Your brother was also suspicious," Arnold added. "Ford hired the new accountant."

Eva and Red exchanged anguished glances. Red squeezed his wife's hand tight.

Max shook his head. "But with Grant dead, Henschel has to do his own dirty work. He must have Skye."

Arnold slumped in his chair. "I never dreamed my simple mistake would cause so much trouble. I never thought Henschel would resort to murder and kidnapping." While Arnold rambled, Max and Brooke headed for the door.

The doctor mumbled into his drink. "You'd better approach Henschel with caution. He may have hired more help. And he has his own private jet. If he thinks anyone is closing in on him, he'll flee the country."

A surge of electricity shot through Brooke. She wrenched open the door. "We can't let him get away."

"We won't," Max assured her, his mouth tightening into a grim line. He spoke to his folks over his shoulder as he and Brooke ran for the garage. "Call the police. Tell them everything. Have them watch the airports."

Brooke suspected Arnold had told them all he knew and that the police would move too slowly to find Skye. She and Max had to do something fast. She climbed into the truck thinking Henschel wasn't stupid. He may have heard news reports of Grant's death. Even if Henschel hadn't, when Grant didn't return, Henschel would suspect their plans had gone awry. Had he abandoned Skye somewhere while he went about his business? Or was Skye still with him? Or— no, she wouldn't allow herself to consider that possibility. Her daughter was alive and Brooke was going to find her.

She looked to Max for answers. He jammed the key into the ignition and the truck roared to life. At the dangerous glint in his eyes, her heart thumped. She recognized that look. Max had a plan. "What are we going to do?"

Max slammed his foot on the accelerator. "Let's

figure that out when we get to Henschel's house. After Mom and Dad's call, the police will cover the airports and stop him from leaving the country. But we can get to his house faster than the cops. Henschel lives in the Garden District, remember?''

"Suppose he's not there?"

Max didn't hesitate for a moment. "We'll ask questions until we find him."

Fear, clammy and icy, stole under her skin. "Henschel could have already—"

"No. Skye's safe. If Henschel knows Grant failed and we're on to him, the only way he can escape is with a hostage. He won't hurt her."

Her stomach grew tighter and drawing her next breath didn't come easy. "If we find Henschel, what'll we do then? Suppose Skye isn't there and he has her locked away someplace? He's not going to admit what he did."

A dark, murderous hardness that she'd never seen before reflected in Max's eyes. "That's where we have an advantage over the cops. There are ways to make a man talk."

A bad taste coated the lining of her mouth. She'd wanted Max to lose his calm—but not like this. She had a terrible feeling that if they pursued Henschel, something awful would happen.

When Arnold had told his story, she'd been so full of hope they would find Skye. Now it was as if someone had tilted the floor beneath her feet and she couldn't maintain her balance. Her entire world had shifted, and she was no longer sure of the right thing to do.

Max rounded a corner toward Dr. Henschel's house. She held her breath as a police car, siren screaming, gained on them from behind. Getting pulled over for a minor violation could turn into a major disaster if the cop asked a lot of questions.

When the police car passed without slowing, she let out her breath in a rush. A throng of butterflies fluttered in her stomach when she thought of how many things could go wrong. Henschel could flee before they found him, take Skye with him, or do something worse.

If it weren't for Max's help and support and love, she didn't know how she would get through this. He'd move heaven and earth to find Skye and she trusted him with all her heart. He was going to make Skye a wonderful father—once they found her.

As he drove, vigilantly checking the mirrors, she noted the tense set of his shoulders and his tight grip on the steering wheel. With the patrol car out of sight, Max ignored the speed limit and slammed his foot to the floor.

The giant mansions of the Garden District loomed in the dark like medieval battlements. This late at night, many of the homes appeared lonely and desolate, empty shells. A brittle silence stretched like icy cords down the long row of houses.

Interrupting the silence, wind gusted through oak branches and keened a high-pitched moan that prickled the hairs on the back of her neck. The wrought-iron gates spaced out in ordered formality along the road reminded her of jailhouse bars. The dark and starless sky smothered the earth with thick thunderclouds that bore down with the weight of a coffin lid.

She rubbed slick palms on her thighs. "I don't think Skye's near here. I have a bad feeling about this."

"We're almost there."

Before he turned past the gates and into the driveway, Max cut the lights. A black cat darted around the corner of the house, but there was no other movement. None of the draperies or blinds stirred. She didn't spot a light peeking out of the windows.

She whispered, trying to control the trembling in her voice, "What are we going to do?"

Max pressed the car keys into her hand. "I'll ring the bell. If he answers, use my cell phone to call the police."

He stepped out of the car and walked the brick path to the veranda. She slid into the driver's seat and fumbled to insert the keys in the ignition without taking her gaze off Max. She squirmed, ready to jump at the first sign of trouble.

At the thud of Max's fist pounding the front door, she stifled a scream. She didn't know which she feared more—that Henschel would open the door, or that he'd already gone.

The stress of waiting in the car grew to intolerable proportions. If they didn't find Skye here, they had no idea where else to look. Sitting and fretting was too hard on her already frayed nerves.

Max peered in the windowpane on the front door, then spoke to her over his shoulder. "Henschel's gone."

Her stomach clenched into a fist. "Maybe he's just a heavy sleeper. Maybe—"

"The house is empty of furniture. I doubt he's redecorating," Max muttered in frustration. He practically growled and tension radiated from him in pulsating waves. To think he'd once appeared so laid-back seemed impossible now.

"Max, look!"

A light had come on inside the house. Max spun to face the front door. A woman stood in the doorway. "Why are you disturbing the neighborhood at this time of night?"

"I need to speak to Dr. Henschel. It's urgent."

"He's not here." The woman started to close the door.

Max stuck his foot on the threshold. "Wait. This is an emergency."

"Call an ambulance. I told you, the doctor isn't here."

Max eased his way across the threshold but his voice carried easily in the still air. "I'd like to see that for myself, if you don't mind?"

"I do mind. As head housekeeper, it is my job to prevent the likes of you from barging in on Dr. Henschel's privacy."

"Do you realize you may be an accessory to a kidnapping? Has the doctor brought a child here in the last twenty-four hours?"

"Certainly not. No one has been here but me," the housekeeper huffed, but then protested with a bit of uncertainty, "And the doctor is not a kidnapper. That's absurd."

Since Max had accused her of being party to a crime, the woman's tone had lost a bit of vehemence. While she might be telling the truth, the housekeeper clearly had her own suspicions about the doctor.

Max gentled his tone. "If Henschel is innocent, he has nothing to fear. I just want to find my little girl and she may be with Henschel. Please, ma'am, if you know where he is, tell me."

The housekeeper hesitated, then spoke crisply. "You didn't hear this from me. But the doctor often stays nights with Karen Forester, his lady friend."

Max sprinted back to the truck and gunned the engine. "We're going to talk to Karen. This time, even if I have to break the door down, we're not taking no for an answer."

AT THEIR KNOCK, Karen, wearing a thin robe, opened the door as if she'd been waiting for them. They walked into a dark room, the only light a pink shade over a dim bulb. But the dimness couldn't hide the remains of an intimate dinner. Candles still burned on a table and two wineglasses remained on the coffee table.

"We're looking for Dr. Henschel. Is he here?" Brooke asked.

Karen's dark, waist-length hair hung in strings about a face distraught with tears. "Henschel's left me. After all I've done for him, he's left me."

"Where and when did he go?" Max asked.

Karen's fingers twisted in the belt of her robe. She refused to meet their eyes, hanging her head and staring at the carpet. "He left here about half an hour ago.

I'm not sure where he was going. My guess would be the clinic—to clean out his safe and clear the computer records of this month's thefts.''

"Did he have Skye with him?" Brooke asked, desperate for news.

Karen's head jerked up. "Skye? He's already found another woman?''

"Skye is my little girl," Max said.

"Oh. I haven't seen a kid, but he mentioned he had *insurance.*''

Dear God! Brooke's thoughts raced. "Could Skye be Henschel's insurance? We have to stop him at the clinic. Once he gets on his plane he won't need her anymore.''

"I had no part in this!" Karen backed away, horror in her eyes. "I had no idea. You've got to believe me.'' She bent over the coffee table, picked up her keys and worked several off the ring. She pressed them into Brooke's hand. "Here. These are the keys to the clinic. Go stop the bastard.''

Chapter Twelve

Feelings of déjà vu hit Brooke the moment Max turned into the clinic parking lot. The lofty building, blacker than the sky around it, brought back memories of the night of Callie's murder. This time her nerves were raw with fear. Skye's life was at stake.

Max pulled around the building, and the truck's headlights beamed onto a low-slung sports car in the reserved parking section. They exited the truck and approached the empty vehicle hand-in-hand.

Excitement coursed through her. Each of the reserved spots had names painted on the curb. Max bent and shone a flashlight on the lettering. "Bingo. Henschel's still in the building."

He shone the light into the car's interior and her hopes rose. Was Skye there? But only a dark suitcase lay on the passenger seat.

Brooke banged on the trunk. "Skye! It's Mommy, sweetie. Are you in there?"

No one answered. But she tried again, remembering how deeply Skye slept. Hopefully her daughter hadn't awakened when the kidnapper stole her out of bed.

She could be peacefully sleeping still with no idea what had happened to her.

Brooke looked up at the hiss of air. Max had slashed the tires.

Grim satisfaction entered his tone. "Henschel's not escaping with Skye in this car."

Brooke tugged Max's hand and picked up his cell phone. "Give me a minute to call the cops. How long do you think they'll take to get here?"

"Not long. Mom and Dad have already alerted them."

She held the phone, knowing these next moments could be critical. "What should I say?"

"Tell them our names and location. Stress we believe Henschel is inside with our kidnapped daughter."

Two minutes later, she waited impatiently for Max to unlock the clinic's front door. She hoped the security guard was in the basement. It wouldn't do for the guard to catch them before they found Henschel and Skye.

Their footsteps echoed in the lobby. They made their way toward the bank of elevators and her eyes adjusted to the darkness.

Max steered her toward the stairs. "He'll hear the elevator. Let's walk up to his office. Maybe we can surprise him."

She took the stairs two at a time and still sensed Max's impatience. To his credit, he let her set the pace. Six flights later, while she caught her breath, Max cracked open the door into the dark hall.

Motioning her to follow, he stepped into the corridor. A water cooler cycled on. A fax machine somewhere to their left beeped. Max turned right. With her pulse racing, she walked silently behind him.

No light peeked beneath the crack of Henschel's door. Unless the man had decided to sleep in his office, she didn't think they'd find him here. Diligently, Max turned the doorknob and opened the door.

She stifled a gasp at the chaos in the room. The contents of filing cabinets had been dumped on the floor, open file folders and papers strewn everywhere. Desk drawers had been flung across the room, office supplies scattered helter-skelter. Glass crunched beneath their feet from broken picture frames that had once held doctoral degrees.

"What happened?"

"I suspect Henschel vandalized his office. Tomorrow, the latest month's overbilling that we need to prove he's stealing will be missing." Max leaned to look out the window. "Come on. His car's still here. We can catch him."

"Wait." Brooke grabbed Max's arm. "Henschel probably wouldn't have taken the stairs especially if he's in a hurry and if Skye is with him. And if he'd ridden the elevator down while we climbed, we would have heard."

Max cocked his head to the side, clearly considering her suggestion. "You think he's in another part of the building?"

"Maybe we should split up."

He took her hand. "We're staying together."

She appreciated that he wanted to protect her, but the police would be here soon. She wanted to find

Skye before they arrived. "We don't have much time. If we each searched—"

"We'll have more time if you stop arguing. We stay together."

The thought of searching the dark building alone gave her the heebie-jeebies, so she gave in with a sigh. "Where to?"

"Let's try the lab."

Once again Max peeked through the doorway before they exited the stairwell into the dark. The lab doors stood closed. When Max tried to open them, they didn't budge.

As he took the keys from his pockets, the keys jingled and jarred her already taut nerves. Was that the security guard's footsteps she heard, or just her pulse roaring in her ears? If she called out, would Skye answer? Or would she be foolishly alerting Henschel to their presence?

She shifted her weight from foot to foot while Max tried one key after another. Every moment counted. If they'd guessed wrong, Henschel could exit the front door and drive away with Skye.

Remembering the slashed tires, she realized he wouldn't get far.

Finally, the key clicked. Max thrust open the door to find a dark, deserted laboratory. Disappointment coursed through her. Where could the doctor be? Would Skye be with him?

Think. Think like a criminal out to hide his tracks. Where would she go? What would she do?

She tugged on Max's sleeve. "Let's try Grant's office. Henschel needs to erase this month's computer records.''

''Good thinking.''

Max's praise gave her the strength to reclimb the stairs on legs trembling with fatigue. As a siren screamed in the distance, she tripped and missed a step. Max's strong grip prevented her from falling.

''We're almost there,'' he whispered encouragingly.

All this skulking around with bated breath was corroding what nerves she had left. Her stomach twisted and somersaulted, spinning out of control. And every time she thought about Skye, her mind whirled with panic.

Henschel has to be here.

Skye has to be here.

She silently repeated the sentences like a mantra, emptying her mind of all thoughts except to place one foot in front of the other. Out of breath, chest heaving, she reached the landing.

Max didn't even bother peeking past the door. There was no time. The police sirens screamed loud enough to be just one block away.

Sprinting toward Grant's office, her hopes rose. This was the first light they'd seen in the entire building.

She heard a soft popping noise, the tinkle of falling glass. Darkness suffocated her as she ran, with Max close behind.

She'd lost her night vision from staring into the brightness, but she maintained her frantic pace. Ahead of Max, she crossed the threshold into the room lit only by the neon glow of the soda machine.

The light hadn't gone out by itself. Someone must be in here.

"Skye? Are you here, sweetie?"

A swish of air from behind was her only warning. An object sliced through the air and thudded against flesh. Max's hand released hers. He let out a muffled groan and collapsed in a heap.

"Max!"

He was down, hurt. Slipping and sliding through the litter of trash strewn on the floor, she knelt at Max's side and groped for his wrist or his neck to check his pulse.

Her hand landed on his thigh. Behind her, paper rustled. *Oh, God!*

She wanted to flee, but Skye might be here. And she couldn't leave Max to the mercy of Henschel. Behind her, the man's heavy breathing stung her nerves like nettles. Before she could locate Max's pulse or decide what to do, a strong arm wound around her neck and jerked her to her feet.

She tried to stamp his foot. The arm around her throat tightened, cut off her air.

Raising her hands to the arm at her throat, she yanked hard. And couldn't budge it.

Rotating blue lights of police cars in the parking lot below splashed dimly through the window. Help was so close, yet so faraway. The building covered half a city block. The police wouldn't find her in time.

Henschel would strangle her. Kill Max and Skye. Blame the break-in on them.

Painfully, she turned her chin toward the crook of his elbow. The extra space she found there allowed her to suck air into her lungs. Henschel backed toward the window and looked down.

Instead of trying to strangle her, he opened the window with his free hand. She took the opportunity to breathe deeply.

Below, she could hear the police fanning out through the building, doors opening and closing. As oxygen hit her starved brain cells, she realized strangulation was too slow and too suspicious a way for Henschel to kill her. He meant to toss her out the window.

With her last remaining strength, Brooke slipped to one side and rammed her elbow into Henschel's stomach. He expelled air with an oof, but he didn't release his grip on her neck. She twisted violently, wishing she could scream.

A shadow rose out of the blackness. Was she hallucinating? Or had Max regained consciousness and risen to his feet?

Henschel bent her sideways over the windowsill until her feet dangled off the floor. "Take one step closer and I'll throw her out the window."

Max stood a good ten feet away. With a desk between them, he couldn't reach her before Henschel made good his threat. Her lungs burned. Stars exploded in her head. Her vision blurred. If only she could do something to help herself.

And Skye.

Who would help her baby?

Woozy, Max fought for balance. He felt as if a battle-ax had slammed into his head, but all he could think about were the awful gasping noises coming from Brooke's throat. He couldn't let Henschel hurt her. He'd die first. "Let her breathe, or I've no choice but to kill you," Max ordered, trying to sound stronger than he felt.

He swept his foot across the floor in search of a weapon until he snagged his foot on a canvas bag and pulled it toward him. Maybe he could toss the bag at Henschel.

The doctor's arm must have eased around Brooke's throat, since Max heard her gulp air greedily. Slowly, he reeled in the bag, and all the while kept talking. "You're not a killer, Henschel. Why don't you let her go and tell us where Skye is?"

"You broke into this building and dare to accuse me of—"

"Come on, Doctor." Max tried to lift the bag with his foot. Surprisingly heavy, it slipped away. "Why do you think the police are here?"

"To arrest you and this woman."

The eerie calm with which he made the statement rocked Max. Even surrounded by police, the doctor still thought he could kill Brooke and bluff his way out. He must be damn sure he'd covered his tracks if he thought he could toss Brooke out the window and claim self-defense.

Every muscle in Max's body tensed. Sweat trickled down his forehead.

He had to outthink the doctor. To protect Brooke and find Skye, he had to cut off his feelings, concentrate on distracting Henschel.

"Shove that bag to me," Henschel ordered.

Max shook his head, and stooped to pick up the bag,

stalling for time, searching for an opening to rescue Brooke, praying Henschel wouldn't do anything foolish.

"I don't think so." He hefted the bag. Maybe if he rattled the doctor, he could make him forget his threats. "I'll bet what's in here contains enough evidence to put you away for a long time."

"That money can't be traced to me."

"On the contrary. Dr. Arnold just told us how Grant set up the computer billing to skim profits."

"Arnold killed himself!"

"Arnold faked his suicide." Sensing he'd distracted Henschel, Max waited for a chance to pounce. Bottling his emotion so he wouldn't get sloppy, he edged closer.

"If Grant was stealing money, I knew nothing about it."

"We have a computer statement that proves you paid Grant to do your dirty work," Max lied, and inched a little closer, knowing he had to be creative, promise anything to save Brooke's life. "A copy was sent to the police this afternoon. That's why the police are here—to arrest you. Right now, you're only an accessory to Callie's murder. If Skye is safe, we'll drop the kidnapping charge. Don't make this worse. Let Brooke go."

"This is all a big mistake," Henschel blustered, but he no longer sounded as if he believed his own lies.

Praying Henschel would release Brooke, Max hardened his tone and cracked his words like a whip in the hope Henschel would reply without thinking. "Where is our daughter?"

Once Henchel's words started, they ran as fast and as cold as a bloated mountain river. "I never intended to hurt anyone. When Grant offered to take care of things, I thought he would use some of our profits to keep any dissatisfied patients quiet. I don't know if Grant murdered Brooke's sister and husband. I never asked. I didn't want to know. Even after Callie started to blackmail Grant, he told me he'd keep her in line. I assumed he would do so in the same way I kept Karen quiet—with promises of marriage. But then he killed her. And I knew I could also be charged with her murder. Something had to be done. Someone had to take charge."

The glittery triumph in his eyes and the twisted admission spoken in a singsong tone forced Max to see the doctor was precariously on edge and apt to take chances.

Brooke's life was at stake. He had to reach her. The separation was a physical barrier he had to overcome. But how? Through their entire conversation he'd only inched forward a half meter. If he threw the bag at Henschel, the doctor might toss her out that window.

The police pounded up the stairs. Brooke dipped her head. In the blue lights reflecting through the open window, Max caught sight of her teeth biting Henschel's arm.

The doctor screamed in surprise and pain.

Sensing opportunity, Max heaved the heavy bag at the closed window several feet from where Henschel and Brooke struggled. The window shattered. The bag opened and hundred dollar bills floated across the room and out the window.

"Nooo!" Henschel dropped Brooke and scrambled for the satchel, which had fallen back into the room.

Brooke landed on the sill with only her legs dangling inside the room. Just as she started to slide out, Max leapt over the desk.

God, no. He wouldn't reach her in time. Her hips slid over the ledge, her feet tilted skyward and caught on the window frame with a thud. For a heart-stopping instant, he thought she'd caught herself. Then she plunged from sight.

He grabbed for her leg, her jeans, a shoe. Too late. He slammed into the wall. His hands came up empty. Empty.

Shocked and shaken, in so much pain he couldn't breathe, he fought to regain his balance, attempting to reach through the window and somehow catch her. As he lunged toward the window, the horrific image of her death exploded in his mind.

From behind, the doctor seized Max's shoulder and yanked him around. Numbed by grief, Max couldn't respond to the attack until his peripheral vision picked up a sharp glinting instrument arching toward his neck. Survival instincts kicked in. Fury quickened his pumped reflexes. Deflecting the scalpel with a block to his opponent's wrist, Max struck the doctor a solid blow to the gut with his right hand and followed with an uppercut to the jaw with his left. God, it felt so good to hit him. Over and over and over. For Brooke…for Skye…for himself.

Sobbing, the doctor rolled away and crawled to his money bag. Furious the man had ceased to put up a fight, Max contained his rage before he committed murder. Still, no way would he allow Henschel to escape after what he'd done to Brooke and before he told him about Skye.

Grabbing the phone that lay in the mess next to him on the floor, Max heaved it at Henschel's head. Bent over a stack of money, the doctor never saw the knockout blow. He keeled over and collapsed with a groan. Max only hoped the doctor lived long enough to suffer the indignation of an arrest, a trial, and jail time. But first he would tell him what he had done with Skye.

Skye had to be alive. He refused to think otherwise. He would find their daughter.

At least he could do that for Brooke. He would raise the child she'd loved with all her heart, the daughter she would never see grow up and marry. He would make sure Skye never forgot her.

God, he ached to do so much more. Selfishly, he wanted to hear Brooke laugh while he tossed rose petals into her bath. He wanted to dance with her at their wedding. He wanted to raise their daughter together.

He slammed his bruised knuckles into his palm, welcoming the pain. He staggered toward the window.

She was gone.

He had to face it. A bruising loss engulfed Max as if a great weight pressed on his chest and splintered his heart. A sob caught in his throat. He didn't bother to blink back the tears that rained down his cheeks.

She was gone.

An odd scrabbling sound jerked him from his thoughts. Henschel hadn't moved.

A disembodied voice—Brooke's voice—floated into the room. "Max! Max, get me out of here."

She was alive!

Max bolted to his feet, leaned out the window, and peered down. Relief flooded through him. Brooke hung from a ledge just below the windowsill.

Reaching down, he snared the waist of her jeans with one hand, placed the other around the back of her thigh and dragged her inside. Overcome with a fierce surge of love, he clung to her, running his hands over her arms, shoulders and back to convince himself she was really here.

"I thought you were dead."

Her voice cracked. "I decided to hang around a while longer."

"Don't ever scare me like that again." He embraced her, and she'd never felt so good in his arms. He'd never known a feeling to equal what he felt for her—a love so fierce he wouldn't get enough of her if they lived into their nineties.

"I'm fine." She kissed him, at the same time shoving one of his stray locks from his face. Her fingers gently wiped away his tears.

Unembarrassed by his emotions, he hugged her tighter. "I thought I'd lost you."

"I'm not going anywhere," she promised as she pulled back. "Except to find Skye. Where is she?"

"Where in the building could he have put her?"

"There's a day-care center for patients' children on the third floor."

"Let's go."

BROOKE AND MAX found Skye sleeping on a cot in the nursery. None the worse for her ordeal, she barely opened her sleepy eyes as Brooke scooped her daughter into her arms, her heart fluttering with relief. "She's okay."

"Hi, Mommy." Skye raised her head sleepily. "Where is my bed? What happened?"

"Go back to sleep, sweetie. Everything's going to be just fine," she assured her through tears of happiness. Not only was Skye safe, her daughter had slept through the kidnapping. She would have no memories of the horror of this night and Brooke couldn't have been more thankful. As much as she ached to hold Skye, her weight took its toll and Max eagerly took the sleeping child.

"Did you mean it when you said you wouldn't go anywhere, wouldn't leave me?" he asked huskily.

"I'll stay as long as you want me."

Max sat in a chair and settled Skye on his lap. He tugged Brooke beside him, needing to hold them both. He'd come too close to losing them to let them go. Brooke cuddled against Max, placed her arm around his waist, the other on their daughter, and lay her head on his chest. "Hold me."

"I can do better than that."

He kissed her, his hot flesh radiating heat that melted the last of her fears. She looked straight into his eyes. "I love you, Max."

"Good."

"Good? I tell you I love you and all you can say is 'good'?" She tried to remain stern, but her lips betrayed her and twitched at the corners. "You can do better than good."

He kissed her nose, his eyes twinkling.

She tapped her foot impatiently. "I'm waiting, Max."

He shrugged. "Waiting for what?"

"For a smart man, you can really be dumb sometimes." His brow arched as if he didn't have a clue what she wanted from him. "I'm waiting for you to tell me you love me."

"Oh, that. Of course I do."

"Not good enough." She challenged him with a look. "I know you love me. I want to hear you say the words."

He chuckled. "That's it. Keep your feelings back. Play mysterious. Don't tell me what you really want."

In his way, he'd just admitted he loved her, but she'd known that when he didn't hesitate to risk his life to save her from Henschel. She knew he loved her from the tender and generous way he'd made love to her, leaving her feeling cherished and desired. His love was evident in his caring looks, his sensual touch—designed to please, in the frenzy of passion that exploded whenever they kissed. He'd told her repeatedly without words how much he wanted all of her. Sure, she recognized the lust, but what she and Max shared was evident in his eyes alight with unspoken promises. What she hadn't known until just now was he'd admitted to himself that he loved her.

She wound her arms around his neck. "Would you rather I was coy?"

His hand closed over her hair. Gently he tugged her

lips to his. "Don't change a thing. I love you just the way you are."

Five minutes later, after a thoroughly satisfying kiss that left her blood humming and her nerves singing, he asked, "Did you really mean you'd stay with me as long as I want?"

"Silly man. I don't say things I don't mean."

"Suppose I want you forever?"

Her lips turned up in a dazzling smile. "Then forever is what you'll get."

Epilogue

One month later

"Daddy. Daddy!" Skye raced into the laboratory that Max kept on the back forty acres of their new home.

He was puttering with a new type of filter that would clean the exhaust before the muffler released fumes into the atmosphere. Yet he always had time to make his daughter feel special.

Whenever he thought about his life, his heart burst with pride. Skye and Brooke were more precious to him than he'd ever thought possible. A month ago, when Brooke had almost died after Henschel dropped her out that window, he'd thought he couldn't have loved her more. But during these past few weeks, his love had grown stronger. His life was enriched beyond his dreams, and he'd settled down contentedly, with nothing more important to him than his soon-to-be wife and his child. The experiment could wait.

Sensing Skye had run all the way from the house, he waited for her to catch her breath. Picking her up, he smoothed her hair off her face and kissed her fore-head. "Who's Daddy's favorite little girl?"

Instead of playing their game and teasing him back, she squirmed.

"What is it, sweetheart?"

Skye's cheeks flushed red and her eyes sparkled with excitement. "Mommy said you should come quick. She has a surprise."

"Now?" His palms broke into an immediate sweat. As he and Skye left the lab and headed toward the house he thought back to the last time Brooke had surprised him. They could have more children. The doctors had located Brooke's missing eggs that Arnold had frozen so long ago, and Max had learned the fro-zen eggs could survive for a decade. Max, Brooke and Skye had celebrated the possibility of adding to their family. But first they had to make the family official and the wedding was still two months away.

He entered the house wondering what surprise Brooke had cooked up now. Skye urged him into the kitchen. "Come on, Daddy. Mommy said this surprise is a really, really, really big one."

He found Brooke on the phone, her eyes filled with happy tears.

His heart lurched. "What is it?"

"It's your mother. Ford just came out of the coma. He's going to be fine."

IN THE HOSPITAL for an implantation of her eggs, Brooke watched her husband marvel at the sonogram that showed their soon-to-be twins, and elation swept through her that the successful medical procedure had enabled her and Max to have more children. Max seemed just as pleased. He couldn't seem to take his gaze off the sonogram picture.

During the past months since the wedding, Max had doted on Skye, spoiling her shamelessly. If the old restlessness sneaked into his thoughts occasionally, he wasn't saying so. But he had mentioned with a mischievous twinkle in his eyes that if wanderlust struck, he could afford to take the whole family with him.

Ford ducked through the door of the hospital room, clapped his brother on the back, and stuck two cigars in his mouth. Now that her brother-in-law had regained the weight he'd lost during his days in a coma, he looked almost identical to Max. Except for the eyes—a sadness he tried to hide lingered there—and she wondered how long it would take to go away.

Ford added another box of Godiva chocolates to the two Max had already given her. "So how's the little mother?"

"I suspect I'm more rested than you." Tired but happy, Brooke winked at Skye's doting uncle who had volunteered to watch Skye until she and Max returned home. Before letting her out of bed, the doctors wanted her to stay another night—just to be sure the embryos took, and Max refused to leave her side. "Girls her age can be a handful. Are you keeping up with her?"

"Barely."

Max looked up from the sonogram, for the first time, a brazen grin twitching his lips. "If that's the case, she's the first woman you can't keep up with."

Ford laughed, his forehead crinkling—but the grief

never left his haunted blue eyes. When Max sat by Brooke and put his arm over her shoulders, Ford's face clouded and his voice choked. "Rhonda would have enjoyed being an aunt."

She was grateful to Rhonda for her daughter, and when Skye was old enough to understand, Brooke intended to explain Rhonda's relation to her. In the meantime, she'd asked Ford to save pictures, mementos and medical records for that time.

Brooke nestled against Max and squeezed his hand while she spoke to his brother. "I'm sorry I never had a chance to meet your wife."

"She would have approved of the way you're raising Skye. Rhonda was a great lady and didn't deserve to die the way she did."

"Henschel ruined a lot of people's lives." Arnold had turned state's evidence and received probation and a suspended medical license. Callie and Rhonda had lost their lives. Karen Forester had left the state. And Henschel? She didn't want to think about him. He'd gotten what he'd deserved.

Brooke kept to herself how much she'd almost lost. If Max hadn't insisted they go after Henschel, they could have lost Skye and the twins would never be born. Instead she had the best of husbands, Skye and children she hadn't thought she could have. Life was good. The best.

Unfortunately fate hadn't been as kind to Ford. He stoically tried to hide the pain, but his eyes frequently stared off into space with a grief he couldn't seem to shake.

He clenched his fist, his voice tight. "Henschel was responsible for the avalanche that killed Rhonda."

Brooke looked up in surprise. Once she'd decided to become pregnant, Max had kept news he'd thought would upset her to himself. She'd reveled in his over-protectiveness, but now she wanted to know the truth. "But Henschel never left New Orleans. He paid someone to set off the avalanche."

Ford frowned, his cheekbones all harsh angles. "If it takes the rest of my life, I'll find out who murdered Rhonda."

Max stood and put his arm over his brother's shoulder. He knew when words were needed and when to be quiet, and nothing could be said to comfort Ford. Brooke hoped the passage of time would heal Max's twin.

As if realizing he'd put a damper on a happy occasion, Ford slapped Max on the back. "Hey, I've a great little lady waiting for me. Skye and I have a date to go roller-blading. Besides, she wants details on *her* babies."

After Ford left, Max took his seat at her side on the bed. "Maybe it wasn't such a good idea to tell Skye we were having the twins for her. She thinks these babies are hers."

"At least she's not jealous, like her daddy."

His eyes widened as if he thought she'd gone crazy. "What?"

"Don't deny it, mister." Although she attempted to scold, her lips broke into a grin. "When I was talking to the nurse about breast feeding, you were smacking your lips."

Max rolled his eyes at the ceiling. "Did not. I was just thirsty."

She giggled at his ridiculous excuse. "Uh-huh. I'm sure the hospital has a cafeteria."

"I'm very particular. Nothing in a cafeteria will quench my thirst for you."

She looked up into his eyes and caught her breath at the love reflecting there. A love great enough to last a lifetime. "If that's your way of saying I love you—"

"No." He drew her into his arms for a kiss. "This is the way I say I love you."

She chuckled as happiness and contentment swept through her. "Ah, Max, dear. You really do have a way with words."

Look for Ford's story,

SWEET DECEPTION,

by Susan Kearney,

in July 1997.

Only from Harlequin Intrigue.
Here's a peek.

Prologue

All she had left to do was kidnap the groom. Denise
Ward had finished the distasteful chore of paying the
bride to leave town. She'd called the guests to inform
them of the wedding's cancellation and had made a
donation to the minister's favorite charity.

Consulting the notes on her desk, she reread the
schedule she'd committed to memory. Since Ford
Braddack's private jet wasn't due in New Orleans
from Beijing until tomorrow morning, the groom
shouldn't learn of the changes she'd made in his wedding plans until it was too late.

Denise shifted in her lumpy chair, hoping Ford
didn't kill her once he discovered what she'd done.
Ford Braddack had the devil's own temper. According
to her investigations, his wife's death last year had
made him even more abrupt, demanding and domi-
neering than usual, so she had no way to predict how
he'd respond to his canceled wedding—or his kidnapping.

Not only did he work impossibly long hours, the
man drove his employees hard, and he played hard,

too. Ford had grieved deeply after Rhonda's death, disappearing for a while, then throwing himself into the business with a ruthlessness that shot Norton Industries' stock soaring. His business exploits hadn't slowed during the past six months. Although he'd escorted a variety of debutantes to business functions, charity events, and to his home in the exclusive Garden District, no woman ever stayed the night in his mansion.

Denise closed the file on her desk and stared unseeing out the window. One month ago, Lindsay Betancourt had whirled into Ford's life with the force of a hurricane. Two weeks ago, Ford had announced his engagement. Denise had been hired to contain the destruction. She imagined him furiously conducting business now, fully expecting to marry Lindsay tomorrow.

But Denise had canceled the wedding.

Abductions weren't her regular line of work. Her usual cases involved following cheating husbands and chasing down hiding divorcés behind on alimony and child support—a far less dangerous task. While her P.I. firm might be in desperate need of the cash this assignment had provided, Denise had accepted the contract only after discovering Miss Lindsay Betancourt didn't care one whit for Ford Braddack. While the scheming woman had claimed a deep affection for Ford, she'd jumped at the substantial bribe Denise's client had offered her to leave New Orleans for Hollywood.

Only God knew how Ford would react once he discovered the betrayal—not only Denise's, but her client's. Ford was unpredictable. Apprehension, mixed with the thrill of anticipation, clutched her stomach. She'd better watch her step and keep her distance. When Ford's business ran smoothly, he was a man to be reckoned with. She shuddered to think how he'd react to her kidnapping him from his own wedding.

She smiled, her foreboding layered with a reckless twinge of excitement.

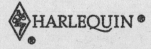

To my grandson, Michael Fox. I owed you one!
To my own Annie Bauer, our miracle baby.
To Patricia Campbell, for the nanny.
And to Julie Fox, whose blithe spirit is the
basis for the nanny.

ISBN 0-373-16682-6

NANNY & THE BODYGUARD

Copyright © 1997 by Mollie Molé

This edition published by arrangement with Harlequin Books S.A.

® and TM are trademarks of the publisher. Trademarks indicated with ® are registered in the United States Patent and Trademark Office, the Canadian Trade Marks Office and in other countries.

Printed in U.S.A.

Prologue

She felt like a criminal.

Studying her reflection in the bathroom mirror, she couldn't help but be amazed that her life had actually come to this. But, she reminded herself, what choice did she have?

The hair color had lived up to its promise. She was a brunette now—and the deep, dark brown hair made her look like a new woman. After she got finished with all the other changes she planned, no one would recognize her.

A noise at the front door startled her. She froze. She couldn't answer it; she didn't dare let anyone see her until the transformation was complete. Barely breathing, she waited a few minutes, hoping whoever was there would just go away.

When it was safe again, she went into the bedroom to pack. The dresses hanging in the closet certainly fit her old identity, but the bright yellow sundress wouldn't do. Nor would the lavender linen with the low neckline that revealed more than it concealed. One thing was for sure: She would need

a new wardrobe in keeping with her new persona. Not that she was aware what *would* be appropriate, but what she owned now definitely wasn't suitable for the role she was about to play.

While she waited for her hair to dry, she emptied her bag on the dresser to remove anything that might give her away. In quick succession, she set aside her driver's license, checkbook, credit cards, and a small plastic folder of family snapshots. Her pulse beat faster as she studied the familiar smiling faces. *Soon,* her heart said. *Soon.* She stuffed the remaining innocuous items into the colorful cloth bag she usually carried.

In went her new social-security card, an envelope containing several important letters and a new wallet made of flowered material.

A quick glance at her discarded pocket calendar reassured her she'd finished and delivered all the commercial artwork she'd been commissioned for the month. She'd canceled future contracts with a promise to resume work soon.

Before a final check in the mirror she extracted contact lenses from a small container and carefully inserted them in her eyes. Her now brown eyes. Then, assured that no one would recognize her, she dressed to go out to the local thrift shop to buy appropriate clothing. All the while, she rehearsed getting her story straight.

So much depended on her being able to get through the next few months as a new woman. And to carry out her masquerade undetected.

She had promises to keep.

Chapter One

Annie Kramer felt she was about to embark on the performance of her life.

She took a deep breath and rang the doorbell of the red brick mansion in Fairfax, Virginia, that was the home of well-known Congressman Robert Matthews. Moments later, she heard footsteps, then the door swung open and a man stood there.

Not just any man.

This one looked armed and dangerous. The expression in his steel-gray eyes was cool, his body language clear: She was on his territory and she wasn't all that welcome.

He was clean-cut, his wavy ebony hair cropped close. His athletic body radiated vitality. In black slacks and a sport jacket, with a shirt open at his neck, he looked ready, willing and able to take on any unwelcome intruder.

When he stepped out and closed the door behind him, Annie's first instinct was to turn on her heel and hightail it out of there. She took an automatic step backward.

Her second instinct was one of defiance. Too much depended upon his acceptance to give up at this early stage of the game. She was here for a job interview and she intended to get hired. Today.

As she tried to pull her thoughts together, the cool look on his face changed to one of annoyance. She dug in her heels, raised her chin and looked him squarely in those intimidating eyes.

"What can I do for you?" he prompted, his gaze roaming over her as if he were searching her for a hidden weapon. It took all of Annie's willpower to meet his eyes.

"My name is Annie Kin—Kramer," she stammered. "I've come regarding the position of nanny." Good Lord, she thought, as his eyes narrowed and took on the color of cold granite, she'd been here less than two minutes and she was already in trouble!

He leaned casually against the doorjamb and seemed to inventory her vintage cotton dress and sensible "nanny" shoes. A knowing half-smile broke over his face. "Is that so, Mz. er...Kramer?"

From the cynical look that came over his face, she realized he'd noticed her tripping over her identity. No matter how much she practiced, she still hadn't gotten accustomed to using her new name.

Annie tried hard to smile, but it wasn't easy. She hid an inward quiver and returned the man's watchful look with a noncommittal one of her own. Whatever he thought she was selling, it was obvious he wasn't buying. Not that it mattered, really.

Whoever this man was, he wasn't the one who was going to hire her. Mrs. Edythe Matthews was her prospective employer. No matter what this hulk might think of her, she intended to carry through the charade and to cinch the job of nanny. Until then, she had to be careful not to give him an inch. From the looks of this guy, he would probably want a mile.

"So you want to be the new nanny, do you?" he asked.

It was clear he wasn't ready to let her inside. So much for the spiel she'd been rehearsing all morning.

"First of all," he commented lazily into her silence, "the children aren't mine. They're the children of Robert Matthews. However, I'm their bodyguard and you'll have to deal with me. And, more important," he said, straightening and raising an eyebrow, "how did you know the position of nanny was open?"

Annie's heart took a nosedive. Why hadn't she been told there was a bodyguard on the premises? And what had happened to necessitate one? She pulled herself together. Now was no time to fall apart.

"If you don't mind, I'd rather discuss this with Mrs. Matthews," she answered.

"Try me first," he suggested lazily. "After all, you have nothing to lose and everything to gain."

"Look here, Mr....whatever-your-name-is..."

"Cassidy."

"Cassidy?" Annie repeated. "That's all?"

"It's all you need to know. By the way," he said with a look that told her he wasn't ready to accept her or her story, "before you go any further, you might keep in mind I know the decision to hire a nanny was made only last night."

Annie thought fast. Since it looked as if he could read her thoughts, she had to be careful while she skirted the truth.

"I happened to be in the employment office when the call came in from Mrs. Matthews." Annie mentally crossed her fingers when he didn't look all that convinced. She tried again. "Because of the urgency, they agreed to let me have an interview immediately. I've already spoken to Mrs. Matthews on the telephone. She's expecting me."

"Great timing, wasn't it?" he answered cynically as he eyed her oversize bag. "Got any identification in there?"

Confident she was almost home free, Annie rummaged in her large cloth bag for the letters of reference she'd composed and typed up that morning. After contacting three of her friends and swearing them to secrecy, the rest had been easy. She'd read enough recommendations to know just what an employer would be looking for. *Please, God, she thought as she handed them to the bodyguard, don't let him ask me for anything more than this.*

He read the references. When he was through, he regarded her thoughtfully. Maybe it was her appearance that bothered him, Annie thought, meet-

ing his gaze. Perhaps, in her attempt to change her identity, she'd overdone it. But dyeing her blond hair brown and wearing colored contacts had seemed important at the time.

"Any other identification?" he finally asked after he handed the letters over.

"My social-security card, if you need to know."

"I need to know," he responded. When he raised an expectant eyebrow, she gave the card to him.

"Driver's license?"

"Actually," she added in a rush, "my driver's license was suspended when I didn't pay a parking ticket."

He looked behind her as he handed back her documents. "So, how did you get here?"

"I came in a cab," she said hurriedly. Before he could question how an unemployed nanny could afford to be taking cabs, she continued, "I'd like to meet Mrs. Matthews now, if you don't mind. I'd like to get the position before someone else shows up."

He glanced down in time to see her set one tentative foot toward the door. At his frown, she froze.

"All right, Ms. Kramer," he said. "We'll go inside just as soon as you let me look in that bag of yours."

Before she had a chance to react, he reached for the colorful cloth bag hanging from her arm. For pete's sake, she thought angrily, did he suspect she was some kind of threat?

"Heavy, isn't it?" he observed, a frown creasing his forehead. He hefted her bag a couple of times. "What in blazes do you have in here, anyway?"

Annie mentally inventoried the bag's contents. If it was the only way he would let her in, so be it. Not that there was anything incriminating in there. "Oh, only the usual things."

She followed his eyes as he glanced around him. A large new pottery bowl, a bag of planting mix and several small gardening tools were on the steps waiting for planting. "Guess this will have to do," he muttered, upending her bag into the bowl before she could stop him.

A red and purple wallet, an empty matching glasses case, six tubes of lipstick, what looked like a fistful of loose coins, combs, brushes, expired newspaper coupons, an assortment of loose keys, a flashlight, a small bottle of vanilla, a plastic bag of chocolate-chip cookies, and a can of pepper spray all fell into the empty planter with a clang.

"You don't believe in traveling light, do you?" he inquired as he looked at the array of items. He picked up the bottle of vanilla, unscrewed the cap and took a sniff. "What do you do with this?"

"It's my perfume," she replied.

His eyebrows lifted in silent judgment before he reached for the can of pepper spray. "Pepper spray? You were expecting trouble?"

"You never know when you might need to defend yourself," she answered primly.

"Of course," he agreed. His raised eyebrows

told her he thought anyone would be stupid to accost a woman who looked like she did.

"Do you have any other goodies like this on you?" he inquired, holding up the "weapon" and eyeing her with a frown.

"No," she returned, becoming more and more annoyed. "Are you going to search me to make sure?"

"Don't tempt me," he warned as he replaced the loose items and the can of pepper spray in her bag and handed the bag back to her. "It can be arranged."

Who did he think he was, anyway? Annie was about to tell him what she thought of him when he reached behind to open the door.

"Go on in. You'll find Mrs. Matthews in the library."

"The library?"

"Try the first door to the left," he instructed. "I'll be right behind you."

Annie could feel his eyes examining her as they walked into the house. She felt uncomfortable at the glint of interest that had come into his eyes before he stepped aside to allow her entry.

Knowing they would be thrown together for the duration of the Matthewses' political-campaign travels made her feel flushed. Granted, he was handsome. Granted, he had a dangerous edge about him that promised excitement. But the last thing she wanted was for him to try to turn their relationship into something more personal. If he

thought she was going to be an easy mark, he had another think coming.

The marble entrance hall felt cool and welcoming, especially after having spent ten minutes on the front step in the hot sun. Her own new home might not be nearly as grand as the Matthews mansion, but she was more than happy with her Cape Cod cottage.

Edythe Matthews rose from behind a cherry-wood desk when Annie entered the library. She was slim and of medium height, with obviously bleached blond hair that was meticulously styled in a fashionable straight bob with wisps of bangs across her forehead. She wore a studied, polite smile that didn't reach her eyes as she waited for Annie to approach. The consummate political wife of the consummate politician, Annie thought. No wonder Robert Matthews had married her.

"This is Annie Kramer," the bodyguard said as he sauntered into the room behind Annie. "She tells me she's applying for the position as nanny to Bobby and Joey. Why don't you give Mrs. Matthews your references, Ms. Kramer?" For her prospective employer's benefit, he added, "I've glanced over them, but you might want to have me check them out a little further before you make a final decision."

Annie ignored him and handed the envelope to Mrs. Matthews. While she waited, Annie glanced at the self-assured man who had stationed himself by the closed French doors. "I can speak for my-

self, if you don't mind," she told him quietly. She caught herself before she went any further. She couldn't afford to antagonize him, or Mrs. Matthews, either. She had to get this job; more depended on it than he could have known.

He gestured airily. "Of course. Be my guest."

Mrs. Matthews cleared her throat. "I see you've met our bodyguard, Mike Cassidy. We hired him last week to watch over the boys." She indicated a love seat in front of the desk and moved back around behind it. "That's just as well. You'll be working together taking care of the children."

Mike? His name was Mike Cassidy? Annie glanced at the bodyguard. Now that she knew his whole name, he sounded more human, less threatening. A lone last name had sounded like a hero in a Clint Eastwood movie; detached, cold. Even so, the description fit him, she decided, as she took his measure. He was a man to watch out for.

He cleared his throat. "What Mrs. Matthews is saying is that you'll report to me," he clarified. "On all matters pertaining to the children, that is. As for the rest..." He left the sentence unfinished, but the implication was clear: He was not only in charge of the children, he intended to be in charge of everything else, as well.

Her face impassive, Annie nodded. She'd had enough of men telling her what to do. He might be in charge now, she thought, but she wasn't the type to put up with his high-handed ways easily. If it

weren't for the sake of her intended charges, she wouldn't put up with them at all.

"Of course—" Annie's prospective employer smiled at Mike and Annie "—I'm sure you'll get along just fine. Now, let's get down to business, Ms. Kramer, or is that Mrs.?"

"Mrs.," Annie answered in time to hear the bodyguard grunt his skepticism.

"Good. I prefer my help be married, with the exception of Mike, you understand. He needs to devote all his time to the boys. Married women are so much more reliable where children are concerned. Don't you agree?" Annie nodded. "And where is Mr. Kramer?"

"Overseas, in the service," Annie answered. She covered her unadorned ring finger with her right hand and cast a defiant look at the skeptical bodyguard. That doubting look still covered his face. His eyes remained noncommittal. She would have to buy a new wedding ring and get a snapshot of her "husband" in case anyone asked to see him.

"Oh, dear, that must be hard on you, isn't it?" Mrs. Matthews put the references aside and finally gave Annie a genuine smile. "I know just how you must feel. My own husband, Robert Matthews, is away campaigning just now. That's one reason we've needed Mike, and now a nanny. Robert is a member of the House of Representatives, you know, and I'm sure you're aware of how greatly his country needs him."

Annie nodded. His country needed him more

than his family? That statement had a familiar ring to it.

"I take it you have no children?"

Annie thought for a moment. "I did," she said quietly. Her private life had to stay private for the duration of her employment. The new Mrs. Matthews's interest in her was the last thing Annie needed or wanted, but it *did* make her feel a little more friendly toward the woman whom she knew Robert Matthews had married only three months ago.

"In our telephone conversation this morning, you indicated you've had extensive experience with children," Mrs. Matthews continued.

"Yes." The less Annie said, the better.

"Does that include boys? They do seem to be different from the few little girls of my acquaintance," she added doubtfully. "Not that I have any children of my own, you understand. The boys are from my husband's first marriage."

"Yes, boys are different," Annie replied with a smile. "Although, personally, I've never found that to be a problem. All it takes is to show the children you care about them. Children respond to affection."

"Yes, well..." Edythe Matthews didn't look convinced. "Now, do you have any questions of your own?" She gazed expectantly at Annie.

Annie realized the prominent Matthews family's connections and wealth could warrant protection

for her prospective charges. But Robert Matthews hadn't hired a bodyguard before this; why now?

"Just one," she answered, turning her gaze on Mike Cassidy. "Why do you need a bodyguard?"

"You really don't need to know the details," Cassidy interjected impatiently. "It should be enough for you to know I'm here."

"That's where you're wrong," Annie countered firmly. "If I'm to be responsible for my charges, I should be aware if something is going on. It's the only way I can take proper care of the children."

"Well said," Cassidy admitted with a grudging smile. He glanced at Mrs. Matthews. When she nodded her agreement, he crossed the room to sit down beside Annie.

"I expect you to keep your own counsel about what I'm going to tell you," he began quietly. "I don't want the boys frightened."

His words sounded ominous. Annie hid her hands beneath her bag to hide their trembling.

"There have been rumors of threats against the congressman's extended family. Nothing tangible, you understand. But to sum it up, they amount to possible kidnap threats for ransom. I'm here in case someone gets the idea to include Matthews's own sons in that threat while he's away from home."

Annie looked at the new Mrs. Matthews for confirmation.

"I'm afraid Mike is right," she agreed, "although I don't think you have anything to worry about, now that he's here. Besides, they're only

rumors. My husband has his own bodyguards assigned to him for the duration of the campaign, so Mike is here only for the children. Not that there have been specific threats against the boys, but in the current circumstances, my husband felt it wise to provide them with their own bodyguard."

Annie decided to voice her thoughts. "Forgive me for being so blunt, Mrs. Matthews, but it *is* well-known that Mr. Matthews's children are from a previous marriage."

"Yes, they are. As I said earlier, I don't have any children of my own."

"Then, under the circumstances, why weren't the children returned to their mother if their father is going to be absent?" Annie knew she was out of line, but it was a question she had to ask.

"Surely, you must realize this is the era of family values, my dear. And this is an election year," Mrs. Matthews replied, staring at Annie as if everyone should be aware of today's political climate. "My husband felt it best to have his family around him, especially at election time. I agreed."

Of course he would, Annie thought. Political ambitions could sometimes come first with a certain type of man. Not that she herself agreed. Annie studied the woman who she hoped was about to hire her to take over a mother's duties. "And you intend to join him while he's away campaigning?"

Mrs. Matthews nodded complacently. "I worked with Robert as his administrative assistant before we married. We're a great team," she added

proudly. "In fact, we make all his career decisions together. Actually, we both agree I'm a greater asset to him on the campaign trail than I am staying home with the children. Especially since I'm not used to the role of mother. Not that the boys are a problem, you understand." This time her smile was genuine—a smile that included Mike Cassidy. "I'm sure Mike and you can take care of everything very well without Robert and myself. We have a cook, a maid and twice-weekly visits from a cleaning crew to help you."

A bodyguard, a nanny, a maid, a cook and a cleaning crew! How could anyone believe they could take the place of a loving father or a loving mother? Annie silently wondered.

If getting reelected was more important than fatherhood, in her opinion, Matthews *should* have sent the children back to their mother.

Annie felt the bodyguard's eyes on her. The speculation in his gaze told her now was no time to comment any further on something that was none of her business.

"If there's nothing else you want to know, as far as I'm concerned you have the position, Mrs. Kramer," Annie's new employer said.

"Wait a minute," Cassidy protested. "I haven't had a chance to check her references!"

"I'll take care of that when I return from our current campaign swing around the state," Mrs. Matthews replied. "Right now, I'm anxious to join

my husband. When can you start, Mrs. Kramer, or may I call you Annie?''

''Annie will be fine, thank you. I can start as soon as you want me.'' Annie was about to tell her eager employer she was ready to start right now, but with the bodyguard steadily scowling at her, she couldn't afford to act too enthusiastic. It would only add fuel to the fire of his obvious suspicion.

''Tomorrow, then?''

Annie nodded.

''Wonderful! I'll call my husband right now and tell him to expect me. In the meantime, Mike can answer any questions you might have about the boys.'' Mrs. Matthews rose, smiled her relief and put Annie's references in a desk drawer. ''I'm sure I'll see you before I leave. If not...'' Her mind obviously elsewhere, she left the rest of the sentence unsaid.

''Aren't you interested in the salary or *are* you actually independently wealthy?'' a quiet voice at Annie's side inquired as soon as they were alone.

Annie was more than ready for Mike Cassidy. She turned to meet his cynical smile. ''I'm sure it will be adequate. Where children are concerned, and especially if they are in jeopardy, any salary would be sufficient. However, I want to meet the children first. If there *is* a problem, then I might want to discuss salary.''

She had no idea what salary had been offered, nor did she know the name of the employment

agency that supposedly had sent her. And she didn't dare guess. She couldn't afford to give him any reason to check on her—not at this stage of the game. She resolved to find out the agency's name as soon as possible and call and tell them the opening had been filled.

"I'm not in this for the money, no matter what you might think." She looked him squarely in the eye. If he continued to doubt her, that was his problem, not hers. "I happen to love children."

"A regular Mary Poppins, aren't you? Where's your umbrella?" He got to his feet and stared down at her. His expression told her he wasn't completely convinced of her identity, or anything else about her.

"I only carry one when it's raining. And I usually keep both my feet on the ground," Annie answered as she rose to meet his cynical gaze. "But I do sing, now and again." She looked around the elegant book-lined room. Everything looked worn and as if they'd been in place for years. Either the new Mrs. Matthews hadn't had time to redecorate or she wasn't the nesting type. Judging from the employment interview, it was obvious she was too involved in the game of politics to nest. And as far as Annie was concerned, Mrs. Matthews wasn't the maternal type, either.

"When can I meet the children?" Annie inquired. "I'd rather not be sprung on them as a complete surprise."

"You won't be. They're aware a nanny is being

hired, although it seems sooner than we all expected. Right now, they're in the kitchen with Mrs. Swenson, our cook. She's keeping them busy making a batch of gingerbread men."

"You've asked me a lot of questions," Annie said. "Now I'd like to ask you one."

His brow lifted in surprise. Annie was pleased. If he thought he'd put her in her place, he was mistaken. He had a lot to learn about her. She wasn't the type to be intimidated that easily.

"Depends on what you want to know," he returned cautiously. Obviously, his answer was going to depend on how personal she intended to get.

"How do you feel about being a bodyguard to two small boys, Mr. Cassidy?"

"Mike," he instructed automatically. "A job is a job." At her frown, he continued. "Make no mistake, Annie Kramer—if that's your real name, which I doubt—it makes no difference whom I guard. Not their age or their size. Whatever it takes," he said, unknowingly echoing her own private sentiments about the safety and well-being of the Matthews children, "you can be sure I'm here to guard them with my life, if necessary."

Annie looked Mike Cassidy right in the eye. Whatever else she might feel about him, she had to admit he sounded sincere about his responsibilities. The children were safe with him.

All that was left now was the moment she'd been waiting for.

"I'd like to meet my charges now, if you don't

mind,'' she said. From the looks of him he did mind, but he shrugged.

"Okay, Annie, follow me."

A large wooden butcher block in the center of the kitchen was covered with flour, spices, eggs, milk and two mixing bowls. Standing on stools and stirring vigorously, were two young boys and a bosomy middle-aged woman.

Tears threatened to come into Annie's eyes as she took in every detail of the children's happy faces, their short blond hair that fell over their large blue eyes and their sturdy young bodies with over-size aprons hanging from their necks to below their knees. The scent of ginger and freshly baked cookies hung in the air.

The woman—surely Mrs. Swenson, the cook—looked up from the large pottery bowl. She wiped her hands on a towel and smiled a warm welcome. "Look who we have here. I'll bet this pretty lady is the nanny Mrs. Matthews promised you this morning."

The younger boy was the first to look up. When he didn't react immediately, Annie knew, with a deep sense of relief, that her disguise was working. She smiled and a moment later, his mouth opened in a soundless whistle as he recognized Annie. Overcome, he jumped off the stool and headed for her with open arms. "You came! You came!"

"Joey!" The older boy bounded after him and put his hand on his brother's shoulder. Then, sud-

denly shy, Joey hung back while his brother came forward and waited for Mike to introduce him.

"This is Mrs. Annie Kramer," Mike announced. "She's come to take care of you while your father and his wife are away. Annie, this young man is Bobby Matthews. He's nine years old. That little guy over there is his brother, Joey. He's seven."

Bobby held out his hand. "I'm pleased to meet you, Mrs. Kramer."

Annie's heart was ready to break with pride. She could hardly believe Bobby's grown-up demeanor. "I'm pleased to meet you, too. You may call me Miss Annie," she replied, shaking his hand. She hungered to do more, but Mike was watching.

"Really?"

"Really," she agreed. "Unless you'd rather not?"

"Oh, I do. It's cool!" Bobby breathlessly assured her.

"Me, too?"

"Of course, you, too." Annie solemnly extended her hand for Joey to shake. She held on for dear life. More than anything, she wanted to pick the boys up and hug them to her pounding heart. She wanted to never let go. But that would come later, when they were alone.

Right now, she lifted her eyes to the two pairs of blue ones looking down at her—and smiled at her sons.

Chapter Two

He had to give her credit.

Within minutes, Annie Kramer had sailed into the house and charmed everyone she met. She'd even managed to bring big genuine smiles to the boys' faces—the first in days.

Judging by the glowing look that came over Annie's face and the reflexive way she reached out toward the boys, Mike had to admit if ever a woman looked like a natural mother, it was Annie Kramer.

Strange, he thought, how the boys took to her. In fact, unusual for a first meeting.

In his experience, however limited, children were taught not to speak or make friends with strangers. Annie Kramer didn't look or behave if she were a stranger. And the boys certainly didn't act as if she were one.

It wasn't only Annie's instantaneous bonding with the boys that bothered him. There was something about her that troubled him even more.

Maybe it was her appearance. For sure, no mod-

ern American woman under the age of seventy-five would be caught dead in an outfit like the one Annie Kramer was wearing—not even his sainted grandmother. She wouldn't have considered wearing clothes like Annie's in public—and from what he remembered of that lovable, feisty woman who had raised him, not in private, either.

To his mind's eye, the long, full dress didn't begin to hide Annie's long legs, narrow waist and shapely shoulders. It was beyond belief that she would even try to hide herself when she had a much greater share of interesting attributes than met the casual glance.

He would be the first to admit Annie was attractive in spite of the way she dressed. Especially with those almond-shaped eyes and long lashes. Her brown eyes revealed a depth of sensuality that took him by surprise. Even the prim lace collar of her dress couldn't hide the long, slender neck where he could glimpse her pulse throbbing, or the tempting curves that strained against the buttons on her blouse.

There was her peaches-and-cream complexion, somehow out of place with her dark brown hair, dark eyes and light eyebrows and eyelashes. Incongruous? Maybe, maybe not.

He stirred uneasily. The problem with thinking about the way a woman appeared dressed was that it became very tempting to consider her undressed, as well. The idea was unthinkable, wasn't it?

He watched her bend over Bobby and his little

brother and shake their hands. The woman was here as a nanny, nothing more. He intended to keep that in mind.

He stopped short and willed away the picture of her with her collar unbuttoned. Where did those thoughts come from, he wondered uneasily? Until now, Annie Kramer hadn't given any indication she was capable of anything more than a friendly, dazzling smile. And he wasn't all that sure it was meant to be friendly—not after her reaction when he'd practically accused her of lying about her identity. Why was she trying to be so friendly, anyway? They were going to be working partners—no more, no less.

Slow up there, Mike, my man, a small voice whispered in his ear. *Slow up before you get in trouble, again.* He'd been trained by professionals not to become involved with or attached to his charges. Or to anyone else on the job, for that matter. It was the only way he could remain objective, able to spot hidden danger signals before they erupted into trouble.

He forced his thoughts back to Annie's credentials. If she was as good at her job as the references indicated, why had she been out looking for work through an employment agency? Surely, there must have been dozens of women eager to find a nanny who came so highly recommended. Word of mouth should have gotten her a new job even before the old one was over.

Then, too, she had said she was married, albeit

to an absent husband. A glance at her left hand showed him she wasn't wearing a wedding ring. Nor did she have the pale circle around her sun-tanned ring finger that would have told him she'd worn a ring at some time.

It was just as well she'd said she was married. And that she had had children, he mused thoughtfully. Maybe that was why she was so taken with the Matthews boys. He was too polite to ask her what had happened to her own children, but he wondered just the same.

No matter how he cut it, or how lovely she was, his sixth sense kept telling him there was something wrong about Annie Kramer. Positive his intuition wasn't failing him, he made up his mind to dog her footsteps until he was satisfied. It was part of the job he'd been hired for, after all.

"Ready for the two-bit tour of the house before you come back tomorrow?" he inquired. He glanced down to where Joey was holding Annie's hand as if he never wanted to let it go. "That is, provided Joey is willing to give you your hand back."

Joey dropped Annie's hand as if he'd been burned. "Maybe I ought to go back and finish the cookies," he said, throwing an appealing look at his brother. Bobby promptly came and put his arm around his shoulders.

"Good idea, but be sure and save some for me," Mike told him. "In fact, maybe you ought to save a few for Miss Annie, too, while you're at it."

The protective way Bobby took care of his younger brother impressed Mike. Then and there, he decided he could tell Bobby just enough about the reason for a bodyguard without frightening him. Up until now, he'd put the kids off with vague answers but maybe with the older boy's help, watching over them would become that much easier. Especially since their new nanny was in the picture to distract them from the truth.

Not that he intended to relax his vigilance when it came to the boys. He knew from his own early experience that boys their age were often bent on finding adventure—and didn't always stop, look or listen before they did so.

As for their new nanny, she was an unknown quantity. And, considering the way his sixth sense was vibrating, Mike intended to keep both eyes on her.

"Ready?"

Annie nodded. She was in no hurry to leave the warm and homey kitchen—or her sons. Particularly since it had been two long and lonely weeks since she had seen them or held them in her arms. But turning down the ever-watchful man beside her would have invited his curiosity. The one mistake she'd already made in stumbling over her new name was one mistake too many.

"Thank you, yes," she answered, her eyes fixed on Bobbie and Joey.

With Mike leading the way, Annie dutifully followed. He led her through the sunny breakfast

room, a formal dining room, large living room and, finally, a family room with a large television and various electronic equipment. Off to the side of the house, in the shape of an L, he told her, as if she didn't already know, were the servants' quarters. Along the way, he cautioned her that the windows and doors leading to the outside of the property were to remain locked at all times.

Upstairs, he pointed out the master suite—a sitting room, double bathroom and a large bedroom; rooms she'd decorated in Laura Ashley hunter green and rose three years ago and that seemed to have remained unchanged.

Edythe Matthews was definitely not a woman who nested.

He led the way down the hall, indicating four adjoining bedrooms, bathrooms included, and a set of service stairs leading down into the kitchen and breakfast area. In keeping with her new identity, Annie conscientiously nodded her head.

"The boys' rooms are here," he said as he opened a door leading to a sunny suite of two bedrooms, each with a large double bed. Baseball bats, softballs, two sets of in-line skates and their favorite word game, Scrabble, were lodged in a large wicker basket. Nothing here surprised her; it was comforting to see her boys surrounded by their favorite things. Then her eyes lit on the bedside table.

What she saw there didn't surprise her—it horrified her. A snapshot of herself and the boys taken at a family picnic. She'd given it to them just be-

fore they left to spend the summer with their father, never thinking the time would come when she would come here to take care of the boys. She had to get rid of the picture—fast. Forcing a calm expression on her face, she feigned interest in what Mike was saying, all the time waiting for an opportunity to shove the frame under a pillow. She tried not to think of her boys gazing at her smiling face in the photo as they lay in bed, saying goodnight to her before they closed their eyes. Had they missed her terribly?

"The boys each have their own room, with a bathroom in between. But, to tell you the truth," Mike continued, "they've been bunking in here together since I started a week ago. Either they haven't settled in yet, or they're homesick."

"Wouldn't you be?" Annie asked quietly. "After all, from what I understand, this is the first time they've been away from their mother."

Mike shrugged his shoulders. "I wouldn't know."

"Really?" The question was out before she could stop it. Instead of engaging Mike in conversation, she should be trying to hurry him out of the boys' room. But, in spite of herself, she was interested in this man.

Mike shrugged before he replied in an offhand manner. "It's the usual story. My parents were divorced when I was ten. My grandmother raised me on the work ethic, figuring I had to learn early how to get along. There wasn't much time to play or to

miss my folks.'' He glanced at her, then turned his somber gaze on the basket of toys. ''But you might be right, at that.''

That could account for some of the disillusionment in his eyes, Annie thought as she watched him open a closet door, look inside and close it behind him. But something told her it was more than that.

A product of a happy two-parent home, she was working hard to make her own sons' lives as normal as she could without their father at home. Robert had been a decent father in his own detached way. Until he'd become too involved with politics to bond with his sons. But she believed boys needed a male influence in their lives. That was the reason she'd agreed to let their father have them for the summer months.

As Mike continued his inspection of the room, making sure the windows were closed and the sashes firmly locked, Annie edged closer to the bedside table, looking for her chance. He finally came to a stop in front of her. Up close, he looked every inch a suspicious, vigilant detective, every inch a man. Her body instinctively responded to his maleness in a way that took her by surprise.

''You've sure learned at lot about the Matthews family in a short time, haven't you, Annie Kramer? Now, I wonder how that is and why?''

Annie was caught off guard, trapped between the revealing photo behind her and Mike's broad chest before her. Thank goodness she had a viable reason ready for him. ''Representative Robert Matthews

has been front-page news for a long time around Virginia," she said, proud of the even tone in her voice. "Especially now that he's campaigning for reelection."

"Really? I haven't paid that much attention. I guess I'm not into politics," he said, studying her. Somehow, he didn't look convinced.

She tried to change the subject. "Which room will be mine?"

"Right next door to the boys, where you can be near and hear them if they need you. Now, as I was saying—"

"And where's your room?" Annie interrupted before he could get in another word. He had that look in his eye again that told her he was full of questions.

"Next to yours. I'm two doors down." He gestured, but he didn't take his eyes off her.

Next to hers! Where she could hear him and imagine what he was doing and what he looked like as he was getting dressed. Next door where he could hear her and the boys if they went in and out of her room! She would have to be extra careful not to let the boys into her room where he might overhear their conversation. And extra careful not to let herself get involved with him. She reminded herself that she was here for her children, period.

Her heart did a somersault just thinking about his presence next door to her. She carefully schooled her expression to remain professionally interested but personally remote.

"I guess that's it," he said. He looked as if he had something more to say, but chose not to say it. From the way he'd been acting, he probably wanted to tell her just what areas were off-limits. She would find out for herself.

When it was obvious he was finished with the tour, she made a mental note to come back to the boys' room and hide the picture. "Thank you," she said. "I'll see you tomorrow."

"Tomorrow," he echoed, as he flipped his hand and turned away. "And hey, Mary Poppins, don't forget your umbrella."

IT WAS NOON WHEN Annie arrived at the Matthews residence. This time the maid, Sharon, opened the door.

"No Mr. Cassidy?" Annie inquired as she entered. "I thought he was the only one allowed to open the doors."

"I saw your taxi coming up the drive," Sharon replied hastily. "I usually call him when someone comes, if he doesn't know already. I wouldn't open the door for just anyone, I swear, but you're different. Are you going to tell Mike?"

"No, of course not," Annie assured her. She might need all the friends she could get. "Where are the boys?"

"Out in back with Mike." The maid picked up Annie's suitcase and carried it inside. "The three of them are playing baseball with the cleaning crew."

"Baseball? In this heat?"

"No one out there seems to mind. In fact, it sounds as if they're having a lot of fun. I wouldn't have minded playing myself, only it seems to be a male bonding exercise," Sharon said wistfully. "I used to play baseball with my little brothers. I still do, when I go home. Anyway, the game should be over soon. The crew is on lunch break."

As she took in Annie's wilted appearance her expression was one of sympathy. "I'm sorry. The air conditioner isn't working too well. We have a call in for a repairman."

Sharon was right on target. Annie squirmed under her loose dress and tried to ignore a rivulet of perspiration making its way down between her breasts. The dress had long sleeves that covered every available inch of skin and ended just short of her ankles. The saleswoman in the thrift shop had assured her it had been the "in thing" during the late thirties. Since no one else had been willing to buy the dress, and two others just like it, she'd given Annie a huge discount.

As far as Annie was concerned, now that she'd worn the dresses for the past two days, she felt she should have been given a medal just for being foolish enough to wear them in public.

From the way the maid was looking at her, Annie suspected she looked as odd as she felt. The last thing she'd wanted was to attract undue attention. Maybe dressing this way hadn't been such a

good idea, after all. But then, her usual style wouldn't have been much better.

She picked up her suitcase and her overnight case and struggled up the stairs to her room. On the second floor it was hotter than it was outdoors.

It took only a minute to wriggle out of her dress, strip down to her slip and hurry to open the window overlooking the back lawn. She breathed a deep sigh of relief as a slight breeze blew through the branches of a tree outside her window and stirred the sheer curtains.

Too late, she remembered Mike's admonition to keep the windows and outside doors of the house locked. She started to close the window and paused. The air-conditioning definitely wasn't working well enough to cool her off. And what Mike didn't know wouldn't hurt him. With a temperature of at least ninety degrees inside her bedroom, she intended to leave the window open no matter what he'd said. She'd take her lumps later. Besides, she thought as she measured the distance from the tree to her window and down to the immaculate lawn, it didn't look as if anyone could climb the tree and gain entry to her bedroom, anyway.

"Run, Joey, run!"

Annie leaned out the window when she heard someone shout her son's name. A ball came bounding across the lawn and Joey came into sight running as fast as his short legs could carry him. Wav-

ing his arms, he rounded a box that was obviously intended to be third base.

Laughing, Mike ran after Joey, cheering him on. The bodyguard was wearing jeans and a tank top that left his shoulders and a large part of his chest bare. He looked like an ordinary man, she thought, as he raised his hands to Joey in a victory salute. Well, maybe not so ordinary at that, she added as she took a longer look. Not when the sight of him tall, bare and laughing was sending waves of pleasurable shivers washing over her.

"Cool!" she heard Mike shout. "That was good for another run! We won!"

Good-natured laughter filled the air and three men wearing the blue uniform trousers of the cleaning service came into sight putting on their shirts. "Yeah, they won, all right. Are you sure we were trying to win, Eli?"

"Face it, Ed. Those kids beat us fair and square." With a wave, they disappeared around the side of the house.

Annie sat on the broad windowsill and gazed out over the yard. However Mike had reacted to her yesterday, it was clear he was fond of her sons. He was giving them the attention they needed, encouraging them, playing with them. It was more than their own father had taken the time to do.

Under different circumstances, she might have revealed herself and her story to Mike. She would have asked for his understanding, explaining that her boys wanted and needed their mother now that

their father was going to be away. But Mike's obvious suspicion of her kept her from baring her soul.

Granted, his proximity was making her blood heat in sensual ways it seemed she hadn't entirely forgotten. She didn't need the added complication of his attraction. After all, his loyalty surely must lie with his employer, her ex-husband. If she told him who she was and why she was here, she would be courting trouble. And, if he gave her away to Robert, as he probably would, she would undoubtedly be sent packing. Or worse, knowing Robert's strong, rigid sense of right and wrong. She could lose custody of her children for violating their agreement.

She was here for her children and no one else. She would have to go it alone and hope no one found her out.

Mike paused in the act of collecting the errant baseball. A movement at an upstairs window drew his attention. His first reaction was annoyance that a window had been opened in spite of his express orders to keep them all closed.

Until he caught sight of Annie.

One hand leaned on the window frame as she looked out over to where the boys were picking up their baseball gear. The other hand was raised as she shaded her eyes from the sun.

Her shoulders were bare; the strap of the skimpy undergarment she wore had fallen down over one shoulder and just barely covered the area over her

heart. A creamy expanse of skin curved down to the hollow between her breasts.

While he gazed up at her, she took a deep breath and wiped her forehead with a small handkerchief. It was obvious to his more-than-interested scrutiny that she'd removed her brassiere, since the tips of her breasts were showing firm and round through the thin material of her slip. There was a wide smile on her rosy lips.

Annie Kramer looked more interesting than she had yesterday, and never more off-limits.

His senses responded to the sight of her bare skin as they hadn't responded in a long time. And never, at least in recent memory, like this. He wanted to kiss her, to taste her. To brush the tender flesh of her throat with his lips, to savor the scent of her, to feel her heart throb against his chest. To feel her against him, bare skin to bare skin.

He closed his eyes and took a deep breath to cool himself down before his thoughts could go any further. *This is all wrong,* he told himself as he turned to go into the house. He had a job to do protecting two young boys. He couldn't allow anything or anyone to interfere with that. Outside of the boys' welfare, nothing else mattered.

He'd taken the job as a favor to a friend who owned a security service. And to give himself some breathing space. He'd even figured the summer was going to be a piece of cake; that it would give him the time he needed to restore his credibility and his confidence. To prove to himself he *could* do a good

job as a law-enforcement officer without letting his testosterone get in the way of his judgment. Now, he wasn't so sure everything was working as he'd planned.

With the Matthews family money and their prominent political connections, he'd reasoned no one would possibly be stupid enough to intrude on their lives, no matter what rumors were circulating. Matthews certainly hadn't taken the rumors seriously, or he would have called in the FBI. Instead, he'd hired Mike, more like an insurance policy.

Mike had honestly believed there wouldn't be any danger connected with the job of guarding the two small children for a few months. When the summer was over, he would take his generous salary and head back to a more challenging job.

He'd been dead wrong. There *was* danger—and her name was Annie Kramer.

Chapter Three

"Have you seen the new nanny today, Mike?"

"You might say so," he answered casually as he stopped in the service porch to wash up. The cook was the last person he was going to discuss his sexual fantasies with. "Why do you ask?"

"She arrived while you and the boys were out playing ball."

"Where is she now?" Dressed, he hoped.

"Upstairs. She cornered the boys as soon as they came into the house. One look at them and she marched them upstairs to clean them up."

Mrs. Swenson handed him a towel to dry himself. "The little ones sure have taken to her. They're like a couple of bees who've found honey."

"Yeah, I imagined they would," Mike answered dryly. "Maybe they just haven't met anyone like her before."

Deep in thought, Mike pulled on the shirt he'd taken off before the ball game and wandered into the kitchen with the cook trailing behind him. He took the lid off the cookie jar, extracted a ginger-

bread man and munched thoughtfully. There *was* something about Annie that seemed to draw people to her, especially those two kids. Just what that something was was what he intended to find out.

"Now, don't go ruining your appetite," Mrs. Swenson cautioned as he reached for another cookie. "I made your favorite lunch—angel-hair pasta with shrimp."

"You're a doll," Mike replied with a smile, wiping gingerbread crumbs from his chin. "After all the exercise I've had this morning, I'm starving."

"You'll have to wait until Annie comes down with the boys. She told me she wasn't going to let them come to the table until they'd cleaned themselves up."

Mike dusted the crumbs off his hands and shook his head. Now was his chance to see what the nanny looked like today. Yesterday's outfit had been one for the books.

"The poor woman doesn't know what she's getting into," he said. "Joey behaves as if using soap is going to take off his skin. I'd better go on up and rescue her. It's the least I can do since it's her first day on the job."

"Sounds to me like they're having a great time." Sharon swayed her way into the kitchen. "I just took some towels up to them and the kids were giggling fit to burst."

"Giggling? You have to be mistaken. They were probably crying." Mike started for the door. "If I

know Joey, he's giving her a bad time. He hates to clean up.''

"No," Sharon assured him. "I'm positive they were giggling. I never did hear such goings-on, and I have three younger brothers. All of them hated soap and water when they were little guys and, from the way they looked the last time I saw the three devils, I'm not so sure they like them any better now." She shot Mike an inviting look. "Now that the nanny's here, maybe you'll have more free time for other things than watching the boys?"

"Free time isn't in the job description," Mike informed her. "I'm going upstairs."

Mike took the back stairs two at a time and made for the boys' bedroom. A loud burst of laughter stopped him as he reached for the doorknob.

"Don't forget to use the soap, Joey," Annie said, laughing at her son's antics. "No, I don't care if it floats, it's not a boat. Now use it." Then she added in a false threatening voice, "Or I'll have to do it for you."

"Ah, you wouldn't really do that, would you?"

"Try me!"

The impish look on Joey's face was almost too much for Annie. She planted a quick kiss on his upturned nose and handed him the soap. "Go ahead, now. Mrs. Swenson is waiting for us. I wouldn't want to be late the first day on the job."

"I will, I promise!" Joey grinned at her as he

dabbed at the bar of soap with the washcloth and rubbed his cheeks. "I love you, Miss Annie!"

"Don't forget me!" Bobby shouted as he wrung out his washcloth over his head. "I love you, too."

Annie sat back on her heels and smiled at the boys. It felt so good to be with them again.

It had been Joey's plaintive voice on the telephone telling her his father and his wife were going to travel through Virginia on a campaign trip and were planning to leave them alone with a nanny that had brought her here. He'd wanted to know why she couldn't come and be with him and Bobby instead. She couldn't bring herself to say no—not when she pictured his earnest face and eyes she had never been able to resist. The scheme to masquerade as a nanny had been the only way she could think of to get here. But if she were exposed, she was certain their father wouldn't be that understanding.

"I'm ready!" Joey finally announced.

Annie reached for a bath towel. "Okay, you both can come out now." She dried Joey off, knowing that if she left it up to him, he would only curl up in the bath towel and daydream. "Now, hurry. I have your clean clothes ready in the other room."

They loved her? Already? Mike stood with his hand on the bathroom door. Obviously, Annie was doing more than okay and didn't need him to help out with two wiggling bodies.

After meeting their new nanny for the first time

less than twenty-four hours ago, the boys *loved* her? It was too much and too soon.

Like most kids, Bobby and Joey were sure they knew it all. And like most kids, they resented any adult voice of reason. And they wouldn't have given up an argument before there'd been a battle of wills, or at least, something that had happened between Annie and the boys to win their admiration. But love?

He debated going back and asking the three of them what was going on. On the other hand he didn't actually have anything to hang his suspicions on. But he would keep his eyes and ears on the trio. Right now, he frowned and turned away to his own room to change.

LUNCH WAS A MORE subdued affair. Maybe it was because the kids were tired out after the ball game, but Mike suspected it might be something more.

He silently ate his pasta and shrimp, waving away seconds. His mind was on more important things: what he was going to do about Annie Kramer. Occasionally glancing up at the new nanny, he mentally summed up the observations he'd made about her.

For one thing, there had been her momentary discomfiture when she'd introduced herself.

Secondly, there had been her timely appearance with references almost too good to be true.

Then this bonding with the boys.

To top it off, except for an obviously new social-

security card that anyone could buy at the nearest underworld location, she had no identification that would hold water. Not even a driver's license with her picture on it.

Given time, he was sure there would be a few other questions he was going to have to ask before he was satisfied. He would spring them on her before she had a chance to make up a story— because that was what he was beginning to think her explanations were: a story.

He glanced over at the enigma. Dressed in another of her "quaint" outfits, she was conversing quietly with Mrs. Swenson. The sexy woman who'd watched the ball game from the upstairs window was gone; she was no longer the sultry woman from his imagination.

Bobby and Joey, freshly washed and smelling of soap, were behaving like two little angels. Every request they made for more milk, more garlic bread, or even for more grated cheese was prefaced by a "please" and ended with a "thank you."

It was even "Miss Annie" this and "Miss Annie" that.

The boys' behavior was too good to be true.

And so was their nanny.

If Annie was a nanny by choice and by profession, he was willing to eat the hat he didn't own.

The first thing he was going to do was give her space to let her trip herself up. And, at the rate she was going, he had a strong hunch it wouldn't take her long.

The trouble was, he was in danger of getting tripped up himself by what Annie was doing to his psyche.

He wiped perspiration from his forehead and glared at the central air-conditioning vent in the wall. In spite of two calls for a repairman, the damn air conditioner was still on the blink.

On second thought, he was sorry it was working at all. If this heat and humidity kept up, sooner or later Annie would have to shed her head-to-toe clothing and put on something a little more revealing. Something that would expose the silky skin he had glimpsed before. Skin he sensed would be as soft and warm as velvet.

"What did you boys have in mind for the afternoon?" Mike inquired when lunch was over. After a vigorous morning of baseball, he was hoping for a quiet game of Scrabble or two and time to make a few telephone calls.

"The boys and I thought we'd ask you to take us to the zoo in D.C." Annie replied. "It's a bit warm, but it's such a lovely afternoon it's a shame to stay inside."

"No," he said firmly.

"No?" She looked at him as if he'd lost his mind. Which was precisely what he was trying hard not to do. It wasn't easy keeping his mind on his job—not when there were so many unanswered questions and her sexy image kept intruding in his thoughts.

"And why not?"

"Too many people." When he saw storm clouds gathering on Joey's face, he decided to explain. "It's summer vacation. D.C. is full of visiting families. The zoo is bound to be crowded with thousands of visitors."

"No one could possibly know who the boys are," she protested.

"*I* would know," he countered, folding his napkin and taking a last swallow of lemonade. "And since the boys are my responsibility, the zoo is out."

Bobby and Joey renewed their clamor for a visit to the zoo. If he hadn't been so annoyed at having his decisions questioned, Mike would have admired the way Annie quieted the boys with a single direct look. He was annoyed. After all, *he* was in charge, and he expected to be listened to.

"We used to do lots of fun things when we lived at home," Joey chimed in. His lower lip quivered.

"Maybe so," Mike answered. "But things have changed. This is home now."

Bobby looked rebellious. Mike briefly wondered what had happened to the cooperative and friendly little guy he'd been entertaining for the past week.

"Well, then, maybe we can go to the park," Annie offered.

"No to that idea, too."

"What's wrong with a neighborhood park?" She looked and sounded incredulous.

"Same reason. Too many strangers around,"

Mike said shortly, feeling an edge come into his voice in spite of his attempt to hide it. He had a job to do and he intended to do it. He wasn't here to make friends.

"Are you saying the boys are going to be prisoners in their own home?" Annie looked horrified.

"Not at all. We'll just have to plan our outings ahead." Mike glanced sternly over at the boys before he pushed back his chair and rose to his feet. "Right now, I'll be in the library catching up with some paperwork. Don't leave the house."

Annie looked at him as if he'd grown horns. Well, he thought, he sure as hell couldn't please them all and still ensure the boys' safety. He intended to follow his better judgment no matter what they thought of him. Even if he wasn't going to be the most popular man on the block.

"Maybe you and the boys can find something to do around here for now," Mike offered in the way of a compromise.

The nanny and the boys stared at him silently. What had he said that they didn't understand?

He gazed at drooping mouths and tearful eyes and Annie's troubled expression. Too bad. He wasn't going to be dissuaded from doing what he knew to be right no matter how unhappy they looked.

He could see trouble coming around the bend like a train that was late at the station. Only, this time, he wasn't going to get in its way. The kids weren't going to be exposed to crowds and that was

that. With a final glance around him to make sure the troops understood he meant what he said, he thanked Mrs. Swenson for lunch and headed for the library.

Annie was troubled as she watched him stride out of the kitchen. Until now, she'd responded to life's choices with "Why not?" instead of "Why?" When he'd first met her, her ex-husband had said he found the trait and her blithe spirit charming. Later, Robert had complained they were some of the many things about her personality that had driven his pragmatic self to distraction. When he'd suggested a divorce, she'd been more than relieved to take him up on it.

From the exasperated look on Mike's face, he wasn't taking her decision-making kindly, either.

It wasn't as if she was asking for the moon, she reasoned. Considering the poor air-conditioning in the house, all she wanted to do was to take the boys out for some fresh air. She was just as interested in the children's safety as he was. She'd been prepared to tell him just that when he turned on his heel and left.

Annie lined up arguments in favor of allowing herself and the boys some greater measure of freedom. After all, according to Mike himself, no real threats had been made to the children and they *were* forewarned. Not only had they been alerted to possible danger, they had their own personal bodyguard in tow. None of the arguments she came up with seemed to hold water. Instead, her common

sense told her she should be grateful for Mike's caution. After all, it was *her* children Mike was guarding.

"Okay, guys," she finally announced, leaning over Joey and wiping a limp strand of pasta from his ear, "it's time to help Mrs. Swenson clean up. When we're through, we'll go outside to the gazebo. You can fill me in on what you've been doing lately."

Bobby looked about to burst by the time they stepped outside.

"Mom, what are we going to do about my baseball team's exhibition game at home next week? From what Mike just said, I'll bet Dad forgot to tell him it's okay to go."

Annie held her breath and thanked God nobody was around to overhear Bobby's slip. She put her arm around him and hugged him tightly. How could she convince her son his father meant well, but that he had more important things on his mind right now? Of course, she mused with more than a little compassion for her sons, if the boys had been old enough to vote...

"I'm not sure yet, Bobby. I'll have to talk to Mike and see what can be arranged." Annie sighed as she figured their chances of being allowed to go to the ball game were slim to none. "But I'm sure if there's a way, Mike will find it."

She brushed his blond curls away from his forehead. Of her two sons, Bobby looked the most like her, although Joey had inherited her free spirit and

imagination. Bobby was the more serious of the two. "In the meantime, you and Joey had better try harder and stick to calling me Miss Annie. No one was here this time, but there's no use looking for trouble."

Once outside, Annie remembered their nearest neighbor, Lyle Houston, had a miniature farm and petting zoo at the back of his acreage. The zoo and the animal sounds coming from it had driven her ex-husband to distraction more than once.

"Let's go over and ask Mr. Houston if we can visit with the animals in his petting zoo," she suggested. "It may not be as much fun as a big one, but you used to like to go over there when we lived here."

"Cool," Joey said. His eyes lit up. "His baby goat liked me."

"You don't remember anything," Bobby said. "You were too little. It was *me* the goat liked."

"I do so remember," Joey rejoined. "I'm the one he used to like."

"He didn't!"

"He did so!"

Annie regarded her two sons fondly. The party was over. The boys were back to being boys; it sounded like old times. Her heart warmed with happiness.

"Bobby, Joey, that will be enough! The goat likes everyone. Wait up. I've got to go back in the house for a minute."

She found the cook putting dishes away. "Is Mike around, Mrs. Swenson?"

The friendly cook smiled. "Why don't you call me Clara, dear? You don't have to be so formal, now that you're going to be with us for a while. Mike's in the library with the door closed. That usually means he doesn't want to be interrupted."

"Then would you tell him we've gone next door the next time you see him?"

"You're sure you want to be going that far? Mike said..." Dubious, Clara stood watching Annie.

"The zoo is only next door," Annie told her. "I'm sure it's not that far away that you need to disturb him."

"Surely you're not going to walk in this heat?"

"It's better than staying cooped up in the house. We'll see you later."

ANNIE FELT HERSELF blanch when Lyle Houston greeted the boys. He was home, after all. What if he recognized her? What if he told Mike or Robert? She should have listened to Mike.

"Hi, fellas! Heard you were going to spend the summer with the congressman. How've you been?"

"Great, Mr. Houston! We came to see the animals," Joey said.

"Come right along, then. They're back here. And who's this young lady?"

"Miss Annie. She's going to take care of us

while Dad is away," Bobby explained under Annie's watchful eye.

"Pleased to meet you. I'm Lyle Houston. We'll be back in a minute." With a friendly nod at Annie, he led the boys away.

She let out a sigh of relief. Thank goodness Houston hadn't recognized her, or her masquerade would have been short-lived.

IT DIDN'T TAKE LONG for Mike to discover something else about the new nanny: She couldn't take orders worth a damn!

She may have told Mrs. Swenson where she was going, but she should have waited and asked him before she took off.

When he'd found the nanny and the kids gone, his first thought was that she'd made off with them. That was before Mrs. Swenson had had a chance to tell him Annie and the boys had gone next door to visit the Houstons' petting zoo. Not that he figured there was any problem there; he'd checked on Houston the day he was hired. The guy was okay.

As for Annie, he should have known she wasn't dumb enough to kidnap the boys the very first day on the job. But she sure was giving him premature gray hairs.

He made his way across the Matthews property. It was small, by Fairfax County standards, but large enough to take him fifteen minutes to check it out as he walked. By the time he'd reached the property boundaries, he'd had a chance for his temper

to cool. In fact, he thought wryly, it was the only cool thing about him.

Maybe he'd been too quick to pass judgment, he decided, when he heard the children's laughter and animal squeaks and squeals coming from a fenced-off area. In fact, he thought sourly, he hadn't been thinking clearly ever since he'd laid eyes on the new nanny.

He couldn't believe his eyes when he finally came upon Annie. She was sitting on the ground holding a baby pig, of all things! Two other little pigs were trying to get into her lap. Hair flying, laughing with abandon, the formerly prim Annie was busy trying to fend off the critters.

"Why didn't you wait for me?" Mike demanded as he planted his feet in front of her and fixed her with a cold stare. He dodged a pig trying to take a bite out of his shoe as he waited for an answer.

"You were busy. Mrs. Swenson said she'd tell you where to find us."

"I wasn't that far away, just in the library," Mike replied. "But that's not the point. You could have waited until I was through. I was only making a few telephone calls."

"I didn't want to disturb you," she said, petting the squirming piglet before she set it down and picked up another one to fondle. "And we were only going next door."

"You disturb me more by going off without me." He was trying to keep a lid on his temper, but it wasn't easy. Not when he had an audience.

"Mike! Did you see the new little potbellied pigs?" Joey climbed down from the fence railing and ran to join him. "Mr. Houston says I can have one. Do you think Dad will let me, Miss Annie?"

"Me, too!" Bobby hollered from inside the pigpen. "Me, too!"

Well," Annie answered helplessly, setting the squealing pig on the ground and struggling to her feet, "I'm not too sure about that."

"Potbellied pigs?" Mike felt his temper rise like a rocket. The thought of potbellied pigs roaming the Matthews estate with the kids chasing after them was almost more than he could bear. He would probably end up having to take care of the lot of them. "Why would anyone want to keep a potbellied pig in his backyard?"

Lyle Houston, a tall, lanky man in blue jeans, rejoined them in time to hear Mike's question. "Guess you could say it's because they're awfully cute when they're babies. Smarter than dogs, too, if you ask me. I've heard some people swear pigs can be trained to do all sorts of things."

Mike felt a leaden premonition at what he suspected was coming next. "What happens when they grow up?"

"You make their pen a little larger," Houston replied with a laugh. "Or let 'em run loose, if you have enough room." The little pig in his arms screeched its distress. He scratched the squirming pig behind its ears and set it down in the pen where it ran squealing for its mother. "They're more in-

teresting than the horses I board. In fact, I've just about decided to raise 'em and sell them for pets.''

"Horses, I can understand,'' Mike muttered with a sidelong glance at Annie. "But why pigs?''

"There's a market for them, that's why. And it's a lot more humane than raising them for food.''

"I want a little pig, Miss Annie!''

Annie quickly glanced away when she noticed Mike's eyes on her. In her other life, she wouldn't have hesitated to say yes to the boys. The little piglets *were* appealing and the boys could use something to occupy them. But at the time she was hired, she'd agreed to let Mike call the shots. From his expression, the adoption of a pig or two was the last thing he was going to consider.

"We'll talk more about that later,'' she said, stalling for time. "For now, why don't you each pick out a favorite pig and we'll come to visit it every day? But hurry up,'' she said with a sidelong glance at Mike. "I think it's time for us to leave.''

The boys rushed off to choose their pets, followed by their owner, Lyle Houston.

Annie didn't *think* it was time to leave; she knew it. Especially when she could practically see steam coming out of Mike's ears.

Why hadn't she thought more carefully before she'd brought the boys over? she wondered, glancing cautiously at Mike. Why had she done something she should have known would antagonize him? Maybe it was because coming here was something she wouldn't have hesitated to do in her other

life. But this wasn't her other life, she thought with a wary eye on Mike. It was a whole new ball game and he was the umpire calling the shots.

"Why are you looking at me like that?" Annie demanded when Mike's silence became unbearable.

"I'm trying to keep a lid on my temper while I try to figure out what you're going to come up with next," Mike replied. His eyes narrowed as he studied her; his expression was forbidding.

Mike's anger registered loud and clear. But so did the lines of his very lithe, masculine body. If she weren't so put out by his male arrogance, she might have appreciated it more. She could see his temper was about to boil over unless she could find a way to placate him.

"I don't know why you're so upset," she told him. "You should have known I wouldn't do anything to harm Bobby and Joey. I'm trying to take care of them the best way I know how. Or is it yourself you're really worried about? Maybe you're afraid you're not doing a good enough job of looking after the boys?"

"Whatever gave you that idea?" he countered, remembering his past experiences with a woman as fiercely determined and as appealing as Annie. Annie was closer to the truth than she realized, but he wasn't buying. "It's just that you're not making it any easier for me to do the job."

"All I'm asking is that you be reasonable," Annie retorted, opening and closing her fists. If he

didn't know better, she looked ready to take him on.

"Look here, Annie," he persisted, undecided whether he should tell her that in his opinion she was the unreasonable one. It would only make her angrier than ever. "Things would be a lot easier for both of us if you just listened to me when I tell you something. I do it for a reason, not just to be arbitrary."

"I'm sure," Annie returned. "But at least you could give me the benefit of the doubt."

Mike snorted. "For the last time, I'm going to tell you not to leave the Matthews property unless I'm with you and the boys! I don't want to have to tell you to never do it again."

Her expression hardened. The good-natured nanny disappeared. In a way, he didn't blame her. No one liked to be treated like a child. Not that she was one, he thought, eyeing the dress that she'd pulled awry getting up. But no matter how she felt, he did expect her to listen to him.

"I'll try," she answered.

He didn't believe her for a minute.

Chapter Four

Annie headed for the boys' bedroom as soon as they returned home. She had to remove the photo from the boys' bedside table before Sharon or, perish the thought, Mike studied it too hard. Even though she'd substantially altered her appearance, she was taking no chances.

But the framed snapshot was nowhere in sight. If she was lucky, the boys had realized they should take it away. In the meantime, she had something else to worry about: She'd remembered seeing a favorite book of hers on the library shelf behind the desk. Worse yet, the bookplate on the inside cover of the book was hers.

She hurried down the stairway and into the library. The book was there in the bookcase behind the desk. She opened the cover. Sure enough, there was the bookplate with her name: Annie Kincaid Matthews. Engrossed in her good luck at finding it before someone else did, she didn't hear the library door open.

"What are you doing in here?"

Annie spun around. Mike stood at the library door, a frown on his face.

"Finding something to read," she said innocently. "Why? Is the library out-of-bounds, too?"

"Not at all," he answered, strolling into the room. "It's just that I saw you head up the back stairs a minute ago."

"I wanted to borrow a book to read." Annie hastily closed the book and held it close to her chest. If it came to that, he would have to fight her to get it away from her.

He glanced at the book and then at a partially open desk drawer. Her eyes followed his. She smiled innocently, knowing full well he suspected her of rifling the desk.

"Looking for something?" he asked, pointedly eyeing the open drawer.

"Only for a book, and I've found it," she replied, edging her way past him to the door. She could feel his calculating gaze centered on the book she hugged to her chest. She hugged it closer. The man had eyes like a hawk.

Mike waited while Annie inched her way past him. Her unusual perfume lingered long after she disappeared from sight. If all she'd wanted in the library was a book, why had she been so nervous? he wondered. In his experience, people usually didn't act that way unless they had something to be nervous about.

It was long past time to check Annie Kramer's references, to find out who she really was, where

she came from and maybe even why she had such
a strong influence on the boys.

Until today, decisions he'd made had been
obeyed without too many protests. In fact, things
had been going so well, he'd even begun to feel
like Bobby and Joey's big brother.

The thought stopped him cold. After his last assignment, he'd made it a rule not to become involved with or attached to his charges. To trust no
one but himself. It was a rule he seemed to have
forgotten. Maybe it was just as well the nanny had
come on board to distract the boys and before his
attachment to Joey and Bobby became too strong.
But there was one thing the three of them were
going to have to accept: He was the one in charge
around here.

He closed the door to the library behind him and
took the chair behind the desk. Opening the center
drawer, he drew out the envelope containing the
nanny's references. Next he looked for Mrs. Matthews's personal telephone book. Damn! She'd
taken it with her. Without the book, he didn't have
a clue which employment agency she'd called. It
would take at least a week before he could arrange
to get a copy of the Matthews phone bill and check
out telephone numbers.

Mike studied the first of the references. "Annie
Kramer is a hardworking, intelligent woman who
loves children." He was tempted to agree. She appeared to be hardworking and she obviously loved
children. As for being intelligent, now that was a

horse of another color. After checking her large cloth bag filled with as eclectic an assortment of items as he'd ever seen in one woman's possession, he wasn't prepared to vouch for that part of her reference.

He punched out the telephone number listed on the letter. No one was home. He moved on to the next reference.

It said much the same. It also noted Annie was trustworthy and had a wonderful imagination that children loved about her. Well, he would give her that much. She had an imagination that promised trouble if he didn't keep an eye on her.

He tried the noted telephone number. Again, there was no answer—not even a recording that would allow him to leave a message.

The third reference was just like the others. This time, when he made his call, he got lucky. A feminine voice answered.

"Mrs. Hitchcock?"

"Yes?"

"This is Mike Cassidy. I work for Congressman Bob Matthews. He's just hired a nanny for his boys, Annie Kramer. She's given you as a reference. I hope you don't mind answering a few questions about her."

"Not at all," Mrs. Hitchcock intoned. "I was sorry to let her go, but we decided to put my son in boarding school for the summer while we travel. He sure loves her. We all do, for that matter. She's promised to come back when we need her."

"Could you describe her for me?"

"What a strange question!" There was a pause. "Well, she's about five feet seven or eight, slender, brown hair, brown eyes. She's such a free spirit— we all got a kick out of her. What else do you want to know?"

Mike sighed. With a description like that, it could be none other than the Annie Kramer currently in residence in the Matthews household. The unconventional Annie who sat in the dirt playing with piglets, who wore clothing that was fashionable sixty years ago, and whom everyone loved.

He thanked Annie's former employer, hung up the phone and studied the references again.

There it was in black and white. In addition to Annie herself, there was the repetition of what bothered him about her: the word *Love.*

The way "love" kept appearing with regard to Annie Kramer, both in the letters of reference and in Mrs. Swenson's observation, bothered him. He wouldn't be surprised to find, if they *did* adopt two little potbellied pigs, that they loved her, too.

Even so, he had the strangest feeling there was something personal in the way the new nanny felt about Joey and his brother and in the way they obviously felt about her.

What really worried him was the possibility the nanny's reason for ingratiating herself with the boys so quickly would turn out to be for some ulterior purpose of her own.

"I DON'T UNDERSTAND why Mike is so sure there's something wrong with me," Annie said as she shared a cup of tea with the cook. "He watches me like a hawk."

Clara Swenson sat back and surveyed Annie. "In my opinion, if you're trying to keep Mike from being curious about you, you're going about it in the wrong way."

"I am?" Annie fingered her hair uneasily and gazed at the cook in surprise. "How?"

"To tell the truth, I think it's the way you look." Clara Swenson eyed Annie with a smile. "With those old-fashioned dresses and the way you wear your hair, you were bound to attract his attention. I wondered about you myself."

"My goodness." Annie managed to laugh. She thought of the unadorned ponytail she'd decided fitted the role of nanny. "I don't look much different than most working women."

"Shows how wrong you were," Clara replied. "If you don't mind my saying so, I've noticed the way Mike keeps looking at you. As if he's trying to figure you out," she added with a whimsical smile. "In my opinion, if you looked like the rest of the women your age, he wouldn't give you a second glance."

"He wouldn't?" Annie felt confused and, surprisingly, a little hurt. She'd been the target of enough second glances not to believe Mike Cassidy wasn't a red-blooded American man just like the rest. Maybe all he needed was a wake-up call.

"He only thinks he isn't interested. Take a good look at Sharon when she's near Mike. She's dying to have him notice her, but as pretty a young thing as she is, he doesn't give her a second look. Not that I can give you a reason, considering he's young and handsome enough to attract any woman he might be interested in."

She rose, turned off the whistling teakettle, and set about making more tea. "It's almost as if he's sworn off being interested in women. That is, until you came along. Now I've seen the two of you together, I've changed my mind." Clara smiled at Annie. "He's a different man since you arrived."

"Different?" Annie asked. "I don't know what he was like before I showed up, but he's been arbitrary and suspicious of me from the first minute he laid eyes on me. Not that I care, anyway. The boys are the only males I care about."

That wasn't strictly true, Annie thought, embarrassed when she remembered this morning's ball game and her reaction to the sight of the bodyguard's muscular body. And even the way he'd looked earlier when he'd laid down the law. What was there about a dangerous man that was so appealing, anyway? In fact, the only male opinion she didn't care about was her ex-husband's.

She wouldn't have admitted it to just anyone, but she did care, especially after he'd rejected her. And now there was Mike, acting much the same way. Maybe she was woman enough to want Mike to notice her. A wicked part of her wouldn't mind

teasing stuffy, good-looking Mike. She hadn't realized how hard it was to act a part that wasn't true to herself.

"We'll see." Mrs. Swenson brought the teapot to the table. "Why don't you join me in another cup of tea, Annie? It helps a body relax and think clearly. And, from the looks of you, you could use a little of both."

Annie sighed and passed her empty cup to Clara. She looked down at her grass-stained, dirt-spattered dress. One of the baby potbellied pigs had spread his muddy hoofprints over the front and left a long tear in the hem. "This dress and two others like it are all I brought with me. If you're right about Mike, Clara, what am I going to do to change the way I look?"

The cook sipped her tea before she answered. "If you're asking me for advice, I think you should buy some new clothing when you have an afternoon off. Or bring your own from home. The sooner the better," she advised. "Something that won't make you look old and out of place. That just feeds his suspicions. Remember, Mike's no fool. He knows the truth as well as the rest of us do—we older women today want to look young. There's no point in a woman looking old when she doesn't have to."

"Good heavens," Annie exclaimed, laughing at her own naiveté. "I've been so stupid!"

Annie had only to look at Clara to see it was true. The cook wore a pretty flowered-cotton dress,

makeup and a perky pink ribbon to keep her hair neatly in a twist at the back of her neck. Her only concession to her occupation was the ever-present white denim apron.

"Why don't you take Sharon into your confidence, too?" Clara suggested. "Once she knows you're not in competition for Mike, I'm sure she'll be more than happy to help you. She hasn't given up on him herself yet, you know," she added with a wink.

"I hadn't noticed, but she can have him with my blessing." Annie thought for a moment. "But maybe I *will* ask her for advice until I can go shopping."

"MISS ANNIE?"

"Yes, sweetheart?" Annie looked up from the dress she was altering. After the piglet attack, the dress was going to have to be shortened by at least five inches, maybe more. That and the few extra touches Sharon had suggested should do the trick, she thought. Although she still wasn't convinced she was doing the right thing. Mike looked too intelligent to be influenced by reverse psychology.

Joey shuffled unhappily into Annie's room. "When are we going to go home? We've been here long enough."

"Soon." Annie forgot her sewing and folded him in her arms. "I'll take you home soon."

"Bobby wants to go home, too," Joey said in a muffled voice as he burrowed closer. "He misses

his computer and I want my toys. And we don't have any friends here to play with, either."

"I'm afraid we'll have to wait until your father comes home to answer that question, sweetheart. In the meantime, you have me."

"Are you going to stay here with us forever?"

"As long as I can." She couldn't promise "forever," no matter how much she wanted to see a smile on Joey's face. Poor little guy, his world had changed so abruptly. It broke her heart to see the difficulty he was having coping.

She hadn't realized the emotional trauma the boys would suffer under the shared-custody agreement she had with their father. After all, he was their father. And, in his own way, a decent enough one. But she knew in her heart Robert's relationship with his sons was polite and distant. As for next year, she doubted that once the elections were over, Robert and his wife would want to play at parenthood.

The less they talked about the future, the better off they all would be, she decided as she stroked his blond curls. Until then, it was more important than ever for her to get Mike's mind off her and back on the boys.

She had a plan.

MIKE GLANCED UP from the breakfast table in time to see a pair of shapely ankles and trim feet shod in open sandals with vivid purple toenails making their way down the service staircase. A moment

later, their owner came into sight. Mike took a closer look.

This was Annie the nanny?

She wore the enveloping dress of yesterday, but it had been altered. The results were staggering. In spite of his earlier negative response to the dress and the woman who wore it, parts of his body were reacting in a way they had no business reacting. He watched her reach the bottom of the stairs. Unless his eyes were failing him, the nanny of yesterday was gone.

Freshly laundered, the once-drab garment she wore was at least six inches shorter than it had been yesterday. In fact, it was short enough to reveal the beginnings of long, bare, shapely legs that brought visions to his mind that were better off left unseen.

His astonished gaze rose, past her enticing breasts to her shoulders, to her arms and beyond. The dress's long sleeves had been shortened to end above her elbows. Under his rapt gaze, her elbows looked pretty enticing, too.

Even the neckline had been altered—its high lace collar removed to reveal more of that slender neck and golden skin he'd seen framed in her bedroom window. Her hair fell in soft waves to her shoulders.

"A concession to the heat?" he inquired casually as she walked across the room and joined him at the kitchen table.

"Not really," she answered. "I hadn't noticed it was particularly warm."

As far as Mike was concerned, it was definitely warm and getting warmer by the minute.

This was a whole new ball game, even if the players hadn't changed, he thought as he determinedly willed his body to cool. He would have to be more watchful than ever to remember the purpose of the chase: He still intended to prove Annie wasn't telling the whole truth, no matter how much he was attracted to her.

His sensible side told him to ignore his reaction to the new nanny. His wild side refused to listen.

He heard a murmur of approval behind him. A quick glance told him he wasn't the only one impressed with the change in the nanny. Coffeepot in one hand and a plate of toast in the other, Clara Swenson stood beaming at Annie. Even Sharon sat wide-eyed. Annie's transformation from a drab matron into a sexy young woman was striking. Except for those purple toenails and silver sandals. On second thought, he decided they were striking, too. And right in character.

He shifted uneasily. He had to do something to lighten the atmosphere in the kitchen. No way was he going to let this new Annie Kramer soften him up again. Not when he'd worked so hard to put the past behind him.

"Where are the boys?" he finally inquired. "I heard them talking with you in your room earlier and figured you'd bring them down with you."

"I sent them back to finish getting dressed. They'll be down in a minute."

"By the way, the dress looks great," Mike remarked casually.

"You really noticed?" Annie answered cautiously. Clara's theory had been backward. "I didn't think you would."

"I'd have to wear blinders not to notice. The question is, why?"

Annie shrugged.

"Never mind," Mike replied under his breath. The reason really didn't matter. What did matter to him was that it was becoming increasingly difficult to stay one step ahead of Annie.

Annie smiled at Mrs. Swenson. "Can I help you, Clara?"

"Clara?" As nice as she'd been to him since his arrival, Mrs. Swenson had never invited Mike to call her by her first name. Not even when she'd fussed over him and fed him homemade cookies. There was a certain dignity about the motherly woman that called for respect, and in his frame of reference, that meant calling her Mrs. Swenson. Not even Sharon called her by any other name.

But not Annie. She'd been here two days and she was on first-name terms and was being treated as if she and the cook had known each other for years. Providing she wasn't practicing witchcraft, there was definitely more to this Annie Kramer than met the eye!

"Good morning, Mrs. Swenson. You too, Mike!" Bobby shouted as he came bounding down the stairs, his brother chattering at his heels.

Mike relaxed. If the boys' behavior was any criterion, maybe everything was normal, after all.

"What did you have in mind for today?" he asked Annie when the boys had joined them at the table.

"Whatever you think is best," she replied primly. "Coffee?" she asked as she poised the coffeepot over his cup.

"Yeah, sure," he answered cautiously, not convinced Annie had changed her ways. Not entirely, and not the Annie he knew. A nagging feeling told him she was out to teach him a lesson, but he wasn't sure on which subject.

He hid a frown as he dug into his breakfast. It was only eight o'clock in the morning and she'd ruined his day with another mind-blowing incident.

More important, he'd overheard Joey asking her when she would take him and his brother home. He'd intended to question her about that the first minute he laid eyes on her, but her mind-boggling appearance had gotten in the way. Why had they asked her a question like that? Where was "home"? And what had she meant when she'd answered, "Soon"?

He intended to find out, now.

"Annie, I'd like to speak to you in the library after breakfast," he said casually. She raised an eyebrow. "Just a few little things I need to clear up."

"You can ask me now, if you like."

"No, thanks. I'd rather do it in private."

He headed for the library door, with only a backward glance to make sure she'd taken him up on his invitation and was following him.

"Now what?" Annie asked, steeling herself for the worst. Bobby had already told her he'd put the missing snapshot in his duffel bag. Something else was bothering Mike. What had she done now? For as surely as the sun would set tonight, from the way he was watching her, she'd done something to feed his suspicions.

His eyes were cold, his body tense when he asked her abruptly, "Where's home, Annie?"

"Home?" Annie frantically tried to think of why he would ask her a question like that. "I don't understand."

"Then let me explain," he said tightly. "I heard Joey ask you when you were going to take him and Bobby home. Whose home? Where? And why would he ask you a question like that?"

Annie knew her stay with her children rode on her answer. Determined to remain with her sons, no matter what Mike thought of her, she locked her gaze with his.

"We both know the boys are here only for the summer, and as a result of a divorce custody agreement," she answered as reasonably as she could. "I'm told it was a decision made *for* them, not *by* them. They're young and they're lonely. They want their mother. I don't blame them. Do you?"

"Of course not," he replied. "What kind of a

man do you think I am? But what has that got to
do with you promising to take the boys home?''

"A decent man, I hope," she said first. "As for
taking them home, you misunderstood. I was only
trying to reassure Joey he and Bobby would be
allowed to go home at the end of the summer.''

She eyed him with as innocent a look as she
could muster. Inside, every nerve in her body was
on alert. Mike was no fool, she knew that by now.
She couldn't give him any reason to believe she
was anything but bewildered by his reaction to the
conversation he'd overheard.

"Why? What did you think I had in mind?" she
questioned as calmly as she was able under the circumstances. He was doing his job as the boys'
bodyguard too well and getting too close for comfort. If ever she needed Lady Luck, it was now.
"You act as though you thought I was planning to
spirit the kids away.''

"Something like that," he answered, studying
her more closely than she cared him to. "Your explanation makes sense, but, let's face it, I don't
really know anything about you. You came here
out of nowhere like a genie out of a bottle and
you've taken over the kids like nothing I've ever
seen before.''

"I'm only giving them the attention every child
should have to make them feel secure. With their
father away, they need affection more than ever.''

"Maybe," he admitted. "But you can't blame

me for picking up on what I heard. For all I knew, you could have been trying to—"

"Nothing," she interrupted before he could finish his sentence. "I wasn't trying to do anything to them or with them. The conversation was nothing more than an attempt to make the boys' lives a little easier, a little happier. I don't have to be their mother to want to make them happy."

But she *was* their mother and their happiness came first with her—no matter what Mike thought of the way she went about it.

That was what she was here for and that was what she was going to do. It was just a matter of praying hard and staying one step ahead of him.

Chapter Five

One look at his face told her there was trouble ahead.

The sound of the truck had gotten everyone's attention, even breaking through Annie's reverie as she sat in the kitchen. It was Lyle Houston, and in the bed of the truck she could see two potbellied pigs.

Mike's lips were set in hard lines, his expression as he eyed the contents of the truck, disgusted. If she didn't get out there right away, she would have another strike against her. After all, the animals had been her idea.

She grabbed paper cups and a pitcher of lemonade and hurried outside to join the gathering.

"Hi, Miss Annie!" Joey rushed to meet her. "Mr. Houston brought us our pigs. And a portable pigpen, too!"

"I thought we agreed the pigs were to stay across the way," Mike said sourly. "How come they're here?"

"I figured the pigs were better off where the kids

could enjoy them all the time,'' Houston replied. ''You can return them anytime you like.'' His jovial attitude prevented Mike from making any other caustic comments.

Anytime he liked? If he had his way, the pigs would be on a return trip to Houston's property right now.

Lyle Houston climbed into the flatbed and handed down a baby pig into Mike's arms.

''That one's Frank, he's mine! I picked him out yesterday,'' Bobby shouted.

''And that one is Hannibal'' Joey hollered as Mike reached for the second pig. ''He's mine!''

''Hannibal?''

''Yeah. He's cool.''

''Who named it, you?''

''Sure,'' Joey replied. ''Bobby named his pig so I named mine.''

''Are you sure you want to call it Hannibal?'' Mike asked.

''Sure, I am. I like it. It's my favorite name for a pig,'' Joey insisted, looking ready to fight. ''Why not?''

''Because this Hannibal's a girl pig,'' Mike answered with a straight face. ''That's why not. Maybe you'd better call her Hannah.''

Wide-eyed, Joey stared at his squirming pig. ''I like Hannibal better,'' he said doubtfully. ''Who cares if it's an old girl pig, anyway?''

''Maybe Frank does.''

''Mike!'' Annie warned. He shrugged his shoul-

ders. The opportunity had been too good to pass up.

"It doesn't make a difference if the pigs are male or female," Annie declared. "It's all the same. After all, they're only pigs."

Mike swallowed a smile as he waved goodbye to Houston. If Annie thought there was no difference between genders, there was a big surprise in store for her.

Just then Hannibal squirmed loose, rolled through the mud and started to run in circles. Joey chased after her. Bobby howled with laughter, until his own piglet got away from him. Shouting for the pigs to stop, both boys started running after them. Joey tripped in the mud, and in seconds was followed by his brother.

Under other circumstances, Mike could have laughed, but the situation wasn't funny. Not to him. Not when he could see he had his work cut out for him.

"Oh, no! Bobby, Joey, stop this instant!" Annie hollered. She shot Mike a disgusted look as she started after the runaways.

And tripped over a shovel lying on the ground.

Mike rushed to her side and caught her by her arms before she could fall into the mud.

He'd never known skin could be so soft. So warm and silky, like the feel of velvet that had been left in the sunshine. He wanted to inhale her vanilla scent, to hold her, to taste her lips. To hold her close.

He was stunned at the direction his thoughts were taking. Maybe he shouldn't have touched her in the first place, or held her longer than it took to set her back on her feet. Most definitely not.

Not when he'd been lost the moment he met her eyes, felt her body instinctively mold itself to his, saw her tempting lips part in surprise. With a sinking feeling, he knew he should let her go, set her out of his arms before he did something foolish. Again.

Instead, he kissed her.

And she kissed him back.

Annie's lips were everything he'd imagined they would be: warm, vibrant, giving. And the kiss, at first hesitant, then fervent, was the kind of kiss that made a man think he'd surely died and gone to heaven.

He felt as though he'd captured the sun, an elusive moonbeam and a wood sprite, all rolled into the tantalizing body of one slender, golden-skinned woman. Everything he didn't need, everything he couldn't let himself want.

What sudden impulse had prompted him to keep her in his arms longer than he should have?

She'd looked up at him with parted lips, and the overwhelming impulse had taken its natural course—and had ended in a heart-stopping kiss that had taken him by surprise.

Annie Kramer might be eccentric and unpredictable, but she was beautiful to look at and more than satisfactory to hold. He held her close for several

moments, savored her unusual scent and the novelty of finding her in his arms.

He gazed in wonder into her dark eyes—eyes that sparkled in the sun, eyes that deepened as her gaze locked with his. Her bewildered expression told him she was as taken aback as he was at the turn of events and at the intensity of the unexpected kiss.

She was a woman he'd never seriously thought he would want to hold—until now. And now was too soon.

A few short hours ago he'd thought he'd had enough of her to last him a lifetime. He'd been looking forward to finding a way to get rid of her and go back to his carefully ordered routine. Instead, he'd given in to an impulse to taste her tempting lips, her honeyed mouth. And now, of all things, he found himself holding her close to him as if he never wanted to let her go.

What in the hell had he been thinking of?

He was stunned by his response to Annie. He'd learned the hard way not to get involved with the people it was his duty to protect. Never to take on their problems. To stay objective, to keep his distance. And never, *never* to let emotion cloud his thinking. He'd made the mistake of forgetting those cardinal rules of law enforcement once before—a mistake that had cost him his self-respect and his career.

Caring had gotten him nothing but heartache.

So what was he doing with the nanny from Venus in his arms?

Especially when he still sensed—no, *knew* as surely as he knew his own name—she wasn't the woman she claimed to be. The fatal attraction between them was dead wrong. She was a fake, or his name wasn't Mike Cassidy. And, heaven help him, he still wasn't even certain she was a harmless one.

Granted, she was lovable; or at least the kids thought so. Granted, one of her references had checked out. And granted, everyone in the household had taken to her. Maybe they weren't any more objective than he seemed to be when it came to Annie.

His sixth sense clamored for attention, reminding him he was in danger of being caught in another dangerous web of his own making. He had to end it here and now. There was too much at risk. He couldn't go through that agony again.

"Sorry," he said. He dropped his hands and stepped away from her. A relieved glance at the kids told him they were too busy with the pigs to be watching. "I didn't mean to do that."

"You didn't?" Her voice seemed to be caught in her throat— she was clearly as surprised as he was by the kiss.

"No. I guess I wasn't thinking too clearly at the time," Mike answered truthfully. "It was a mistake, right?" He felt a twinge of regret at the hurt expression that crossed her face, but he hardened

his heart. He couldn't afford to soften, to be taken in by bewildered eyes, trembling lips and his male need to protect. Not again. Instead of kissing her, what he should have done was run for his life.

"I guess I wasn't thinking too clearly, either," Annie finally replied. Shaken to her core, she could only meet his troubled gaze. For a man who hadn't meant to kiss her, he'd done a very thorough job.

"Maybe it's a condition that's catching," he said gruffly.

If he was trying to lighten the tension between them, it wasn't working.

Annie hadn't counted on finding a man like him guarding her sons. And certainly not a man who would stir her senses the way this one did. Bodyguards weren't supposed to be so handsome, so virile, so human; nor to kiss with an intensity that awakened unwelcome desire.

She'd expected to find him cold, dispassionate and definitely not interested in women after what Clara had said about him. She certainly hadn't expected him to kiss her so passionately. Nor had she expected to respond to him in the surprising way she had. No man had ever prompted such a heated reaction, she realized as she looked back at him in a daze of uncertainty. But then, her husband had never kissed her the way Mike had.

Once the original attraction between them had worn off, Robert had made love to her as if she were an amusing toy to be taken out, briefly held, and admired now and then. His lovemaking, if she

could call it that, had become routine, his mind
being elsewhere. Until he'd decided she was too
much of a free spirit and that she didn't fit his idea
of what a politician's wife should be. She'd agreed
to an amicable divorce and had never once regret-
ted the decision. But she was grateful to him for
her children.

As for what had just taken place between herself
and Mike, she knew enough to recognize sexual
tension when she felt it. The trouble was, she didn't
know what to do about it.

To her growing dismay, nothing had gone the
way she'd anticipated since she'd arrived to take
care of her sons. In fact, nothing had gone *right*
with her masquerade, either, or Mike wouldn't be
dogging her footsteps.

It definitely looked as if Clara's advice had been
the worst advice she could have taken.

Annie had noticed the look in his eyes when
she'd come into the kitchen that morning wearing
her altered dress and bright ribbon in her hair.
She'd felt the heat of his studied gaze—and, truth
be told, she'd felt a sudden warmth in her middle
and a quickening of her breath as she met his eyes.
She knew, as surely as she knew the moon would
rise in the night sky, she'd attracted his attention
as never before.

"Are you going to be okay with this?" Mike
asked, breaking into her thoughts. She could see he
was as surprised as she was at what had happened.

"Yes," Annie assured him before she could give

herself away. *No*, a little voice told her as she drew back from him. She had a sinking feeling nothing was going to be okay again, and maybe would be even worse than ever. She wasn't upset that he had kissed her. She was upset by the way she was beginning to feel about him.

No matter what Clara had said, Mike Cassidy had a passion inside him. A passion he didn't want anyone to see.

He might be meticulous in his ways, seemingly unaffected and starkly objective in his thinking, but was that the real man? In spite of his serious and sometimes-gruff exterior, she'd seen a softer side of him when he was with Bobby and Joey. And now with her.

Mike wasn't the man he appeared to be, any more than she was the woman she was trying to portray.

The noise and excitement around them drew her attention away from Mike.

The surrounding scene was sheer bedlam. The baby pigs were running around in circles, more agitated than ever. The boys were making their version of pig noises and trying to herd the piglets into the little portable pigpen Houston had brought with him.

"Come on, Hannibal!" Joey shouted as he jumped up and down. "Come on home!"

"You, too, Frank! Come on in here," Bobby coaxed. "I'll give you something good to eat if you do!"

Annie could see the waving and the frenzied shouting only served to bewilder the little pigs more than ever. Squealing, they kept running in ever-widening circles.

"Do something to help, don't just stand there!" Annie shouted at Mike.

"I told you, I don't know a thing about pigs," he answered. "Except, of course, how to identify their gender."

"Oh, stop that nonsense and try to catch Hannibal and Frank. If you don't do something, they'll get away!"

Gender was nonsense?

If she thought the differences between male and female were nonsense, no wonder Annie was a mixture of hot and cold femininity.

As for the little potbellied pigs getting away, that was fine with him, Mike thought as he watched the melee. The last thing he needed was to take charge of two hysterical animals and, unless he was mistaken, their progeny to come.

Except that he would have two unhappy young boys on his hands.

"Tell you what," he finally agreed, drawing on his crowd-control training. "You go on over there to the left side of them and I'll take the right side. Bobby, you keep trying to herd the pigs toward the pen. With Joey herding them from behind, maybe we'll be able to get them going in the right direction."

She nodded and took off like a streak of lightning.

He'd liked the way she'd kissed him. Now he even liked the way she ran. Her long legs flashed in the sun, her arms flailed in the air as she narrowed the distance between herself and the runaways. Even the sound of her voice trying to sweet-talk the piglets into slowing down and heading for their pen was pleasurable. Considering her track record of drawing instant admiration, he had no doubt the pigs would soon succumb.

"Mike!" Annie shouted when she saw him stop cold. "Don't give up now. The pigs are headed in your direction!"

Mike joined in the chase, trying hard to keep his eyes and mind on the job at hand. It was tough, especially since he had a full view of Annie at her uninhibited best. She was lunging from side to side, making pig noises and calling the pigs by name. Sparkling, vivacious, she was more woman than he'd ever thought possible after his first glimpse of her.

He couldn't believe the change in her. She was light-years from the way she'd appeared when he'd opened the door to find her insisting on a job interview. She'd been drab, uninteresting and, in his opinion, had looked as if she were from another planet.

After examining the contents of her bag, he wouldn't have guessed she had a sensible thought in her head. But in two short days in her company

he'd discovered she could be downright manipulative, shrewd and a fighter.

And as sexually tempting as hell.

She was going to be hard to get rid of—and even harder to forget.

"SORRY, MIKE, I've checked with the state motor-vehicle department. No driver's license has been issued to an Annie Kramer in Virginia."

"And the social-security records?"

"I couldn't find anything there, either," the voice over the phone confessed. "Are you sure you have the right name?"

"That's the one she's given, although I don't have much faith in its validity."

"She doesn't have a record, either. What did you say she's done?"

"Nothing, yet." Mike paused. The truth was the nanny hadn't done anything wrong, but, in his opinion, she also hadn't done anything right. "And, if I have any say about it, she's not going to be around here long enough to cause any more problems."

"How's that?"

"Oh, nothing that wouldn't sound as if I'm making it all up," Mike responded. "Thanks, Eric. I'll have to do some more digging and get back to you, if you don't mind."

"Sure, pal," his friend, Eric Cord, agreed. "Say, we sure miss you around here. You disappeared in such a hurry, I never had the chance to tell you I

wish things could have turned out differently. Besides checking into this woman, what else have you been up to lately?''

Mike scowled into the telephone receiver. If he told his former partner he was reduced to guarding two little potbellied pigs and their young owners, he would be the butt of jokes for the rest of his life.

"Oh, not much. At least, nothing exciting," he replied, thinking wryly of his current pig-control problem. "You might say, a little bit here and there. Thanks, again. I'll talk to you soon."

He settled back and studied the telephone. Eric's empty search ruled out confronting Annie. But there had to be some other way he could pin her down.

She had to have come from somewhere nearby to have registered with an employment agency in Annandale or in D.C. Until a driver's license or some other document could expose her, he would have to think of something else—even if he had to go through the telephone books and call employment agencies one by one until he found the one that had sent her to the Matthewses.

He wanted to identify the agency without calling on Mrs. Matthews and possibly upsetting everyone for nothing. He would look like a damn fool if Annie's story turned out to be true, even if he had growing doubts about that.

He suddenly remembered one of his grandmother's favorite expressions: "If one door closes, an-

other opens." It was just a matter of finding the open door. After a few moments' reflection, the "door" he found led to the kitchen.

"You're just in time to do a taste test for me," Mrs. Swenson announced when he strolled into her view. "It's a new recipe and I want to get it right."

Life was full of happy little surprises, Mike decided as he joined the cook by the stove. She'd given him a reason to spend some time with her. Maybe now he would be able to learn the name of the employment agency Mrs. Matthews used.

"Mrs. Swenson," he began as he sampled the curry sauce that was destined for tonight's dinner. "How was Mrs. Matthews lucky enough to find you?"

"Oh, go on with you." Mrs. Swenson blushed. "I worked for her cousin, Rose, until the poor soul passed away several months ago."

"How about Sharon? Did she come with you or was she hired through an employment agency?"

Before she answered, Mrs. Swenson put the wooden mixing spoon in the sink and rinsed it off. "Sharon came with me," she said. He could see speculation grow in her eyes. "Why don't you sit down, young man, and tell me just what all of this is about? You didn't come in here to sample my cooking, or my name isn't Clara Swenson."

"I just wanted to know the name of the employment agency Mrs. Matthews uses when she needs help," Mike replied honestly. He had too much respect for Mrs. Swenson to lie to her.

The cook stared at him for a long moment. "Why didn't you just come right out and ask her?"

Mike shrugged.

"In the first place, Mrs. Matthews and Sharon and I have only been here for a short time," the cook continued. "The congressman's previous help quit when he remarried three months ago. Like I told you, Sharon and I used to work for Mrs. Matthews's late cousin. I don't know how Annie was hired."

"Why do you suppose the previous help quit when they did?" Mike prompted.

"I'm no gossip," the cook demurred, but she went on anyway. "I heard it was out of loyalty to the first Mrs. Matthews. I gather they thought a lot of her and stayed after the divorce only because they hoped she'd reconcile with her husband."

That bit of information didn't surprise Mike. Some people inspired loyalty. After all, look at the way everyone had cozied into Annie's arms since her arrival. Maybe the previous Mrs. Matthews had been the same type of woman.

"About the employment agency Mrs. Matthews used to hire the nanny." Mike maneuvered the conversation back to his original question. "Do you happen to know which one it was?"

"I don't understand why you aren't asking Annie."

"No concrete reason, I'm afraid," he answered. "I suppose I'll have to take you into my confidence, but I have to ask you not to repeat what I

tell you. Not to anyone, and especially not to Annie.''

Mrs. Swenson's eyes narrowed as she waited for him to continue.

"There's something about Annie that doesn't ring true," he confided. "Not the timing of her arrival, her odd appearance, her references, or anything else about her. And not that she's done anything wrong. It's just a feeling I have about her.''

"And what do you intend to do about it?''

"Whatever it takes. After all, I'm here to protect the boys and that's what I intend to do. I wouldn't be taking care of them properly if I didn't look into the little things that bother me. And Annie bothers me.'' *In more ways than one,* he thought silently as he waited for Mrs. Swenson's reaction.

Her reaction wasn't long in coming. She folded her arms across her bosom, frowned and looked him straight in the eye.

"You can take it from me, young man. Annie isn't here to harm the boys. I could bet my life on it.''

He should have known better. Annie had made another fan.

He should have been satisfied by Mrs. Swenson's answer. Only when he went looking for Annie and the boys did he realize she hadn't given him her promise not to tell Annie.

Chapter Six

"What are you going to do with those?" Mike inquired when he found Annie in the family room filling slender tubes of black material with cotton batting. The boys were in the corner, busy arguing over a game of Scrabble and not paying attention to them. Even before she answered, he had a familiar premonition. This was going to be another day in a string of stranger-than-fiction days. He wasn't sure he wasn't going to like the answer any more than he'd liked any of the answers to his earlier questions.

"I'm making horns."

After a few days with Annie, he was resigned to her strange way of thinking and her zany ideas. But horns?

"I'm getting ready for a Halloween party," she added before he could comment. "I'm making costumes and masks."

"A Halloween party?" Mike took a firm grip on his sanity. "This is July, or hadn't you noticed?"

"Of course. But that shouldn't make a differ-

ence. Halloween is just a date on a calendar. It seems to me a person ought to be able to have a party anytime they feel like it. Maybe you'd like me to help you with a costume, too.''

"Me, in a Halloween costume? Not on your life! I didn't have one when I was a kid and I'm not going to dress up in one now, either.''

"You didn't?'' Her pitying look suddenly made him wonder if he had had a deprived childhood. He thought back to the days when Halloween had meant he could hand out penny peppermint sticks for trick-or-treat. They had been too poor to do anything else. From what he recalled, at least that part of it had been fun. He'd probably eaten as much of the sweet stuff as he'd given out. As for wearing a costume, if not dressing up in sheets and scaring the hell out of himself made him deprived, then he was guilty. He stopped his reflection. His childhood wasn't the issue here. Annie had to be up to something.

He studied her carefully. Nothing about Annie added up, but he was sure about one thing: She didn't have a sensible idea in her head.

What could have brought on this off-the-wall idea of celebrating Halloween in July? In his mind, there was only one reason: She was trying to throw him and his suspicions of her off track.

"You aren't serious, are you?" he asked.

"Of course, I am."

"Holy cow!" he exclaimed. "If I hadn't heard it from your lips, I would never have believed it."

After the way Mike had been behaving, his negative reaction didn't come as a surprise to Annie. But she hadn't expected anything like this. Celebrating Halloween in July was a bit unusual, she was willing to concede, but it wasn't a crime.

"I'm just trying to keep the boys occupied, just as you asked me to," she replied innocently.

Mike snorted. "You really don't see anything weird about celebrating Halloween in the middle of the summer, do you?"

"Of course not. I've done it for years with the children."

It wasn't a custom she could expect Mike to understand, but she and the boys had celebrated holidays whenever the fancy had suited them. It was little enough to do for them.

She tried to give Bobby and Joey traditions of their own, to give them happy memories of their childhood. And she believed in giving them free rein to their imaginations, provided they earned what they wanted and didn't hurt anyone in the process.

She looked up to see Mike studying her closely. If he'd asked her something, she hadn't heard it.

"With your own children?" he repeated. His gaze locked with hers as he waited for her answer.

Stabbed by his piercing eyes, Annie felt her heart start to race. Somehow she managed a smile. "With the children I care for," she replied in what she hoped was an even voice. After all, it was the truth.

"It's not only the Halloween party I'm talking about," he said after a moment's pause. "It's everything, including going over next door without telling me and our winding up with pigs in the backyard."

"Maybe that was a mistake," she conceded. "But a Halloween party isn't."

Silenced but not cowed, Annie stood her ground. He was too annoyed for her to make him understand the boys' welfare was more important to her than it was to him. As for taking the boys outside the property boundaries, he was right. If the rumors were correct—and she prayed they weren't—it wasn't safe. But, it was also wrong to turn her children into prisoners.

"I've only been trying to keep the boys too busy to miss their friends and familiar surroundings. I should think you'd feel grateful to me for doing what you told me to do!"

"True," he admitted. "But I didn't expect something like this." She looked like innocence personified, but after a few days spent in her company Mike still doubted that innocence. There couldn't possibly be a person like Annie, unless it was in storybooks or in the movies; even Mary Poppins was a figment of someone's imagination.

He had to admit she was right about the Halloween party and he was wrong, but he wasn't prepared to tell her so. The truth was, he *was* upset. It was becoming harder and harder to concentrate

on the job he was getting paid to do with her around as a distraction.

"I'm not taking any chances," he finally said. "If you have to have a Halloween party, then go ahead. But it's just for you and the boys, unless Mrs. Swenson and Sharon are in the mood to go along with you. And no masks," he ordered. "I want to be able to see everyone's faces. And while I'm making the ground rules for this great event, let's get this straight: I'm just watching on the sidelines. I am *not* going to wear a costume or play games."

Clara Swenson came to the door. "Annie, can I see you in the kitchen for a moment?"

As soon as she and Annie were out of Mike's hearing, she whispered, "I'd be careful about upsetting Mike, if I were you, dear. The madder he gets, the more he wonders about you. He's already been asking me questions about the employment agency and where you came from. I told him I don't know anything about you and I don't want to. But I thought you should know."

Annie nodded. "Maybe I'd better go back and try to be friendly."

"That's my girl." Mrs. Swenson hugged Annie. "You can get more—"

"Bees with honey than with vinegar," Annie finished. "It's one of my mother's favorite expressions. I do try to remember that, but Mike has the strangest way of getting to me."

"I don't doubt that for a minute." Clara smiled at her and turned away.

Now what did Clara mean by that remark? Annie wondered as she headed back to the family room. And why had there been a twinkle in her eye when she'd said it? She gazed thoughtfully at the closed kitchen door. Had Clara seen the embrace she and Mike had exchanged earlier?

Annie blushed just remembering the kiss, the texture of his firm lips and hard, muscled arms that had held her close. Her lips began to tingle at the memory.

This had to stop, she thought firmly. She was here for the boys, not to become romantically involved with the bodyguard. After all, she'd been there, done that with her ex-husband. The difference, said a little voice inside her head, was that Mike kissed her as though he meant it. Angry and all, he had looked at her as if she was a real person, worthy of consideration. That was more than her ex had done.

Yes, something told her she would be far better off having Mike as a friend than an adversary.

MIKE'S FEARS WERE realized when Annie and the boys showed up the next afternoon wearing their Halloween costumes.

After getting a look at Annie's costume, Mike couldn't take his eyes off her.

She was wearing a skintight black bodysuit, unadorned except for a white collar, a black bow tie,

and two golden chains around her waist. She carried a real pitchfork and, apart from a few loose tendrils, a black kerchief held back her hair from her face. Every enticing inch of her was hidden and at the same time clearly revealed to his fascinated gaze. He took another look. She was even wearing the horns she'd made.

The costume was not only breathtaking, it was something he would have expected Sharon to wear—not thrift-shop Annie. A quick look at Sharon's beaming face gave away the costume's donor.

"Don't you think the weather is a little too hot and sultry for that getup?" he inquired when he could catch his breath. He would have thought Annie would have come up with a cooler costume, but then, that was probably too logical for her. If she took any time to stop and think, it didn't show.

"Oh, I feel fine." She smiled happily. "Absolutely great."

Sure as hell, she'd found another way to torment him.

He glanced over at Bobby and Joey as they trailed into the kitchen. The boys wore matching black pajamas. White collars and small black bow ties had been added to their costumes, just as they had to their nanny's. Each of them carried a miniature pitchfork made out of starched red napkins.

Annie must have been working overtime last night and this morning.

It was easy to see the boys were supposed to be little devils, although until they'd come under An-

nie's influence, they'd been pretty quiet. Now their eyes sparkled, their young bodies were animated. And as for their nanny, he thought as he took in her costume, she was right in character as a she-devil. Especially with the braided black tail she'd pinned to the back of her perfectly formed derriere.

The three of them looked too pleased with themselves for Mike's peace of mind. He wasn't so pleased. Especially when he got the message. In her own not-so-innocent way, he was willing to bet Annie was trying to tell him he had three devils to contend with today. Hell, he could handle that. It was Annie's sex appeal he was having difficulty coping with.

"Hi." Annie smiled tentatively at him as she handed him a miniature pumpkin fashioned out of an orange napkin. "Happy Halloween."

"Thanks," he muttered, trying hard not to stare at her, but it was almost impossible. Not when she was only inches away from him. Her costume fit as if it had been painted on her, breathing when she breathed. Nothing was left to his imagination.

Afraid of what might come next, he started for the door. "I've got to go upstairs for a minute," he told Mrs. Swenson. "I'll be right back."

He took the stairs two at a time, anxious to get his mind off Annie the she-devil.

He'd intended to remain upstairs just long enough to cool off, but it was a good opportunity to check her room for incriminating evidence.

The nanny's bedroom was neat as a pin—too

neat, considering her normally breezy personality. She'd seemed to be the kind of woman who needed a maid, not to mention a cook and a bodyguard of her own to keep her out of trouble.

The bathroom was next. Bathrooms could be tidied up, but his experience told him people had an odd way of leaving revealing clues behind them that gave them away. Fresh towels and a washcloth hung neatly on the towel racks. The tub and the washbasin had been wiped dry. If he hadn't known better, he wouldn't have believed the room had been in use at all.

He rummaged fruitlessly through the empty wastepaper basket and the few items on the shelves behind the bathroom mirror: toothbrush, toothpaste, aspirin, lipstick. He even went back into the bedroom and began to carefully check through the dresser drawers.

As far as he was concerned, the very neatness of the rooms was incriminating. And, to his way of thinking, it made the Annie he knew more of an enigma than ever.

What he eventually did find sent his blood racing. Annie might normally be staid and stuffy on the outside, but her lingerie told another story. In one of the dresser drawers were lacy bras and matching skimpy briefs. And they weren't just plain colors. No, sir. They were purple and pink, red and black— definitely not the type of garments the Annie Kramer of four days ago would have worn. That Annie would have worn long johns,

even in the heat of summer. The Annie of today, yes, but that didn't add up, either. Unless she'd been dressing in a costume all along.

He checked further. Carefully concealed among her underwear, but not concealed enough, he found eyedrops and a kit for storing and cleaning contact lenses.

Why would anyone try to hide such commonly used items? Unless she didn't want anyone to know she wore contact lenses, which didn't make much sense. Or unless she was disguising the true color of her eyes.

One and one began to add up.

"DID YOU FIND WHAT you were looking for?" Annie asked, all innocence when he came back into the kitchen.

Too innocent, Mike mused. It was obvious she'd anticipated he would search her room. No wonder he couldn't find anything that might give her away.

He glanced sharply at the nanny. She looked as if butter could melt in her mouth, but he knew better. There wasn't an inch of her black-clad body and dark eyes that rang true. Not outwardly, that was. As for what he'd gathered from her sexy underwear, that didn't ring true, either.

"Who said I was looking for something?"

"Why, you did."

"No, ma'am. I just said I was going upstairs for a minute." He watched Annie exchange a quick glance with Mrs. Swenson before a blush came

over Annie's face. The contrast between Annie's now rosy complexion and her black kerchief made her look sexier than ever.

He didn't know what he'd done to deserve another woman in his life like this, sensual and appealing. One should have been more than enough. If he was being punished for his sin of having been too soft on a needy woman before, he'd been punished enough. He was a bodyguard now instead of police detective only because he'd made the fatal mistake of trusting a woman.

"Let's get on with the party," Mrs. Swenson announced. "I have everything ready and waiting to take outside."

Party? Outside? Mike had been so busy thinking about his past mistake he hadn't had time to check out everyone else's costume. He looked at the cook and finally realized she'd made a few changes in her own appearance, too. The white apron was still there, but this morning, she resembled a character out of a nursery rhyme: Mother Hubbard?

And there was Sharon, in sharp contrast with Annie, quaintly dressed as a shepherdess. It should have been the other way around.

He looked around the kitchen where preparations for the festivities were evident. There was a small tub of water with apples bobbing on the surface, a platter of cookies decorated with smiling black-and-orange faces, and an assortment of games. A shopping bag held prizes. There was definitely going to be a party.

He was going to have to be twice as careful as usual to ensure the boys' safety, and three times as careful to keep out of Annie's possible plans to include him in the party.

Outside, he prowled the perimeter of the fenced kitchen yard, checked the latch on the pigpen to make sure the pigs didn't join in the fun. A quick glance told him the driveway leading to the yard was empty. No cars were around. Satisfied everything was in order, he leaned against the wall and watched the hijinks going on in the kitchen yard.

Annie had pinned a picture of a donkey on the trunk of a tree. With an apologetic glance in his direction, she blindfolded the boys one by one, spun them around and instructed them to pin a paper tail on the donkey. Even Mrs. Swenson and Sharon each took a turn. Everyone cheered when Joey pinned the tail four inches from the donkey's rear and took the prize, a hand-knit key chain.

"We could use you in the next game, Mike," Annie invited. "We're going to have a sack race and we need one more body."

"Sack race?"

"Sure. We all pair off, one foot of each partner inside the sack, and then we race each other. We need one more person to make things even."

Clara grabbed Joey. "Joey, you can race with me. Bobby, you race with Sharon." She handed Mike an empty burlap bag. "And you can race with Annie."

"I don't think so," he answered, frowning at the

cook. Enough was enough. "I'm not very good at that sort of thing."

"Try it," Clara coaxed. "Otherwise Annie can't play. You might like it."

He would like it, Mike knew. In fact, he would probably like it too much. But, as the cook had pointed out, if he didn't participate, Annie would be left on the sidelines.

"Okay." Mike smothered a false sigh. It was four to one. He didn't have a chance, not that he wanted one. He held the sack until Annie could put one shapely black-clad leg inside it and then stepped in. Mike bit back a smart remark and joined her.

"Now, put your arm around your partner," Clara instructed, "and hold on tight."

Mike dutifully put his arm around Annie's shoulders. She responded by putting her arm around his waist. The silky material, warmed by the sun, rubbed against his bare arm, and her faint vanilla scent assailed his senses. At the rate he was going, he doubted he would ever make the finish line.

At a sharp "Go!" from Clara, they set off.

Annie's shoulder fell against his with every hop. Her soft arm bumped against his and took his mind off the race and put it squarely on Annie. He'd never been so aware of a woman before.

For sure, he wasn't going to let it happen again, he vowed. After the race, he wasn't going to get within ten feet of Annie.

So preoccupied by his partner, he was surprised

to find they'd won. A quick kiss on his cheek and a set of colored pencils were his reward. Too bad the donor was Mrs. Swenson.

Bobbing for apples was next.

He watched Bobby put his arms behind him and try to catch a floating apple in his teeth. Several tries later, the kid caught the apple by its stem. A giggling Sharon and Clara were more successful. Not Joey—he was soaking from the top of his head to his toes in no time. Poor kid, this time he was going to get the booby prize. And sure enough, Annie had one waiting.

"Now you, Miss Annie!"

Annie set aside her pitchfork, pushed back her horns and made ready to bob for an apple.

Mike held his breath until she lifted her head, an apple safely between her teeth. Her flushed face glowed with her success, her laughter filled the air as she held up the apple and took a bite of the shining red fruit. Mike couldn't help but feel like Adam to her Eve.

Afterward, Sharon offered cold apple cider, the cook her homemade pumpkin cookies. Annie hugged the boys to her and soon everyone was laughing and joking.

Ever since Annie had shown up, Bobby and Joey had been smiling. Before then, Mike suddenly realized, they'd been too well-mannered and subdued to be real. Well, whatever she was doing, she definitely was a good influence on them.

By the time the partygoers trudged back to the

house, he was left with a wistful longing for the Halloweens past he'd never taken time to enjoy. And he wondered what other brilliant ideas Annie had planned.

He asked her while they gathered up the games and headed for the house.

"That's all for today. Halloween is over," she announced as she slunk past him in the costume. "Tomorrow is another day."

"Thanks a bunch for that bit of news," he muttered as he stared after her. Maybe Annie wasn't aware of what she was doing to him, but he wouldn't take bets on it.

"We'll talk later about what the boys want to do tomorrow. Right now we all need to change," Annie called over her shoulder as she started up the stairs, her tail tantalizing him as she disappeared from sight.

He was grateful to her for leaving. He couldn't stand a full day with her in that costume. After all, a man could take only so much.

Mike was torn between his growing fascination for the way Annie's mind worked and his uneasy suspicions that she was up to no good. In her own eccentric way, she was funny. And when she wasn't making him angry, she made him laugh— laughter he took great pains to hide; it would only have encouraged her to greater heights of creativity.

He kept that confession to himself, prepared to deny it if anyone asked.

Actually, in spite of his growing suspicions about her true identity, he found it difficult to resist the golden glow of love and affection that surrounded Annie. Whatever it was about her that drew Mrs. Swenson, Sharon, and everyone who came in contact with her, it was beginning to work on him, too. In her own unconventional way, Annie Kramer was the most interesting woman he'd ever met. And one of the most confusing.

And definitely the sexiest.

But how could he be so attracted to Annie, with her zany ideas and quick mind, when she spelled trouble? Trouble so thick he could almost taste it.

Chapter Seven

She'd already knocked the hell out of most of his professional credos, but "Don't leave yourself open to surprises" was one Mike wasn't going to let Annie demolish, too.

He waited in the family room while she put the boys to bed. Whatever ideas she'd come up with for tomorrow, he intended to know about them tonight.

"The boys in bed?" he asked when she appeared and dropped into a chintz-covered armchair opposite him. Thank goodness she was back to the makeshift sundress. He didn't know how he could have stood it if she'd still been wearing the she-devil outfit.

"Yes," she answered absently. "It took me longer to get them settled than I thought it would."

"You were great with them today, you know." In the interests of peace and harmony, he was going to try to be more open-minded and give credit where credit was due. "I haven't seen the boys so happy before now. In fact," he added with a wry

grin, "they're behaving more like kids since you arrived."

"Thank you," she said as if he'd been discussing the weather.

"Maybe it helps to think like a kid?"

"Yes," she answered. "It's something grown-ups sometimes forget." This time her smile was real.

He could see her thoughts were elsewhere, that she had something to say and didn't quite know how to say it. If she was that undecided, it probably had something to do with him. Not that he blamed her for being cautious.

"Well, what's next?" he asked. The sooner she came out with it, the better. He would have more time to get his own ducks in order.

"The boys want to go to the beach tomorrow. I told them you'd probably be willing to go along with them."

No matter what she'd told the boys, he knew, from the tone of her voice, she wasn't too sure she would be right about his reaction.

Hell! She was at it again, trying to get him to let the kids have their own way. Even after he'd explained why he didn't want them out in the open or in crowded areas!

He should have known that any idea on Annie's agenda wouldn't be a simple, uncomplicated request. Although he had to give her some credit. The air-conditioning had finally been fixed, but with the continued heat and humidity still almost intolera-

ble, this latest idea made a little more sense than her previous ones. Short of keeping the kids in the house every day, there was no way out.

"First of all, the closest beach is Rehoboth, Delaware, and that's at least ninety miles way," he rationalized as patiently as he could. "Secondly, kids are notoriously poor auto travelers. And most important, there are bound to be hundreds of beachgoers swarming the place. Maybe we could overcome the first and second problems, but the third is out of my hands."

"We could go early in the morning, before the crowds come," she suggested hopefully. "And, after all, you'll be there."

No matter how hard he'd tried to make Annie listen to reason, it was obvious to Mike that she and the boys had their hearts set on going to the beach. Cool ocean breezes were tempting. Crowded beaches were not. Under different conditions, he might have said yes.

"We've been to Rehoboth Beach plenty of times," Annie added. "Actually, we enjoyed it so much we've always felt it was worth the time it takes to get there."

"We?" Mike inquired, treading carefully now that his sixth sense was back clamoring for attention. He was getting somewhere at last. Maybe now he would find out who the "we" was she'd mentioned once before. "Who's we?"

"Er…"

Got her! Mike thought as he noted her hesitation. "Yes?" he prompted.

"With my previous charges!" she finished with a flourish.

"'Previous charges,' sure," he agreed solemnly. "You did the driving yourself, did you?"

"Of course."

"Of course," he echoed. "So you *do* have a driver's license?"

"I told you I had one the day I got here," she answered. "It's just been suspended for sixty days." Under his undisguised close scrutiny, a blush crossed her face.

She might not be truthful, but as far as Mike could tell, Annie wasn't a professional liar. Whoever she was, and whatever she was up to, she was an amateur.

"So you said." He studied her for a long moment before he abruptly inquired, "And in what state did you get your driver's license?"

"This one, of course—Virginia." She replied without hesitation as she looked down at her lap and twisted and untwisted a fold of her skirt with her fingers.

It was a sure sign of stress if he ever saw one, Mike thought as he watched her slender white fingers smooth the creases in the cloth. His instinctive reaction was to wonder what it would be like to have her fingers stroking his in the same sensuous motion. Just the thought made his body stir. His second reaction was to wonder just what she had

to be so nervous about. And how did it affect the boys?

"Under what name, Mary Poppins?" Experience had taught him to be blunt, to catch his adversaries off guard before they had a chance to come up with an alibi. But he had to keep his cool or he would only scare her off.

"My maiden name, Anna Sanders."

He didn't believe that one, either, but he would check as soon as he could. It was just a matter of time before she tripped herself up. In fact, he was sure Annie was some kind of fake. He intended to mention it to the congressman when he called. *If* he called. In the meantime, he intended to be more on his guard than ever.

"So tell me, what other names do you use?"

At the cornered look that came over her face, he felt cruel for baiting her. But he'd been taken in once before by a woman like her and he didn't intend to be taken in again.

Still, it was almost as though he *didn't* want her to be guilty of something, whatever that something was. For the first time in his life, he *wanted* to be wrong. In fact, when she remained silent, he felt strangely relieved. After all, his suspicions were only that. He hadn't found any real proof she wasn't who she said she was.

Not that it mattered; not at the moment, anyway. He had to expose her for the sake of the boys. It was his job.

"Cat got your tongue, I see." When she still

didn't reply, he said, "Have it your way. I'm going to find out, sooner or later." He smiled and settled back in his chair. He had ways to find the truth, now that he was sure she was hiding something. At her look of relief, he thought again. She'd gotten the message all wrong. No matter how he was beginning to feel about her, he was determined to get his answers, one way or another. Getting the truth out of her was another story.

"Now, about this trip to the beach. I'm willing to go along with anything that's reasonable. But this isn't reasonable. I figure it would take us almost two hours just to get there and another two hours to get back. Besides, it's bound to be crowded. I'm sure we'd have problems with antsy kids," he added.

She sat listening politely. He gave up. Reasoning with Annie was futile.

When had she done anything he thought was normal or reasonable since he'd met up with her?

All he could envision as they spoke was Annie in her skintight black she-devil costume. Or, now that she'd brought up the beach, Annie in a brief bathing suit. All he could recall was how sweet she'd tasted when he'd kissed her. And all he could think about was when he could kiss her again. From the heartfelt look he remembered in her eyes, he was willing to bet the feeling was mutual.

Too bad she was married. Considering how she'd reacted to their kiss, either she'd been away from her husband too long or she was one of those

women who trade on their sensuality to bring a man to his knees. If so, she had another think coming. No matter how attracted he was to her, he wasn't going to get stupid.

"Try again," he finally told her. "I'm sure you could find something to do around here if you put your mind to it. I'm going up to explain to the boys why we can't go. Maybe they'll see it my way, even if you don't."

"SO YOU SEE," he ended after explaining to the boys that the reason for not going to the beach was out of concern for their welfare, "it's not that I have anything against going to the beach. I care about you guys."

"Didn't you get to go to the beach when you were little, either?" Joey asked. His piquant little face was troubled, his blue eyes clouded.

"Not too often, although it was for a different reason," Mike told him. He wished things were otherwise for the little guy, but they weren't. "I started working summers when I was twelve, mowing lawns and taking care of other people's pets to help out at home."

"Didn't you want to go?"

"Sure, but we didn't have a lot of money. I knew I had to help my grandmother."

"We used to go to the beach when we lived with our mom," Bobby said, a wistful look on his face. "Everything's changed since we came to live with Dad. I wish we could go again."

"Me, too," Joey added. "I wish we lived with Mom. She'd let us go."

"OKAY, BOBBY. START BY counting all the vans we see on the road. Joey, you count the cars. And silently, to yourselves," Annie admonished. "I'll ask for a count in twenty minutes. The winner will get to choose a prize I have in my bag. Now remember, no fighting."

Mike was grateful. He wasn't looking forward to a shouting match between the boys. Not when he was trapped in the car for two hours. How had he gotten into this? But the boys had looked so sad last night that more than anything, Mike wanted to put smiles back on their faces. And as long as Annie was going to come up with a prize every twenty minutes to keep the boys happy, it was okay.

He glanced in the rearview mirror and saw the boys engrossed in their activity, their lips moving as they counted the vehicles. Beside him, Annie was rummaging in that giant bag of hers for prizes. The bag bulged with nonsensical stuff she'd spent at least half an hour rounding up.

There was more paraphernalia in the trunk of the car. Mrs. Swenson had sent them off with enough food for days instead of one afternoon. There were even two beach chairs, blankets, pillows and a cooler loaded with cold drinks. Joey had put up such a fuss over leaving his favorite beach ball in the trunk, he'd been allowed to keep it on his lap.

When it bounced into the front set, Annie grabbed it and put in on the floor under her feet.

As she leaned over, a stolen glance revealed golden skin and a tantalizing mole between her breasts. Mike swallowed hard before he turned his attention back to the road.

Even so, he was taken by the picture Annie and the boys made. The loving looks and smiles being exchanged were enough to make even a cynical man like himself believe in marriage and fatherhood.

If ever a woman was meant to be a mother, Mike thought, it was Annie. Too bad she no longer had children of her own.

IT WAS STILL EARLY when Mike gratefully pulled up in a parking lot by the boardwalk. The ocean shimmered in the early-morning sun and, thank goodness, it was still relatively cool. Only a smattering of people marred the pristine white sandy beach.

In the distance, he could see the amusement center and people waiting for the rides to start. As far as he was concerned, the amusement area was definitely out of bounds.

"Race you down to the Ferris wheel!" Bobby shouted as he started off down the boardwalk.

"No fair!" Joey hollered, getting ready to chase after his brother. "You had a head start!"

"Stop right there, both of you!" Annie raised her voice above the verbal exchange. "First things

first. Come back here and help carry our things to the beach. You can play later!''

She went around to the back of the car to help Mike. ''Come to think of it, you're not dressed for the beach,'' she said, taking in the light jacket Mike wore over his jeans.

''Of course not,'' he replied. ''Just where did you expect me to keep my holster?''

''Holster?'' Annie felt herself blanch. ''Like in gun holster?''

''You bet,'' he replied. ''But keep your voice down, please. We don't want to attract attention.''

''Don't you need a permit to carry a concealed weapon?'' she whispered.

''Got one,'' Mike answered shortly. ''The better to protect the boys with.''

The mere thought of guns around her children made Annie shiver. At least the boys were immune to Mike's presence. They'd been hurt enough by her and Robert's divorce; she didn't want any more unhappiness or worry in their lives. Shaking off these unpleasant thoughts and determining to give them a great day, she grabbed a load of towels and a blanket and started for the front of the car.

On her way, she sent cautious glances around her in case there might be someone nearby who would recognize her. So far, her disguise had been holding up but her nerves couldn't take worrying over whether she'd bump into someone who knew her. She felt uncomfortable living a lie—but it had been

a risk she'd taken for the boys' sake. She would do it and more for them, if she had to.

Bobby and Joey were nowhere in sight when she rounded the car. She froze. After all she'd told them, the boys should have known better. Heaven only knew what Mike would think if they disappeared now. He would have her head on a silver platter. She had to find them and bring them back before Mike had a chance to be really upset.

"Mike! I'm going to get the boys!" she shouted. Without so much as a fleeting look behind her, she dropped her bundle on the hood of the car and streaked down the boardwalk toward the amusement area.

Mike heard Annie's shout and a wave of icy fear ran over him. Instinct told him something was wrong, very wrong. He dropped the beach chairs and blankets into the trunk and ran around to the front of the car. In spite of his repeated warnings to stay with him, Annie and the boys were nowhere in sight! She must have taken this opportunity to carry out some kind of plan. But how, where? he wondered as he frantically looked around him. He'd only taken his eyes off them for a few minutes. Did she have an accomplice waiting for her?

Damn! So Annie *was* a fraud! He'd been taken in by her innocent ways and empty promises. The realization she'd had more than enough time between last night and this morning to line up accomplices didn't help. She must have had them waiting

for him to show up. He should have suspected something when he'd parked in the place she'd pointed out as the perfect spot for swimming.

Whoever had taken the boys, Annie had vanished along with them. He cursed himself up and down, backward and forward, as he searched the horizon for their familiar figures.

His worst fears were realized. The past had repeated itself. He'd been betrayed by another woman, and worst of all, by one he'd actually started to admire, had even begun to like.

He pulled his cellular phone out of his jacket pocket, ready to call the Rehoboth Beach police, the state troopers and the D.C. police, if he had to. Annie wasn't going to get away with this, unless it was over his dead body.

"SO TELL ME, MR. CASSIDY. Just what does this woman look like?" The local policeman held a pencil poised above his notebook.

Mike pondered the question. What identifiable information could he provide about Annie? Not that he was sure anymore just what she did look like. Was she the plain-Jane nanny with the old-fashioned dresses, or the seductress who had his emotions in a tailspin?

How could he go about describing Annie? And who would believe him, anyway?

"She's tall, about five feet eight," he began. "Brown eyes, maybe, and brown hair. Her purple finger- and toenail polish is enough to blind you

and she's wearing a dress no woman in her right mind would want to be seen in.''

"I see," the policeman answered, writing rapidly. "Not exactly your everyday type, is she?"

"Definitely not!" Torn between anger at himself and worry over the boys, Mike was ready to wring Annie's neck if she ever came within arm's reach again.

"And the boys?"

"Joey is seven, Bobby is nine. I have their picture right here." Mike dug into his jacket pocket for the snapshot he always carried with him just in case—and one he'd hoped he would never have to use. It looked as if this was the "just in case."

"How long has this Annie Kramer been their nanny?"

"Not quite a week."

"And they went with her without a struggle? Seems kind of strange, doesn't it?"

"Not if you knew the nanny," Mike growled. "She has the damndest way of getting people to like her right away. Before you know what's hit you, she's got you, sure and fast. In fact, she charms people the first time they meet her."

The policeman regarded him closely. "You sound a little bitter. You included?"

"Hell, no!" Mike retorted, knowing damn well he was lying through his teeth. "She's charming enough, but I've got a job to do."

The man raised an eyebrow after he looked at the snapshot. "Did you say they're the children of

a congressman? Hmm. Just how popular is the guy?''

"It's not his popularity, it's his money," Mike replied. "The Matthews family is loaded."

"*The* Matthews family?"

"Unfortunately, yes."

"Well, that puts a more serious light on their disappearance." The policeman closed his notebook and put it in his pocket. "I'm going to call this one in on my car radio—straight to the top. I'll be back in a minute."

Before Mike could respond, a large rubber beach ball bounced into his back and a familiar voice called his name.

"Mike! Look what I found in the sand near the Ferris wheel!"

It was Joey holding up a dried starfish. Close on his heels came Bobby. Their nanny brought up the rear of the parade. The boys were laughing, Annie was not. She looked troubled.

Mike wasn't laughing, either.

Now that she was safely back with the kids, his first instinct was to call off the cop and apologize. His second one was to grab Annie, shake her to see if she was real and to kiss her senseless. He wished he could give in to the insane impulse, but they had company. Besides, he was too damn angry.

He grabbed her around her shoulders and pulled her to him, ready to shake her. His relief quickly turned to anger. "Where the hell have you been?"

he ground out between set lips. "How could you do this to me after you agreed to follow my rules if I brought you here?" He looked into the tempting eyes that troubled him and breathed in her now familiar vanilla scent. With a sigh, he buried his face in her silken hair.

Under the brilliant sunshine, her hair blowing slightly in the ocean breeze, Mike couldn't help but notice that the roots of her hair looked blond—and the rest was becoming decidedly lighter. She dyed her hair. His heart damn near stopped as he held her away from him and searched her face. Unbidden, one thought clamored in his mind: If Annie dyed her hair, what else was she hiding? She was going to have to do a lot of explaining when they returned home, and so were the kids. And this time, he wasn't going to give up until he'd gotten the truth out of them. "Guess this must be the lady you were so worried about." The voice of the Rehoboth Beach lawman came from behind Mike's shoulder.

"You called the police?" There was a note of horror in Annie's voice.

"Of course," Mike retorted. If she was so afraid of the police, she definitely was hiding something. "Isn't that what you'd expect me to do under the circumstances?"

"I told you where I was going! You've only managed to frighten the boys, and me, too."

"Then you and the boys should have listened to me when I told you to stay put."

Mike glanced over his shoulder. "It looks as if we've attracted an audience, worse luck. I was hoping no one would notice we were here. Now the whole damn beach knows."

He took a deep breath. The rest of the lecture would have to wait for later when they were alone. If she didn't promise to tell him the truth and nothing but the truth, he would arrange to give her her walking papers. No matter how much he was attracted to her.

"You were right," Annie agreed. With a last look at Mike, she moved away. His rigid body stance told her she was in more trouble than she might be able to handle. And that it wasn't only her chasing after the boys.

She eyed the growing crowd of curiosity seekers. Good Lord, if this got into the papers, her whole masquerade would surely blow up in her face. She refused to even think what Robert would do when he found out.

And what was she going to do about Mike? Not only had she come to respect him for the conscientious job he was doing as bodyguard to Bobby and Joey, she was taken by his obvious compassion for them. A compassion that had prompted him to play baseball with them and to bring them to the beach when he had good reason not to.

As for herself, she was drawn to his strength, his dark and dangerous appearance and the way he gazed at her when he thought she wasn't looking. The one kiss they'd shared had remained with her.

She'd hoped there could be others. But now, maybe not.

It wasn't fair to Mike to continue this way—not when she was a fraud and living a lie.

"Don't be mad at Miss Annie, Mike," Bobby said as he and his brother clutched Annie's hands. "It was all my fault. I wanted to race Joey to the Ferris wheel."

"Yeah, and I had to go after my beach ball when it got away from me." Joey eyed Mike manfully ready to take his punishment. "It's me you should be mad at. I guess it was partly my fault, too."

"After being cooped up in the car for two hours, it was just instinct to run," Annie offered in her children's defense. She put her arms around the boys and hugged them to her. "If we'd stopped a couple of times along the way this wouldn't have happened."

"You didn't ask, or I would have. Anything would have been better than this," Mike commented with a wry look at the policeman.

"I was afraid you'd get impatient," Annie explained. "I didn't want you to call the whole thing off."

"Better impatient than this. Considering what just happened, stopping once or twice would have been worth it."

"You're right. It won't happen again." She was apologizing for more than rest stops; Mike was the last man she wanted to hurt, but her sons' happiness came first. "I'll remember for the next time."

"Don't hold your breath," he answered with a fatalistic shrug. "I'm not anxious to repeat this experience."

"Well, folks," the police officer called out to the onlookers, "I guess it was just a false alarm. Go along and enjoy yourselves."

He waited until the spectators drifted away. "If it's okay with you, Mr. Cassidy, I'm going to put this down on my report as a family misunderstanding. Let's just hope it doesn't happen again." He eyed Bobby and Joey sternly. "You guys stick close to Mr. Cassidy. No more running away. I don't want to have to come looking for you."

As he left, he winked broadly at Mike.

Annie felt sorry for Bobby and Joey as they stood there openmouthed and wide-eyed. From their expressions, she was certain they thought they would be put in jail the next time they got into trouble. She was going to have another motherly heart-to-heart with them. She knew from experience that lengthy lectures didn't work, so she would do it in a sentence or two they wouldn't forget.

She took another look at Mike. He wasn't through with the kids. Somehow she knew he wasn't through with her yet, either.

"WHAT DO YOU MEAN you didn't bring along a bathing suit?"

Annie hesitated. Her lack of a bathing suit was

only a cover. Really, she was afraid the salt water would rinse out whatever hair color she had left.

As for the bathing suit, she had one in her bag, just in case. But after the way Mike had eyed her the past few days, she wasn't about to let him see her in it. The last thing she wanted to do was whet his appetite—or her own.

"Well, I guess I'll have to take the boys into the water. They certainly can't go in alone. You never know who might be out there."

"Good heavens, you don't expect kidnappers to be lurking in the ocean, do you?"

She knew that was exactly what Mike thought. And after what she and the boys had just put him through, she really couldn't blame him. But putting on the bathing suit and exposing herself to his gaze was definitely out.

"Maybe it's just as well that you're going to take them," Annie said, newly aware of dangerous possibilities. "Be careful."

"*Now* you're worried?" Mike replied after giving her a long look followed by a what-am-I-going-to-do-with-you shrug of his shoulders. The kind her ex-husband had subjected her to almost daily. "I guess it'll be okay." He sighed. "I have bathing trunks in the car."

While Mike went to change, Annie looked around the area. The spot she'd chosen was adjacent to a rock formation and was still fairly clear of people. The lifeguard station was close by in case of trouble.

"I don't think we have anything to worry about," she told him when he returned. "You take the boys in the water and I'll stand watch from these rocks," she said in the most decisive voice she could muster. "I'll shout if I see anything out of the ordinary."

Her take-no-prisoners tone of voice worked for the boys, maybe it would work on Mike, too.

"Okay," he said, dropping his linen jacket onto her lap. "But stay on alert. And use this in case you see trouble."

From the weight of the carefully folded jacket, Annie was sure Mike had changed his mind about leaving her his gun. As if it were aflame, she picked up the jacket and squinted up at him, horrified at the mere thought. She'd never touched a gun, let alone shot one.

What was she going to do if trouble started?

Chapter Eight

"You must be crazy?" Annie tried to keep her voice down, but the shock was obvious. "You expect me to handle a gun?"

Mike grabbed the jacket from her hand. "I wouldn't leave a loaded gun with *you*." The emphasis on the word "you" didn't go unnoticed. He opened the jacket and pulled out an object from the inside breast pocket. "Here's my cell phone. Dial 911 if you spot any trouble. It's a lot safer."

Annie felt like a fool as she reached out for the phone. "You were serious about leaving the gun in the trunk, weren't you?"

From his vantage point, standing above her, Mike peered down at her. "I'm always serious, Annie, or hadn't you noticed?"

She'd noticed, all right. Mike hadn't so much as cracked a smile; in fact his expression was tight and there were lines around his mouth as he held his lips taut. "You know, you could still do your job even if you lightened up a bit."

"Lightened up?" He looked at her as if she'd

lost her mind. "Being a bodyguard is a serious job, especially when vulnerable young children are involved. And I'm here to tell you you're not helping with some of your ideas." As he knelt down to put his watch inside his jacket pocket, his face was mere inches from hers. He didn't look particularly happy with her.

"What's wrong about coming to the beach? I understand the risks as well as you do, but there's still room to let the boys breathe a little. If you keep acting as if danger dogs their footsteps, you'll only frighten the boys, and me, too."

If they weren't so far from home, and the kids so excited about going in the water, she thought sourly, she would have insisted they leave.

"We've already been over that ground," Mike answered in a measured voice. "I wasn't trying to frighten anyone, just to make you think twice. If you'd had your way, we would have been here before dawn waiting for the sun to come up. You're not alone—the beach is crowded at this time of the year. Everyone who can get out of D.C. has the same idea as you have."

Annie glanced over at the lightly populated beach. "I only suggested it because the beach is deserted early in the morning and you wouldn't have had anything to worry about. Anyway, watching the sun come up over the ocean is a special treat."

"Maybe for lovers," Mike countered. "But not for me."

Lovers. Annie averted her eyes from his muscular chest, strong shoulders and flashing gray eyes. Mike's appeal for her was strong and getting stronger. She had to remember she and the boys were only a job for him, no matter how he looked at her when he wasn't angry.

The children's excited voices drifted across the sand. She had to go along with Mike, if only because the boys were so happy.

"They don't need to hear this," she commented under her breath. "Can we continue this discussion later? I don't want to ruin their day."

"Fine with me." He shrugged, got to his feet and looked over at Bobby and Joey. "Just as long as you realize the dangerous position they might be in. So keep a careful watch while we're in the water. And don't forget to use the phone to call for help, if something should happen to me or the boys...."

Or the boys. A cold chill ran down Annie's spine at his last phrase. "I'm sorry," Annie told him. "I didn't realize you'd be so concerned about being caught unarmed, or I wouldn't have suggested you be the one to go in the water." For the first time, she was afraid. "It's just that I never saw you with a gun on you at the house."

"That's because the house is as safe as I know how to make it," he explained as he watched the boys approach. "Outside, it's a different story. I always carry a gun, even if you're not aware of it. I keep it on me for a reason: I have no control over

what's going on around us out in the open and I don't care to be caught off guard.''

Annie shivered. "I'm sorry," she said, unable to argue the point. He was right; she was wrong.

"Don't be sorry," he assured her. "You haven't done anything I can't handle. But now that you know why I take the precautions I do, maybe you'll be more practical with those ideas of yours after today."

She looked up, past his long lean legs and narrow hips to his solid, flat waist. The trunks he wore had seen better days before they had shrunk to show his masculine figure. Her gaze continued all the way up his muscular chest and shoulders to his set lips and thoughtful gray eyes.

Studying him so closely was a big mistake. She became more aware of his masculinity and the dangerous edge in his gaze that seemed to attract her rather than turn her off.

She struggled to her feet. "Actually, I thought the whole idea of coming to the beach was pretty harmless."

When the sleeve of his jacket trailed on the sand, he grabbed her arm. "Don't get sand in the cell phone."

She looked down at the strong hand that held her and up into his eyes—eyes that were a mixture of suspicion and desire.

"That phone's not just for show," he told her, dropping her arm abruptly. "In an emergency it could make a difference, so be very careful."

"Careful!" she repeated with a shiver, as much from the look of desire in his eyes as from apprehension. "Here." She held out the bundle. "I've changed my mind."

"What are you so worried about? It's only a telephone."

"I don't care. It still feels like a gun!"

Mike was disgusted. If he *did* need help—a thought that left him cold—it was obvious Annie would be next to useless. So much for giving in to nostalgic memories of himself as a young boy and to Joey's beseeching blue eyes.

"Your imagination is working overtime," he assured her. "Pull yourself together. The boys are coming this way. It would be a shame if we have to leave now that we've gotten this far. Or am I wrong about who we're here for?" he asked her from under a raised brow.

"For the children, of course," Annie replied. The beach was a favorite place of hers, but the boys loved it, too. She glanced over to where Joey and Bobby were climbing off the rock formation. "I don't know why you're always suggesting I don't take care of the boys properly, or maybe something even worse," she added darkly. "It's just that you and I don't see their care in the same way."

"Really? And which way is that?"

"I agree you need to be concerned about their safety, but the boys have other needs, too."

"I thought their safety was what I'm here for. What else did you have in mind?"

"Not you. Me," Annie explained patiently. "Naturally, I look after their welfare, but I also try to teach them to be responsible and to appreciate what they have."

"And they don't?" Mike questioned. "I didn't hear any complaints until you came along. Except maybe to wish their father was home."

"I know," Annie replied. "I've asked them to try to understand that their father has a life, too, and that he loves them in his own way even if he's not around all the time."

"And *my* job is seeing to it that they're kept safe so you'll have a body to take care of," Mike declared. "It might be easier if they would rein in their imaginations."

"Imagination is what gives them their personalities," Annie countered.

"And yours seems to have worn off on them," Mike retorted. "Potbellied pigs and Halloween parties are okay when they take place at home, but something like today is different. When you encourage the boys with outings like this, you make it damn difficult for me to keep them out of harm's way."

"Then maybe we should be partners in taking care of the boys instead of your suspecting me of goodness-knows-what," Annie finally offered in the interests of peace and getting on with the day. "It's obvious we both have the safety and welfare of the boys at heart."

She knew it wasn't wise to antagonize him—it

would only feed his suspicions. Even Clara had reminded her of that. Mike might not know she was the boys' mother, but surely he ought to be able to realize she really cared about them.

"Partners, you said?" His dubious gaze took her in from the top of her head to her toes.

She could almost feel his eyes touching her, and her insides began to warm. "Yes, partners."

"Well..." He sighed and seemed to consider her proposal. "It might work, at that. As long as we play by my rules, understand?"

His crystal-clear eyes studied her as if he could see into her mind. His frown told her he wasn't all that sure about what he saw—or was there something else that bothered him?

The question remained unanswered, but she was becoming more and more intrigued with Mike Cassidy, the man. Especially after his impulsive kiss and the unspoken promise that had seemed to hang in the air between them.

If she could only trust him to understand how much the boys meant to her, she might have told him the whole truth. But from the hot-and-cold way he reacted to her, it was too soon for trust.

Why was he so afraid of being friendly, she wondered. Did he have a wife or children of his own somewhere in his background?

Physical attraction aside, she had to admire the way he approached his responsibilities. It was plain he wouldn't allow any attraction he might feel for her to get in his way of doing his job. She felt a

pang of regret. She would much rather have him for a friend than an enemy.

Fate in the form of her son Bobby intervened. "Can we go in the water now?" he hollered from the water's edge.

Mike waved to him to wait. "How about sitting over there and keeping watch?" he asked Annie as he motioned to where the rock formation met the waterline. "Arguing over who's right and who's wrong about watching over the kids isn't going to get us anywhere. You can keep watch while I take them into the water. We won't be staying long. Think you can handle it?"

She nodded and hugged the jacket closer. "Stay close to Mike," she called to the boys with as bright a smile as she could muster. "Lunch in half an hour?"

"Fine. We'll be ready." With a last hard look at her, Mike loped across the sand to the water.

Annie sat on a flat rock and watched him and the boys run into the ocean. Striding ahead, Mike dove under a wave and, like a seal at play, swam back with it to come up beside an unsuspecting Joey. She could hear Joey's shrieks of laughter when Mike picked him up and tossed him in the air and caught him before he fell into the ocean.

"Me, too!" Bobby called, struggling through the water. "Me, too!"

Mike lifted Bobby out of the water with his free arm when another wave tumbled toward shore. The boys held him around his neck while the wave

broke against them and sprays of water swirled
over them.

Annie smiled fondly at the scene. The difference
between Mike and her ex-husband had never
seemed more real. Mike was the type of man who
would make a good father, she reflected wistfully
as he bent his head to hear something Joey was
telling him. A father who listened to and laughed
with his children. Unlike their own father, Mike
wouldn't see them as possessions or put his own
needs first.

The appeal of the waves sliding gently to shore
became too great to ignore. Annie took off her sandals. Clutching Mike's jacket, she walked to the
water's edge where she let the cool water sluice
between her toes. She laughed when the foam
swirled around her ankles before it ebbed back.

Soon, every inch of her seemed to be attuned to
the sun's rays sparkling on the ocean, the waves
sliding to shore and the sound of her children's
voices calling back and forth.

From where she stood, she could see water glis-
ten on Mike's muscled chest. As she watched him
gambol in the surf, her body warmed and her
thoughts turned to imagining erotic play between
the two of them. The more abandoned he became,
the more she was filled with a longing to join him,
to be held in his arms; to share his laughter, to see
a sparkle come into his eyes. Heat swept over her
like an ocean wave cresting before it tumbled and
glided to shore. She closed her eyes and envisioned

herself diving into deep, dangerous waters, losing herself in Mike's welcoming embrace.

When she opened her eyes again, it was to see Mike staring at her. He stood motionless, outlined against the sun like some bronzed pagan god. Under his gaze, she felt more like a woman than she had in ten years of marriage.

She tried to look away but the electricity that seemed to arc over the water held her fast. Sensual thoughts tumbled through her mind like the ocean waves that formed in the distance and swept slowly and surely to shore.

She had to stop daydreaming, she told herself wistfully. It was simply a matter of her imagination working overtime, and she had to stop. The simple truth was that Mike was a flesh-and-blood man, and she was a flesh-and-blood woman. They were opposites, as different as oil and water, the sun and the moon, the earth and the heavens. They could never belong together.

And she was still a mother to the two small boys who needed her. They came first.

But someday she was going to ask Mike what had made him suspicious of her and why he sometimes appeared to be angry.

SHE'D FOUND ANOTHER way to drive him out of his mind.

Mike was transfixed by the sight of Annie as she unpacked the picnic hamper. He'd been taken by

the image of her standing at the water's edge, and he was taken by her now.

She'd hugged the dripping-wet Joey to her chest while she'd dried the kid off. The front of her dress was soaking wet and clung to her like a second skin. Every womanly curve was outlined to his unabashed gaze. He couldn't look away. He was man enough to enjoy the view no matter how puzzled he was over the woman who was Annie. Obviously, one thing had nothing to do with the other.

He still didn't have a clue as to what there was about her that continued to puzzle him. Sure, there was her odd view of life that managed to frustrate him one moment and her convoluted logic that intrigued him the next. In a crazy way, whatever she came up with was beginning to make sense. That scared him more than anything.

He had to solve the mystery of who Annie really was rather than who she appeared to be. Either that, or he was going to have to put her out of his mind until the congressman came home to stay and his job would be over.

He suspected by becoming intrigued by Annie's behavior, he'd probably overlooked a passing clue or two that would have solved the puzzle of Annie Kramer's true identity, and that the sexual tension building between them was getting in the way of his thinking rationally.

"Here," he said abruptly when he realized he was heading into murky waters, "how about handing me my jacket. I'm going to go and change.

Keep a close watch on the boys—I'll be back in a minute.''

Annie looked up from where she was unpacking the picnic basket. ''Are you sure you don't want to eat lunch first? Clara sent turkey sandwiches, chips and lemonade. And some of her cookies.''

''Later. I'm too cold and wet right now. I have to change,'' he said shortly, his uneasiness over his growing sexual tension slowly turning into frustration. Even though he knew she hadn't been guilty of enticing him deliberately, a soaking-wet Annie was too much for him to handle right now.

''Not to worry. The heat of the sun will dry you off if you give it a chance,'' she said, handing him a clean towel.

He took the towel, but shook his head at the offer of lunch. There was a heat burning inside him that would dry him off faster than any towel. He didn't dare stick around—not when he was wearing nothing more than skimpy bathing trunks and a feeble smile.

WHEN HE RETURNED to the picnic, he was fully dressed and his gun was firmly in its holster under his loose cotton jacket. His only concession to the locale was his bare feet and rolled-up jeans. The heat was still there, burning inside him.

''Ready for lunch?''

A quick glance at Annie's face told him she found his behavior puzzling. She wasn't alone. He found his behavior puzzling, too. After all, he was

old enough and experienced enough to control his traitorous body, and not to get involved with a "harmless" woman—not twice.

He reached for the sandwich and cold drink Annie offered him. When their hands touched, he experienced a sinking sensation.

He'd definitely broken another of his cardinal rules—"Don't become involved with a suspect." It was damn clear he *had* allowed himself to become emotionally involved with Annie and his young clients. He should have known better as soon as he realized Annie was more than a bright, loving, caring woman: She was damned attractive.

With the exception of some of her New Age thinking, Annie was everything a woman ought to be. But, if given a choice, he would have wished she was more realistic.

He wondered about her obviously misnamed profession, since sure as hell she was no more a professional nanny than he was. To his way of thinking, nannies had to be as objective as bodyguards in order to take care of their charges properly. This nanny seemed to be moved purely by whatever her imagination and her heart dictated.

Surely her creativity, intelligence and people skills, though a little offbeat, qualified her for something more.

He looked forward to the real woman when he unmasked her. If he ever satisfied himself that she was indeed harmless, he intended to hold her in his arms and to take care of unfinished business.

"Eat up, boys," he said, checking his watch and hoping Annie couldn't read his mind. "We'll be driving home soon."

Joey dropped his soda in the sand and screwed up his face in protest. "You mean we can't go over to the Ferris wheel and the roller coaster?"

"Not today." *Or any day he was in charge of the boys.*

"And what about the merry-go-round?"

"No, not that, either. I'm sorry, guys, but that's out, too."

Mike cast a quick look over at Annie as he spoke. *Didn't anyone care about safety precautions but him?* She looked mutinous, but at least she kept her silence. With her encouragement, he had a good chance of getting his charges home before the crowds arrived.

He was wrong.

Again.

He should have known he wasn't going to win an argument with the boys now that they had an ally. And, for sure, from the look on her face, Annie was on their side, even if she hadn't opened her mouth.

"I want to go on the roller coaster," Bobby announced when he'd finished his sandwich.

"And I want to go on the merry-go-round!" Joey added.

"Sorry, kids. It's like I told you before. I don't want you guys around crowds." Mike checked his

wristwatch. "There're bound to be hordes of people over at the rides by noon."

"Is it noon yet?" Bobby asked.

Mike shook his head.

"Then why can't we go over there now before
the crowd gets bigger?" Bobby insisted. "I thought
that's why Miss Annie woke us up and made us
come early."

Mike glanced at Annie for support. A faint smile
hovered at her lips. Damn it! She looked as if she
was as pleased with the boys' logic as if she'd
thought of the argument for staying herself. He
couldn't believe it. But, to give Bobby credit, it
was a more sensible question than usual.

It was barely eleven-thirty, and a weekday at
that. Maybe he could take the boys down the
boardwalk long enough to get their craving for excitement out of their system—especially if it would
wear them out and make the ride home that much
easier.

"Okay," he announced reluctantly. "But only
for half an hour. And when I say it's time to go,
it's time to go. I don't want any problems about
this. Got it?"

"Got it," Bobby said reluctantly. Mike could
see the kid wasn't too happy about the compromise.

"Got it," Joey echoed. He didn't look any more
enthusiastic than his brother.

Out of the corner of his eye, Mike could see the
faint smile on Annie's face become a happy grin.

He began to worry. In his mind, that smile meant more trouble. With his luck, he was afraid the happier she became, the less objective and careful she would be. To add insult to injury, as every inch of her glowed with pleasure, every inch of her became more desirable.

As if he didn't have enough on his hands keeping an eye out for two small boys, now he would have to keep a watchful eye on her, too.

"If you want to go on the ride, you'll have to put on your thongs and your shirts and wait for me," Annie told the boys. She gathered the remains of their lunch into the picnic basket.

"You coming along?" Mike asked. He knew the answer before he asked the question. Annie wasn't the type to pass up a chance to play on a carousel. As for himself, he hadn't been on one since he was twelve. It was a little late in life to try again. He would let them take a ride or two, but the rest of the rides were definitely out! And someday, the Good Lord willing, he was going to win an argument with Annie.

"Of course. There's nothing more exciting than a ride on the merry-go-round and trying for the brass ring," she answered happily.

"The brass ring?" Mike scoffed. "That's for kids."

"You're wrong, you know. All you have to be is a kid at heart. Besides, if you catch the brass ring, you get another ride."

Maybe that was what was wrong with him—he

wasn't a kid. And maybe, looking back, he had never had the luxury of being one.

In spite of his good intentions, cardinal rules, or whatever else he tried to fool himself with, Mike actually found himself looking forward to watching the boys ride the merry-go-round. And Annie, too. To see their laughing faces, and to know that, just for today, there was innocence in the world after all.

And he was looking forward to watching Annie catch the coveted brass ring. Surely fate wouldn't deny her anything as simple as that.

He was going along only because he'd managed to frighten them earlier. He'd wanted them to be cautious, aware of their surroundings, but he hadn't wanted them to become paranoid. As for himself, he was paid to be paranoid. With a sigh, he checked his shoulder holster to make sure his gun was in place.

"Of course," he told Annie, "by going along with you and the boys, I'm probably violating every rule in the bodyguard handbook."

"There's a bodyguard handbook?"

"If there isn't, there ought to be," he answered, feeling foolish—the way he always felt after a verbal exchange with Annie.

"And once they hear about this morning, if there's a bodyguards' union, my membership will probably be revoked," he added, until he realized she might have been taking him seriously. All he'd wanted to do was lessen the tension.

If he'd ever needed a guardian angel, he needed one now.

"Don't worry, Annie. I was only kidding, anyway," he finally said. "Let's get going. The sooner we get over there, the sooner we can start for home."

He couldn't recognize himself as the trained professional he'd been before Annie arrived, Mike thought, as he carried their belongings to the car. Maybe it was Annie's people skills, or maybe it was witchcraft, but he'd been turned into a man he probably wouldn't recognize even if he looked into a mirror.

Defeated, he shrugged his shoulders and looked up at the shimmering summer sky. Surely by now, someone up there was laughing at him for bending the rules to their max. But then, they didn't have to deal with Annie.

"Okay, now," he addressed the boys. "Just remember we stick together so I can keep an eye on you."

"To the merry-go-round!" Joey cried.

Mike exchanged a fatalistic glance with Annie. "To the merry-go-round," he agreed. "Remember, we just have a little over half an hour." He felt like a hero when he saw her face break into a smile of anticipation as wide as its mirror image on Joey's face.

OVER THE BOYS' PROTESTS, he made certain they rode inside horses. He had Annie take the outside horse.

"This is the wrong horse!" Joey hollered. "No fair!

"Yeah, yeah, I know you both want to ride on the outside," he agreed when Bobby added to his brother's protest, "but this way I can keep an eye on you."

As for Annie, he wanted her where he could watch her try for a brass ring.

To the tune of "Lara's Theme" from *Doctor Zhivago*, the merry-go-round set off. Annie clung to the carousel pole, humming as the horse moved up and down in time to the music, even periodically casting a happy smile at him over her shoulder. He felt pretty pleased with himself, too, in spite of the reproachful looks Joey kept giving him.

He was especially pleased when, on the third round, Annie leaned away from the horse and caught the brass ring. She waved it in the air.

"Free ride!" she called to Mike.

Mike swallowed hard when her exuberance pulled her dress taut and her breasts strained against the thin material. Visions of her in her she-devil costume swam in front of his eyes. Maybe it was just as well she wore those shapeless dresses.

The kids shouted their congratulations and began to bounce up and down with happiness.

"Aw-right!" Joey hollered. "Now get one for me, Mommy!"

Chapter Nine

"You have some explaining to do," Mike said curtly when he cornered Annie alone in the family room.

After hearing Joey call her "mommy" on the merry-go-round, all his earlier suspicions about her had jelled. He'd been troubled over the possibility that Annie might be trying to ingratiate herself deeply enough to entice the boys away from their father. If she *was* their mother, the possibility could become a certainty.

In the short time she'd been here with the boys, she'd been like a mother to them. She'd held them, soothed them, played games with them, made them laugh and tucked them into bed each night. Everything he associated with a mother's love...

But could she actually *be* their mother?

Despite the evidence, there was some part of Mike that refused to believe it. Deep down inside, he didn't want to believe it. He studied Annie from the top of her loose brown hair to her silver san-

dals. No, she wasn't the type Matthews would have married—not a man with his political ambitions.

But it was his job to find out the truth, and tonight, no amount of explaining was going to change his mind. And neither was the sensual attraction surrounding her going to cloud his thinking.

Whoever she was and whatever her reason for being here, there was something at the bottom of Annie's behavior. And he was going to find it out before he called in Matthews.

Annie felt apprehensive, but not surprised. She'd heard the hesitation in his voice that morning at the beach when he'd reluctantly agreed to work together as partners. Now he didn't act as if he was interested in a partnership. How much of the truth could she tell Mike to ease his obvious suspicions? More important, was he ready to believe her?

"The boys may need me," Annie told him through the lump in her throat. "Surely, whatever is bothering you this time can wait until they're in bed." If her voice sounded unnatural to her own ears, she could imagine how she must sound to him.

"You don't have to worry about the boys. They're in the kitchen getting enough TLC from Mrs. Swenson to last them until bedtime."

"Later, after the boys are asleep?" Annie glanced at the door leading to the kitchen, hoping no one was listening. She needed time to get her thoughts together, to keep her stories straight.

"Now, if you don't mind. What I have to say won't take long," he answered firmly. He put his hand under her elbow and pulled her after him out of the family room and down the hall. "We can talk in the library."

At his unbending look, Annie felt a cold foreboding flood through her. She searched her memory, trying to remember what could have set him off again.

After their trip to the beach this morning, she'd thought he would ease up on her. Instead, the harsh sound of his voice told her he'd gone from thinking she was up to something to actually believing it. He obviously wanted answers and he wanted them now.

Annie felt threatened as never before. She was afraid her charade was about to play itself out. With a last glance in the direction of the kitchen, she followed him to the library.

"I'll get right to the point," he said as he closed the door behind them. "I heard Bobby call you 'Mommy.'"

Shaken by the abruptness of his accusation, Annie forced herself to laugh. "You probably did, but then, I don't pay much attention to what they call me. It's been my experience young boys call their caretakers 'Mommy' out of habit when they're excited."

Mike's eyes were as cold as granite as he confronted her. Although Annie knew his eyes could be as deep and rich as velvet, today they were sharp

and cold. The intimidating expression remained on his face in spite of her ready explanation. His lips and his square jaw tightened. His cold look told her his questions weren't over and that she hadn't satisfied him. She steeled herself for more and prayed she had the answers.

"So you're not the boys' mother?"

"That's a stretch of the imagination, isn't it?" Annie returned as she met his frigid gaze. She'd learned years ago from her former husband to answer a question with a question in order to avoid confrontation.

Even if it broke her heart, she loved Bobby and Joey enough to deny she was their mother. She wanted more than anything to claim the boys as hers, to tell Mike how much she loved her children and what she was doing for that love. She wanted to make him understand, to realize she wasn't a sneak or a schemer—just a mother.

"Not at all," he replied, looking her over in a way that made her feel he was searching out her secret. "You might not look like the kids, but you sure act like their mother."

"I thought I'd explained all that once before," Annie said reasonably, although her heart beat wildly. "The boys are just responding to me because they miss their own mother."

His eyes bored through her, uncertain, still not satisfied. "I have another question for you," he said. "But before I go any further, I think it's only fair to tell you I've checked on your references."

Annie's heart took another leap into her throat. She'd covered that base, too, but it looked as if she wasn't home free, after all.

"I'm not surprised," she answered. "I expected Mrs. Matthews to give them to you."

"I was only able to contact one of your former employers, a Mrs. Hitchcock. She verified your previous employment."

"Of course," she retorted, pretending surprise and more than a little indignation. "Why in heaven's name would I have lied about something so easily proved?"

"Beats me," he said, running his hand through his hair. Annie knew from experience it was a sign of his frustration. "Except that since a lot of things about you don't add up, it does make a man wonder. Anyway, I'm going to keep trying to contact your other two former employers. One reference isn't enough to satisfy me."

"Anything else? If not, I have to check on the boys."

"Relax, the boys are doing fine without you." The frown on his forehead deepened. "There are still some things about you that bother me."

There were a few things about the bodyguard that bothered her, too, Annie reflected silently. But since most of them were of a personal nature, she kept her thoughts to herself.

Suddenly, he did a double take, took another step toward her and stared down into her hair. "You color your hair, don't you?"

Annie instinctively folded her arms across her chest. She was ready for that question, too. The fact that her hair had lightened considerably and that the roots had begun to show after her daily shampoo hadn't been lost on her.

"I'm blond," she replied with a rueful tone under his searching gaze. "I was tired of being thought of as a blond bimbo, so I decided to try brown." She rumpled the back of her hair and managed to laugh. "I used a home coloring kit, but I guess I didn't do a very good job, did I?"

"No, you didn't," he said sharply. "And you didn't do any better a job with the rest of your makeover, either. How much of the rest of you is real?"

A chill crept over her at his curt remark. The chill grew colder as his eyes studied her more closely. She felt the hair on her arms tingle.

"I was trying to get people to stop taking me for granted," she explained, hoping her inner turmoil wasn't transparent. "As a matter of fact, sometimes I had trouble making people take me seriously." Her ex-husband, most of all.

"Take it from me, Annie Kramer, it's not easy for me to take you seriously, either. No matter what color your hair is." He eyed her purple toenails. "You're the only woman I've ever met as uninhibited as you. And as far as that goes, I've never met anyone who would dress the way you did the day you showed up and expected to be taken se-

riously. Although," he added dryly, "I have to agree there's been some improvement recently."

"Thank you, I think," she responded to the cryptic compliment. At least it was better than his reaction when he'd first laid eyes on her. "Any more questions?"

"Yes." Mike hesitated. "It doesn't have anything to do with your identity, actually, but the answer is important.... Are you married?"

Annie stiffened. "I don't know what that has to do with it, but actually, I'm divorced."

"And the children you mentioned you once had?"

"I have two. They're just not with me anymore."

"So, why the story of the husband overseas?"

"If you have to know, I didn't elaborate on my marriage because I wasn't sure how Mrs. Matthews would feel about a divorcée as a nanny," she answered defiantly, standing, ready to leave. "And I still don't know what that has to do with anything!"

"Don't go yet," he said, interrupting her in midstride. "I'm not finished with you yet."

He eyed her in a quizzical manner as if he still couldn't figure her out. Well, she thought angrily, she couldn't understand herself for putting up with him, either.

"While we're on the subject of your personal history, I haven't met a woman yet who would think adopting potbellied pigs or celebrating holi-

days anytime she felt like it was remotely normal. Of course," he added thoughtfully, "it's difficult for me to believe all of that nonsense wasn't a ploy to throw me off."

"Nonsense?" Annie blurted, offended at the idea she would try to use feminine wiles to lull his suspicions, or for any other reason, for that matter. Of all women to be accused of using her sexuality to get what she wanted, she was the least likely. After all, hadn't Robert told her that many times?

"Just because I'm a woman who doesn't believe in living by the calendar, or in high fashion, either, you suspect me of some crime?" she retorted, angry in spite of herself. She might know what he was accusing her of, but the best defense was a strong offense.

"As a matter of fact," she countered, hands on her hips and ready to do battle, "my dresses are comfortable. Now, tell me. How in heaven's name is that trading on my femininity?"

"It's not only the way you dress," he replied, carefully studying her in a way that made butterflies cavort in her middle. "I think it's quite possibly more than that."

"Then what?" Annie held her breath as the pulse at his neck noticeably stepped up its beat and his now warm gaze surrounded her.

"Something tells me you're afraid of being recognized."

"Recognized?" Surely, she thought, now the other shoe was going to drop. Her charade was

over. She would be sent packing, or something worse.

"Recognized for the woman you really are," he clarified as he closed the distance between them.

The butterflies in Annie's stomach hung suspended in midair, as surprised as she was by his unexpected revelation. Until she realized he wasn't talking about her identity.

"What you're looking at is the real me," she finally answered, backing away from him. *A mother doing her best to look after her children, and putting her integrity on the line to do it. Or, was that all she was? Was she hiding her sexual needs behind her "mommy" needs?*

"No matter how you might deny it," Mike continued on, "it's pretty plain to me that you're trying to use the attraction between us to throw me off track." He took another step toward her. "I want to..." His sentence unfinished, he started to reach for her.

Bobby's excited voice sounded outside the closed door. "Miss Annie! Miss Annie! Come and see what Mrs. Swenson made for us!"

Annie quickly moved out of Mike's grasp and made for the door, more than grateful her sensuality wasn't going to be tested. "I have to go. The boys are calling me."

Mike put his hand on the door above her head, staying her. "I'm sorry if I've upset you, but there's something I still need to know."

She shook her head. From his actions, it looked

as if Mike was about to test the attraction he said they felt for each other. She couldn't allow him to take her in his arms. Not now, and not when she was more aware of his masculinity than she had any right to be. It was no time to test his theory, to find out if what her body was telling her was true. If it was, Mike was dangerous—now more than ever.

She ducked under his arm, threw open the door and left without a backward glance.

THE BOYS IN BED, Annie went outside to sit in the swing that hung in the gazebo. As she worried her lips, a dozen scenarios played out in her mind. All of them involved Mike. He was getting too close for comfort, both to her secret and to her heart.

Under his steady probing, she'd already admitted too much. Even that she was the mother of two children. He was bound to put one and one together. It was just a matter of time. But why had he asked her if she was married? Was it because of the embrace she'd sensed would follow if she answered that she was not?

She drew a quick breath to calm herself. It had come down to a matter of choices. She had only two left to her. She could cool the way she was beginning to feel about Mike and bluster her way through her masquerade for the rest of the summer. Or she could leave the boys in someone else's care before he decided he was right and told Robert.

Bobby was old enough to understand if she ex-

plained why she had to leave. But Joey? She knew without asking that it would break his little heart.

"Annie?" Clara Swenson stood in the doorway. "I was straightening up in the kitchen when I saw you come out here. From the way you looked, I knew something was wrong."

"Yes, I'm afraid there is." Annie wiped the tears from her eyes and nodded her head.

"It's Mike, isn't it?"

"I'm afraid you're right," Annie said unhappily. "He watches me like a hawk and has questions for me whenever we're alone. Nothing seems to satisfy him. It upsets me, and I'm not sure what I should do about it."

"Maybe it's because he suspects the truth?"

"The truth?" Annie gasped. She was shaken by the realization she was so transparent that first Mike, and now Clara, had guessed she was a fraud. And if both Mike and Clara had guessed, had Sharon? And would Robert know if he came home?

"Yes." Clara smiled sympathetically. "That you're actually the boys' mother. You are, aren't you?"

"What makes you think so?" she asked, wary of telling the truth even though Clara had shown that she was a friend.

If ever Annie needed a friend, she needed one now. Someone to share her thoughts with, someone to ease the fear of exposure she lived with every hour, everyday.

"I can recognize a mother's love when I see it,

my dear. As for anyone else, I'm sure there's no doubt in their minds you love the boys. It's obvious that the boys love you, much more than they would if they'd only seen you for the first time a week ago. I'm afraid it all adds up."

"And Mike?"

"I'm sure he senses it, too. But, professional that he is, he has to prove it first."

"My children mean everything to me. I would do anything I have to do to stay with the boys," Annie told her, "including masquerading as a nanny."

Clara nodded and dusted a speck of flour from her apron. "I understand, but I have a feeling there's something more than the boys involved here."

"You may be right about that, too," Annie said ruefully, gazing off into the distance where she could see Mike walking the perimeter of the property. He was wearing his jacket, a sure sign a gun and its holster were underneath. "I have to admit I've come to care for Mike, but it's hopeless. He thinks I'm just playing on feminine wiles to get him off my back."

"I don't doubt that you care for him. He's an honorable young man, and a handsome one, too. But sometimes there's a certain strange expression that comes into his eyes. A certain watchfulness, an uneasiness. As if he's afraid to let himself feel." Clara sighed and shook her head. "It's too bad. But if you ask me, you're not the only one with some-

thing to hide. I think Mike has something to hide, too.''

"I've wondered about that, too," Annie said, her eyes following Mike. "Especially when he becomes angry so easily."

"Seems to me, you'd both be better off if you told him the truth about yourself. If Mike cares about you, and it sounds as if he does, I'm sure he'll understand."

Annie shook her head. "I don't know if I dare risk it. The attraction between us may not last. I can't jeopardize my chance to remain with Bobby and Joey."

"Unless I'm mistaken, he'll come here to find you as soon as he's through his rounds," Clara advised, getting to her feet. "Tell him the truth about who you are. And tell him how you feel about him. Ask him to be truthful with you, too. It might heal the both of you. If you're honest with each other, maybe you won't have to be afraid of what might happen next."

Annie nodded reluctantly. Clara had been wrong before. She was afraid she might lose everything if she took her advice again.

SHE HEARD HIS FOOTSTEPS before he stepped into the light.

"Hi, there," Mike said as he strolled over to the swing. "Are you okay?"

"Yes." Annie looked up and forced herself to

smile. She could sense things weren't over between them.

"I thought maybe we could finish our conversation now that there's no one around to interrupt us."

Her smile faded. Instinct told her that if she ever decided to bare her soul and put her trust in Mike, now wasn't the time. "More questions?"

"Not really." He stood regarding her, a determined look on his face.

"Don't tell me you're going to apologize for this afternoon?"

"Apologize? For what?"

"That kiss. I realize it must have been just an impulse and didn't mean a thing."

"I'm never going to apologize for wanting to kiss you," he answered as he grasped her by her shoulders and drew her to her feet. "In fact I intend to pick up where we left off. I have something to prove. To prove to both of us that you've been putting on an act to throw me off my guard."

"An act?" Annie felt confused. His moods changed faster than her mind could follow.

"Yes. But let me warn you. No matter the outcome, I still intend to find out who you really are and what you're doing here."

Before she could tell him what she thought of his single-mindedness, he took her in his arms, clasped the back of her head between his hands and lowered his lips to hers. This time his lips were hard, seeking, searching—demanding a response.

His fingers stroked the nape of her neck, brushed the sides of her cheeks.

If the first kiss had come out of nowhere, this one seemed to come from the depths of his being. All thoughts and fears for the future flew out of her mind. This was Mike. She wanted him as much as he wanted her. Her arms rose to tangle themselves around his neck. Her lips sought his, seeking something she'd needed for a long time. She couldn't get enough of him.

He tasted of fresh water and soap, and of pure male sexuality.

Annie had been waiting an eternity for this moment. She thought of bare skin against bare skin. Of hands touching her in her most sensitive places, of lips sliding against her breasts. Of a magic that could take them both to places she had only dreamed about when she had nothing left but dreams.

She was enraptured by the taste of him, the feel of him. His lips lifted from hers to explore her eyelids, her lips again, the corners of her mouth. After a searching glance into his eyes to assure herself he wasn't just testing her, she parted her lips to give him entry.

With a breathless sigh, she buried her fingers in his hair where the salty scent of the ocean still clung. Every inch of her responded to the touch of his hands as they caressed her shoulders, drawing her closer and closer until she could feel his heartbeat.

Her own heart was filled with the yearning she'd lulled to sleep when she'd realized life with Robert wasn't going to be the fairy tale she'd expected it would be. He'd blamed his loss of interest on her, never bothering to nurture the sensuality she had in her. He hadn't even seemed to care.

Sensing a yearning of his own behind Mike's kiss, she turned off her thoughts of the past and lost herself in his embrace.

When he finally released her, she was unable to stand alone. She leaned into him, rested her cheek against his chest, felt his heartbeat echo her own. She heard him whisper her name like an unspoken question into her hair. It was as if he couldn't believe what was happening to them any more than she could. His voice was tender, but unsure. She heard a note of regret as he started to tell her he was sorry for doubting her, before he fell silent.

If he'd been trying to prove there was nothing between them, he'd been wrong.

"This doesn't change anything," she heard him say, as if to himself.

He was wrong. Now that he'd proved to them both how deeply they were attracted to each other, everything had changed.

Chapter Ten

Alone in her room, Annie sank into the maple rocking chair to mull over the day's events.

She gazed around the bedroom with a wistful smile. During her marriage it had been a guest room and she'd decorated it with the cozy rose-and-green motif she loved. She'd never dreamed she would one day occupy it as nanny to her own children. Tonight, it was a refuge. A place to gather her thoughts, to take a deep breath, and to take stock of her growing affection for Mike and the possible consequences.

After accusing her of subterfuge and using feminine wiles to throw him off track, he'd proceeded to demonstrate his point all too well.

He may have shown her how much they wanted each other, but what he'd also proved was that their attraction for each other was turning into something more than physical desire. Or at least, it was for her. The cold, hard edge to him that had been there the past few days was gone. There was his strength, his integrity and the tender way he regarded her

when he thought she wasn't noticing that warmed her heart. And then there was his obvious affection for her children.

Even though he seemed to have softened, there were still those unanswered questions between them—questions he would surely get around to asking again. This time, she would have to answer with the truth he must already know.

The time had come when she would have to pay the piper. Or to make the choice to leave before disaster struck.

She leaned her head back against the rocker. Its gentle sway turned her thoughts back to the swing where she had gone willingly into his embrace a short time ago. Even now, after realizing how much she wanted him, there were still the depths of the troubled waters that separated them.

Maybe Clara was right: She and Mike had to talk before much longer. It was the only way to put her mind at ease and to settle what was between them.

A soft knock on her door startled her. She glanced at the clock beside the bed before she hurried to the door. Who could be at her door past midnight?

Mike stood there, one hand poised to knock again. In the other, he held a pink rose.

It was as though she'd willed him to walk out of her thoughts and come to her.

"I have a confession to make," he said somberly. "I was wrong about you before."

"Wrong?"

"Yes. You weren't playing a game after all, and, I guess, neither was I. But then, you knew that all along, didn't you?" he added softly as he offered her the rose. His rueful smile caught at her heart.

"I was pretty sure about myself," she agreed hesitantly. "But I wasn't so sure about you."

Mixed emotions ran through Annie as she looked into Mike's smile. Surely he must know from the way her breathing quickened that he'd caught her unaware. That she'd expected far different than this.

"Neither was I until an hour ago," he said as he glanced around the room. "I heard you moving around. It sounded as if you're as restless as I am. Is there a problem or...?"

"No. I just couldn't sleep," she replied, her heart racing. The heat inside her grew at the husky question in his voice. She knew as well as he did that his concern for her was an excuse to continue where they'd left off.

He hesitated in the doorway. "I couldn't sleep, either. I hope you like the rose. You might say it's a peace offering."

She caught her breath as his gaze swept her brief cotton pajamas. She trembled at the desire that stirred as her eyes locked with his. He waited in the doorway, the next move was up to her.

He wore jeans, a shirt unbuttoned to his waist and an uncertain smile. His feet were bare. The shock of rumpled hair that fell over his forehead only partially hid the desire shining in his eyes.

When she brushed the shock of hair away, he caught her hand and brought it to his lips. The question in his eyes remained as he kissed her palm.

He was seductive and tender, a mixture of all she'd dreamed about before marriage to Robert Matthews had disillusioned her. He was also a danger that drew her in spite of the voice at the back of her mind warning her she was getting in too deep.

"Do you mind if I join you?" he asked softly.

For a breathtaking moment their eyes locked again. She could feel the pull of passion surge between them. She hadn't had to think about sexual play since before her divorce two years ago, let alone slept with a man. Besides, thinking about sex and having it were two different things, she reflected fleetingly.

Did she know how to do this? she wondered. Would Mike think she was a fool if she told him about her fears, her self-doubts about how much of a woman she was? Doubts that marriage to Robert had instilled.

She hesitated, but looking into his eyes, she knew she was lost. Her awakened desire drew her into his arms as surely as the moon drew the tides. If ever she was going to fulfill the yearning for his strong arms to hold her again, his searching lips to taste hers, the time was now. She glanced over his shoulder.

"There's no one else around, except the kids,"

he said quietly as his gaze followed hers. "I checked on them a few minutes ago. They're fast asleep."

"Clara and Sharon?"

"I said good-night to them half an hour ago when I was making a final check in the servants' wing. I was about to go to bed myself when I heard you moving around." He quirked an eyebrow to acknowledge it was only an excuse. "I decided coming here might be a better idea. How about you?"

Annie's heart went into instant meltdown. He was honest about wanting her, but it was her choice to make.

She held the door open. "You can come in for a few minutes, if you like."

"I'd like," he answered with the lopsided grin that put the butterflies in her middle on full alert.

She closed the door behind him and turned to watch him as he strode into the bedroom and swung around to face her. His tight jeans rode low on his lean hips, the tanned flesh of his chest under his open shirt glistened in the dim light of the lamp.

Her mind took her back to where she'd waited on the shore of the beach at Rehoboth. The image was so vivid, she couldn't concentrate on what he was saying, let alone answer him. His chuckle broke into her reverie.

"You weren't listening," he chided. "I was trying to tell you something before we go any further."

"No," she agreed. "I'm afraid I had something else on my mind." *A bronze pagan god rising, dripping, out of the sea... Dreams coming true...*

"I want to be honest with you," he repeated softly. "I really hadn't planned on staying for just a few minutes. But I guess you know that too, don't you?"

She glanced down at the rose he'd given her— a gift so out of character for the cold man she'd met just days ago—and she had to smile.

"I have another confession to make," he said cheerfully. "The rose was Mrs. Swenson's idea."

"Oh, no!" Annie felt her face turn crimson.

He grinned sheepishly. "After she got through with me, she had me believing bringing it to you was my idea and the greatest idea I'd ever had. And that I was the smartest guy in the world for thinking of it."

"Thank you. Roses have always been my favorite flower," she answered as she buried her nose in soft petals and inhaled their fragrance.

"I'll keep it in mind for future reference." With that wry comment, he closed the distance between them, pulled her into his arms and smiled down into her eyes.

For future reference?

Annie leaned into his solid chest and laid her cheek against his bare skin. Why was she hesitating? she wondered. After all, this was what she'd longed for only moments ago.

As intensely as she wanted him, and as much as

she'd yearned for this to be for more than just to-night, Annie knew it was impossible.

Not when she knew she wouldn't be able to re-main with her children and become involved with Mike at the same time; she sensed it wasn't in his character to love a woman who lived a lie.

But she couldn't turn him away; she had to have tonight. She ached to have his hands slide over her flushed body, to have his tongue caress the breasts that hungered for his searching lips, to taste of him as he tasted of her. To finally know the full mean-ing of the love of a man for a woman.

No matter what happened between them in the next few hours, she resolved to hide her real iden-tity and the reason behind it.

"I'll go if you want me to," he whispered as he brushed his fingertips over the nape of her neck and smiled down into her eyes. "But I'm afraid not without a protest or two. You have thirty seconds to change your mind."

Too late, her heart cried when he finally drew her hair aside and bent to kiss the sensitive spot on her neck.

"You can stay for a little while," she whispered. She would take the gift fate had offered her and pray for a miracle—a time when Mike would un-derstand her mother's heart.

Fears for the past, the present and the future faded away in a haze of sensation under his kisses. Wherever these few precious hours with Mike would take her, she would go gladly.

She would let tomorrow take care of itself.

Mike sensed her hesitation, but the smoky look in her eyes gave her away. As surely as if he were looking into a mirror, he could see his own desire reflected there. With a reassuring murmur, he bent to his task of convincing her tonight belonged to them.

She tasted of sunshine, moonbeams and rainbows. Her faint scent of vanilla was more provocative than the finest perfume. She was a temptress, a mistress of seduction, and an elusive blithe spirit all rolled into one. And, maybe not even the woman she seemed to be. But tonight she was his. Tonight he would reach for his own brass ring.

"You won't ever be sorry," he whispered into her hair. "I would never do anything to hurt you."

He drew the thin straps of her pajama top from her shoulders and slowly rained feathery kisses along her throat until her breasts were bared to his hungry gaze. He kissed each breast reverently, ran his tongue around its nipple and worshiped it until she stirred under his lips.

He murmured his reassurance as he hooked his thumbs beneath the waistband of her boxer pajama shorts and slid them down her silken legs, leaving her fully exposed to his hungry gaze.

She had long legs meant to curve around a man, to hold him tight, and to draw him into heaven, Mike mused as he held her to him; a slender waist he could almost span with his two hands, and full, tight breasts that begged for the return of his lips.

"You'd better hold on for a minute before it's too late." He laughed unsteadily as he briefly held her away from him. When she groaned her frustration, he quickly added, "Only for a minute. I promise." He reached into the pocket of his jeans, took out a foil packet and tossed it on the nightstand.

She shook her head. "A minute is too long," she protested. She reached for his open shirt and pulled it out of his jeans. "I have some business I want to take care of, too."

"I'm all yours," he answered, helping her shrug the shirt off his shoulders. "Do with me what you will, sweetheart. The night is still young and I'm more than willing."

"I intend to," she replied pertly while she slid his shirt off as if she couldn't wait to feel the texture of his skin under her lips.

Then she tugged at his leather belt, fumbled over its buckle and muttered her frustration when she couldn't manage to release it.

"Here, let me," he said, stilling her hands and working the buckle by himself. "You can practice on me some other time. Right now, I'm more than ready to find out what you have in mind."

"Only this," she said as she slid her hands over his shoulders, down his chest to his lean hips. She tongued his chest, tasting the salty sheen of him. "Fair is fair. Off with these," she continued, struggling to slide the jeans off his hips.

Laughing, he grabbed her hands in one of his and held her still while he did the job himself.

"Any more of that," he told her with a rueful smile, "and this will be over before we begin."

He lifted her into his arms and placed her gently on the antique quilt.

When he stood there gazing down at her, she blushed and instinctively reached for the quilt to cover herself.

"No," he said, stilling her seeking hands. "Don't. I want to look at you."

She was beautiful, anywhere and everywhere he looked, Mike thought with growing desire. Even to the series of small birthmarks on her hip. And, she'd been honest with him, he observed with a tender smile. She was a blonde.

He couldn't wait any longer. From the look in her expressive eyes, and from the way her body trembled under his hands, neither could Annie. It took him only a moment to prepare and lower himself to the bed and take her in his arms.

He told himself to go slowly. To savor each moment, to thoroughly explore her. To pleasure her until he heard her soft moans of arousal. To see rapture growing in her eyes. The night was long and it belonged to them.

"Tell me what you like," he whispered into her seeking lips. "I want this to be a night you'll remember."

"Everything," she told him, opening her arms to draw him closer to her. "I want everything."

Sensing that her need was real, and that tonight had a meaning for her at which he could only

guess, he gave her her heart's desire. Her response told him she was as virginal in the ways of sexual gratification as if she'd never been married, never had a child.

The minutes melted into hours. The hours into the night. And at the end, the joy on her face mirrored the joy in his heart.

Only when the dew appeared on the roses beneath her window did Mike reluctantly put a sleeping Annie from his arms and cover her with the quilt.

He gazed down at her with a soft smile. The woman who had spent the night in his arms was a million light-years away from the one who had turned up out of nowhere to capture him, body and soul. When had he stopped looking at her with suspicion and seen the woman inside?

She sighed and turned over onto her side. How could he have suspected this lovely nurturing and caring woman was up to no good? How could he have ignored the magic of the love she created around her? There had to be good reason for her disguise, her odd behavior.

He had to follow the course his job demanded of him. But Annie was the last person in the world he would willingly hurt.

He would remember this night, he thought as he heard her murmur his name in her sleep, even though there was still tomorrow and new memories to make. He wanted the night to always be special to her, too.

As he looked down at Annie, he had a feeling they had created memories.

The intercom sounded. With a quick glance at the sleeping Annie, Mike flicked the button on the wall. "Cassidy, here."

"Good. There's a call for you," Clara said. "I tried your room first. I wouldn't have disturbed you, but it's very important. The mister just called. He and the missus are on their way from the airport. They'll be home in about forty-five minutes." She went on to fill him in with the details Mrs. Matthews had given her. "And don't forget to warn Annie," she cautioned before she hung up.

Puzzled, Mike glanced over at the bed. Warn Annie? Warn her of what—and why?

Annie was waking. "Who was that?"

"Clara." Damn, Mike thought, just when the relationship between himself and Annie had started on a new course, reality had to intrude. How could he confront her with questions when they had just spent the most wonderful night of his life together?

"What did she want?" Annie asked, rubbing sleep from her eyes. "And how did she know you were in my room, anyway?"

"Nothing important." He eyed her golden skin, her cheeks still flushed from sleep, and started toward her to take her into his arms. Questions could wait. "At least, nothing that will change anything," he said, grinning as he reached for her. "Just delay it for a while."

"What do you mean, nothing important?" Annie

yawned and stretched. "Clara would never have called you here if it wasn't important."

"Maybe you're right," he answered ruefully. He and Annie could explore their new relationship tonight. "It seems the Matthewses are on their way home. There's an unexpected important campaign meeting set for tonight. They'll probably only be here for a few hours, to check on the boys and make a few telephone calls."

A few hours? Annie drew the sheet around her, sat up in bed and looked frantically at Mike. "They're coming home today?"

"Sure, why not?"

"You don't understand!" Annie cried.

"What don't I understand?" he asked. Suspicion stirred in the back of his mind and a frown creased his forehead as he gazed down at her. "What *is* there to understand?"

"Nothing," she muttered. "Nothing, really. You just took me unaware."

"Come on, now," he replied. "You look as if you'd just been through an earthquake. How could nothing be wrong?"

"Maybe I just realized how it would look if Matthews found you here."

"Not on your life," he assured her. "I wouldn't do anything to jeopardize you."

She looked so appealing, so forlorn, with her tousled hair and eyes still slumberous. He headed for the bed, intending to kiss her again, and maybe

more. After all, forty-five minutes left them plenty of time to do what he had in mind.

Until he saw the apprehension on her face. She was as white as the sheet she clutched to her breasts. "They were calling from their limo. In fact, they ought to be here by the time we're dressed and downstairs. Is something wrong?"

Nothing had changed, he'd said? Annie threw aside the covers and scrambled for fresh clothing. If Mike only knew, more than just their relationship had changed. If she didn't think of something quickly, Robert would surely recognize her when he came home and found her here. And once he did, she might lose more than Mike: Her custody of the children could be in jeopardy.

She knew from experience that her ex-husband's giant ego couldn't take being bruised—and perhaps even less, now that he was preoccupied with his reelection campaign. He would believe she was out to make a fool of him. If anything, he would construe her presence as a betrayal of what he'd considered a magnanimous offer to let her have the boys nine months out of the year.

True, she'd had the children for twelve months last year, but now that Robert had decided he needed window dressing for his reelection campaign, things were different. Not that he really cared for fatherhood, but the role was convenient for him right now. Family values was the name of the political game he played.

"What's the matter, Annie?" Mike inquired. "You look as white as a ghost."

Annie tried to force herself to smile. A look at Mike's face and she knew she'd failed miserably. "I'm afraid I'm not feeling too well," she improvised, running a trembling hand across her forehead. "I think I may have a fever."

"Really?" he said, leaning over her. "You were fine last night. I hope I didn't do anything to hurt you."

"No. I think it may be just a touch of the flu."

Mike put his hand on her forehead. "You do feel warm, at that. Maybe you ought to stay in bed for a few hours. I'll ask Sharon to look after Bobby and Joey. The kids won't mind—maybe because she has three younger brothers of her own. She and the kids get along great."

"Maybe I will, at that," Annie replied as she settled back against the pillows. Last night's lingering rapture evaporated at the new crisis. Ice water flooded in her veins at the thought of what might happen unless she figured out a way to prevent it. But at least pretending to be ill would give her some time to think, to figure a way out of this unexpected turn of events.

Ignoring the worried look on Mike's face, she burrowed under the blanket—and muttered a prayer for a miracle.

She wouldn't think about Mike and their wonderful night of making love. She had to concentrate on the almost-impossible task waiting for her. Rob-

ert had to be made to listen. He had to be made to realize that the happiness of their children came before his own reaction to her masquerade. That she hadn't pretended to be a nanny to make a fool of him or to challenge his custody rights. That she'd done it for their children when they'd asked her to.

She would take her lumps if she had to, but not without a fight.

Chapter Eleven

No matter how hard she tried, Annie couldn't think of a way to keep her former husband from recognizing her if she went downstairs. She might have been able to fool everyone else for a while, but she knew she couldn't fool Robert.

This bit about the flu wouldn't fool him, either. He was meticulous and organized to a fault. Every player in his life was scrutinized and programmed or they weren't allowed to play at all. That would include the children's nanny.

She had only to remember their relationship. As soon as he'd decided she didn't fit in with his lifestyle, he'd asked for a divorce. Children included, he'd been willing to let her go with only the shared-custody agreement. If he saw through her disguise, it would be over. After all, as he'd told her more than once, he and the boys were part of the prestigious Matthews family, and as such, he had a role to play.

"Miss Annie! Can we come in?"

Annie started. The boys! Of course! As soon as

Mike had announced she wasn't feeling well, they were bound to come and check on her.

"In a minute!" She scrambled to pull on a robe, brush her hair and put on a smile. "The door's open. Come on in!" she called, after a quick look around to make sure Mike hadn't left anything of his behind that might give them away.

"Mike said you were sick," Bobby began as he inched his way into the room. "Do you have a temperature?"

"Is it catching?" Joey asked, hanging back. The forlorn look on his face was too much for Annie. She held out her arms.

"No," she assured him when he ran to her. "I'm just tired. But I hope this is catching," she added as she smothered him with kisses.

Joey giggled and put his arms around her. "Can I call you Mommy when we're here alone in your room with you?"

A sense of danger smote Annie's heartstrings. "No, sweetheart, I'm afraid not. Not even here," she replied, smoothing the frown from his little forehead. "Even the walls have ears."

"They do?" he asked apprehensively, and cuddled closer to Annie. "How come I can't see them?"

"No, not really." She laughed and nuzzled his chin. She'd forgotten how literal-minded small children were. "That's just a saying. But sometimes it's easy for someone to overhear us talking, especially if they're right outside the door. As a

matter of fact,'' she continued with a quick kiss on his nose, ''Mike told me he heard you call me Mommy on the merry-go-around yesterday. I had to tell him you only think of me as your mother because you're lonesome for her.''

''Gosh!'' Bobby muttered. Even at nine he seemed to be aware of the danger of losing his mother if the truth were to be known. ''What are we gonna do now?''

''Pretend, sweetheart. Pretend nothing is wrong. And if anyone asks you about me, just tell them the same thing I told Mike.''

''Anyone?''

''Mrs. Swenson knows the truth,'' Annie clarified. ''She told me she recognizes a mommy's love when she sees it. But I don't want you to think about that,'' she hurried to add when he looked alarmed. ''Mrs. Swenson won't tell anyone. But it might be a good idea to play down the way we care for each other just in case.''

''Don't worry, Bobby and I will protect you,'' Joey said stoutly as he clenched a fist. ''We won't let anyone try to hurt you!''

''No one's going to hurt me,'' Annie assured him, ''but they might try make me go home.''

''Even Dad?''

''Even Dad,'' Annie confirmed. ''But he has his reasons, and they have nothing to do with you. You boys mustn't forget he loves you, even if he doesn't show it.''

It was hard to explain to the boys that their father

loved them when he'd been too busy to spend time with them until now, but she had to try.

"No one's going to make you go home, either," Bobby announced, his jaw clenched. He glared at the door as if ready to take on anyone who came in. "You're our mom! Joey and I will make sure of that!"

Annie's heart swelled with love for her two wonderful children. If they'd learned anything during their young lives, they'd learn to protect each other. Every instinct reminded her not to let her guard down where they were concerned. How could she have allowed her desire for Mike to cloud her thinking? The boys came first. She was their security blanket, just as they were hers. She wasn't going to let them down. As for Mike, he knew how to take care of himself.

Now that Robert was home, it was time to have a heart-to-heart talk with him. Maybe he would be reasonable if she told him herself before he had a chance to find out she was here. The way things were going, the truth might leak out, anyway.

"Why don't you boys go on outside? I'll come down as soon as I get dressed," she announced.

"You promise?" Joey asked.

"I promise," she replied and sealed her promise with a kiss.

"It's good to see you, Mike." Robert Matthews shook the bodyguard's hand. "How have things been going the last few days? I meant to call home,

but my wife told me she'd arranged for things to go smoothly in our absence.''

"Just fine, sir," Mike answered. He rapidly inventoried the events of the past six days. Maybe he ought to tell his employer about Annie, and maybe even about the addition of two potbellied pigs to the Matthews household. A glance at the congressman busily flipping through an accumulation of mail told him the man had already forgotten Mike was here. "Nothing unusual," Mike added, tongue in cheek. The week had been one of the most unusual in his life, including Annie. But something told him the congressman wouldn't look at it the same way.

Maybe he ought to tell Matthews he was pretty sure Annie was the boys' mother. He dismissed the idea out of hand. After all, she was really harmless and hadn't done anything threatening. The boys were happy with her, weren't they? And he *was* keeping a very close eye on her.

"And the new nanny?" Mrs. Matthews asked as she handed her purse and jacket to Sharon. "Have you checked out her references? Are you satisfied with her performance?"

Mike felt a wave of embarrassment flood through him. If Edythe Matthews only knew. Annie had more than "satisfied" him— not that he intended to say so.

"She checked out okay," he answered. He would be damned if he got into a discussion of

Annie's qualifications. So far, she suited him just fine.

"And the boys?" Matthews asked, almost as an afterthought. "How are they doing?"

"They're doing okay, too. As a matter of fact, they're playing outside. If you want to see them," Mike offered, "I'll bring them in."

"Not now. I'll be in my den taking an important conference call. Please see to it I'm not disturbed," Matthews added. "When my campaign chairman, Dick Harper, shows up, show him right in."

"I'll come with you, dear," his wife announced, taking the mail from her husband. "I'm sure I can be of help with the new changes in strategy Dick has suggested. Please make up a light lunch and some coffee, Mrs. Swenson," she called over her shoulder as she followed her husband into his den. "This may take a while."

Annie stood frozen at the top of the stairs. She'd started down just as the door to the den slammed behind her ex-husband. Robert was evidently too busy to listen to anything she had to say. So much for her resolution to confront him with the truth and to ask him to let her stay.

Mike bounded up the stairs. "I was just coming up to check on you," he said when they met on the landing. "Are you feeling any better?"

"Yes, I am. It was nothing, really," Annie answered. "A brief weakness came over me. I'm fine, now." Her mind was awhirl. Even though Robert

had asked not to be disturbed, should she go down and corner him anyway?

"You're sure?" he asked softly. "I'd hate to think last night was too much for you."

"I'm not really sure about anything right now," she replied, glancing at the closed den door. "And as for last night," she muttered under her breath, "I'd rather we kept it to ourselves."

"Of course," he agreed. "I just wanted to make certain you haven't forgotten what we shared."

How could she forget when the look he gave her was hot enough to melt an iceberg?

"We'll keep it our secret," he said into her silence. "That is, if it's possible to have any secrets around here."

Annie flushed. She could feel herself turn fiery red. "Clara's calling you in my room was your fault."

"Maybe it was because Clara knew the rose would do the trick. Before that, she must have thought I was moving too slowly," Mike retorted. "But now that I have the hang of it..."

He left the rest of his sentence unsaid.

"I have to talk to Robert," Annie announced, ignoring him and looking over the stair rail. "How long did he say he would be here?"

"Just for today." Mike looked at her curiously, as if something she'd said had caught his attention. She held her breath.

"What did you want to talk to him about?"

"I'll let you know later. As a matter of fact, I

think I'll just go on in and talk with him right now.'' Annie ran downstairs and started toward the closed den door.

''No, I don't think you'd better.'' Mike grabbed her by her elbow. ''You'll probably just get thrown out on your ear and we'll all be in the soup.''

''Well, maybe,'' Annie replied with a last long look at the closed door. She could hear Robert shouting into the telephone. Mike was right; maybe it wasn't the time for her to talk to him. But she was determined to corner him before he left and put an end to this nonsense. After all, she *was* the children's mother. ''I'll be outside with the boys. Please call me when Robert's free.''

As he watched her leave the house, Mike was puzzled. When had the congressman become ''Robert''? And what could have caused the change in Annie from the lovable woman of last night to the grim-faced woman of a moment ago?

Now that he thought about it, it had all started with Matthews's phone call. The smile on her face had disappeared and dark clouds had gathered behind her eyes. In the space of a few minutes, she'd gone from being a seductive woman to one with a mission. The look in her eyes boded trouble for someone.

He'd been around long enough to know she had the look of someone with a score to settle.

Lucky for Matthews he hadn't been available to take the brunt of whatever was bothering her. Or was Matthews behind the problem?

That left him. She couldn't actually be angry with him, could she?

He thought back to last night. There hadn't been an inch of her intriguing body he hadn't explored, just as she'd explored his. There'd been a smile on her face to match the one in his heart.

Come to think of it, except for a few soft words of need and affection, there hadn't been a confidence they'd exchanged all night, either. He didn't know her any better in the morning than before he'd taken her to bed. Lord knew, he'd been too preoccupied to ask her any questions at the time.

Maybe he didn't know the real Annie after all.

But, he was willing to bet, there *was* someone who did. Actually, *two* someones. And he intended to question them both.

ANNIE'S LAUGHTER DREW him outside.

He found her on the front lawn with bath towels in her hands. She was watching Bobby and Joey frolic in the lawn sprinklers. In a short blue granny dress, her hair caught up in a barrette at the back of her head, she looked as young and carefree as the boys.

The sprinkler shower looked so inviting, he was tempted to put on his bathing trunks and join them. But he had a job to do and he couldn't do it romping in the spray. Even playing with the boys at Rehoboth Beach should have been out-of-bounds. Not that he hadn't enjoyed it, but he'd been there to guard the boys, not to play with them.

He'd sometimes wondered why the wealthy and influential congressman hadn't put in a swimming pool. He wouldn't have had to drive to the beach in Delaware or to any other place to keep cool, for that matter. If the weather continued to be so hot and sultry, it was going to be just a matter of time before Annie cooked up another bright idea to cool everyone off. As far as he was concerned, one outing had been enough.

"You'd think there'd be a swimming pool on the property, wouldn't you?" he casually remarked as he came up alongside Annie. "There's certainly plenty of room."

"The children were too small. We were concerned about their safety," she said absently, waving to the boys when they hollered at her to watch.

"*You* were concerned?" Mike asked. Alarm bells started to ring. He glanced down at Annie in surprise. Her smile faded as she must have realized what she'd said.

She swung around to face him. "Not really," she said with a nervous laugh. "I'm afraid I pictured myself in their parents' place. I know I would have thought they were too young."

Mike studied her silently. Her answer may have seemed logical to her, but her laughter had a false ring to it.

Why was it that every time he decided to bury any of his suspicions about Annie, and even though he was positive he knew who she was, she did something new to bring the suspicions back? Why

was he finding it so difficult to believe she was harmless, no matter who she appeared to be?

Maybe it was because he'd already decided she wasn't a professional liar. Maybe it was because he really believed she was basically an honest woman with an overripe imagination. And maybe, even though he was positive he was right about her real identity, it was because he wanted to believe what she told him was the truth.

He remembered the old adage "Love is blind." There was another one—"Love is blind, and only for fools"—which his father had quoted when he'd found out about Mike's big mistake. He'd been right; Mike had been on the verge of being taken by the con artist, Christiana Wells—a woman with two small children, just like Annie.

Mike had believed he'd learned his lesson until he'd succumbed to Annie's smile and loving ways. And yet...

"Annie?"

Her smile faded. She put a hand on his arm and gazed up into his questioning eyes. "Please don't ask me any more questions. Not until I get a chance to talk to Robert. If all goes well, I'll tell you then," she begged. "Just trust me. Just believe in me for now."

He wanted to. Lord, how he wanted to. Just as he wanted to take her in his arms, to feel her melt against him. To taste again the honey of her mouth, to inhale the quirky scent of vanilla that never

failed to quicken his heartbeat. And to protect her from whatever was bothering her.

To complicate matters, he was actually beginning to feel that he was a coconspirator of Annie's.

After a quick glance at the boys playing tag under the sprinklers, he cupped her face with his hands and bent to kiss her trembling lips. "For now," he agreed, although perhaps he shouldn't have. "But promise me you'll tell me tonight what's bothering you. I'll try to listen without prejudice, but I *am* the boys' bodyguard. I have a job to do, and I take it seriously."

"I promise," she whispered into his kiss. "I don't know how to thank you."

"Thank me with another kiss," he replied, brushing her forehead with his lips.

It was at that moment Mike became committed—committed to Annie who had brought laughter into his life. She'd begun to cure the self-doubt and anger he'd carried within him for the past two years. Now he would find out if what he knew in his heart was the truth, even if his mind still had questions: He was falling in love with her.

ANNIE FELT WRETCHED. Mike had always been honest and aboveboard in his dealings with her. She'd repaid him with lies and half-truths. In her heart, she knew she owed him that truth, no matter what his reaction to it might be.

She longed to be able to tell him about her marriage to Robert—that they'd divorced when their

life-styles became too incompatible. To tell Mike the boys were hers and that she was here caring for them because their father would not. That two little boys needed their mother to love them and nourish them instead of a stranger. And that she needed them as much as they needed her.

But she knew how much she would hurt Mike in the telling.

"Tonight?" he asked softly.

"Tonight," she agreed with a heavy heart.

"Will you let me make love to you again?" he asked as he took her hand in his and caressed her cold fingers.

"Yes," she murmured softly. Even though the unsaid truth hung between them, she wanted—no, needed—to taste again the new life he offered her. To know rapture at least one more time. Because she knew the moment was fast approaching when she would give herself away. And when that time came, the precious bond that had grown between them would surely shatter.

"Mike," she began as she looked up into his eyes, "maybe we need to..." Her voice trailed off. How could she deny him anything when his gaze burned her skin with its wanting? And when her own senses responded to that wanting with a surge of her own desire for him?

"Maybe we need to what?" he prompted until he was greeted by howls of protest. The automatic sprinklers had turned off and Bobby and Joey were headed for Annie. It would be seconds before they

threw themselves into her arms, begging to have the sprinklers turned back on. Annie knew she would agree, if only to give herself time to frame her confession.

"Ask me later," she answered.

"By the way, I meant to tell you the congress-man's meeting is over."

She seemed to wither before his eyes. "Some-thing *is* bothering you," he said.

"It's nothing," she replied. "How about keep-ing an eye on the boys while I go upstairs to freshen up before I find Robert?"

"Sure." As he gazed after Annie, he grew more troubled than before. Again, Annie had called their employer by his first name.

Mrs. Matthews came out of the house. The stud-ied smile on her face faded. She froze and pointed to the pigs in their pen. "What in heaven's name do you call those?" she screeched. "Robert, come out here this instant!" she called over her shoulder. "I want to see you now!"

Her husband rushed out of the house. "Really, Edythe. I still have several calls to make before we leave for the television studio. What could possibly be so important..." His voice trailed off as he no-ticed the pigpen and its occupants.

"Pigs?"

"Yes, sir," Mike hurried to explain. "Frank and Miss Hannibal are the boys' pets. You might say they're on loan from your neighbor for the rest of the summer."

"Pets? Frank and Miss Hannibal? Since when are pigs pets?" Edythe Matthews cried. "Who knows what those children will want to do next? Boys," she said, turning on Bobby and Joey, "go find your nanny and bring her out here. I want her and Mike to get rid of those filthy animals right now!"

At the mention of their nanny, the boys sent up a howl that could have been heard clear across the river and into the capital. Bobby backed into the pigpen gate. The gate flew open and Frank darted out and into the yard. Within seconds, Miss Hannibal followed him. The boys hollered for them to stop. Edythe Matthews screamed. Pandemonium broke out.

"Quick, let's catch them before they get away!" Bobby shouted as he and his brother took off after the pigs.

Mike stood rooted to the ground. From previous experience, he knew just how to help, but he'd quickly realized Bobby had opened the door to the pen to create a diversion.

A diversion for what? A glance at Annie's open window suggested the truth. They were trying to protect her from the Matthewses.

"Mike!" Matthews shouted. "Don't just stand there! Get those pigs back in the pen and take them to where you found them. I don't want to find them here when we come back!"

"I told you we should have given the children back to their mother!" The irate Mrs. Matthews

turned on her husband. "But no, you always know better. You wouldn't believe me. Now look!"

"But we decided on the family thing for the campaign," Matthews protested.

"It's been nothing but a big headache since they got here," his wife replied. "And, what with a bodyguard and a nanny, it seems to me to be a needless expense."

"Now, Edythe..."

"No, this won't work at all. Besides, if we need them for a photo shoot, I'm sure their mother will let you borrow them."

From her open window above the Matthewses' heads, Annie could see the melee, hear her former husband's threats and his wife's remarks. She gasped. "Borrow" her children whenever Robert's publicist thought it was a good idea? The boys weren't a cup of sugar to be passed back and forth!

She was about to dash downstairs to put him straight when she heard the blast of a car horn.

"We've got to leave for the television station right now!" Robert Matthews announced loudly over the excitement. "Take care of those pigs, Mike. And you and their nanny do something about making those boys behave. I'll call you in a couple of days to see how things turn out. Come, Edythe," he called to his wife. "We're going to be late as it is."

Annie saw Mike glance up at her window. She knew enough about him by now to know his sus-

picions had been aroused again.

"INTO THE HOUSE, boys," Mike ordered. "Go on up and get yourselves cleaned up before Miss Annie gets a good look at you, After that, we're going to have a talk."

"A talk?" Joey echoed with a quick glance at his brother.

"A talk," Mike repeated firmly. "Now, go on. I'll be up in a minute."

Mike hid a smile when the boys started into the house. The boys' grumbling was loud and clearly designed for him to hear. Not that he blamed them; he'd hated soap and water when he was their age, too.

He thought of the expressions on the Matthewses' faces when Bobby had crashed into the pigpen gate and all hell had broken loose. It had been a downright brilliant diversion and funny as hell. And very calculated. He intended to ask about their quick action to deflect their father's anger.

He waited until the kids disappeared into the house before he went back to fixing the pigpen gate. If he hadn't known better, he would have sworn the two pigs grinned at him. He started to smile back before he caught himself. Pigs couldn't grin, he told himself, anymore than they could fly.

Maybe it was Annie's influence that had softened him, but he'd actually grown fond of the two potbellied pigs. They'd gotten to him, for sure. The same way the Halloween party, the morning sun-

light on the ocean and Annie's catching the brass ring on the carousel ride had gotten to him.

With a last look to make sure the gate was firmly closed and the yard empty, Mike headed for the house. It was time to tackle the boys.

SMELLING OF SOAP and dressed in clean bathing trunks, Bobby and Joey were seated side by side on the edge of their bed, waiting for him. The fact that they'd cleaned up by themselves without any prompting was an indication of how determined they were to stay out of trouble. Which didn't stop them from casting longing glances at the open bedroom door when he came in. Mike closed it firmly behind him.

"Okay, guys, it's time to talk," he said, throwing Bobby a softball. "We'll talk a bit and then we'll go on outside and throw the ball around."

"What do you want to talk about?" Bobby questioned. "If it's about the pigs, we're sorry. Honest."

"No. It's not about the pigs. Let's talk about Miss Annie, shall we?"

"We don't know anything," Bobby announced with a dark look. He started to edge his way to the floor. "Can we go outside now?"

"Me neither," Joey seconded. "I want to go back outside, too."

"I haven't asked you any questions, yet," Mike remarked, swallowing a smile. "But I promise, you don't have anything to worry about. Okay?"

The boys nodded, sat back down and moved closer together.

"I just wanted to know how long you've known Miss Annie."

"Seems like forever," Bobby replied cautiously.

"Yeah, forever," Joey echoed.

"Did you know her from someplace before?"

"Feels like it, don't it?" Bobby asked his brother.

"Yeah," Joey agreed.

"Maybe she and your mother are friends?"

Bobby blinked. Joey covered his mouth with his hands.

"You like her a lot, don't you?" Mike asked gently, prepared to take one small step at a time.

"We love her," Joey said impulsively. His brother poked him in his ribs.

"We should all love each other," Mike agreed. "So how come you called her Mommy on the merry-go-round yesterday, Joey?"

"I forget," Joey replied, his lower lip starting to quiver.

"Maybe because she's so nice and reminds you of your mother?" Mike prompted.

Joey nodded, but his tears threatened to flow.

Mike felt like a heel. He'd known the kids would clam up when he started asking questions, but he'd had to try. Nowhere in his training at the police academy had they taught him how to interrogate small children. Now, if they'd been hardened criminals...

"You aren't going to tell me anything about Miss Annie, are you?" he finally observed when he couldn't think of anything to ask that wouldn't set Joey off. Something that wouldn't make himself feel guiltier than ever.

The two heads shook as one.

The boys' love and loyalty to Annie was obviously strong. Children had a way of knowing when someone loved them. He knew that much. And, surely, no child could love someone who intended to do them harm, could they? But then, they weren't the only ones taken in by a tender smile.

He had only to look at himself. It had taken him most of his life to learn the hard way when love was real and when it was a subterfuge.

"Would you like to call your mother?" Mike asked, trying one last time. "I'm sure I could arrange it."

"Maybe later," Bobby replied after a wild glance at his brother.

"Okay, boys," Mike finally said. "You can go now."

As they tumbled over each other to get out the door, their relief was so apparent it almost made Mike laugh. Maybe that was what he needed to put his suspicions to rest—more smiles. After all, that's what they were. Only suspicions.

Maybe he should accept Annie at her word. She would tell him everything when she was ready. In the meantime, he had to take her for who she appeared to be, and to enjoy her as long as they were together.

Chapter Twelve

Annie waited for Mike to come to her and fought the dread that threatened to tear her world apart.

In his arms, she'd discovered she was a sensual woman worthy of a man's love. And that, in spite of her ex-husband's disinterest even before their divorce, she was still desirable. With the discovery, her marriage to Robert faded into the background where it belonged.

She paced the floor, straightening the items on the dresser that had already been straightened, and trying to still her growing fears.

Tonight was going to be the gamble of her life. Tonight could mark the end of the new relationship that was starting to grow between herself and Mike, or, if luck was with her, it could be the beginning of a greater bond—a bond based on truth and trust.

A sound brought her to the door. The moment of reckoning had come.

But it wasn't Mike at the door. It was Joey.

"I'm sick, Mommy," he announced. "Can I come in?"

"Of course, sweetheart." She'd said good-night to Joey little more than half an hour ago. At the time, he'd seemed his usual happy self, especially when Bobby had offered to read him the latest R. L. Stine horror story. "How sick?" she asked as he came into her open arms, ready to remind him again that he should call her Miss Annie. One look at his flushed face told her he was too sleepy to remember her warning.

"My stomach hurts," he said, glancing hopefully over at the bed. "Maybe I have the flu like you did."

Annie swallowed a smile and led him inside her room. The three varieties of ice cream and several tempting toppings he'd had as a treat that afternoon were making their presence felt in her young son's stomach. Or perhaps the bedtime story Bobby had chosen had frightened him. Either way, he needed her.

"Does this make it better?" she asked as she tucked him into her bed. She slid in beside him and cuddled him in her arms.

"Yes," he said sleepily. "Can I stay in here with you tonight?"

"Of course." Annie gently rubbed her son's stomach. "But maybe you shouldn't eat so much ice cream at one time. What do you think?"

Joey seemed to consider her question before he reluctantly agreed. "Mike ate a lot more than I did. Do you think he's not feeling too good, either?" he asked.

"Let's hope not," Annie replied.

"Me, too. He doesn't have anyone to make him feel better, does he?"

"No, Mike doesn't have anyone to make him feel better," Annie agreed. Except possibly her. And tonight, tired of her subterfuge, she might even hurt him more.

Tonight was to have belonged to her and Mike. It was to have been a night to reaffirm their new relationship—a relationship that had given birth to her latent sensuality. A night when she would have confided in Mike and asked him to trust her.

Somehow, when he showed up, she would have to make him understand that Joey came first.

Softly humming her young son's favorite song, she looked down at him with compassion. His fingers were tightly laced in hers as if he was afraid she would disappear. His eyes were slowly closing. She kissed the top of his tousled hair and whispered words of comfort.

"Good night, son," she said when he sighed.

"Good night, Mommy," Joey answered as he turned on his side and fell asleep.

She heard a sound. Mike was standing in the doorway, the smile on his face slowly fading. In seconds, it was replaced by a look of pure anger.

Annie held a finger to her lips and slowly disengaged herself from Joey. She tucked the covers around him, drew a deep breath and prepared for the worst.

HE'D BEEN HAD.

Mike seethed inside as he watched the scene unfold in front of him. He'd known Annie was a fraud right along, hadn't he? So why did the proof facing him and the verbal exchange he'd just overheard anger him and make him feel as though he'd been cut off at the knees?

It wasn't as if he hadn't seen telltale signs pointing to something wrong about Annie before now. Hardened from his earlier experience, he'd suspected her from the day she'd been hired. He'd been so busy trying to be fair and objective about her, he'd ignored his gut reaction. In the process he'd swept aside her incongruous appearance and a dozen other clues.

Right off, he'd sensed Annie's arrival had been too on the button to have been a coincidence. So why, instead of following his instincts, had he allowed himself to fall under her spell? Especially since it hadn't taken him long before he'd already decided there was a good chance Annie *was* the boys' mother. What he'd heard tonight only proved what he already knew.

Why hadn't she trusted him enough to tell him the truth?

One thing was clear: He'd gone about solving the mystery of Annie the wrong way.

Looking back over his actions during the past week, it had been as though he was trying to prove himself wrong and Annie right. And all because

he'd been attracted to her blithe spirit, her quick mind and way the boys loved her.

Sure, it had all started with physical attraction. But it had moved beyond that so fast it made his head spin just thinking about it. In spite of himself, he'd become fascinated by Annie's fey appearance, the love that emanated from her and the way she'd kept changing. He'd even been too intrigued to pursue the obvious when it had stared him in the face.

It wasn't as if he hadn't seen through her. He had. After watching her with the kids, he'd known deep down inside him she was their mother, even if she'd hadn't admitted it. But now that he'd seen Joey in her arms and heard the affectionate exchange between them, the truth was impossible for him to ignore.

He didn't have to be an art critic to see the similarity between the picture Annie had made with Joey asleep in her arms and the Madonna and Child hanging in museums. Love between mothers and their children was universal.

Annie *was* Joey and Bobby's mother.

She was also a fraud. She'd taken him in as easily as a spider ensnared prey in its web.

As for his needing someone to comfort him, he thought with growing disgust, he was a grown man and he didn't need to be comforted.

What he needed was a woman he could trust.

It didn't look as if Annie was that woman.

Annie held her breath while Mike glanced over at the bed as if to reassure himself Joey was asleep.

Images of heated lips, arms that had held her and eyes that had swept over her with the look of love danced before her. Those same eyes now pierced her with a cold, unforgiving look.

Her last hope for telling him why she was here and gaining his understanding died.

If only she'd had a chance to explain before he'd found out for himself.

"You know the truth, don't you?" she asked quietly.

"Yes, I do," he replied bitterly. "As a matter of fact, I guessed days ago, but you confirmed it just now. I thought you cared for me, trusted me. I'd say what I saw tonight is the only truth in this entire misbegotten caper."

His cold, sharp gaze hurt her as deeply as if he'd wielded a knife to her heart.

"If you have anything to tell me, you'd better say it now," Mike continued. "Because I want you to pack up and be gone first thing in the morning. I'd want you out of here tonight, if it weren't for the kids. I'll give you a chance to say goodbye."

His steel-gray eyes grew colder as he spoke.

"There's only so much to tell, and it's really not very complicated," she answered. She looked down at his clenched hands. The same hands had roamed over her burning skin and had brought her to heights of passion she'd never dreamed were possible. Now they were clenched, knuckles white; the hands of a stranger.

"Why don't you start from the beginning and let

me be the judge,'' he prompted. ''Not that it's going to make any difference. You still have to go.''

Her heart pierced by his cruel words, Annie could only nod. At least, he intended to let her explain and say goodbye to the boys.

''Let's start with your real identity,'' he said impatiently as he glanced over at the sleeping Joey. ''Is Annie Kramer your real name?''

''No. My real name is Leandra Kincaid Matthews,'' she began slowly. Every word she uttered might be another reason for him to hate her, but she wasn't going to go quietly. Any mother would have done what she had done, given the opportunity.

''Not Annie?''

''No, but I've been called Annie since I was born. It's the name by which most people know me. That's why I naturally used it to get the position.''

''Naturally,'' he echoed dryly. ''So Leandra Matthews is the name you used on the driver's license you claim not to have had?''

''Yes, and no, I *didn't* have it with me. I was afraid it might give my true identity away if anyone saw it.''

''So, *that's* why I couldn't find any record of a license issued to an Annie Kramer in Virginia.'' Mike studied Annie coldly. ''And the employment agency was just a gimmick?''

''I'm afraid so.''

''The references you gave Mrs. Matthews?''

"I wrote them myself."

"There weren't any past employers, either, were there?"

"No. The three names I used are friends of mine."

"That was quite an elaborate setup you went through to get the job," Mike finally observed. "Who else around here knows the truth about you?"

"Clara Swenson. She said she'd never tell Robert or his wife."

"How did she find out?" He questioned her rapidly so she wouldn't have a chance to dream up any more lies.

"She just knew. Said she could tell a mother's love…" Annie look up at him, her eyes making tentative contact with his. "I'm sorry I had to lie to you, Mike. But I did what I felt I had to do at the time."

"I should have known there was something you were hiding when you called the congressman 'Robert,'" he said bitterly. "Seems to me you should have told Matthews the truth. Maybe he would have gone along with you."

What he was saying was logical, but then, nothing about Annie was logical.

"When Frank and Miss Hannibal fly," she retorted sharply. "Robert would never have agreed. He hasn't been reasonable for years where I'm concerned. His ego wouldn't let him. But the truth is,

I finally decided to tell him yesterday. Only I never got the chance.''

''So *that* was what you were so emotional about?'' Mike demanded with a cool glance. ''After last night, I was fool enough to think it might be me.''

''Last night was made of treasured moments I'll never forget.'' Her voice lowered, sounded more wistful. ''It was the happiest night of my life.''

It had been one of the happiest of his life, too, Mike thought as he saw tears come into her eyes. He remembered the way she'd responded to him. How her silken skin had tasted under his searching lips. How her flesh had burned under his touch. And how the faint vanilla scent of her had sent his senses reeling. Fool that he was, he couldn't help wanting her. Not even now, when he knew the truth.

Mike became more and more disgusted. Not so much with Annie as with himself. He'd known from the start that Annie was too good to be true. What he didn't know was why he hadn't been smart enough to do something about it before now.

''And you were Robert Matthews's first wife?''
''Yes.''

Mike glanced at Joey sleeping peacefully in his mother's bed. ''What in heaven's name possessed you to disguise yourself as the boys' nanny if you are their mother?''

The dispassionate tone of Mike's voice broke her heart. She could have understood if he'd been an-

gry. Maybe she deserved his anger, but not the remote gaze that dismissed her as if she were a stranger. Not after last night.

"Knowing that their father wouldn't agree to my coming here." Tears spilled down her cheeks now and she swiped at them with the back of her hand. "Bobby called me and begged me to come and stay with them while their dad was away. Since I realized that during his absence they would be surrounded by strangers who wouldn't recognize me, I agreed. But I changed my identity to make certain."

"I wasn't exactly a stranger by then," Mike said dryly. "The boys seemed happy enough to have me around until you came along. But why didn't you just come right out and ask Matthews if he would let the boys go back to you? Or allow you to come here to take care of them? It would have been a lot easier on all of us."

"Because it was clear he wanted them around, but not me. He wanted to play the family man for the media," Annie replied with a touch of bitterness she couldn't hide. "The boys had never been away from me before, not even for a day. I had to come when Bobby called. You do understand, don't you?" she asked.

"Yeah, I understand, all right," Mike answered harshly as he willed memories of last night away. "As a matter of fact, I understand too well. I've been through this type of experience before." At the bitter memory, he rubbed his forehead to clear

the ache that was starting to roar through his head. He thrust his hands into his pockets and, with another glance at Joey, he started to pace the floor.

"I was once a detective in the L.A.P.D., assigned to the missing-persons division. Two years ago, I was assigned to locate a woman who had kidnapped her own children from her former husband after a court gave him custody."

Annie gasped and covered her lips with her fingertips. Mike barely noticed, he was so intent on explaining his decision to have her leave—to himself and to her.

"I found her eventually. She appeared to be so young, so helpless. And very appealing. She gave me a song and dance about child abuse being the reason she'd kidnapped her children. I believed her. Maybe it's because I wanted to believe her. Hell, I don't remember anymore."

"What did you do then?" Annie asked him.

A glance showed him she looked as lost and as vulnerable as his nemesis had been. Only this time, Annie was real. Mike hardened his heart, telling himself he couldn't afford to soften—not again.

"I let her play me like a violin. I helped her and her two children hide. It was only a matter of days before I was caught in the act of seeking shelter for her. It turned out she was guilty of writing false checks and maybe even transporting some kind of drugs."

"You were only trying to help someone who

needed help,'' Annie interjected. ''Surely that's no crime.''

''The law is the law.'' He shot her a cold glance as if to say he wasn't surprised at her willingness to break the law. ''I should have turned her in. Instead, I was caught and scheduled for an internal investigation. I resigned from the force before that could happen. I couldn't bring myself to stick around and get caught up in the media frenzy.'' He shook his head. ''And all because I'd let my heart get in the way of my head.''

''What happened to the woman and her children? Surely the children weren't punished!''

''No, of course not. As it turned out, she got time and the kids went back to their father.''

''And with that experience behind you, why did you take this job?''

''I told myself I was doing it as a favor to a friend. The truth is, I had to do something to restore my confidence in myself and in my judgment.'' He laughed harshly. ''How wrong I was.''

''So that's why you're so angry,'' Annie said. ''You feel betrayed again.''

''You might say that,'' Mike replied. ''But this time, I'm going to end it differently.'' He stopped in front of Annie. She looked so lost, so vulnerable, he decided to make a concession. ''I will do one thing for you, though. If you leave quietly, I won't expose you to Matthews.''

The hurt in Annie's eyes was obvious. ''You still

want me to leave after I told you the reason I came here?''

"I can understand your reasons, all right," Mike assured her, "but I don't think Matthews would. I still think it was a fool idea. If you'd been honest with me from the beginning, none of this would have happened."

"You never would have let me in the door," she told him. "I sensed your anger from the first time you spoke to me, but I couldn't account for it. Now I can. It wasn't me you were angry with as much as you were angry at that other woman who betrayed you. And, from what you've just told me and from the way you're acting, I can see I've been tried and convicted in your mind. What difference would it have made if I had told you the truth back then?''

He shrugged. She was right. His earlier experience had made him suspicious of women like her— too friendly, too loving, too seductive. So far, her story seemed harmless enough. Her reason for coming here to be with her children might have been an understandable one, even if she'd chosen the hard way to accomplish it. But the fact remained: She'd lied. And she'd taken him in, even after he'd sworn never to be taken in by a woman's guile again.

For that matter, now he wasn't even sure about last night.

Annie's loving, blithe ways and her novel view of the world had almost converted him. A view that

had shown him there was goodness everywhere if he would only give himself a chance to look for it. Even in things he'd accepted all his life without thinking—like a simple sunrise.

Of course, he knew there was nothing simple about a beautiful sunrise. Any more than there was anything simple about Annie. She was a mixture of woman and child, mother and lover, student and teacher.

She'd even made him wonder what the hell was the matter with him that he couldn't accept her at face value. In fact, he could have listed a thousand little ways that made Annie special—until the moment when he'd seen and heard her with Joey and the truth could no longer be ignored.

Had she been playing a role all along? Had she seduced him only to ensure he wouldn't turn her in to Matthews?

"I meant what I said, Annie," he said as he shook off empathy for Annie's plight. "You have to leave. I work for Robert Matthews. He trusts me and I can't betray that trust."

He paced the room, glancing at the crystal vase that held the rose he'd brought her. A token of the love he had begun to feel for her, fool that he was. "I'm sorry, but you'll have to go. The most I can do for you is to wait to tell Matthews about this until after you've gone."

A sense of loss overwhelmed him as he went to the door and opened it.

"Don't forget, I want you gone as soon as you

tell the boys. I don't care what you tell them, but I suggest you be honest with them. After all, I have to live with them after you're gone and I'm not looking forward to any problems.''

He tried to keep himself from looking at her, but he failed. Annie stood there, in shock or in pain—he couldn't tell. Her eyes refused to meet his. With a deep breath, he collected himself and walked out the door. And out of her life.

MIKE PACED HIS ROOM, hating himself for what he'd done and hating Annie for driving him to do it.

In spite of wanting to believe her, he found her story about the boys calling her and asking her to come unbelievable. After all, when he'd been hired, he'd been told the children were going to be with their father only through the summer months; that the boys were to go back to their mother when school started. Hell, it was common knowledge the arrangement had obviously never been meant to be permanent.

So why had Annie felt the need for the masquerade?

He considered the man who was the boys' father. He might not be the father of the year, but he'd been good to the boys before he left on his reelection campaign. Granted, neither Matthews nor his current wife were ideal parents, but the kids hadn't been neglected. They'd had himself, Sharon and Mrs. Swenson at their beck and call. And Mrs.

Matthews until she had opted to travel with her husband.

He finally shrugged, went downstairs and out into the night to walk off his anger and frustration. A shooting star floated across the velvet sky. He didn't even bother to make a wish. There wasn't anything he wanted more than Annie. But, as he watched the falling star, he was certain of one thing.

Annie and her world had slipped through his fingers, as surely as if they had been made of gossamer.

Chapter Thirteen

"We don't want you to go home, Miss Annie! Why can't you just stay here with us?"

Annie felt her heart shatter into a myriad small pieces at Joey's tearful question. Poor little guy, he'd even remembered to call her Miss Annie; but it was too late.

She'd waited until morning to tell him she was leaving. Cuddling him in her arms, she stroked his blond curls and kissed his teary eyes. He was still in his pajamas and only half-awake.

"Miss Annie?"

Bobby, his pajama bottoms sliding down his slim hips, stood in the doorway. "I woke up and Joey was gone. What's the matter with him? Is he sick?"

Annie swallowed the pain that tore at her heart. "No. Come over here and sit down with me, sweetheart," she told her older son. "We have to talk." She lifted Joey and carried him to the rocking chair.

With a half-awake Joey perched on one knee,

and Bobby trying to fit on the other, she attempted a brave smile for their benefit.

"Joey had a stomachache last night and came and stayed in here with me," she told her older son. "He feels better now, don't you, baby?"

"Then why is he crying?"

"Because I told him I have to go home today."

With Joey hiccuping through his tears, it didn't take long for Bobby's face to start to crumple.

"Are you leaving because you're angry with us, Miss Annie?"

"Not at all," she assured him as she kissed his pert nose. "In fact, I love you more than ever."

"Then why are you going away?" Bobby cried. "What did we do wrong?"

"Yeah, what did we do wrong?" Joey echoed. Tears flowed as he looked up into his mother's eyes.

"You boys didn't do anything wrong," Annie told them. "It's just that I have my work to finish. I have clients waiting for me."

Why was it, she wondered as she slowly rocked with the boys leaning against her chest, that children always assumed they were somehow responsible when their parents divorced or one of them had to leave?

"I only came to stay with you long enough for you both to settle in," she continued, kissing each one on their tousled hair. "As soon as you were comfortable with living with your dad, I was going to leave, anyway."

"But why?" Joey persisted. "Why are you going away and leaving us alone?"

"You're not alone, sweetheart," Annie told him, holding back unshed tears of her own. "You have Mike to take care of you. And Mrs. Swenson to teach you how to make cookies. And there's Sharon. She told me she has three little brothers at home. I'm sure she'd be willing to play games with you, if you asked her to."

"No one can play games like you, Miss Annie!" Joey looked up into her eyes, his heart shining through his tearful gaze.

"You don't have to call me Miss Annie anymore, baby. You can call me Mommy."

She smiled when Joey frowned through his tears and bit off an instinctive retort. He hated to be called "baby" and she knew it. He was seven, and in his eyes, at least, he wasn't a baby anymore. But to her, he was still her baby. She suspected she would always think of him that way, even when he was six feet tall and had a family of his own. She gazed down at him wistfully. Every day with him was precious. He would be grown before she knew it.

Bobby's eyes widened as the meaning of her statement sank in. "Why shouldn't we call you Miss Annie? Isn't it a secret anymore?"

"No, it's not," she answered truthfully. "I guess my disguise wasn't good enough. Anyway, Mike figured it out by himself, and so did Mrs. Swenson. Probably Sharon, too, I guess."

"Is that why you're going home and leaving us here?"

"One of the reasons, but not the only one." Annie added another reason she'd spent the night thinking about and one that the boys would understand since she worked out of their home. "I have to get back to work. I have a lot of articles to illustrate for winter sales brochures."

"Mike will let you stay if we asked him to. Dad will never know if you don't want him to."

"Mike isn't making me go. I have my work to finish." Annie knew how important it was that the boys and their bodyguard remained on good terms. Without her, he was the one who would keep the boys safe from harm. And, judging from the way he related to the children, he was the male influence they needed in their lives to teach them to become men. It was too bad he would only have a chance to do it for a few months.

"I don't think you should go, just for some ol' drawings." Joey insisted. "Who's going to do all the fun things with us like you do? Mike didn't know how to have real fun before you came. He only knows how to play baseball and Scrabble."

"Then teach him to do other things," Annie suggested, remembering how Mike had learned to celebrate Halloween and to relate to potbellied pigs. And there had been the envious look in his eyes as he'd watched them ride the merry-go-round. "Maybe he never had anyone to teach him how.

I'll bet he'd like to learn. And if you get lonesome, you can call me whenever you want.''

There was a deep silence as they rocked. Sad as it was, both the boys had learned early on that not everything in life was the way they wanted it to be. After their father had packed up and left, it had taken months for them to get used to the idea he wasn't coming home at night. In fact, outside of a few Matthews family gatherings and the infrequent telephone calls Annie had initiated, they hadn't had much contact with him at all until this summer.

Now they had to get used to being without her, too. Thank goodness it was only going to be for a few months.

''Your dad will be coming home soon,'' she added to placate the boys. ''Wouldn't it be wonderful to have him to yourselves for the rest of the summer? Maybe he can take you to all the places you want to go.''

''Yeah,'' Bobby said thoughtfully. ''Maybe he could even get to love us again.''

Annie was shocked. How could she not have known the children felt unloved by their father?

''Don't even think such a thing!'' she told Bobby. ''Your father loves you! He's just been busy, that's all. You should be proud of him. Not everyone is lucky enough to have a congressman for a father. Congress is going to be in session soon and your dad will have lots of time for you. Wait and see.''

Annie said a silent prayer that Robert *would* re-

alize the treasure he had in his two sons. And that Mike would help ease the boys' separation from her.

"Come on, let's get you guys dressed so you can go downstairs. You need to have breakfast and I need to pack. I'll come down and say goodbye to you when I'm ready to leave."

Clara Swenson's sad eyes greeted Annie when she came into the kitchen to say goodbye. "The boys told me you were leaving," she said as she gave Annie a big hug. "I know they're unhappy now, but children heal quickly enough. Don't worry about them too much. I'll try to keep them busy—we all will. Especially Mike, you can bet on that. He really cares for the boys."

But not enough to give them back their mother, Annie thought sadly. "Where is he now?"

"He called a cab for you. He's waiting out in front with the boys so they can say goodbye."

Annie nodded and gazed around the kitchen where she and her sons had spent so many happy moments. She tried to burn into her memory all the laughter and smiles they'd shared here this week. Then, picking up her bag, she went out to the front step.

Bobby and Joey stood there, Mike's hands on their shoulders. They struggled to hold back their tears, and although she wanted nothing more than to run to them and hold them to her and never let go, she simply knelt in front of them. Taking each of their chins in her hands and smiling as broadly

as she could, she said, "I love you both very much."

And then she walked away to the waiting cab.

HE'D DONE WHAT HE HAD to do. So why did he feel so lousy?

Mike looked at the unhappy faces of the boys, their blue eyes so sad, and he felt like a heel. He wouldn't even let himself recall the pain in Annie's eyes when she'd said goodbye.

"What do you say, guys? Want to do something fun today?" He tried to cheer them up and, despite his own reservations and against his own rules, he suggested, "Still want to go to the National Air and Space Museum? We could take Sharon with us and make an afternoon of it."

"Maybe," Bobby said listlessly. "But it won't be the same without our mom."

"Yeah," Joey echoed. "No fun."

Mike knelt down in front of them. "I overheard you and your mom talking about going to the museum, so I know you want to go. Why don't we give it a try?"

Joey looked at his brother for approval, and when Bobby nodded, he said, "Okay. But—"

"It won't be fun without your mom," Mike finished for him. "But we'll try. We'll take Sharon for company."

Summer vacation had brought families to the museum from all over the United States. To Mike's jaundiced view, every one of them had zillions of

children, all of them squirming or shouting in his ear. He had to be crazy, bringing the boys here in this crowd. Why did he ever let their sad little faces compromise his better judgment? The lines to the new interactive exhibit, "What's New, Columbus?" were long. Tempers were short. Mike's was no exception. Even Sharon looked as if she would rather have been anywhere but here.

"I have to go to the bathroom," Joey announced after they'd been in line for twenty minutes.

"You just got here." Mike scowled down at Joey who was standing with one leg crossed tightly over the other. "Can't it wait?"

"No," Joey answered, looking desperate. "I got to go now."

"I reminded you to go to the bathroom before we left the house," Mike chided.

"I didn't have to go then," he said, his voice quavering. He rolled his eyes heavenward. "But I sure got to go now."

"Not by yourself," Mike told him, resigned to the inevitable. "Come on, Bobby. You might as well give it a try, too."

"I don't have to go!"

"I'm not leaving you here."

"Sharon's with me!"

"I don't care who's with you, I'm not leaving you behind," Mike insisted, grabbing him by the shoulder. "Come on before your brother has an accident."

"I'd rather wait here with Sharon and keep our place in line." Bobby edged closer to Sharon.

"No, you can't," Mike said firmly—he didn't intend to let the kids out of his sight. "Let's get a move on. The sooner we go, the sooner we'll be back." He and Sharon exchanged helpless glances. "Wait here," Mike told her. "We won't be long."

"I HATE CROWDS," Mike muttered under his breath to Sharon when he and the boys came back. "There're too many chances for something to go wrong."

"No one knows who you are," Sharon reassured him. "I'm sure you're worrying for nothing."

"I don't get paid for worrying about nothing." Mike's eyes scanned the throng of people waiting to get in to the exhibit. "I get paid to make sure nothing doesn't turn into something."

He could see Sharon eyeing the slight bulge under the left side of his loose blue cotton jacket. And the other bulge in the jacket pocket. She must know by now he had a gun in the holster nestled under his left arm and a cellular phone in the jacket pocket. He didn't care what she thought of the precautions he had to take—not that he looked forward to having to use the gun, but he intended to be prepared.

Once inside the exhibit hall, Mike was even more disturbed when he saw that the interactive exhibit was for children only. A sign asked adults

to move down to the other end of the room to meet their children.

So much for trying to keep an eye on the boys.

"How about going on to the end of the line and waiting for the boys?" he asked Sharon. "With a crowd this size, I don't want them leaving the area without me. I'll stay behind them on this side of the ropes."

Sharon agreed and started to make her way through the crowded hall to the exit sign.

The crush of parents standing behind their children and watching the interactive play prevented Mike from seeing if Bobby and Joey had reached the end of the exhibits. Frustrated when he couldn't spot them, he finally pushed his way through the throng to join Sharon at the end of the line.

She wasn't there and neither were the boys! And, unless she'd taken them on another bathroom run, it looked as if they were gone.

He could have kicked himself when the thought occurred to him: Sharon and Annie were friends. No doubt Annie had charmed the young woman, just as she had the rest of the household. By inviting Sharon to come with him, Mike had literally asked for trouble. For all he knew now, Sharon and Annie had become collaborators.

Damn, he thought, as he continued to search the crowd for Sharon and the boys. After what he'd been through this past week, he should have known better than to trust Annie. But she'd seemed so sin-

cere when she'd agreed to leave. He'd believed her.
And look how she'd repaid that trust!

As he searched, he recalled their last conversation when he'd told her she had to go. She'd sounded more bitter than usual over Matthews's wanting the kids for publicity purposes, hadn't she? Maybe she'd had enough; had decided to spirit the children away to prevent them from being exploited by their father—either to pay Matthews back or to get even with him for what she felt he'd done to the boys.

He frantically searched the crowded museum, inch by inch, frustrated by the way people kept moving around. If Annie had taken the boys, they were nowhere in sight. *Face it, Cassidy*, Mike told himself, *Annie and the boys are long gone.*

It was his duty to locate Matthews, he finally decided when his search turned up empty; to tell him what had happened. And until Matthews gave him the go-ahead to call in the authorities, he had to search for Annie's familiar face. Wherever she was, the boys and Sharon couldn't be very far behind.

"WHAT DO YOU MEAN, my former wife has been living here for a week? And in a disguise?" Robert Matthews, disheveled and furious from his precipitous rush home, faced Mike. "How could you not have recognized her?"

"I'd never seen her before last week," Mike explained. "And no one else around her worked for

you when she lived here. None of us made the connection.''

"But Bobby and Joey knew her! They could have told you she doesn't have an ounce of brains in her head!''

"And they knew enough to keep quiet, too,'' Mike replied, trying to restrain himself. With Matthews blowing off steam, it was hard to keep his own temper. The boys' disappearance was bad enough, but how could the congressman talk about the mother of his children this way?

"As a matter of fact, Annie told me they'd called her and asked her to come to take care of them while you and Mrs. Matthews were away. That's when she came and applied for the position of nanny.''

Matthews scowled at his wife. "How could you have been taken in by someone like Annie?''

"She never told me she was their mother!'' Edythe Matthews rejoined. "She may have come here under false pretenses, but she had good references. I asked Mike to check them out before I joined you.'' She looked accusingly at the bodyguard. "And he certainly didn't tell me there was anything unusual about this Annie Kramer, as she called herself. If he had, I never would have hired her, no matter how badly I wanted to join you.''

"And you, Mike! What in the hell were you doing all the time she was here?''

"Guarding the boys and trying to check out their nanny at the same time.'' Mike clenched his fists

and damned himself for his own stupidity. "I came up empty. She covered her tracks very well."

"Hell, Annie never had a sane or practical idea in all the years I knew her," Matthews snarled. "How could she have been smart enough to fool you? I thought you were an experienced body-guard. Sounds to me like you were just another sucker taken in by an empty-headed woman."

Mike seethed inside, although he took great pains not to show it. The congressman's disdain for Annie's intelligence and nurturing ways showed Mike just how unaware Matthews was of her rare and remarkable nature. And from what Annie had unconsciously revealed during their lovemaking, Matthews had never treated her like a real woman, nor loved her as a man should love his wife.

No wonder Annie had escaped into a fantasy life.

But wait a minute, he told himself. What was he saying? He was supposed to be angry at Annie for what she'd done, not trying to find reasons to jus-tify it.

"I wasn't taken in at the end," Mike replied. "In fact, when I found out the truth about who she was, I ordered her to leave. It broke hers and the kids' hearts, but she left without an argument."

"I was paying you to keep something like this from happening!" Matthews thundered. "As far as I can tell, you're just as guilty as Annie is in all of this—just by letting her hang around after you started to realize she was up to something!"

Mike kept his silence. After all, Matthews was too close to the truth for comfort.

"You're fired!" Matthews announced. "You were no better than no bodyguard at all. I don't need you any longer. In fact, I've made up my mind to ignore those fool kidnapping rumors. That's all they were. The greater threat to my children was right under my nose—their mother!"

"I wouldn't go that far," Mike countered. "She'd never harm Bobby and Joey. Not Annie."

"What in the hell do you know about my ex-wife?" the congressman demanded. "She's impractical enough to put the boys in jeopardy with some of her crazy ideas."

Mike couldn't contain himself any longer. "If she's that bad, why did you allow her to have custody when you were divorced?"

"Who in the hell do you think you are?" Matthews sputtered. "And just what does Annie mean to you, anyway? It sounds to me as if—"

"You don't have to answer that, Mike. I can take care of myself." Annie's voice was loud and strong as she came into the room. She looked around. "Where are the children?"

"Annie? Is that you?" Matthews stared at Annie with her brown hair and nanny clothes. "You don't look like the same woman."

"No, and you're right," she retorted, looking him squarely in the eye. "I'm not the same woman you knew, and furthermore, I never intend to be."

"What did you think you were doing when you

dyed your hair and dressed up like that?'' he asked with disdain. ''And why are you back again after Mike said he'd told you to leave? Is this another of your fool ideas?''

Mike took a step in Annie's direction. She halted him in his tracks with one direct look.

''I don't have to discuss my reasons with you, Robert. But the fact is I'm the boys' mother and I'm not going to let anyone push me around. Not you, not Mike. No one!'' She took a deep breath. ''Now, I want to see the boys and tell them I'm back.''

''Over my dead body!''

Annie ignored him. ''Where are Bobby and Joey?'' she asked Mike.

''They're gone, that's what!'' Matthews retorted before Mike could answer. ''And what's more, I'm not too sure you didn't have something to do with their disappearance. You're just trying to make me look like a fool!''

''Gone, where?'' she asked Mike, ignoring Robert's comment. She had a sinking suspicion that Mike's apprehension had come true. Fear for her son's safety almost paralyzed her when he shrugged his shoulders.

''You have to do something to find the boys, Mike,'' she cried. ''And as for you—'' she turned to her former husband ''—I love my children too much to use them as pawns, and I respect you too much to do anything like that. And, fool that I

was," she added with a catch in her throat, "I kept telling them you love them, too."

"Of course, he does," Edythe interjected. "It's just that being a congressman is a full-time job."

"And so is being a bodyguard, but it looks to me as if Mike forgot that when you showed up!" Matthews hollered.

"Hold on a minute," Mike shouted above the din as he raised his hands. "We've forgotten the real issue here. The boys are missing and before we lose any more time, we need to find them!"

"And we will, but not with your help! You're fired, Cassidy, remember? And as for you—" Matthews glared at Annie "—even if it turns out you had nothing to do with this, I intend to take you back into court for breaking our agreement. I intend to ask for full custody of Bobby and Joey. I don't want them under your influence any longer. And, furthermore, I'll even make sure you never see the boys again!"

"You couldn't! No judge would go along with you. I'm their mother!" Annie snapped back, although she felt fear shoot through her. Her worst nightmare loomed on the horizon.

"Watch me," her former husband challenged. "Don't forget I have the connections to do it."

"Wait a minute, everyone," Mike interjected before things got out of hand. "Let's stop and think. There may be a reasonable explanation for the boys' disappearance." Fired or not, he intended to

see to it that the children were found and Annie was protected from Matthews's wrath.

"There's a phone call for you, Annie." Clara stood in the doorway. "It came in on the private line in the mister's den."

"I'll take it. It might be about the boys," Matthews said as he pushed past Annie. "As far as she's concerned—" he glanced angrily at Annie "—she's out of here."

Mike stepped in front of the door. "I think you'd better let her take the call," he said firmly. "If it *is* about the boys, whoever has them may have a reason for not wanting to talk to you."

"I'm their father!"

"Right," Mike agreed. "But it's Annie the caller's asked for. Be smart, let her take the call."

"Robert." Edythe caught her husband's hand and pulled him back. "Listen to Mike. You'll know soon enough," she added with an inquiring glance at her predecessor.

Annie nodded. "Of course," she said on her way to the den. She didn't have the time now to think about Robert's wife. Maybe she was a caring woman, after all.

"Annie? Is that you?" the voice on the telephone asked.

"Yes. Sharon? Thank God!" Annie cried as she recognized the voice of the maid who had befriended her. "Where are you? Do you have Bobby and Joey with you?"

"Yeah. I'm sorry, but we got separated from

Mike at the museum. I tried to catch up with him, but I couldn't. I decided to come back and meet him at the house. Only the boys got frightened when they heard all the shouting going on. Especially when their father started shouting at Mike. They were afraid to go in with all that racket. So I did the only thing left for me to do. I brought them home to my house."

"You were right," Annie told her, the fear that had consumed her slowly beginning to fade. "Where are they now? Can I talk to them?

"Right now, they're out in back playing with my brothers. I waited until they settled down before making this call. After Clara told me you were back, I decided to speak to you. At the rate Mr. Matthews was hollering, I was afraid he'd fire me if I tried to talk to him."

"Don't worry about that now," Annie said. "Does Clara know where you live?" She listened for directions. "Stay there, I'll come to you."

"Who was that?" Annie turned around to find Mike standing in the doorway poised to go with her.

"Sharon. She has the boys. They're okay. They're—" Annie's voice caught and suddenly she started to shake. It was as if the fear she'd held in check was instantly replaced by cooling relief that chilled her to the bone. Before she knew what was happening, tears were spilling down her cheeks. "I'm sorry, I—

Mike was at her side in an instant. "I know. You

never cry." He offered her his handkerchief. "But it's okay to cry, and this time you should. Just let it out."

Annie stood there, racked with sobs of relief that her sons were okay. It was just a false alarm and soon she would have them in her arms again. She kept swiping at the tears and finally she was able to talk again. "They're at Sharon's house," was all she could say.

"Come on," Mike said. "Let's go tell Matthews the news. Then you can tell me all about it on the way to Sharon's."

More than anything he'd ever wanted in his life, Mike wanted to take Annie in his arms, to comfort her, to share her happiness. And to tell her he was going to work on making a miracle happen. But first things first.

Chapter Fourteen

"Mommy, Mommy, you came back!"

Annie ran forward to meet Bobby and Joey. She knelt on the grass to catch them in her arms. "I couldn't leave you two, after all," she explained, burying her head in their blond curls and smothering them with kisses. "I missed you both too much."

"We missed you, too," Bobby assured her as he patted her on her shoulder, "but Sharon told us not to worry. She said you were going to come back. How did she know?"

Annie sent Sharon a grateful smile. "Because she called your father's house and told me you were here waiting for me. I came as soon as I could."

Joey looked over her shoulder when a second car with his father in it drew up. "Does Dad know what we did? Is he going to be mad at us for getting lost at the museum?"

"You weren't lost, sweetheart. You had Sharon to take care of you," Annie replied as she hugged

the boys to her again. They were part of her; without them she had no reason to live. From the moment she'd left them that morning, she'd prayed for a miracle, knowing that miracles seldom happened—until a voice had sounded out of nowhere and told her to go back to her children. Realizing that waiting for miracles is sometimes not enough, she'd listened to that inner voice—only to find the boys gone and their father threatening to take them away from her for good.

"Are you going to stay with us forever?" Joey asked when he finally wiggled out of his mother's arms and looked apprehensively at the arriving cars and the group of people headed toward him.

"For now," she answered as she reached to stroke his curls away from his teary eyes. "But I don't know about 'forever.' That's up to your father."

Forever isn't long enough, Mike thought as he witnessed the kisses, smiles and happy tears. The scene tore at his heart. Annie and the boys were a family and clearly they belonged together.

As he watched the touching tableau, he realized what must have been bothering him all along. Even with Annie's offbeat disguise and the children's intermittent "Miss Annie's," he'd sensed almost right off that they *were* a family. And he knew now why it had taken him a week before he could bring himself to turn her in.

He'd grown to love her.

From almost the first time he'd seen her com-

passionate and generous nature, her love for the boys and her zest for adventure, he'd loved her without realizing it. She represented all the good things in life he'd managed to overlook because the profession he'd chosen dealt only with the bad side of life—even though he'd been too dense to see it until it was too late.

But, he thought grimly, maybe it *wasn't* too late, after all.

He owed Annie.

Owed her big.

If only she could someday see her way clear to forgiving him for his stupidity.

A glance at Annie's face told him she'd forgotten everything and everyone now that she and the boys were together again. Including him. He probably didn't have a chance with her. Not after the role he'd played in separating her from her children.

Watching the dramatic reunion unfolding in front of him, he couldn't remember a time when he'd felt more defeated.

"Here, let me in," Robert Matthews said, elbowing his way past Mike and Annie. "I'm the boys' father," he said over his shoulder to a man who followed him with a microphone.

Mike's eyes narrowed when he realized the man was a reporter for a television station. In seconds, a cameraman and an assistant pulled up in a news truck and rushed out to join the growing crowd around Annie and the boys.

"You called the media in on this?" he asked.

"Yes, of course," Matthews answered in a low voice that only Annie and Mike could hear. He moved behind his sons and proudly placed his hands on their shoulders. "When you called and told me the boys were missing, my publicist thought I should make an appeal on television for the return of the boys. But now that I've found them, it'll make an even greater story."

Matthews had found them? Mike grimaced. If not for the audience, he would have punched out the congressman right then and there.

"Edythe!" Matthews called. He led the boys away without a backward glance at Annie or Mike. "Come on over here and get in the interview."

Left behind, Annie stood watching. When the boys looked back at her and hesitated, she waved them on.

Mike could sense the sadness that seemed to envelop her like a black cloud. Surely there was something he could do for her to ease her pain. He moved to her side.

Annie swung away from him when he reached for her arm. "Don't touch me!" she spat out. "Haven't you done enough?"

"Annie, don't," he pleaded. "I only wanted to tell you I'm sorry."

"Too late," she retorted as she gazed after her ex-husband. Bobby and Joey clung to his hands. "Are you satisfied now? No matter how wrong you

knew you were, you did the job Robert hired you to do. You got what you wanted after all."

"I didn't want this, Annie," he protested. "Never this. Give me some credit. I had a job to do and I did it. You need to understand that, after my last experience, I was determined not to mess up again. I never dreamed it would end this way."

"How could you have equated me with that other woman?" she demanded, her anger overcoming her anguish. "You should have realized the only thing I'm guilty of is loving my children!"

"I know that now," he said. "Maybe it's not too late to do something about this. Maybe I can still help."

"The only thing you can do for me is forget we ever met," Annie told him bitterly. "As for me, I'm going to try to do the same. All I care about is having my children returned to me."

She looked over to where her former husband was being interviewed. At least, the boys were safe. Perhaps now, Robert would realize that being a real father was just as important as serving his country. Maybe more so.

She gazed over to where the boys were speaking into a separate microphone. "There *is* one thing you can do for me, after all."

"Anything, Annie. Just name it."

"Tell the boys I love them." With a last, long look, she turned and walked away.

THE FOLLOWING DAY, Mike went back to the Matthews house to collect his things. "I guess this is

goodbye, Mrs. Swenson," he told the unhappy cook. "You've been great to work with."

He turned to Sharon who was watching. "And I'd like to thank you, Sharon. I'm glad Matthews decided not to fire you. After all, you *were* the heroine in all of this. You saved the day."

"I'm sorry. I guess I should have brought the boys into the house," she told him, "but they were frightened at the hollering going on. I didn't want them to hear any more in case it got worse. But maybe I was wrong. I guess I made Mr. Matthews angrier than ever. I never dreamed he'd treat Annie that way. After all, she is their mother."

"Don't worry about it anymore," Mike assured her. "I understand, and I'm sure their mother does, too."

"You're not going to forget the boys, are you, Mike?" Mrs. Swenson asked. "They're crazy about you."

"No," Mike answered. "I'm not going to forget them." *Or Annie, either.*

There had to be a way to help her, he told himself as he drove away. And if there was the slightest chance of doing it, he would find it. As for telling the boys their mother loved them, he wasn't going to do that. No, sir. He was going to do his damnedest to have her say it to them in person.

IT WAS A FEW DAYS before things settled down and Matthews was back in his local campaign office.

At the risk of getting thrown out on his ear, Mike decided it was time to pay him a visit.

"Sorry, the congressman isn't seeing anyone this afternoon. He's in a strategy meeting," a bright-eyed volunteer informed Mike when he handed her his card. "But if you care to leave a donation to the campaign, I'm sure he'll drop you a thank-you note as soon as he finds time."

"Strategy meeting?" Mike inquired with a broad smile intended to throw the receptionist off track. He'd used that smile before on his job to lull suspicion, and with far less reason than the one that had brought him here. "Great. Strategy is exactly what I was hoping to talk to him about."

"Are you a member of the planning committee?" she asked doubtfully as she took a closer look at him. "I don't remember seeing you around the office before."

"Oh, I've been around the congressman, all right. He knows me very well," he assured her. He eyed her name tag. "Just give him my card, Julie, and tell him I have a suggestion for him he can't refuse. I'm positive he'll want to see me."

"You're sure?" she inquired in a voice that was definitely weakening now that he'd called her by name. "I wouldn't want to disturb him."

"On the contrary, I imagine he'll be very grateful to you after he's heard what I have to say," Mike told her with another encouraging smile.

"Well, if you say so. I'll be back in a minute."

The minute stretched into three. Mike could hear angry male voices and feminine protests. Casting Mike a reproachful look, Julie reappeared. Behind her, Matthews came storming out of his office.

"What are you doing here, Cassidy? I thought I fired you!"

"Let's look at it this way," Mike offered in as reasonable a manner as he could. He was here on a mission and he intended to accomplish it. "Let's just say I'm here as a volunteer to help you get reelected, not as an employee."

"Volunteer? That'll be the day. I don't trust you one damn bit," Matthews snorted. "Now, get out of here and don't come back."

"Let him spit it out, Bob," a voice called from the office behind Matthews. "Maybe his idea is worthwhile."

"Well, all right. Come on inside," Matthews reluctantly agreed. "I'll give you two minutes of my time. I'm very busy right now."

"How would you like to be a hero, Mr. Congressman?" Mike asked as soon as the door closed behind him.

"A hero?" Dick Harper, the "Re-Elect Robert Matthews to Congress" campaign manager asked as he gestured Matthews to silence. "What kind of hero?"

"The kind of hero who gets all the feminine votes in the state of Virginia."

Matthews dropped into his chair and eyed Mike

suspiciously. "And how do you propose I do that?"

"By returning Bobby and Joey to their mother."

Mike waited while his words sank in. From the look on Matthews's face, he wasn't taking the suggestion too well. On the other hand, Harper looked interested.

"Go on," Harper prompted.

Mike sat down, steepled his hands and went for broke. "For one thing, there are a lot of single mothers out there struggling to raise their children alone. Some even lost custody because some judge decided fathers know best."

Matthews waved his dismissal and rose to his feet. Mike knew then that was precisely what the congressman intended to do—remove Annie completely from the children's lives.

"Let the man finish what he has to say," Harper said quietly. "He may have a point."

"Some have ex-husbands who help out, but too many of them forget the joy of fatherhood," Mike continued. "Just think of how you would come off if you returned the boys to Annie instead of asking for full custody. And not only returned them, traded your summer custody rights for, let's say, one weekend a month. After all, you and I know how much the children love their mother and how much they miss you. Send the boys back to their mother and I'm willing to bet every woman in Virginia will vote for you in the next election. You

can even announce it on television. Think of all the publicity you'll get.''

Harper stared at Mike, no doubt mentally assessing the campaign mileage his candidate would get out of the maneuver. After a moment of silence he nodded. "Yes, I think that would work. Bob, I think you should do it.''

"But what would Edythe say?'' Matthews frowned. "She promised to keep an eye on the kids now that they're about to live with us permanently.''

"Edythe would probably be ecstatic,'' Harper said wryly. "She's one hell of a campaigner. On the other hand, who knows what kind of a mother she'd make?''

"Why don't you talk it over with your wife, Mr. Congressman?'' Mike suggested. "I'm sure she'll be willing to listen to reason if you tell her how important she is to your campaign.''

As Mike watched the broad smile on Harper's face and the rapidly changing expressions on the congressman's, he was willing to bet the farm on Edythe opting for the campaign trail.

THE DRIVE TO REHOBOTH Beach was the longest ninety minutes of Mike's life. And, unlike the last trip, the quietest, Mike thought with gratitude as looked through the rearview mirror at his precious cargo.

The sunshine had just started to light up the horizon when Mike pulled into the beachfront parking

lot. Its rays reflected off the ocean, strangely as calm today as a glass mirror. A light morning breeze drifted its way across the sand, bringing with it the sounds and scents of the awakening midway.

Mike inhaled the mixture of salt water and sunshine and thought back to the day when he'd seen Annie waiting at the water's edge and laughing as the water ran over her toes.

She'd been the picture of innocence—crazy clothing and all. Why hadn't he realized the truth sooner, instead of letting his past experience color his opinion of her?

He understood betrayal all too well, and had the emotional scars to prove it. But he'd had no right to inflict those same scars on Annie.

He hadn't tried to find her before this, to make it up to her—not until he had fulfilled his promise to himself to help her. Even if she'd told him she didn't want his help.

Today was the time to mend his fences and heal her aching heart.

With a quiet word to his two small passengers, he took off for the merry-go-round where the attendant had just arrived.

"How about starting up a little early?" Mike inquired.

The attendant looked around. "There's hardly anyone around to make it worthwhile. I just came early to do some preventative maintenance."

"Will this help?" Mike handed over a fifty-dollar bill.

"You mean you want me to start this thing up just for you?"

"Only two of us, for now," Mike told him with a glance at his companions. "Maybe two more, later."

"Okay," the attendant said, pocketing the money and laughing. "Maybe it'll attract a few more customers, at that."

"I don't doubt it for a minute," Mike replied as he gestured toward the silent horses. "Choose your mounts, fellows. I'll be back."

The haunting music from *Doctor Zhivago* floated through the air, played on to the end of the record, paused and started up again. The bittersweet melody and the tender, hopeful words brought Annie to mind more than ever.

"Somewhere, My Love..." A song of lost love, and hope for its return.

Annie had loved riding the carousel. Surely, this was the place where he would find her. The place where she would try to find solace—and, if it were up to him, to find the promise of love, happiness and fulfillment.

He found her sitting on a bench alongside the carousel, her eyes closed and softly humming along with the music.

"Annie? It's me. May I talk to you?"

She opened her eyes and studied him wearily.

"What is there to talk about? Haven't you done enough?"

"Not until yesterday," he answered. "Just give me a few minutes to explain. If you're not interested in what I have to say, I'll go."

She looked at him silently, contemplating her response. "You've come a long way," she finally replied. "I suppose I could listen."

Mike sat down beside her. He knew the next few minutes were going to be the most important in his life. No matter the outcome, he had to try to bring a smile back to her face.

The carousel music played in the background as he said, "This is the place where I first started to realize how much I cared about you. And where I realized how much I'd changed from the man I was when I first met you."

"Evidently not enough," she whispered, looking away from him and out over the sand.

"Perhaps not at the time," he admitted, "but since then you've made the process complete. You helped me see a side of life I wasn't willing or able to recognize before I met you. So, I figured this ought to be the place where I'd tell you I've fallen in love with you."

"Love," she retorted bitterly. "That's a strange word coming from you, all things considered."

"Maybe so," Mike replied. "As a matter of fact, almost everything in the past weeks have been strange. Except for today."

"What makes today different?" she asked, looking at him at last.

"Because today," he said, raising his right hand, "I'm finally willing to swear I believe in celebrating Halloween in July, potbellied pigs for pets, carousel rides and a sunrise over the ocean. I'm even ready to swear that I believe in you."

"You do?"

"Yes," he assured her. For the first time, he dared to hope. "I do. I don't want you ever to change. I want you to be your fascinating self." He gazed into the blue eyes she shared with her children. "Let your imagination fly as high as you want to. Just let me be your anchor."

"Oh, Mike!" Annie cried. "Even after all the terrible things I've said to you?"

"I deserved them," he told her as he took her in his arms. "But I'm a different man. Just tell me you love me back. And that you're willing to marry me as soon as possible."

"Mike, I love you, too. But I told you once before, it's too late. I don't know why you would want me, anyway," she added, looking into his eyes. "I've been only half a person since Robert told me he was going to take the boys away from me. I don't even know when he'll allow me to see them again."

"You haven't lost the boys at all," he told her. He stood and signaled to the now silent merry-go-round.

Annie's joy exploded when she saw Bobby and

Joey dash from between the horses. She laughed and ran across the sand to meet them.

"Mommy, Mommy, we're back!"

Mike watched her. The happiness on their faces when the kids threw themselves into her arms was a sight he would remember for the rest of his life.

"How did you get here? And does your father know?" Annie asked when the boys finally freed her and she could catch her breath. She ran her hands over their bodies as if she couldn't believe they were actually there, couldn't get enough of them. As if on cue, Bobby and Joey pointed at Mike. Annie turned to look at him through happy tears. "You?" she asked.

Mike nodded. "I owed you, but the truth is I got Matthews to agree for myself, as well."

"Yeah!" Bobby shouted, hopping up and down in his excitement. "Dad said we can live with you all the time from now on."

"And he's going to let us come and visit him some weekends as soon as the election is over!" Joey added happily.

Annie stood in front of Mike, her eyes brimming with tears. "I don't know what to say." She smiled at him. "Thank you for doing this for us."

"I told you, I did it for me, too," he said as he reached for her hand. "If there's room enough for me, I'd like to be part of your family. That is, if you'll let me."

"Cool!" Bobby cried.

"Cool!" Joey echoed as he looked up at Mike.

"When are you and Mommy going to get married?"

"As soon as your mother will have me," Mike told him, with a sidelong glance at Annie.

"I'll have you, Mike Cassidy," she said around a smile. "Right now."

"Tomorrow, Mommy," Joey ordered. "Now let's go back on the merry-go-round."

Mike laughed when Annie agreed and the boys scampered away to choose their horses. "Would you like to ride, too?" he asked Annie. "Maybe grab another brass ring?"

"Why don't we let the boys ride alone? Look at them. They're so happy, they've probably already forgotten I'm here."

Mike looked over to where the boys were laughing and calling for him and Annie to watch them. "You're sure?"

"Yes. I'll watch them from here," Annie replied with a twinkle in her eyes. "We might not get too many chances to be alone later. After all," she said as she put her arms around his neck and raised her lips for his kiss, "I've already caught the brass ring. I don't need another one as long as I have you."

He changes diapers, mixes formula and
tells wonderful bedtime stories—he's

Mr. Mom

Three totally different stories of sexy, single
heroes each raising another man's child...
from three of your favorite authors:

MEMORIES OF THE PAST
by Carole Mortimer

THE MARRIAGE TICKET
by Sharon Brondos

TELL ME A STORY
by Dallas Schulze

Available this June wherever
Harlequin and Silhouette books are sold.

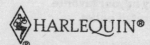 

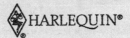

It's hot...and it's out of control!

Beginning this spring, Temptation turns up the
heat. Look for these bold, provocative,
*ultra*sexy books!

#629 OUTRAGEOUS
by Lori Foster (April 1997)

#639 RESTLESS NIGHTS
by Tiffany White (June 1997)

#649 NIGHT RHYTHMS
by Elda Minger (Sept. 1997)

BLAZE: Red-hot reads—only from

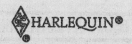
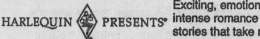

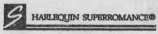

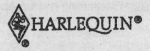

LOVE *or* MONEY?
Why not Love *and* Money!
After all, millionaires
need love, too!

How to Marry a
MILLIONAIRE

Suzanne Forster,
Muriel Jensen
and
Judith Arnold

bring you three original stories
about finding that one-in-a million man!

Harlequin also brings you
a million-dollar sweepstakes—enter
for your chance to win a fortune!

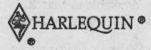

HARLEQUIN ®

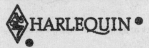

Mollie Molay

NANNY & THE BODYGUARD

Harlequin Books

TORONTO • NEW YORK • LONDON
AMSTERDAM • PARIS • SYDNEY • HAMBURG
STOCKHOLM • ATHENS • TOKYO • MILAN
MADRID • WARSAW • BUDAPEST • AUCKLAND

ABOUT THE AUTHOR

Mollie Molay started writing years ago when, as a
going-away present, her co-workers gave her an
electric typewriter. Since then, she's gone on to
become president of the Los Angeles Romance
Writers of America. A part-time travel agent,
Mollie loves to travel, and spends whatever spare
time she has volunteering; she's grateful for her
good fortune and wants to give back to those
around her. She lives in California.

Books by Mollie Molay

HARLEQUIN AMERICAN ROMANCE
560—FROM DRIFTER TO DADDY
597—HER TWO HUSBANDS
616—MARRIAGE BY MISTAKE
638—LIKE FATHER, LIKE SON

Don't miss any of our special offers. Write to us at the
following address for information on our newest releases.

Harlequin Reader Service
U.S.: 3010 Walden Ave., P.O. Box 1325, Buffalo, NY 14269
Canadian: P.O. Box 609, Fort Erie, Ont. L2A 5X3

> ## "I won't apologize for kissing you."

Mike grasped her by her shoulders and drew Annie to her feet. "In fact, I intend to pick up where we left off. I have something to prove. To prove to both of us you've been putting on an act to throw me off guard."

"An act?" Annie felt confused.

"And let me warn you, no matter the outcome, I intend to find out who you really are." And with that, he took her in his arms and claimed her lips, searching, demanding a response.

And respond was all Annie could do. She'd waited an eternity for this moment, to feel his hands touch her in her most sensitive places. With a breathless sigh, she buried her fingers in his hair and let herself be drawn closer and closer, until she was lost in his embrace. When he finally released her, she was unable to stand. She leaned into him and rested her cheek against his chest, felt his heartbeat echo her own. She heard him whisper her name like an unspoken question into her hair, as if he couldn't believe what was happening to them any more than she could. Then he fell silent and pulled away.

"This doesn't change anything," he said.

But he was wrong. Now everything had changed.

"The doctors aren't crazy. This could be danger-ous," he insisted.

"It's not as bad as they make it seem. Besides, you sound like someone who honestly cares," his father pointed out with a smirk. "Considering this is the first time I've seen your face since you told me to shove my money and my parental rights seven-teen years ago, I guess I should take you seriously."

The dig wasn't unjustified. This *was* the first time Blake had set foot in his father's house since he was eighteen years old. If he had never again walked through the doors of the infamous Boudreaux planta-tion house, he would never have missed it. He could have continued to live in the most luxurious settings in Europe, rather than return to this arctic tundra of a house despite the sultry heat of the Louisiana summer outside.

He would never have met his father's much younger second wife, Marisa, and his then five-year-old half sister if said wife hadn't been on a trip in Germany at the same time Blake had been involved with the princess of a small, nearby principality.

That's when he'd discovered that Marisa loved to travel to exotic places and be seen by the most impor-tant people. Abigail's care was relegated to a nanny while her mother spent her days exploring her next big adventure. She'd only taken Abigail along be-cause Armand had refused to let her leave the child at home. Marisa matched his father in narcissism, though she lacked his vindictive streak.

Blake had never thought he would ever care about

children in any capacity that had an impact on his life. His playboy reputation was widely known and accepted by all but those women who tried—and failed—to change him. Children were something that existed and were cute…as long as they belonged to someone else.

But one charming afternoon with the little girl with soft ringlets, wide brown eyes and a keen curiosity about everything around her had this playboy hooked. Luckily, Marisa had facilitated his attempts to stay in touch with his half sister until a few months ago. Blake would have had no idea about the present situation if his half sister's former nanny hadn't called out of the blue two days ago with the distressing news. Blake had rented a private jet and gone to New Orleans immediately.

Thank goodness he had an inheritance outside of his father's reach. His mother's exclusive gift had given him the chance to live a carefree life without a thought to money…or his father's opinion. The fact that he successfully supplemented that income with an avid interest in producing and distributing art was a bonus known only to him.

"I do care about Abigail," Blake finally said. Better to keep it simple than give his father any ammunition to use against him. "Someone should."

"She's weak. Life will toughen her up."

His father turned his laser-focused gaze on Blake, studying him in a way that made Blake want to squirm. He resisted the urge, of course. He was long past the point where he would allow his father to direct his actions in any way. Showing any sign of weakness would be seen as a victory by the old man, and Blake wasn't giving an inch.

"But since you're here, I might consider giving you the job."

That wasn't what Blake expected at all. "Excuse me?"

"The job of looking after her. Though you're hardly qualified for childcare, now, are you?"

At least I'm willing to try. Blake simply locked his jaw and waited. If his father was willing to about-face, there would be a price to pay. Might as well wait for the bill.

"I don't know," the older man said, fiddling with his diamond cuff links as he pretended to consider the situation. "I haven't decided if I'll let you see her at all."

A sudden tiny gasp sounded from behind a chair tucked into the far corner of the room. Unfortunately it echoed off the vaulted ceiling, and was magnified for the listeners nearby. His father's gaze swung immediately to the shadows.

"I told you to stay in your room," he yelled, his booming voice forcing Blake to suppress a wince.

A little girl slid out from behind the piece of furniture. Despite a little extra height on her, Blake would have said she was unchanged in the last two years. She had the same brown ringlet curls, though they were currently a tangled mess. The same vulnerable gaze. She hesitated before obeying, her brown eyes, flecked with green, seeming to memorize every inch of Blake as if afraid she would never see him again. Blake could certainly relate. His father was just enough of a jerk to forbid him to ever see her if he realized how much it meant to Blake.

So he hid his own emotions, gave Abigail the barest of smiles and motioned for her to go upstairs… before she heard more from her father about what a problem she was. Blake had grown up with a lifetime of those abusive rants stuck in his brain. He didn't want that for Abigail.

While her mother was here, Blake had thought she would be protected from the harsh reality of Armand Boudreaux's judgments. Now there would be no one in a position to protect her. The housekeeper, Sherry, might be able to check in, but she still had a job to do. Would that be enough?

Blake hadn't even had that much. He remembered long, endless days when he barely saw anyone except the cook, who would fix him a plate. He'd been healthy, but lonely. Except having his father take an interest in him had usually meant an hour of yelling about how horrible Blake was.

Blake couldn't allow that to happen to Abigail. Two years ago, he never gave his terrible childhood a second thought, but Abigail's situation was bringing a lot of bad memories to the forefront of his brain.

Turning his gaze back to his father, he continued as if they hadn't been interrupted. "You were saying I could help with Abigail's care?" Caution was the name of the game here.

"Sure. You care so much about her—" Armand

narrowed his gaze on Blake, a thin smile stretching his lips. "It might be worth something for you to see her."

Oh boy. "Don't you have enough money?"

The seconds-long hesitation sent a spear of worry through Blake. Money had never been an issue for his father. Not growing up. And, Blake assumed, not now. But that hesitation made him wonder.

Then his father said, "Not money, son. *Freedom*."

A pretty significant bargaining chip for Blake. It always had been. This would not end well. "I'm not following."

His father paced back and forth across the marble floor, the click of his dress shoes echoing off the vaulted ceiling. Blake's stomach sank. This was his father's move whenever he was plotting…planning. Definitely not good.

His father paused, tapping his index finger against his bottom lip. "I think there might be a solution to this situation that will benefit us both."

Hell, no. "I know how this works. Your solutions only benefit you."

"It depends on how you look at it." His father's smile was cold. "This could definitely benefit Abigail. Isn't that what you *say* you want?"

"I never said any such thing."

"Your actions speak loud enough for you."

And he'd thought he'd shown remarkable restraint… Remaining silent would keep Blake from incriminating himself further. So he kept his trap shut and his gaze glued to the man before him. Armand fitted in so well with the sterile beauty of the Boudreaux plantation. It was his perfect backdrop.

"Yes, I believe this will definitely work. I've waited a long time for this." Armand nodded as if confirming the thought to himself. His full head of silver hair glinted in the sun from the arched window behind him. "And you're gonna give me exactly what I want."

Blake turned away, panic running through him at the thought of going back to being that eighteen-year-old boy who had no defenses against his father. But just when he thought he would stride right over to the door and disappear through it, he caught a glimpse of tangled brown hair and pink leggings at the top of the stairs.

What choice do I have?

He could report Armand for neglect, but Blake doubted that would do more than dent his father's reputation. Armand knew too many people in high places for any charges to go far. Abigail probably wouldn't even be removed from the home.

He could take her with him now, but that would probably lead to him being accused of kidnapping... and she'd end up right back home.

He needed more time, more resources...but he could not let Abigail down, even if it meant turning his own life inside out to help her. Who would have guessed this playboy would grow a conscience?

He turned back to his father. "What do you want me to do?"

With a grin that said he knew he'd gotten his way,

Armand slipped through the double doors at the far end of the room leading to his office, then returned with a file folder in his hand. Blake didn't dare look up the stairs and give away Abigail's continued presence. But he was conscious of her sitting just out of his father's line of sight.

"There is a woman here in town, Madison Landry. She has something that belongs to me. Something you will retrieve."

"Can't you get a lawyer to take care of that?"

"That route has proved…fruitless. Now it's time for a different approach."

The rare admission of failure was unheard of from his father, which piqued Blake's interest. "So you want me to convince a former…what, lover?…to return something to you?" Obviously legal channels hadn't worked, so his father didn't have a legitimate leg to stand on.

His father smirked. "Hardly." He pulled a photograph out of the file. "Have you ever heard of the Belarus diamond?"

"No." Jewels had never been a major focus for Blake.

"It's a rare, two-carat, fancy vivid blue diamond that was gifted to our family by a Russian prince before we settled in Louisiana after leaving France. When I was young and foolish, I had the diamond placed into a setting for an engagement ring. For a woman who did not deserve anything nearly so special."

Well, this was news to Blake. He studied a photograph of a brilliant blue oval-shaped jewel. "You were engaged before my mother?"

"To the daughter of a now nearly extinct family from Louisiana society, Jacqueline Landry. The engagement lasted less than a year."

"So she dumped you?"

If not, Armand would have taken steps to get back what was his before walking away.

Armand's back went ramrod straight, as if he were affronted by the assumption. His sigh indicated he had no high horse to sit on. "She made the foolish choice to leave, and took the ring with her. That diamond belongs to our family. It is mine to do with as I wish."

But not the ring? This wasn't about a piece of jewelry Armand could hand down to his children. It was about something else... Money? Pride? Surely not after all of these years.

"Then you shouldn't have given it away," Blake reasoned.

"I sent several letters through the years demanding the ring back, all of which were returned unopened."

"From my limited experience with broken engagements, that's her prerogative."

His father's snap to attention told Blake he'd touched a nerve.

"Dammit, this is not the time for your flippant sarcasm. I want that ring and I will have it." Armand smoothed down his hair and jacket in a move utterly familiar to Blake. Growing up, he'd seen it often after his father's rages. Blake steeled himself as a wave of unpleasant emotions washed over him.

"You will get it for me, Blake."

"How? You don't even know if Jacqueline's daughter still has it."

"There's never been any record of it being found or sold. Which means it's still in the family's possession somehow. You will find this woman and get it back from her. With her knowledge or without it."

"You expect me to convince her to just hand over a priceless diamond that belonged to her mother?"

"You'll find a way. I'm sure a man like you, one who has seduced and discarded numerous women through the years, will have no problem with this mission. It should be a perfect use for the very few skills you've actually cultivated in your lifetime."

Blake had to admit, that stung a little. Even if it came from his father, who wouldn't have a nice thing to say about him if he'd used his wealth to become a big-shot CEO, either. Of course, the other skills Blake had developed he kept well disguised behind the facade of his carefree lifestyle. "Those women knew the score going in."

"This one won't. And I forbid you to enlighten her." He narrowed his gaze on his son. "Until afterward, of course. If you want to tell her you stole from her to save your sister, that's your business."

Armand handed over a file with all the confidence of a man who would get his way. "Read it. Let me know."

"I can't do this." *Could he?*

"And there's one more condition," his father went on, as if Blake hadn't spoken. "Access to Abigail will be limited by me until the job is done. But afterward, you can have her all to yourself. I'll sign the paperwork to wash my hands of her, and you can give her the upbringing you claim she needs."

Bile rose in the back of Blake's throat. He wasn't sure what he'd expected when he'd walked back through the Boudreaux plantation's doors, but no part of this conversation had gone according to plan. What business did a man who'd spent his life deliberately avoiding any type of responsibility have raising a young girl with epilepsy?

As if he could read Blake's thoughts, his father smirked. "Are you sure a playboy like you is up to the challenge?"

"Sleepy?"

Madison Landry started awake, embarrassed at being caught sleeping by her boss at Maison de Jardin. "I'm so sorry," she stammered out, "I'm just not sleeping well right now."

"It's not a problem for me," Trinity Hyatt said with one of her trademark gracious smiles, "especially since you're here on your day off. Want to tell me why that is?"

Madison tried to shrug off the question with a lame excuse. "There's always plenty to do around here." And there was.

The charity, which provided a safe haven and life skills training for abused women and children, was in a constant state of managed chaos. If it wasn't laundry that needed doing, it was job applications or fund-raising or any number of things. The desk in front of her in the downstairs office was filled to overflowing with paperwork and records.

Not for anything would Madison admit she'd come over to Maison de Jardin, which shared a border with her family estate, because she needed a distraction. Not because work needed to be done.

The last thing she wanted to discuss were the sleepless nights. The memories of her father's last painful days. Dreams where she could hear him struggle to breathe with the pneumonia clouding his lungs, causing fear to tighten her own chest. Waves of gratitude over the old-fashioned doctor who would still come to the house to treat him after her father's refusal to be moved to a hospital. The stuff of her nightmares.

Though the understanding expression in Trinity's soft gaze said she probably knew already. And her boss wasn't one to shy away from the hard discussions. "Well, I hate to see you suffering from insomnia. I had the same issue after my mom died. Just couldn't turn my brain off for anything."

"That's definitely an issue," Madison agreed, fiddling with her pen as she thought back over so many sleepless nights lately. It was one of the few things Madison felt comfortable discussing. She tried distracting Trinity from any deeper issues. "Besides, it's hard to retrain yourself to sleep well after having to stay alert during the night for so long."

Only her attempt at distraction just gave her boss more fodder for discussion.

"How many years did you take care of your dad?" Trinity asked, leaning against the doorjamb.

Her gaze swept over the room with familiarity, giving Madison a momentary reprieve. After all, the office had last been Trinity's. She'd only moved up to take care of Hyatt Heights, the company started by her late husband. He and his parents had established Maison de Jardin in New Orleans when he'd been a young man. But taking over his company meant Trinity didn't have time to run the charity, too, especially after her late husband's relatives had gone to court to fight over his estate.

Madison just happened to be in the right place at the right time. She'd known Trinity since she was a teenager, coming over to the shelter to help whenever she could. Unfortunately, her dad's illness had prevented that at times. But when Trinity had to move on, she'd trusted Madison to step into the role despite her age, knowing her life experience went way beyond her years.

Trinity's perusal of her old office ended with a look straight at Madison, who squashed the urged to squirm in her seat.

Madison cleared her throat. "Ten. But the sleeping and mobility issues were only a problem for the last five or so."

"Madison," Trinity said in a voice so gentle it eased Madison's instinctive panic. "You realize that it's perfectly normal to *not* be okay. Right?"

Madison knew her answers were clipped, but the dread she'd felt for weeks was clawing at the back of her throat with each word.

Multiple sclerosis was a tough disease. One Madison didn't wish on anyone after dealing with it up close and personal. The thought of what her dad had gone through always made her sad. He'd lost his business when Madison was young, then been diagnosed with MS before losing the love of his life. But they'd had good times together, too, leaning on each other for comfort and joy.

Madison could barely respond above a whisper. "I know." With a hard mental shove, she locked all those roiling emotions away. The more she talked about them, the more power they had. It was better just to move forward. "It's really okay," she said, mentally reminding herself that her restlessness and fear and pain could be normalized. "Last night, I spent the time cleaning and reading some more of my mother's journals." After all, what else was there to do at three in the morning?

There was a gentle caution in Trinity's question. "Are you sure you're ready to clean out the house, Madison? Your father has only been gone six months."

As much as she sometimes wished it didn't, Madison was well aware that life had to go on. "The house has to go on the market soon. With only me to clean it out…" She shrugged, as if this wasn't a discussion she'd had with herself a million times over.

Shuffling the papers on the desk before her didn't distract her from the ache of knowing she would have to sell the only home she'd ever had. It was falling down around her, even after years of doing the best she could with it, but every one of her lifetime of memories involved that house somehow. Knowing she would have to part with it was only making her grief grow exponentially.

But who knew how long it would take to clean out the clutter and sort through her parents' possessions? She discovered new pockets of stuff all the time. Just a couple of months ago she'd found a collection of journals that had belonged to her mother. Reading them had brought her memory back in vivid detail. They brought her a lot of solace as she sorted through more and more stuff.

And she had no idea how she would afford to do any of the repairs the house would need, much less cosmetic work, before she put it on the market. Her job here paid her substantially better than the odd jobs she'd taken to keep her and her dad afloat after her mother's accidental death, but years of neglect had led to some significant damage in what had once been the most beautiful, stately home in New Orleans's Garden District.

Deep down, Madison just wished it was all over and done with. That the house was fixed, sold and being renovated by someone who could afford to return it to its former glory. It might hurt to rip the bandage off, but at least it would be gone.

*I can only do so much...*was the mantra she lived by. All of her life Madison had focused on one task at a time, because she was only one person, usually working without any help. Coming to Maison de Jardin had allowed her to be part of a team. But for much of her life, it had been her…or nobody.

"I'm so sorry, Madison."

"Don't be," she replied with a shaky smile. But at least she still remembered how to form one. "Coming to work here has been the best thing that's ever happened to me. Thank you, Trinity."

"Girl, I couldn't do it without you. Especially right now. I know the women here are in good hands. But—" She grinned. "Enough of all this emotion… I have an exciting surprise for you."

"What?" Madison welcomed the change of subject, relief easing her tense muscles.

"Your dress came in!"

For most women, the news would be exciting. For Madison, it brought on another fit of nervousness. Next week they would be attending a society fundraising event, a first for Madison. She'd never had cause to leave her father's sickroom for such things, nor the funds. But in her new capacity as director for Maison de Jardin, it would be her job to mix and mingle with New Orleans's best and brightest. Though their legacy from Trinity's deceased husband should fund them for a long time to come, it never hurt to have support from others who could afford to help.

Thus, Madison found herself about to be presented to New Orleans high society.

A generation ago, it would have been Madison's rightful place. Her parents both came from established families that had helped found this incredible city. The last of their respective lines, the love merger should have cemented them as a power couple.

But Madison only knew this from a few stories she'd heard from her mother growing up. Her mother had been very secretive about their marriage and choice to live a more isolated life despite their prominent home in New Orleans's Garden District. Something had happened around the time of their marriage, but Madison had never been able to figure out quite what the scandal had been.

Which was why she'd been reading her mother's journals each night after finding them in one of the closed-off rooms on the upper floor of their house. Maybe there she could find some clue to how her parents had met and married. After all, stories like that might replace the sad memories she currently fought off during her sleepless nights.

Trinity took her hand and led her through the halls of Maison de Jardin to the master suite up on the second floor. It was currently empty, having been Trinity's room before she moved out when she married Michael Hyatt a mere two months ago. Michael's tragic death and Trinity's current battle over his estate left her life a little unsettled. Since Madison lived nearby for the time being, she hadn't claimed the space as hers, wanting Trinity to still feel like she had a home here if she needed it.

Laid across the pale blue bedspread was a beautiful lavender dress. Madison gasped, letting her fingers train over the soft flow of material.

"It's an unusual color for a redhead," Trinity said. "I think it's gonna be a fabulous choice."

Madison hoped so.

This was how she would be presented to society. Her stomach churned, though her nerves were a welcome distraction from her earlier grief. First impressions were a big deal. While her family name had been well known in NOLA in the past, history had slowly erased it from the current consciousness. The South still prided itself on its history, and the history of its families, but money stood for a lot more. It was the way of the world. Madison knew that and knew she couldn't change it. With her father's illness, her family had drained its coffers until all they had was social security and what little she could eke out from various odd jobs. Her father's health meant she couldn't go to work full-time.

She had to remember, this was her job now. Making a good impression would allow her to be helpful to the charity—now and in the future. But that didn't ease her nerves.

Should she back out now? Give in to the fear and tell Trinity she would need someone who could better handle this part of the job?

"Let's try it on!" Trinity exclaimed, her excitement puncturing Madison's growing fears.

When she stepped back into the bedroom suite after changing, Madison didn't recognize herself in the mirror. The bodice was fitted, with only one strap made out of fabric flowers that went over her left shoulder. Multiple layers of chiffon allowed the skirt to swing around her legs to right above her knees.

"A killer set of strappy heels and you're all set."

Madison chuckled. "Let's just hope I don't break a leg in them."

"You'll be fine. It just takes practice."

Madison brushed her hands down over the gown, learning the shape with her shaking fingers. She didn't even look like herself. It was hard to take it all in.

"We can do your hair like this," Trinity said as she lifted Madison's mass of thick auburn tresses to the top of her head. "With some drop earrings and curls."

"I feel kind of like Cinderella," Madison said with an unsteady laugh.

"Well, maybe you will meet a Prince Charming at the ball. It's really just a good ol' New Orleans party, but you know good and well there will be dancing. Won't that be fun?"

The very concept was foreign to a practical girl like Madison, but the transformation hinted at in the mirror egged her on. After all, she'd never been someone who backed away from what needed to be done. Ever. "I could use a little fun."

Trinity gave her an exaggerated wide-eyed look in the mirror.

"Okay," Madison conceded, "I need quite a bit of fun."

"As long as it's safe."

And requires nothing that makes me think too hard. In fact, a Prince Charming might be a little too complicated for her right now. Her life had always been and continued to be full of responsibilities and organization and obligations… She needed some space from all of that.

Madison smiled at herself in the mirror.

And who knew? Maybe she could find a *Prince for Now* to have some fun with. A girl could dream, right?

Two

What the hell was he doing here?

Blake should have been perfectly at home at the party being held at the home of one of Louisiana's most famous power couples. It was the type of event where people with money gathered to discuss local gossip and politics, and generally impress others with their money and intelligence...or lack thereof. Blake frequented many such parties all across Europe. The only change was the language and food. The people were mostly the same.

While he usually anticipated getting lucky at such parties, he'd never gone to one for the express purpose of initiating a one-night stand.

Yes, casual sex was a part of his lifestyle, but the women he spent time with were always on the same page. He made sure of that up front. The fact that the only plan he could come up with—in terms of feasibility and expediency—was to get into the Landry home by way of a one-night stand brought on a completely foreign feeling of shame.

But for Abigail, he'd do what he had to.

Hell, even reporting Armand for neglect wasn't an option. His father had more than one city official in his pocket. Besides, could he risk the possibility that Abigail might be forced into foster care before he could get everything worked out? At least at home there was a sympathetic housekeeper to keep an eye on her. Sherry couldn't be with her all the time, but she was always nearby and looking out for Abigail. At least, that's what Blake had gathered from their phone conversations. Given the odds of her ending up some place worse than his father's house, Blake knew his best bet was to get the diamond as soon as absolutely possible.

So, as uncomfortable as the idea made him, his only choice seemed to be seducing Madison Landry to fulfill his father's demands…unless he wanted to resort to breaking and entering.

It hadn't taken him long to spot the woman he sought in the crowd, though she appeared much younger than he'd anticipated.

Even in the photographs in the file, she hadn't looked quite as old as her twenty-six years. Maybe it was her pale complexion or the dusting of freckles across her nose that she hadn't bothered to hide for tonight's occasion. But somehow he'd expected the hard life that had been briefly chronicled in the file to show on her face.

She'd also spent most of her time here barely speaking and rarely venturing from the table she was standing near. He'd been anticipating someone eager to display herself on the marriage market, rather than the quiet woman he saw before him. After all, she was young, single and had too hard of a life to be a party girl. She wasn't dancing, though she moved slightly to the music as if it intrigued her. There was no steady round of interested men introducing themselves. Certainly no flirting.

She appeared to be a species he had no experience with.

He had enough confidence to approach her while she was still surrounded by her friends. But now it looked like he wouldn't have to. She'd just returned from the restroom to her table alone, looking longingly out on the dance floor. A young woman who needed to have some fun…and Blake was the perfect partner in crime.

Glancing down at the napkin in his hand, he grinned. Now he had an interesting opening to approach her.

Blake crossed over to the table and paused beside Madison's chair. She glanced up, then did the double take he was used to. Her eyes widened as she got a good look at him, though she quickly tried to mask her reaction. He'd never been uncomfortable knowing he'd dressed to impress—but for some reason he was tonight; it made him feel like a used car salesman.

"Hello," he said simply.

"Hi there." Her smile wasn't quite firm at the edges.

Then she glanced around as if he surely must be looking for someone else. But he wasn't. Blake knew exactly who he was meeting tonight.

Slowly he slid the napkin in front of her on the table and gave her a moment to get a good look. Her brows went up, then she leaned in for a closer look. Step One accomplished.

He'd made a sketch of her on the white scrap. Her face was in profile, and dead accurate, though the drawing lacked the vibrant color of her auburn hair and the multihued strings of lights decorating the large room.

He pitched his voice slightly louder to be heard over the music. "A woman this beautiful shouldn't be sitting on the sidelines."

The muscles in her throat worked as if she had to swallow a couple of times before she answered. "Is that a remark about my physical appearance or your artistic prowess?"

"Both?" he answered, surprised at her response. Most women would have gushed over the gift or been flattered by his remarks. He'd never been questioned over a drawing before.

Despite that, she rubbed her finger over the edges of the sketch. Finally she looked up with a small smile that seemed genuine. "How long did it take you to draw this?"

He shrugged. "About five minutes."

"At least you aren't too invested as a stalker," she said, raising a single brow as if in challenge.

Blake was shocked enough to laugh. Definitely not what he'd expected. Neither was her voice. On the deep side, slightly husky, it evoked images of mystery and sex. The opposite of her young, bright presence.

She ducked her face down for a moment, before glancing up at him through thick lashes. "I probably wasn't supposed to say that out loud."

"Definitely not." But she could keep talking all she wanted.

"I knew I'd never fit in here."

On their surface, the words could be taken as if she were teasing, just making polite conversation, but the way she worried her bottom lip with the edge of her teeth told him otherwise. "First time?" he asked.

She nodded, causing the colored lights to reflect off the glorious red of her hair. Blake had the sudden urge to see it down around her shoulders, rather than pulled back from the heart shape of her face. His lips suddenly felt dry. "Me, too," he murmured.

To his surprise, she leaned a little closer. "So you're not from around here?"

"Yes—" Suddenly the music cut out, making Blake's voice sound loud. "Yes, I am from here, but it's been a while. Care to be new together?"

Again her teeth pressed against the fullness of

her lower lip, causing blood to rush into the curve as she released it. "My friends will be back soon."

Blake ignored the subtle rejection. "Good, then they can watch me *not* stalk you on the dance floor."

Suddenly the music started up again, this time with an exuberant trumpet player in the lead.

He moved in closer to make himself heard. Leaning toward her ear, he asked, "Would you like to dance?"

Her breath caught, trapped inside her throat as she swallowed once more. Then her body gave a quick shiver, though it was far from cold in the room. Blake should be grateful for her reaction, this confirmation that she wasn't immune to him, but instead he felt a strange mixture of grim determination and melting heat low in his belly. Did she feel the same attraction as he found trickling through his unprepared consciousness?

Madison's gaze swung longingly toward the dance floor. Until now, the lively sound of jazz tunes had filled the air all night but she hadn't once approached the dance floor.

"Well, I don't think so."

To his shock, she pulled back a couple of inches. "What's the matter? Part of coming to a dance party is to dance."

"I think people come to parties for a lot of different reasons," she said, glancing down as she ran her finger over the edge of the drawing once more. "To socialize, to drink, to eat, to be seen..." She paused, and he swore he saw a flush creep over her cheeks, even in the dim light.

A woman who still blushed? Blake couldn't remember the last time he'd dealt with one of those. Before he could confirm it, she glanced the other way. Maybe to look for her friends? Maybe to hide the evidence?

He wasn't sure, but part of him, the part that had been watching her tonight, wanted to know for sure. In fact, the more he watched, the more he wanted to know. And that interest made him even more uncomfortable with what he was doing here tonight.

"I'm Blake Boudreaux, by the way," he said.

To his relief, no recognition showed in her expression.

"I'm Madison." She seemed to relax a little before she asked, "Did you move away for work?"

Oh, she was gonna make him earn that dance, wasn't she? "More like life management."

"Seriously?"

"Yes. Leaving allowed me to have a life." He softened his unexpected answer with as charming a grin as he could muster.

Madison cocked her head to the side, awakening an urge to kiss her delicate chin. He straightened just a little. "I'm just visiting long enough to handle a family issue."

She nodded, the move containing an odd wisdom considering her youth. "Those aren't easy."

"Never, but they are the reason we drink and have fun."

The laugh that came from her surprised him. No giggles for this girl. Instead she gave a full-bodied laugh that made tingles run down his spine. She didn't try to hide her enjoyment of his little joke or keep her response polite.

"So how about that dance?"

Suddenly a strange look came across her face—a combination of surprise and panic and almost fear. This time her retreat was obvious. Blake sat stunned as she mumbled, "I… I don't think that's a good idea. I mean…" She waved her hand in front of her as if to erase her response but inadvertently bumped her drink and knocked it over.

"Oh, my. I'm so sorry."

"It's okay." Blake wasn't sure why, but he reached out to grasp her hands in his. "It's okay, Madison."

She started to smile, but then her face contorted and she jerked her hands away. "Good night," she said, then turned on her heel and ran into the crowd.

Blake stared for a moment in confusion. They'd seemed to be having a good time. She wasn't as comfortable with men coming up to her as he'd expected, but she hadn't shown any signs of hating him during the conversation. What had gone wrong? This was not at all how he'd expected tonight to turn out. But then again, not much about Madison had turned out how he'd expected.

Honestly, this hadn't happened since he'd passed his eighteenth birthday, and he had no idea how to handle it. Something had spooked her. Should he leave it for tonight and try to find another way in?

Thoughts of Abigail and what might happen to her in the amount of time it might take him to find another opening into Madison's life had his heart pounding hard in his chest. He clenched his fists. He would not let her down.

Reaching out, he righted the now-empty wine glass. The small amount of liquid that had been inside had already been absorbed by the tablecloth. Next to the stain lay the napkin with Madison's sketch on it and a small lavender bag.

A bag? As the realization hit that it must be Madison's, so did a renewed sense of purpose. A one-night stand might not be an option, but at least he could arrange a date? It would afford him a chance to impress her and possibly find another way into her house to do some digging.

Plunging into the crowd, Blake didn't give himself time to think or plan. Halfway across the room he saw Madison and her friends near the door, speaking to the hosts as if they were about to leave. Adrenaline quickened his step as he realized his window of opportunity was closing.

The opportunity to find the diamond and save his sister. To understand more about the unusual woman with her emerald green eyes. To explore the strange feelings she called up inside of him.

Blake called out her name when she and her friends were just steps from vanishing through the door into the warm Southern night.

"Madison."

She glanced over her shoulder, her eyes widening

as she saw him. She turned back to her friends, but
Blake wasn't going to let that stop him. He stepped
into the circle without an invitation.

"Madison, I believe this is yours." He held out
the lavender bag.

"Oh, yes." She frowned as she looked at the offering. "Yes, I'm so sorry—"

"I thought you might need it," he said, cutting
off her words, which seemed to just compound her
awkwardness.

"Thank you so much."

He glanced at the couple standing with them, but
the woman simply gave a composed smile. "We'll
meet you at the car, Madison," she said and they
turned to leave.

Madison took the bag from his outstretched hand,
then fiddled with the strap for a moment. "I really
do appreciate this," she murmured.

Luckily, they were far enough away from the
dance floor that he could hear her. "Look, Madison. I think maybe I came on too strong back there."

"No. No, it wasn't you. It's me. I'm just not used
to—" She waved her hand around them. "Please
don't think you did anything wrong."

He could almost feel her need to leave as the feeling came over her. Something about her body language told him she was ready to run. He couldn't
let that happen.

"Tell you what, how about you make it up to me?"

Her gaze flicked up to his, and he gave her a
teasing smile. "Or rather, how can I get a second

chance…an opportunity to get to know you when I don't have to yell to be heard?"

Her muscles relaxed and she smiled, just a little. Why did that smile feel like a big victory?

So let's try this again… "Where can I pick you up?"

"Why in the world did I agree to this?"

Madison looked around at the array of clothes that she'd brought over to try on for Trinity. Never in her life had she done this. She'd never been the girl to worry over what she wore or what her makeup looked like or how other people perceived her outward physical appearance. Because her life didn't have anything to do with that.

It was about helping others and doing what needed to be done for her daddy. Not clothes and shoes. Her daddy had never cared about any of those things. And neither had Trinity. It was easier to do their job in jeans or yoga pants.

Even her mother's journals provided no blueprint for how to date. Madison had found them oddly lacking in information from before her marriage. There were a few comments about a happy childhood but nothing about dating or her engagement.

Right now, it was easier to focus on clothes than to wonder whether she could sit across from a man as suave and charismatic as Blake Boudreaux and be comfortable and happy and…have fun?

The women at Maison de Jardin were grateful for

a helping hand and a friend. That was what made Madison feel fulfilled.

Wasn't it? She had to admit to an unfamiliar restlessness since her daddy had died six months ago. It wasn't that she didn't enjoy helping people. But there was an aching need for something a little *more*. Something only hinted at on the nights she sang at a local nightclub—a hobby that she could indulge now that her father was gone. The pure enjoyment of losing herself in things that didn't require her to meet someone else's needs. That didn't require her to work, to figure out how to fix things. She'd been doing that stuff all her life.

Maybe it was the extra space in her life now that her last living relative was gone. Maybe it was her age, and the realization that most young women were starting to settle down or already had by now. Maybe it was just a quirk of her overactive imagination. But for once, she simply needed enjoyment without any responsibility attached.

Would she find that with Blake? Everything about that man made her nervous and excited and tingly in ways she'd never felt before. He made her feel emotions that weren't exactly comfortable enough to be called fun. He made her feel *too much*. Especially when he moved in close, smelling spicy and exuding heat.

Just thinking about it made her heart thud hard against her ribs.

She hadn't imagined two people could have that much chemistry outside of a bedroom. He made her think of magic and sin and heat all mixed together in the air. Incredible.

Which only made her more awkward, more anxious than she'd ever felt. Her life was built on a definition of success that had become uniquely hers through the years. Not money or fancy cars or expensive clothes, but days and hours and moments of achievement through sheer determination, hard work and action. Not this uncertainty that made her feel paralyzed.

"What am I doing, Trinity?" she asked, unable to resist nibbling at the inside of her lower lip. "Why did I say yes to this?"

But she knew why. It had been a combination of that tingly excitement and the fact that he'd tracked her down and given her purse back. She'd hastily surrendered her phone number, then rushed out the door with burning cheeks and butterflies in her stomach.

"Everything will be fine," her friend assured her. "Did he tell you what y'all were gonna do?"

"No," Madison huffed. "He said he wanted it to be a surprise. All I have is an address and that's about it."

"Which I know is driving you crazy. You're nothing if not prepared."

Trinity knew her too well. "The mystery should be perfect. It should help me step out of my comfort zone. Instead—" Madison pressed her fist against her stomach.

"I know, love." Trinity gave her a quick hug. "What's the address?"

Madison picked up her phone to review Blake's texts. "Looks like it's somewhere down near the river."

"Well, meeting him there is a smart move." Trinity's lips twisted in a small grimace, confirming Madison's belief that she needed to keep her own vehicle nearby. Better to take precautions and be safe than sorry later. "I guess working in this place makes me extra cautious."

Me, too. Madison had tried to be a modern woman—also something she didn't have a lot of experience in—assuring Blake she could get herself where they were going. After all, what did she really know about him besides chemistry? Except now the lack of information made her feel even more ill-prepared for the night ahead.

The array of clothes before her included a relatively small number of articles from her own closet and a few she'd just spent a meager part of her salary on at an upscale secondhand store. "So we'll be near the river, right?" she asked herself more than Trinity. With an impatient sigh, she grabbed a new pair of jean shorts and a casual blouse and forced herself to dress without thinking any more about how she looked.

Trinity offered an understanding smile. "If you need anything, keep your cell phone on you. I'll come get you if you call. No matter what time."

"I will," Madison said as she tried to breathe through her nerves.

"Text me anyway when you get there so I know everything is okay."

This time Madison smiled. "Yes, Mama."

But she was very grateful for Trinity's offer when she arrived at the address and found herself near a marina. She walked along the worn planks of the dock until she found Blake waiting for her halfway down. Next to him in the slip was a very smooth, very elegant boat.

Embarrassed heat washed over her immediately. Only sheer determination kept her feet walking toward him. He was dressed in a designer polo and dress pants, standing next to the nicest boat she'd ever seen—even on television. She tugged down on the hem of her shirt, wishing she'd opted for a summer dress at the very least.

What the heck was she doing here? she asked herself for the bazillionth time that evening.

Blake didn't seem to notice. "Good evening," he said smoothly.

Madison drew her gaze away from the craft, realizing her mouth had dropped open...just a little. But all that gleaming chrome sure was pretty...and way above her pay grade.

"I'm glad to see you made it," Blake said, as if he hadn't noticed her gawking.

Madison could barely meet his eyes. This wasn't a situation she knew how to handle or fix or arrange. What should she say? *Nice boat?* Was it even called that? Or was it a small yacht? *Ugh.* "I'll admit, I almost backed out." *Dang it.* Why did she say that?

But Blake chuckled. "I guess I understand. After all, I'm practically a stranger. Though why you wouldn't want to spend the evening with someone as heroic as me…"

"Heroic?"

With a sheepish grin, he offered a hand to steady her as she stepped onto the craft. "I did return a missing purse."

"That hardly qualifies," she scoffed.

"A guy can hope, right?"

She raised a brow at his begging puppy dog expression, then forced herself to glance around the boat. "The question is, can you pilot this thing without breaking it?"

"You'd be surprised how smooth she is in the water. A captain's dream."

Something about the way he said the words sent a tingle along her spine. The good kind…not the afraid-he's-a-serial-killer kind. To distract herself, she hurriedly took a picture of the boat's name on the prow and texted it to Trinity, much to his bemusement. Even though Blake didn't give her any creepy vibes, she wasn't taking any chances…and he needed to know that.

"A girl can't be too careful," she said with a shrug. "After all, if you are secretly a serial killer and I disappear tonight, at least my friends will know where to start looking."

His shocked expression made her laugh. Normally, Madison never censored herself when it came to laughter. There'd been too many sad times in her life for her not to cherish every happy moment. But here, on this beautiful boat with a beautiful man, her full-bodied laugh suddenly seemed loud, obnoxious. She quickly smothered it.

"That's actually pretty smart."

To her surprise, he didn't seem offended that she might think he was dangerous. She hoped that proved he could handle the quirks that made Madison who she was. Not that she should care. She should have the attitude that if he didn't like her, she could easily walk away.

This was about fun. Not relationships or happily-ever-afters.

So why did her hand in his feel much more important than that?

Blake had clearly spared no expense when it came to tonight. The boat itself was brand-new, with a lot of bells and whistles from what she could tell. It had a large deck, covered access below and several leather-upholstered chairs in the upstairs driving area. It was the on-water equivalent of a luxury car.

Blake cast off, then joined her in the chairs up front. Now it was just the two of them. Maybe she should be happy that there wasn't a captain to navigate and watch their every move all night. She wasn't actually sure if that would have made her happy or not.

Only twenty minutes into this date and settling down seemed impossible. Blake guided the boat smoothly out of the slip and down the channel to where the shore spread out before them. The boat practically glided on the glassy surface.

At this time of year, the breeze at night was cool and comforting, a relief from the midday heat. A recent rain had lowered the humidity, though Madison knew from experience that in a couple weeks it would be uncomfortable no matter what time of day without a breeze and a cold drink.

That was life in the South.

Blake picked up speed as they gained open water, which was when the first bit of uneasiness hit Madison's stomach. Her focus turned inward as she tried to figure out the source. Maybe her nerves? After all, she had experienced plenty of anxiety over the past few days. No, this was something else. Something she couldn't quite put her finger on.

The queasiness rose with each passing minute, forcing Madison to swallow once or twice. She tried to concentrate on the feel of the wind on her skin, praying that the feeling would pass. Of all the things she'd anticipated tonight, feeling sick was not one.

Blake slowed, then stopped the boat out in the middle of the glassy gray water. The wake rocked the boat, sparking a quick surge of nausea. Madison breathed in deeply, then let it out slowly. Maybe she'd be better now that the boat had stopped.

Blake smiled over at her. "Good?"

She nodded with what was hopefully a steady smile. The last thing she wanted was a double helping of embarrassment tonight.

"I'll set up dinner then."

Madison didn't move as Blake made his way to the back. At the press of a button, a portion of the deck floor retracted and a table rose out of the depths. *Well*. She guessed they wouldn't be eating off paper plates from their laps, would they?

She didn't have a lot of experience eating outdoors with formal silverware. More like fast-food wrappers and brown paper napkins.

Madison turned back toward the front of the boat, pretending to be absorbed in the view of the water. But her stomach continued to churn. What should she do?

Ask to go back? The thought of that trip had bile backing up into her throat. She definitely couldn't eat right now. So she simply breathed and prayed whatever this was would go away.

To her relief, the unease in her stomach subsided. She gave herself another minute, then two, but the ticking clock in her head told her he would start to wonder what was going on if she kept delaying. Finally Madison stood to make her way to the back of the boat. The world seemed to tilt as she walked, even though she could swear the boat wasn't rocking. What was wrong with her?

"I'm about ready," Blake said as she approached. Then he looked up from his task. "Are you okay?"

She tried to smile. She really did. Then she glanced down at the table and saw an open container of what appeared to be chicken or crab salad. Two seconds later, she was hanging over the edge of the boat to empty her stomach.

Three

"Are you okay now?" Blake asked.

The ultra-pale cast to Madison's skin worried him. Her freckles stood out even in the dim light from the dock. They'd made it back but the last thirty minutes had been a strain, as he knew the very thing he was doing to quickly get them to land was the thing that was making her sick. It had never occurred to him that she would suffer motion sickness.

He was used to drama like crying, yelling and feigned illness. One look at Madison, with her trembling and careful movements, convinced him this was real. His chest went heavy, filling with an unfamiliar mixture of responsibility and regret.

"No," Madison croaked, her hands tightening around the edge of the dock where she now sat. She swallowed hard enough for him to see. "Actually, I'm good. Just let me not move for a while."

"I'm sorry." Her sheer desperate need to stay still made his own stomach twist. Having ridden everything from a camel to a fighter jet in the name of adventure, Blake could only relate through sympathy. "Why didn't you warn me that you suffered from motion sickness?"

She cracked one eyelid open to peek at him. Even her brilliant green eyes seemed a paler color. "I didn't know. I've never been on a boat before."

That explained that. For the second time since meeting her, Blake found himself in the minor role of rescuer. Without an instructor in sight… "I'm gonna lock everything down. Will you be okay for a few minutes?"

She nodded but didn't speak. Blake left her to get her bearings on the dock while he secured the yacht and packed up their uneaten dinner.

He wasn't sure whether to laugh or rage at his current situation. His only thought when he'd chosen this adventure had been to impress her. He knew she didn't have a lot of money and probably had never seen a vehicle like this one. Add in the reflection of a full moon on the water at night. Instant romance! That was as far as he'd gotten.

He'd been searching for the quick and easy route to accomplish his goal of getting into the house. And maybe the current situation afforded him the perfect opportunity. He could kill two birds with one stone. By taking her home and watching over her, he could make sure she didn't suffer any ill effects from the motion sickness and get some time to search the house. The longer he spent with Madison, the more sleeping with her to accomplish his plan seemed wrong. Madison wasn't a casual girl and he simply couldn't treat her that way.

His frustration sparked as he thought back over the last few days and his father's refusal to let him see Abigail. He'd been worried about how she was, and anxious to do something the old man would see as "progress" so that maybe he could check on her. But looking over at Madison on the steady wooden planks, sunk in on herself to ease the pain in her stomach, made him feel guilty for that, as well.

Blake finished securing the boat, then stepped up onto the dock. "Here," he said, offering both his hands to help her up, "let's get you home."

"Oh, right." Madison pushed her hair back behind one ear. Was her grimace one of discomfort or embarrassment? "You don't have to do that. If you'll just call me a car..."

Blake scoffed. He may be a lot of things, but he wasn't the type of man to send a sick woman home all by herself. Besides, he still had a job to do. "Absolutely not. I'll take you home. Then we'll both know you're safe." He thought back to her insistence that she meet him here. "I promise I'll take you straight to your house."

With great reluctance, Madison put her hands in his and let him lift her to her feet. He waited a moment to make sure she was steady before letting go.

He held her hands just long enough to feel the tremble in them. Was she nervous? Was it him? Or something else?

Part of him was intrigued at the myriad emotions she'd shown tonight. Most women just put the best face on things, presenting him with a facade. But not this one—she was very real.

And overly quiet as they started the drive back to New Orleans proper. Blake had to admit he found himself at a loss.

Which reminded him of exactly where he was and what he was doing. He glanced over at the woman in the seat next to him, who had her gaze trained solidly out the window. She probably was embarrassed by all of this, whereas he was completely focused on his own emotions and complications.

So he softened his voice when he said, "What's the address, Madison?"

He knew exactly where she lived. But taking her straight there would give away too much. Instead, he'd play this out like he knew nothing about her other than what she'd told him. Then he'd go to work on plan B.

"Just take me to Maison de Jardin."

The husky quality of her voice only heightened the panic racing in his veins. Nope, that wasn't a good idea.

"Are you sure? Wouldn't you be more comfortable in your own bed?"

She immediately shook her head. "No," she snapped.

Surprise had him gripping the steering wheel

a little tighter. So she was more spirited than he'd thought at first. As he remained silent, she squirmed just a bit, causing her seat to squeak in the quiet. He glanced over at her, but she continued to face the window.

After letting the silence stretch out for a while, he took a deep breath and said, "Look, I just don't want you to be alone and sick." And that was true, despite his currently conflicted emotions and motives. "This is my fault. Let me drive you to your house. I'll stay with you until you feel better…rest will help."

Please let this work.

The barest sounds of a sniffle caused more panic to shoot through him. But another quick glance at her showed no evidence of tears. He'd dealt with a lot of insincere waterworks through the years, but something about the rawness of Madison's demeanor right now took it to a whole other level he wasn't sure how to handle.

"Just take me to Maison de Jardin. My friend Trinity is there this evening. She'll watch over me."

He felt a wave of disappointment. He actually wanted to be there with Madison. To make this better—though he had no clue how to do that. But he wanted to be there in a way that had nothing to do with his mission. At all.

Remember Abigail… Remember why you're here…

Right.

What could he do to salvage this? He glanced over at Madison, who was in almost total darkness.

True sickness wasn't something he had any experience with. What should he do?

He stewed for a bit, tapping his finger against the steering wheel. By her deep and even breathing, he guessed she'd fallen asleep. Probably the best thing for her.

As soon as the lights of New Orleans appeared in front of them, Blake came up with plan B. Madison slept as he found the local coffee shop he wanted, and locked her inside the car. After a few minutes, he was back. Madison stirred when the internal lights flicked on.

"Where are we?" she asked.

"Not far from the house," he assured her. "I stopped to get you something for your stomach. It probably shouldn't be empty."

She glanced at the cup and frowned. "I don't think coffee is a good idea."

"It's not coffee. It's ginger lemon tea. Supposed to help settle an upset stomach."

Slowly she reached out for the cup, as if scared to believe him. "Thank you. I wouldn't have thought of that."

"Don't be impressed," he said, brushing it off. "You have just witnessed the extent of my knowledge of medicine."

She chuckled, ending with a sigh. Maybe he'd salvaged something of tonight.

A few minutes later, he pulled the car into the circular drive of Maison de Jardin, which he knew bordered her own family land. The house was lit up, assuring Blake that someone was inside.

He unbuckled his seat belt. "Let me just—"

Before he could finish, she had unstrapped herself and was out the door. "No need. Thanks, Blake."

Then the door slammed and she made a quick but unsteady trip to the front door. Blake remained frozen as she unlocked it and slipped inside. Before she did, he caught how the lights along the sidewalk glinted off the wet trails on her cheeks. So much for plan B. He thought about her having someone to look after her, then thought about Abigail, wondering if she was okay tonight.

Would he even be allowed a plan C?

"Oh, Lord. We are in trouble now."

Madison looked over her shoulder to see Trinity and one of the tenants, Tamika, come into the kitchen at Maison de Jardin. She wanted to grin at Trinity's facetious comment but instead turned back to the stand mixer on the granite counter to hide her embarrassment. She was nothing if not predictable. Another strike against her.

"Don't judge," Madison said as she continued adding flour to the mixture. "Besides, everyone benefits."

"Tell that to my waistline," Tamika complained.

"It's totally worth it," Trinity said.

Her boss at the charity completely understood where Madison was coming from. After several years of working together, she could usually recognize when Madison needed some downtime. And showing up here last night after her disaster of a date certainly qualified.

Trinity had been helping out the night before with some budgeting work, which thankfully meant Madison hadn't had to take Blake up on his offer. But she suspected that Trinity hadn't wanted to be at her deceased husband's mansion across town, hounded by memories of her best friend and the business consultant hired to make her an acceptable heir to Michael Hyatt's business empire.

One of Madison's indulgences was to bake in the kitchen at the grand house. She could bake at home, but there were a lot of sad memories associated with her house, her kitchen. It had always been depressing to make micro versions of her father's favorite sweets, because there were only two of them to cook for, and there was barely anything in the cabinets.

Here in Maison's kitchen with its original brick walls, she could focus on the peacefulness of cooking for people who appreciated it. All the amenities didn't hurt, either.

Trinity peeked over Madison's shoulder at the batch already cooling on the counter. "Chocolate chip! My favorite!"

"I'm glad I could help," Madison mumbled.

Tamika said, "I should've known you'd be here baking after your experience yesterday. I guess residual nausea kept you from starting sooner."

Madison whirled around, slapping her hands on her hips. Flour dust floated into the air. "Who told you about that?"

Tamika's eyes went wide. "I guess a little birdie told me," she said before glancing over at Trinity.

Great! The humiliation of her failed date would be all over the building by noon, less than twenty-four hours since the debacle. Word spread fast. Madison gave Trinity a pointed stare.

Her friend had a chagrined look on her face. "Sorry! I was worried about you."

"*We* were worried about you," Tamika corrected. "That's why we're down here now instead of waiting until the cookies are completely done. Besides, we thought you might need somebody to talk to after those new posts."

"What posts?" Madison asked, confused.

Tamika shook her cell phone. "Your boy is the subject of today's *New Orleans Secrets and Scandals* blog."

Trinity groaned. "No, please, no more gossip!"

"Don't blame the messenger," Tamika said with a shrug.

Trinity stomped over to the fridge. "Right about now I could use a gallon of wine."

Unfortunately for her, the charity didn't allow alcohol on the premises. But Madison could fully sympathize. The anonymous owner of the *Secrets and Scandals* blog was in the process of making Trinity's life hell. The site posted all kinds of lies about Trinity's relationship with her late husband and questioned her involvement in his death. There had even been posts digging into Trinity's abusive childhood.

The popular blog had made Trinity's current sticky situation even more complicated.

Madison wished she could help her friend as she sought to learn everything she could from the business consultant the company had hired to make Trinity a better candidate to run the businesses. She knew Trinity was afraid of losing the court case Michael's relatives had initiated to take the estate from her. Trinity didn't discuss it too much, but Madison had a feeling the situation with the consultant, who was living in the Hyatt mansion, had taken a personal turn that had Trinity more than a little unsettled.

When Tamika handed over her phone, Madison couldn't stop her gaze from scanning down the post. Its headline blared, Playboy Home for Good? Various salacious tidbits jumped out at her from there: *Last seen romancing a Greek princess… Making a splash in Rio de Janeiro…* Photographs of him looking like a Scandinavian prince with a blonde model in a bikini…

Feeling a little sick, Madison handed the phone back. That last picture especially left her feeling like a complete washout as a woman. Blake had spent his life surrounded by gorgeous women who were obviously more on his level…and could actually ride in a yacht without losing their lunch. Heck, they probably owned yachts themselves.

What in the world had he been doing with a down-on-her-luck charity director from New Orleans?

"This guy really lived it up in Europe," Tamika crowed. "He's been spotted skiing in the Alps with beautiful women, on all the best beaches, at all the fancy parties. And he doesn't seem to have a day job, so he's got to be loaded."

"Hey, he sounds like a perfect guy to just have fun with," Trinity mumbled around a bite of cookie.

Madison glared at Trinity for a second, who simply shrugged. Bitterness built up in her throat, roughening her voice as she said, "I have no idea what he was looking for on a date with someone like me, but I'm pretty sure it wasn't me hanging over the side of his boat vomiting. I seriously doubt I'll ever hear from Blake Boudreaux again."

Madison stared morosely down into the second batch of chocolate chip cookie dough, hating that she cared so much about this…hating that she couldn't shake it off…hating that she didn't seem to be the type of woman who could just have fun and not care when things went wrong.

Then she heard a slight giggle from her left, then from her right. She glanced up to find her friends desperately struggling to hold in the laughter. "I'm sorry," Trinity said. "But the visual your words call to mind is just…"

Tamika couldn't hold back any longer and burst out in laughter. Madison realized what she'd said and started to smile…then giggle…then laugh. The image of her hanging over the railing, backside in the air, while a sexy, incredibly rich man watched her ralph over the side of his yacht… If she didn't laugh, she was gonna cry.

Eventually they were all indulging in full-on belly

laughs. A sense of gratitude for these good friends who understood her and weren't afraid of a quirky sense of humor warmed her up. All too soon, they were down to a few chuckles and wiping the tears from their faces as they indulged in another spoonful of dough.

"Thanks, guys," Madison said as she tried to catch her breath. "I needed that."

But as she slowly chewed a few chocolate chips, savoring the burst of flavor against her tongue, she sobered. What had a man like that been doing with her? He was obviously sophisticated, and according to the post, he'd been with plenty of women. Model types. Nothing like Madison's red hair and freckles.

Why had he picked the least likely woman at the party to ask on a date?

"Sometimes I wonder if I was being punked the night we met." And yesterday. Except she wasn't anyone anymore. No one would care enough to read about *her*.

Trinity scoffed. "Of course not! You're a bright, attractive woman…"

"With a tendency to fatten up everyone around you," Tamika said with a saucy grin.

"We won't mention that," Madison mumbled.

Trinity raised her voice. "Who bakes the best chocolate chip cookies around…"

Not to be outdone, Tamika added, "Along with chocolate chip Bundt cakes, macaroons, apple fritters…"

"So I like to feed people. So what?"

The teasing felt good, though. Madison had gone a long time feeling alone and unappreciated. Not that her daddy hadn't loved her, but she'd been taking care of him so long that it had become more habit than anything for him to say thank-you. She knew how precious it was to have people in her life who loved her, and she made sure she let them know. Even if it was just by delivering a plate of brownies.

Here, in this kitchen, was the place she'd felt most welcome in her lifetime. That was the most important thing. Not some guy she'd just met and embarrassed herself in front of.

Her phone lit up just then, causing her to glance over at it. Blake's name flashed on the screen. "I thought for sure I'd deleted that number..." she mumbled, remembering her middle-of-the-night intention.

That was wishful thinking. After all, it wasn't like she had that many numbers in her phone. She stared at it, trying to decide what to do.

Tamika leaned over the counter for a look. "Girl, he is interested! You'd better answer that."

With the girls goading her on, Madison reached out and connected the call. The phone was chilly against her ear as she gathered the courage to speak. "Hello," she croaked.

"Hi, Madison."

Wow. How could just hearing that deep voice make her chest ache for what could have been? If only she were a different type of person. The kind who went with the flow instead of diving deep into the tide.

"Uh, hi."

"How are you feeling?"

"Fine." Could she be any more lame? "I mean, everything's good. Just some motion sickness." That she hoped never to experience again. "Boats are definitely not for me," she said, trying to laugh it off.

A glance over at Trinity and Tamika made her cringe. They weren't even pretending to not eavesdrop. Instead they both nibbled on warm cookies, watching while she agonized over what to say.

"I don't blame you," Blake said, then paused. After a long minute of silence, he went on. "Listen, I wondered if you wanted to go out again tomorrow night. Something completely on land this time."

Madison worried the inside of her bottom lip, trying to decide what to do. Even though they couldn't hear him, Trinity had a slightly skeptical look on her face. Tamika, on the other hand, was giving her the thumbs-up. For someone who came to Maison de Jardin after being in an abusive relationship, Tamika had managed to maintain her belief that a happily-ever-after was somehow attainable. Or at the very least, that a couple of good nights could be salvaged from the situation.

"Madison? You there?"

Out of the blue, a wave of nausea hit her. It ebbed, then flowed, just as it had with the motion of the boat. Maybe she just wasn't ready?

She was shaking her head before the words tumbled out of her mouth. "No, I don't think so, Blake. Goodbye."

She stared down at the phone in her hand, wondering what the heck just happened. For a woman who had been determined a few days ago that she needed a little fun in her life, this had been the most stressful attempt at fun she'd ever known.

It reminded her of her attempts throughout the years to carve out time for herself as a caregiver. She'd known she needed to renew her energy, to rest, but it had been too complicated to make it worth her while. By the time she'd hit on the one thing that brought her joy and was easy to fit into their lives, her father had fallen into a rapid decline. Death had followed not a month later.

A glance up showed a mixture of dismay and understanding on her friend's faces. Madison just continued to shake her head. "What the heck is wrong with me?"

Four

So Madison had forced him to move to plan C.

Blake couldn't believe it when Madison turned down his request for another date. What was he, the plague? She was nothing like any of the women he'd dated before, but he was realizing that that was part of what kept him intrigued.

He knew from being with her that Madison wasn't a typical woman, wealthy or otherwise. She'd had a very unique upbringing; she had an altruistic focus in her life. A unique woman called for a unique approach. Somehow he knew he wasn't giving her what she needed.

This was taking him a little while to figure out, because rejection was not his usual experience in life. It wasn't typical in his general daily dealings, in his business interactions and certainly not in his relationships. Not that he'd really call what he had *relationships*.

They were more like encounters, he realized.

Not one-night stands exactly, but his interactions with women rarely got too deep no matter how many times he saw them. He liked it that way. He kept it that way, because then he didn't have to deal with any ugly emotions or pain. The few tantrums or hissy fits he'd encountered had been surface-level, because the last thing he'd allowed was for any woman to get attached.

If there was one thing his father had inadvertently taught him, it was that the more you loved someone, the more they could hurt you.

Blake found a place to park his car, then got out and started to walk. To the casual onlooker, he was just strolling. Blake knew his destination, but he wasn't in any hurry to get there. He'd give Madison time to get settled in, and then he could show up. The edge of the Garden District at night was just as beautiful as it was during the day. The shadows of the stately homes created mystery and intrigue, showcasing a history that was barely hinted at in a casual glance. It was still early, but the heat had dissipated, allowing him to walk in relative comfort.

He was surprised he'd caught this little tidbit of Madison's life in the PI's notes. Though he'd read through the file his father had given him before, Madison's actions had sent him back to the drawing board. Another thorough read had shown him one line that he'd missed the first time around.

Sometime during the last year of her father's illness, Madison had managed to find herself a new side gig: singing. The little neighborhood pub was not too far from her house. As a matter of fact, it was within walking distance. She'd lucked out that it was so close, which had probably given her a chance to sneak away at night…maybe when her father was sleeping. There she spent a couple of hours creating atmosphere for those around her, and dreams for herself.

That little discovery had made having to reread the story of her sad upbringing worth it.

His father had been a big motivator, too. Surprise, surprise. After his continued refusal to let Blake see Abigail, Blake had confronted him to demand proof that she was okay. His father had once again refused, stating that Blake hadn't made any kind of progress that was worth rewarding him for.

He'd later called the housekeeper, who had loudly told him she could give him no updates, then whispered she was fine. But the ticking clock in his brain told him he had to do something soon, or else Abigail might not be there for him to see. He could only hope that Sherry would continue to keep an eye on her. He had a feeling that if time ran out, she'd either have a medical episode, or his father would end up sending her away.

Blake noticed his destination up ahead on the right. The little neighborhood hub was a hole in the wall that only locals would know about. The single door and dusty windows weren't enough to draw in tourists.

As Blake approached, he could smell a whiff of alcohol and a slight smokiness coming from the entrance, even though patrons were no longer allowed to smoke inside. He paused not far from the door, leaning against one of the support posts. A soft amber light glowed behind the milky windowpanes.

The voice hit him in a smooth, insistent way. He would have recognized it anywhere…but Madison's husky tone was enhanced somehow by the song. He closed his eyes and let the wave wash over him. The undertow was so smooth he would have willingly followed it anywhere. Suddenly Blake understood the stories he'd heard about sirens. He could feel himself falling under her spell; the words didn't even need to mean anything. It was simply a sound that filled empty parts of his soul he didn't even know he had.

In a moment of panic, his heart picked up speed. It felt as if something out of the ordinary was happening, and he might never be the same. Logically Blake scoffed at the idea. Still his heart and lungs continued to race.

"Incredible, isn't she?"

With a jerk, Blake realized he wasn't alone. In the dim light beneath the awning, he'd missed the grizzled bouncer seated on a stool on the opposite side of the doorway. His knee-length shorts, button-down shirt, leather vest and chest-length beard announced him as a biker all the way. His smile revealed a couple of broken teeth.

"Our Maddie is something else, right?" he asked again.

Blake nodded, still feeling a bit too unsteady to leave the support of the post. "Sure is," he said simply.

"The regulars love her, for good reason. I've heard a lot of talented voices in New Orleans, but hers is one of the best. Untrained, but still smooth as silk. She could tell you to go to hell and make you enjoy the ride."

Blake chuckled, then straightened up and paid the cover charge.

"Enjoy," the bouncer said.

Blake made his way through the tight quarters right inside the door. The bar was there on the left, the wood smooth and aged but still glossy. A couple of tables on the right were sparsely populated.

Several feet in, the room widened, opening into a much larger space with multiple tables. The crowd had gathered here to listen to Maddie sing.

Blake didn't bother with a table. Instead he slipped along the back wall and stood in the shadows to watch the sexy woman in the spotlight. She wore a simple blue dress that revealed curves he remembered from the first night he'd met her. She barely moved, yet somehow she gave the impression of keeping time with the music. Her gorgeous auburn waves were pulled up and back from her face, revealing the smooth column of her neck.

Once again the words of the song rolled over

him, tempting him to let his eyes drift closed so he could absorb every one. But he couldn't take his gaze from the woman on the stage. Her voice washed over him, luring him to stay, breaking through his barriers piece by piece.

"Can I get you a drink, hon?"

Blake realized he had indeed let his eyes drift shut. He glanced over at the waitress, whose expression was hard to make out in the dim light. He requested a whiskey, then turned back toward the stage, but the mood had been broken. He found himself a table and had a seat. The waitress delivered his drink. He sipped at it every couple minutes, letting the burn coat his throat.

Almost too soon Madison's set was done. He saw the waitress whisper to her and nod in his direction. He wasn't sure how she'd known he was here for her, but even from across the bar he could see the flush that stained Madison's cheeks.

She should be used to men being drawn in by her voice, so was the blush for him in particular?

She approached and slid into the seat across from him.

"Drink?" he asked.

She shook her head, and something inside him became impatient. The urge to hear her speak, to compare that voice to the one he'd heard from the stage, grew as the seconds slid by.

But when she did speak, her voice came out hard. "What are you doing here? You aren't supposed to be here. No one is supposed to know—"

He leaned back in his chair. This wasn't at all what he'd expected. "I'm just glad I did."

"I'm not."

Blake frowned, surprised by the pushback. "Why?"

She drew in a deep breath, glancing around as she slowly released it. "I've just never shared this with anyone before. It's private."

Blake perused the people filling the small bar. But it was the room itself that helped him understand her protest. The stage was lit with a spotlight, but the rest of the room was cast in dusky shadow. Here Madison could have her own space, indulge in something she loved, practically anonymously, and be free of her burdens for a few hours.

"I know it doesn't make sense—"

"No, Madison. It's okay. I'm sorry for intruding."

She swallowed and dropped her gaze to the tabletop. "Why are you here?" she whispered, barely loud enough for him to catch it over the people speaking now that the music had ended.

"I've never explored much of New Orleans, so I decided to take a walk and happened by." Which sounded lame, even to him. "I got drawn right in. Your voice is incredible, Madison." *There you go. Distract her with the partial truth.* "I feel privileged to have heard you sing."

"No. Why are you here with me?" She patted the table with her palms in emphasis. "Why are you even interested in me?"

"Madison..." He wasn't sure what to say. The answer to that became more complicated with every minute he sat here.

"You shouldn't be. I'm not like them."

"Who?"

"The women in the pictures. I saw them online." She shook her head. "I'm not like them. I'm broke and awkward and a caretaker and have obligations. I'm just not a casual kind of person, Blake. I want to be…but I don't know how."

Every word rang in his head, confirming why he was here. She wasn't anything like what he was used to—and he liked that. The fact that her assumptions about him were so close to what he was like any other day made him angry. At himself, for being so shallow. At her, for buying into his public image.

True panic sizzled up until it popped like a champagne cork. "Damn it. Don't you think I know that, Madison? With all those women, nothing about them kept me coming back. But I can't stop coming back to you. Do you even understand what that means?"

Where had that come from? They stared at one another in silence. Blake breathed hard, his mind racing. His brain replayed the words he'd said, words he wished he could take back. It was a truth he hadn't wanted to face…much less blurt out to Madison like that.

But he couldn't take it back…so he waited.

His heart pounded as he kept waiting for her answer. As much as he wanted to convince himself that his nerves hinged on Abigail's fate, that it was about his father's demands, deep down he knew he'd just made it something more. Something personal.

Was that why this felt more real than anything he'd ever experienced before?

Then she spoke. "For something that was supposed to be *just fun,* this has sure gotten complicated."

Her words, so closely echoing his own thoughts, startled him. He quickly hid his reaction and asked, "What do you mean?"

"I don't understand why a guy like you is here with me. You're champagne and caviar. I'm—" she waved her hand "—just not."

"Maybe we need to explore that difference. No obligations."

This was it. This was the key he'd been looking for. So why wasn't he elated? Instead, anticipation and fear sizzled in his veins. "So what do you say?"

"I still don't understand."

He didn't want her to. The truth would be devastating—maybe to both of them.

"But yes," she conceded.

He lifted his glass in a toast, and was relieved when she nodded her consent. The burn centered him once more. He set his glass on the table, rimming the edge with his index finger. He needed this conversation back on a smoother track. "So I guess a hot-air balloon ride is out, right?"

Madison laughed, pressing the palm of her hand against her stomach. "Let's not risk it." She studied him for a moment. "So you haven't seen much of New Orleans? Not even as a kid?"

"No." The pressure of her gaze urged him to elaborate, but for once he kept quiet. His childhood was something he never wanted to relive, even in memories.

"Well, how about I show you my version?"

"Are you sure you want to walk?" Blake asked as he met her on a corner of the outer edge of the Garden District a few nights later. "I'm happy to drive."

"Don't be a baby. It's barely even summer here," Madison teased.

Besides, the June heat was starting to dissipate as evening fell on the Garden District. The only way to get a good feel for this town was to walk it.

"You can't experience the essence of New Orleans in a vehicle," she said, "unless it's a streetcar."

"Those are just tourist traps," Blake scoffed, but he fell into step beside her.

"Those are history," Madison corrected. "And a lot of people use them besides tourists."

"God forbid."

Madison paused to study him, one brow lifted. Blake either hadn't been exposed to the history of New Orleans, as he'd admitted, or he made a habit of not looking at a place too closely. "Just for that, I'm going to make you ride one. A lot of people commute on those things."

"I'm not sure I'd fit in with my designer shoes." He struck a pose, a grin forming on his too-perfect face. His words and actions were a reminder to keep things casual. A reminder she definitely needed.

How was she supposed to manage that?

"Pretty spiffy," she agreed, keeping her tone light, "but you'll be fine. I'm starting to get the feeling you didn't really see all these countries you claim to have visited. Not really."

He shrugged. "Maybe not." But the line that appeared between his brows told her he didn't feel as casual as he let on.

She didn't want to ask what he'd really been doing in them. All those pictures of him with supermodel types told her most of what she didn't want to know. Instead, she resumed her stroll along the sidewalk. As they walked, the tall, stately houses gave way to smaller, crowded buildings that contained businesses.

As they paused on one corner, a bus stopped at the red light. Its door opened and the older man called from the driver's seat, "Hey, Madison."

"Hi, Frankie," she hollered back. "How did your granddaughter's soccer game go?"

"She scored the winning goal," he answered with a toothy grin and a thumbs-up before heading on down the road.

Not too much farther along, ol' Mr. Paddington rounded the corner, walking his golden retriever. Madison paused to say good evening and pat the dog's head as she passed.

At Blake's curious look, she said, "Mr. Paddington lost his wife recently to a stroke. I encouraged him to get the dog to give him something to do. He walks her every evening about this time."

A couple more blocks down, an elderly woman in a floral housedress paused while sweeping her front porch to wave. "Evening, Madison," she yelled.

Madison raised her hand in greeting but didn't stop this time. Maybe this hadn't been the best route. She hadn't thought about how many interruptions they might run into.

They crossed another street to a corner, where a familiar gentleman sat on a stool in the shade. His lovely saxophone blended with the sounds of traffic and commerce around them, and had for more years than Madison could count. She dropped a couple of coins in the open case at his feet. "Night, Bartholomew."

"Thanks, Miss Madison," he said.

They strolled along in silence for a few minutes before Blake glanced over at her. "Is there anyone you don't know around here?"

"I've been walking this area since I was a kid. So honestly, not many. We lost a lot of people during Katrina and afterward, but new ones have moved in and that's been a blessing."

The sights and scents around her drew her in, enveloping her in a cozy feeling that had nothing to do with the fading heat of the day. She nodded at a small bakery, then a hometown pizza restaurant across the street. "All these places have been here for years. My mama used to walk up here when she was busy taking care of my dad. One of the special adventures she would take me on when I was a little kid was to get a free cookie from that bakery. They gave one to every kid who came in the door, and sometimes they'd be nice and give me two. I'd always share with my mama. I think the owner knew that.

"After her death, it was my turn to take care of my daddy." Madison pressed her lips together for a minute. Was she revealing too much?

"What was wrong with him?"

"Multiple sclerosis. At first he thought he was in a severe depression after losing his business in a bankruptcy, but he progressively got worse. You never knew what a day would bring with him. My mother died when I was sixteen. This was the extent of her world, and mine for a long time." She didn't mention that they'd rarely had money for her to go anywhere else. Abruptly Madison paused, realizing just how much she'd said.

She'd intended to introduce Blake to her New Orleans…not spill the details of her sad and meager childhood. The sounds of the cars on the road and music coming from the stores covered their silence for several steps while she tried to figure out how to keep this conversation from getting too deep.

"Speaking of houses, when are you going to invite me over?"

Apparently Blake didn't have the same issues about boundaries. Or most likely, he had no idea what a touchy subject her home had become.

Having him over was the last thing Madison wanted to do. *So much for a modern girl's attitude…* As much as she hated how shallow it sounded, Blake was loaded. Money was not something Madison had ever had. Only now was she able to truly make a living with her job at Maison de Jardin.

The house that had once been a showplace of the area now had overgrown hedges to block the sight of it from the road. The disrepair from years of having to make do with a shoestring budget was something that embarrassed her greatly. She'd done what she could to keep up with the major fixes, but the broken windows, peeling paint, warped flooring and the lack of a new roof were sore issues for her right now.

The very knowledge that she would soon need to sell off her family home made her heart ache, but she knew it was for the best. It was taking every bit of her current salary to get it up to snuff. There was no way she could maintain the house in the glory it deserved.

A lot of people bought houses in the Garden District specifically to renovate them, and she was hoping her house would be lucky enough to have the same fate. Soon, but not yet.

"Are you staying far from here?" she asked, hoping to distract him.

He went along with it for now. "I'm in an apartment in the business district, but my family lives on one of the old plantations."

Madison smiled, taken back to her vivid daydreams of open spaces and old barns as a child. "I bet that was a magical place to grow up."

"It was a hell with no means of escape." A brief glance showed her a fake grin on Blake's face to go with his harsh tone. "But then childhood memories are often exaggerated in our minds, right?"

She wasn't so sure. Memories of the hard years of her childhood had softened with age, but they never went away. She reminded herself that that wasn't why they were here tonight; this was about fun, not digging deep. Luckily, the place she had planned for dinner was just ahead. That should steer the conversation in another direction.

They stepped through the door with its peeling paint and a jingle bell over it into a long, narrow galley kitchen.

"Madison!" An African American woman rushed from behind the counter to hug her. Bebe was old enough to be her grandmother but appeared timeless with her smooth, dark skin. "It's so good to see you. And who's your friend?"

"Bebe, this is Blake. And I told him he needed to have the best po'boy in the city of New Orleans for dinner."

Blake gave the dim conditions of the room the side-eye but seemed to be won over by the woman's smile.

Bebe's grin was contagious, as always. She pulled off her apron to give Madison a hug. "Girl, you are skin and bones. You need a po'boy and then some."

Madison just smiled. "All that mothering instinct coming to the fore."

"Yes, ma'am." Bebe's smile turned down at the edges. "And I'm happy to report Talia is doing better."

Madison gave her friend a little extra squeeze before turning her loose.

Bebe glanced over at Blake. "Love this one like a daughter. She's the same age as my own Talia, whose undergoing cancer treatments right now." She patted Madison's arm while Madison blinked back tears. "This girl can make me smile on the worst of days."

Then Bebe went back behind the counter. As soon as she put her apron back on it was all business. "What can I make you?"

Madison's throat had closed up so that speaking was impossible. Blake stepped up to the counter. "How about Maddie's favorite…times two?"

Bebe beamed her approval and got to work. Soon she handed the food back over the counter, then leaned over to give Madison a kiss on her cheek. "You have a good evening, darling," she said as they headed out the door with their heavy bag.

"This way," Madison said.

A couple of stores down, a narrow alleyway opened to the right. She led him down the space barely wide enough for his shoulders. As they walked, she took a few more deep breaths to try to clear her emotions away. Seeing Bebe was always a mix of happy and sad, but that was how they got through the tough times. Madison just hadn't thought about it before taking him in there. She'd just wanted to show him some of her favorite places.

Finally they reached the end of the alley to face a black wrought iron fence. Taking a few steps to the side, Madison reached for the latch to let them in. And this was her favorite place of all.

"What is this?" Blake asked as they stepped into a lush, overgrown garden.

The centerpiece was a beautiful cherry tree, surrounded by various ferns, hostas and an abundance of moss growing in the shade. Tucked into one corner was a small wrought iron table and chairs.

"This is one of my favorite places in the whole city," she said. "The garden is actually part of the St. Andrew's Catholic Church. My mother brought me here as a child, and we would eat our cookies while enjoying the cool and quiet."

She noticed Blake cock his head to the side like he was listening for something. Sure enough, the buildings and lush foliage blocked out the sound of the busy street not too far away. Despite living in the city, Madison had a deep love of nature and enjoyed these green spaces. Being here gave her a sense of peace and calm that everyday life seemed to withhold. But wasn't that the same for everybody?

Maybe not, but she'd take peace where she could get it. Even now her heart rate was slowing and those unwelcome tears were seeping away.

"The priests don't mind because they knew we would never leave a mess. The church allowed my mother's services here when she died."

"This is beautiful," he said simply.

"You should see the conservatory at Maison de Jardin. It's absolutely gorgeous."

She started to unpack their dinner, needing a distraction from the minefield of memories. How come she couldn't just have fun?

"How did you go to work there?" Blake asked as they settled in. "You're very young to be the director of that large a charity."

In years, maybe. She didn't want to talk about the experience that had made her qualified for her job. "Trinity, the former director, has known me for a long time. Knows what I'm capable of. But she's still very hands-on."

She paused to take a bite of the sandwich, enjoying the resistance of the bread and the crunch of the fried crawfish. "What do you do?"

He immediately popped off, "According to my father, nothing."

Whoa.

Blake jumped to his feet and paced in the small space. Madison held really still. Should she say something? This went way beyond their surface chatter tonight. Not that she'd stuck to her goal of keeping it light very well herself.

He was quiet for so long the back of her neck tightened. Was he looking for a way to blow the statement off? Then she realized she didn't know enough about Blake to counteract his bitter statement in any way. Just as panic set in, he turned back toward her and leaned against the tree trunk behind him.

"Is he right?" she asked, blowing off all of her angst and going with her instincts.

"Partly." He offered a half smile. "But less than he knows."

A lightbulb went off. "Your drawings?"

"How did you—of course, you noticed. You see a lot, don't you?"

"Is that a good thing?"

"Probably not." He pushed away from the tree and crossed to her side. "Definitely not."

Before Madison could blink, Blake had her in his arms, his lips barely meeting hers. But he didn't rush. He waited for her to open, granting him permission to press forward. Then he sampled, testing and tasting her lips in smooth, slow strokes. Madison's spine lit up. The spicy taste of him on her tongue left her ravenous for way more than food.

After long moments he pulled back, leaving her dazed and a little unsteady on her feet. She opened her eyes, blinking once or twice before focusing in on the golden, angular lines of his face. Only to see them softened by his smile as he said, "I'm not comfortable with you seeing things, but I think it's more than worth it."

Five

Blake dove back in for another taste, leaving Madison breathless and gasping. The feel of him intoxicated her. She had the resistance of a rag doll as he pulled her into his lap. More naturally than she would have imagined, she found herself straddling his thighs. Belly to belly. Face to face.

As his mouth traveled from her lips, over her jaw, to her neck, she struggled to pull air into her lungs. The excitement of his touch, the racing of her pulse, the need to press herself closer to him despite the heat in the air…how was this happening?

Something tickled the back of her mind, something she should remember, but nothing intruded on the sensations evoked by the man beneath her. She clutched at his shoulders, kneading the well-defined muscles, not sure whether she was trying to steady herself or imprint him with her touch. A fire rose inside her, forcing her to squirm, needing relief from the intense sensations pooling low in her belly.

Madison rocked forward. Blake gasped against her skin, his hands squeezing her arms. "Madison," he groaned.

Her pulse pounded at the base of her throat. After one last hot, openmouthed kiss, he pulled back. "We have to stop. Right now."

"Why?" she whispered. She should know the answer, but right now it was as far from her as possible.

"We have to," he said. He rested his forehead against her collarbone, breathing heavy in the hush of the garden. "I had no idea how addictive you would be."

Well, no one had ever called her that. She drew in a deep breath, searching for equilibrium. How had this gotten so out of hand?

"May I help you?" a voice asked from the shadows.

Madison started, realizing they weren't alone. Instinctively she jerked back, and lost her balance because she was on Blake's lap. With a cry, she fell, landing on her backside on one of the stone pavers surrounding the table. She ignored the pain. Instead she focused in on the source of the voice. "Father Stephen... I'm so sorry."

The younger of the priests here—at forty-five— gave her a soft smile. "I see that."

Blake reached out and helped Madison to her feet. "Honestly, Father," he added. "I apologize for—"

He broke off and a flush of red tinged the skin right above his magnificent cheekbones. Madison would have giggled if she wasn't aware that her entire face was on fire, too.

"Yes, well, maybe it's time to finish your dinner? Yes, Madison?" the man asked.

Madison guessed it was a good thing he knew her, or else she'd probably have been arrested for... something. But that thought made her embarrassment burn even hotter. "Yes, sir. I'll—we'll do that."

"See that you do," he said. "And I'll see you at mass Saturday night."

Madison choked on her emotions as the man retreated around the corner to the back door of the church. She only dared to glance over at Blake when he chuckled. He shook his head as he said, "Well, that was embarrassing."

"He hasn't known you since you were a baby. Imagine how I feel."

Blake held out her chair for her to sit back down at the table. "Oh, I don't have to imagine."

The suggestive comment should have put her back up. Instead, she covered her face with her hands and let laughter release her tension. Now that her head had cleared somewhat from the kiss, she could finally put her finger on what had been bothering her...they were in public.

It was the first time she'd ever managed to forget that...

Blake simply picked up his sandwich and continued to eat.

"How can you—" Men were obviously very different from women. Or maybe it was just her and her lack of experience with these things.

She simply stared at him until he met her gaze once more. It made her feel a little better when his smile had a sheepish tinge. "Well, I'm not about to let a little embarrassment keep me away from the rest of this po'boy. You weren't wrong about it being the best in New Orleans."

She recognized his attempt to return things to normal, and did her best to relax. "I hope you mean that, because I eat at Bebe's all the time."

"I'm on board for that."

They ate in silence for a few minutes. Madison preferred not to think about the last few minutes. Maybe later tonight, alone in her room, she would. But if she thought about it now, she'd never be able to carry on a conversation. Instead she cast her mind back to what they'd been discussing before.

"I'm sorry that your father can't see the value in your art," she said.

As hard as her life had been, Madison's father had always made his appreciation plain. He'd hated what she had to do to keep them afloat, but he'd always expressed gratitude for her hard work and dedication.

"My father is not an easy man." Blake's smile wasn't as convincing as he probably wanted. "And I would have said that was no longer an issue for me. But, well, family is never easy."

Instantly the picture he'd drawn that first night came to mind. "So you draw for a living?"

He shrugged. "I wouldn't necessarily call it a living. I had a lot of help from my inheritance from my mother, which would have let me live a careful existence without working for the rest of my life. But I'm rarely careful…"

"But you are a very talented artist." Even in her inexperience, she could see that.

"Some people think so, and they are willing to pay for my drawings." He glanced away, studying the lush foliage around them for long moments. "That was a very complicated answer to an easy question."

"Sometimes the easy answer isn't the best." She couldn't keep the words from slipping out. "I'm sorry, Blake."

He studied her for a moment. "Why?"

She shook her head. "I tried to keep whatever this is between us on the surface, just fun, but everything about tonight has run completely counter to that. I don't feel comfortable, like I'm lying to you. This just…isn't me." Her smile was sad, apologetic. "I realize that now. And I'm sorry. I know that's not what you want."

"Are you sure?"

They both seemed equally surprised by the question. Then he cocked up one blond brow. "Quite frankly, I'm willing to hang around until we find out what it *is*. Not what it *should* be."

"Really?"

He winked at her. "Really."

That should be a good thing…so why was she shaking over the prospect?

* * *

"Let me see Abigail. Now."

Blake's father offered him a smile that had nothing to do with being happy. "Slow down," he cautioned. "You didn't seem to be making any progress the last time you checked in. Did you bring me some proof?"

For a moment, Blake just stared in disbelief. Arguing the way he wanted to would probably get him nowhere.

"What kind of proof are you looking for?"

"A pair of panties?"

Gross. Why would he—? "I don't have to sleep with Madison to get the diamond."

"But you do have to spend time with her, and get invited into her house. Which as far as I can tell, hasn't happened, either…"

His father's straight back and braced arms told Blake he wasn't backing down. So instead of saying more, Blake pulled out his phone and offered up a picture of him and Madison together in the garden at the church. His father nodded slowly as he studied it.

"Not the most efficient method in my book, but good job."

Those words grated over every nerve, forcing Blake to clench his teeth. His father had often told him "good job" as a child, usually after berating him for making a choice he wouldn't have, then forcing Blake to do things his way.

His father leaned closer, staring at the phone. Blake was surprised to see his lips tighten. "Let me guess," he finally said, his tone now clipped. "The garden behind St. Andrew's?"

Blake nodded slowly. "How did you know?" After all, he couldn't imagine his father being anywhere near that part of town.

"Her mother and I met there a couple of times."

Whoa. That wasn't what Blake had expected.

Then again, he couldn't imagine his father meeting a woman anywhere other than at a fancy party. There he could easily disguise his narcissistic attitude with fancy clothes and jewelry. Polite small talk. And offers of fancy outings.

That brought Blake up short. Wasn't that exactly what he had tried to offer Madison? To impress her? To keep things polite and on a superficial level?

Well, that approach hadn't lasted with this particular woman, had it? All it had taken was one physical touch to shake him. Madison's response hadn't been practiced or lukewarm. It had been real, full-bodied passion.

And Blake had found it amazing.

His father and a woman anything like Madison? He just couldn't imagine it. "Why are you doing this? Her mother is dead. Revenge is going to accomplish nothing."

Familiar rage seemed to make his father grow larger and more menacing. At least this time Blake was too big to be intimidated. "She should have been mine," he growled as he strode across the tile floor, his dress shoes clicking as he moved.

"And since you couldn't possess her, you now

have to take back what didn't belong to you? After all these years? Come on... I'm not buying that."

He stopped abruptly. "Desperate times call for desperate measures."

"You're never desperate," Blake argued. "Cold. Calculating. But not desperate."

"In this economy, everyone is desperate."

"Money?" He should have known. But his father had always been more than solvent. What had gone wrong?

"Isn't it always about money?"

"No. Usually it's about people." Even when it seemed to be about money, for people like Madison, that money was necessary for keeping her family fed, housed, clothed. Not for fancy cars and travel.

"I made a few bad investments," his father said with a too casual shrug. "With that diamond, I'll be set."

"But it doesn't belong to you."

"I'll take whatever I have to. I did before, and I will continue to as long as necessary."

Suspicion filtered through Blake's consciousness. "Father? I know that tone. You couldn't have had anything to do with her father's illness. And I certainly hope you had nothing to do with her mother's death. What's the deal?" he demanded.

His father brushed at a nonexistent spot on his jacket. "No, unfortunately those issues were beyond me. But I made sure they didn't have the money to do much about them, now, didn't I? I set out to ruin

Jacqueline's husband, and that was one goal I managed to accomplish."

Blake held silent. So this steady downward spiral of Madison's father's business, the bankruptcy that killed his spirit, had been his own father's fault? Why wasn't he surprised?

"So your only plan for pulling yourself out of the red is to steal from a young woman who deserves no punishment whatsoever?"

"She'll never miss what she's never had."

Blake should be surprised, but even after all these years, he remembered that the only person his father cared about was himself. If his finances were in that dire a state, he wouldn't hesitate to strike out, no matter who it was. If it wasn't Madison, it might just be Abigail.

His father turned away, cutting the conversation off. "I guess you deserve a little reward, for what progress you've made. Just make it quick. Abigail might be in her room. She's as slippery as you were when you were a kid. Always where she doesn't belong."

Blake heard the patter of tiny feet as he stepped onto the first stair in the foyer. He moved slower than he should have, considering the concern that had built over the last week. What did he know about talking to a child?

The few times he'd been with Abigail before, her mother and nanny had been present. She'd been cute and engaging, but children were completely out of Blake's league. He moved down the hallway to an open door and glanced inside. The pale pink walls, frilly pictures and a large silver monogram of the girl's initials hanging over the headboard showed that her mother had at least decorated before she left. Abigail sat in a puddle of fluffy blankets on the bed. The dim light in the room didn't reveal much about her, so he reached out to flick on the light switch.

She blinked in the extra brightness.

Those big brown eyes, so reminiscent of her mother's, made her look vulnerable in a way Blake wasn't comfortable with.

What should he say after not seeing her for two years? "How are you, Abigail?" he asked. Lame, but he had to start somewhere.

She shrugged, but Blake remembered that response from his own childhood. He wasn't going to be brushed off.

"Tell me, Abigail." He made sure their gazes met. "I really want to know. Miss Sherry said you'd been sick."

"Those pills make me feel tired."

Was that normal? Blake wasn't even sure whom he would ask.

"But my head doesn't feel funny anymore."

So maybe the medicine was working? Her color looked healthy. Could you tell anything about epilepsy from just watching her? He needed to investigate that more.

"I'm sorry," she whispered.

Distracted from his obsessive worrying, he came closer and sat beside the bed. "Why are you sorry?"

"If I hadn't gotten sick, none of this would've happened."

Blake's heart sank. No child should have to feel responsible for the actions of the adults around them. Blake should not have had to feel responsible for his father's anger, for his mother's incompetence, for the string of stepmothers who moved in and out of his life. "Abigail," he said, searching for the right words. "You don't have to be sorry. Scratch that. You should not be sorry. None of this is your fault."

"But Mommy left me."

"And that's her fault." Blake didn't bring up the fact that her mother simply wasn't strong enough to handle anything outside of his father. He didn't want her more fearful that she already was. "You being sick, it just…is."

"Why?"

"I'm not sure." Man, saying that made him feel inadequate. He was probably screwing this up royally, but he didn't know how else to proceed. "I have to go, but if you need me, you just need to tell Miss Sherry to call me, okay?" The housekeeper had given him frequent updates, even though they'd been short to avoid detection from her boss.

Abigail nodded slowly. The move was solemn enough to make Blake's chest ache. "Look, I don't know when he'll let me come back. But I want you to remember, I *will* be back."

Her deep brown eyes filled with tears, but she blinked them back in an all too familiar move. Blake remembered that vividly from a time or two during his childhood. "Promise?"

"Promise." Even if he had to walk over hot coals. Which would actually be preferable to complying with his father's demands.

Six

Madison took a deep breath, trying to calm the nerves in her stomach.

She always had butterflies at the beginning of a performance, but this was different. This was her first time knowing she was singing in front of Blake. The first time she wasn't craving that chance to close her eyes and lose herself in a different world.

Normally when she was up here on stage, she didn't see the crowd. She didn't hear the clapping. She didn't pay attention to any hecklers. She lost herself in an inner world of melody mixed with darkness. A place where she felt happy and safe.

Tonight she felt the glare of the spotlight. But she needed it, wanted it. She could no longer deny that she wanted to see where this thing between her and

Blake would go. The only way to find out was to dive in deep, and stop questioning every single stroke.

And he'd given her the perfect opportunity by showing up tonight.

Madison caught her cue and opened her mouth to sing. Tonight, instead of losing herself in the darkness, she sang for Blake alone. Every rhythm, every note was for him. As if they were alone in the room.

She braced her heels against the wooden planks of the stage. The mic stand felt cool between her palms.

She couldn't see him, but she could feel him. Feel his gaze as it roamed every inch of the silky green dress she wore. Her blood raced through her veins, as if the very act of singing were foreplay. She was amazed at how good this felt...and at her ability to let go and embrace what she realized she wanted.

A real relationship. Yes, she wanted it to be fun. But she wasn't capable of living on the surface. And if he was okay with it being more, then they'd see where this would go.

If it ended, it would hurt more. But Madison's life had been a series of endings, and she knew she'd survive.

This time when her set was over, she met Blake at his table with a drink of her own and slid into the seat opposite him as if they were strangers. The glass between her hands steadied her. "What brings you here?" she asked with what she hoped was a sexy smile.

His half smile sped up her heartbeat. "I heard there was a very sexy singer that I just had to see."

"I hope she didn't disappoint."

"Never," he said, his tone dropping an octave.

Even in the dark she could see his gaze dip down to the V-neckline of her dress, tracing the arrow down to her cleavage. Secretly she'd wanted to show off and had chosen this dress for that very purpose. Hoping he'd be here. Hoping he'd want more.

It looked like her hope just might turn into reality.

"You look beautiful tonight, Madison."

"You're not so bad yourself, Blake."

"How late will you be—"

A gravelly male voice interrupted. "Well, I should've known you'd be here, sugar."

Blake looked up, but Madison kept her gaze trained on him. Her teeth clenched.

She recognized the voice. One she'd dreaded hearing ever since her daddy had died. The man was a nuisance at best. His visits to their house had always upset her father. As an adult, she'd realized the man had been trying to buy the house out from under them. But he'd never wanted to pay a decent price for it. Or maybe her daddy had been like her. It really didn't matter who the house went to, as long as it didn't go to this obnoxious, self-entitled boob.

Finally Maddie looked away from Blake's enticing blue eyes up at the man's face. His overtanned skin and calculating look repulsed her. "Hello, John Mark. How are you?"

Not that she really wanted to know, but it was polite to ask.

The middle-aged, heavyset man pulled over a

chair from another table and turned it around backward so he could straddle it. He held out his hand to Blake. "Hi there, I'm John Mark. I don't think we've been introduced."

"I don't guess so," Blake said, glancing back and forth between the two of them.

Madison had been raised to have manners, to be accommodating of other people even when you didn't care for them. But somehow she couldn't summon it tonight. Her greeting had used up her store of politeness. She could feel a frown pulling down the edges of her mouth and eyebrows. The energy to lift them just was beyond her. This man was associated with so many irritating memories from when her father was alive, and that gloom settled over her like a weighted blanket.

She didn't bother to contribute to the expected introductions. Hopefully the dim lighting would hide the animosity in her expression.

"I don't think I've ever seen you in here, John Mark," she said instead. That was one good reason to keep coming to the club. It had always felt like her safe place. What was with the sudden invasion?

"Oh, but I knew you would be here," he said. "And it's long past time we talk some business."

"I don't really think this is the time or place—"

"Of course it is," he said with a grin that was too wide. "Besides, you're a hard woman to catch. Always here or there. And nobody's returning calls from the house. In the meantime, that place is gonna fall down around your ears."

Blake cleared his throat. "I don't really think…"

"Oh, she knows what I'm after," John Mark replied with a careless wave of his hand. "I begged her father to sell me that house for years. Now it's time."

The audacity of his words hit Madison the wrong way. Heated pressure grew deep inside her. "Actually, I don't think there's anything for us to talk about."

John Mark wasn't listening. "I will take that house off your hands real easy, young lady. You just sign over the paperwork and the headache is no longer yours."

Madison knew she needed to sell the house, but not to this man. *Never* this man. "The house isn't ready…"

"There's no need to do anything to it. I'm pretty sure I know how bad a shape it's in. I might have to tear it down and start over, but that's a prime piece of land. It's a shame your daddy let it get that bad, but he wouldn't get out when his body gave up on him, would he?"

Madison felt the tips of her ears start to burn. The pressure rose, mixing with grief for her father and anger over this man's casual words. The last thing she wanted was for Blake to find out the true state of affairs with her family like this.

"When I am ready, I'll—"

"You'll never be ready. Just sign the papers."

"No." The pressure erupted. "And do not talk over me."

Madison stood, feeling more in control on her feet. She wasn't sure where the steel in her voice

came from, but she wasn't being railroaded into anything she didn't want to do. "Do not come to my
house. Do not call on the phone. I'm not selling my
place to you. Ever."

John Mark glanced back and forth between them,
a smile spreading across his face. "Now, there's no
need to get into a tizzy, little lady."

"Ev-ver."

Something in her face or tone must've finally told
him she was serious. His thin lips pressed together,
a scowl curving his brows. "Beggars aren't in a position to be choosers. Don't be stupid."

"Back off," Blake said, a growl underlying his
tone.

"Why? She's not going to get a better offer. And
she desperately needs one... I could tell that with one
glance around that place. I always did wonder how
you kept it up." He gave Blake the once-over, clearly
taking in his fancy watch. "Guess now I know, huh?"

Instantly Blake was on his feet, crowding John
Mark away from the table. There was a flurry of activity as the bouncer headed their way, and a low exchange of voices between the men that she couldn't
quite catch. But Blake's advantage in height seemed
to make an impression on the bulky man. He raised
his hands in surrender.

The bouncer grabbed John Mark's arm. "This guy
bothering you, Miss Maddie?"

At first she just nodded, not trusting her voice. As
John Mark started to protest, she stepped in close.
"My daddy was always a good judge of character.

He had you pegged as slimy from the beginning. I do believe I agree." She nodded at the bouncer, who strong-armed him away.

For a moment, Madison stood still, stunned at what had happened, until Blake led her back over to the table. "Are you okay?"

Madison melted into the seat, the starch in her spine washing away. "I just can't catch a break. Every time I'm around you something stupid happens." She plopped back in her seat, trying hard not to let the tears well up. That would just be the icing on the cake.

"It's not stupid. You have no control over him showing up," Blake insisted.

"But why did it have to happen right now, right in the middle of—"

"It's okay, Madison."

She smacked her palm against the table, her voice rising. "It's not okay. I didn't want you to find out about that."

Blake tilted his head to the side in question.

"On the good days, I can handle the fact that I'm going to have to sell my family home. I've done the best that I can. My father did the best that he could. And I know it has to go. That's the way it is, but that doesn't make it hurt any less."

She stared down into her drink. For a moment, she was at a total loss. Her normal go-to was to get up and do something to fix it. And there was no fixing this.

She could walk away, and leave Blake sitting here

by himself. She could hang around and let him convince her that it was all okay. He didn't need to—she knew her own worth. The state of her house embarrassed her, but considering the state of their finances when she was growing up, she knew she had done the best that she could. And if Blake couldn't understand that, then she needed to walk away.

Or she could do what her body and soul had been telling her since she'd met him. She could walk toward him, and let happen whatever happened. Accept his decisions and make the memories she wanted so badly.

She glanced back at him and saw his blue eyes trained steadily on her. No hint of embarrassment, no signs of anger or irritation. Just watching her. Maybe he was looking for the next clue?

Just then the waitress interrupted, drawing Maddie's attention to her with a hand on her shoulder. "Hon, are you going to finish the night out?"

Normally Madison would never walk away from her gig under any circumstances, but tonight she simply couldn't continue. "No, I need to go home."

The waitress squeezed her shoulder before walking away. It was wonderful to work with people who were so understanding.

With a pounding heart, she glanced back over at Blake. "Would you like to go with me?"

Blake stared up at the house as he turned off his car. The silence that surrounded them had almost an echo to it, as if there were unspoken words surrounding them. The history of the place, maybe? Blake wasn't sure, and he was hesitant to look too deeply.

This was what he'd wanted all along. To be inside this house, to be given an opportunity to search through it. Hell, he'd even prepared himself for a one-night stand in order to do it.

But what he was walking into tonight wasn't a one-night stand. He was walking through those doors in an emotional state that he'd never anticipated. Because Maddie was real; she was more real to him than any woman he'd slept with before. And he had a feeling there would be no going back after tonight.

"Everything okay?" she asked.

He could hear the slight tremble in her voice. She was nervous. Blake knew that she was opening herself up in a way that she wouldn't ever have with someone else. That vulnerability, that choice humbled him.

He tried to remind himself about Abigail. He tried to remember his purpose, but all he could think about was Maddie. He glanced over at her in the dark. "Yes," he lied. "I'm fine."

Blake let himself out of the car and crossed around to her side to open the door. The driveway was tight, crowded on each side with an overgrowth of bushes. The oddly planted tree here or there. Was the overgrowth on purpose? Or simply one of those things that hadn't registered in the list of tasks that Madison faced every day?

He gave her just enough room to slip out the door, then closed it behind her. He pressed in close, trapping her between the vehicle and the hardness of his body. "Madison," he whispered, in deference to the quiet surrounding them. "I want you to remember something."

He could feel the shiver that went through her, and knew it had nothing to do with the temperature. The heated night closed in on them, but still her body responded. "Yes?"

That deep huskiness in her murmur shot straight down his spine. "Just remember, I want to be here."

Those simple words felt like more of a commitment than he could ever have imagined. Then he turned quickly toward the house, catching her hand in his.

Madison led him around the back and put her key in the door. The bushes surrounding the house were also out of control, some of them flowering crape myrtles, some overgrown hydrangeas. The heavy scent of flowers on the night air was intoxicating.

The door opened smoothly, to his surprise. A small mudroom opened up into a large kitchen. It was obvious that a lot of time was spent here. It gleamed with scrubbing. A meticulously maintained work surface that could possibly be original to the house gave the room a warm feeling that Blake could honestly say he'd never experienced in any house he'd lived in.

It wasn't until they moved on to other rooms that the wear and tear begin to make itself known. Bits of peeling paint. Cracked floor tile. Dim lighting where the bulbs in the chandeliers were obviously blown. Some rooms were closed off completely.

Madison kept her head down, as if she could ignore the signs of age if she didn't get a close enough look. Moving through the foyer, she did an abrupt turn to go up the stairs. Through the open doorway on the opposite side, Blake caught a glance of multiple pieces of furniture in various states of repair.

"What's this?" he asked, leaning into the doorway.

Madison paused about a quarter of the way up the stairs and looked back down at him. Her reluctance to return was clear, even in the shadows. After a moment's pause, she slowly came down one step at a time before reaching his side.

"What's this?" he asked again, not acknowledging her hesitation.

She stood next to him in the doorway but didn't glance into the room. "It's just a hobby," she said in a rush.

"It's a pretty expensive hobby…" The room had to contain at least ten pieces of furniture that were being refurbished. "That's a lot of elbow grease."

He glanced to the side to see Madison's arms crossed tightly over her rib cage. Apparently he'd waded into another touchy subject. But he really did want to know. This was obviously important to her, which spoke to him on a level he'd never experienced with other women.

"Come on, Maddie," he coaxed. "Tell me the truth."

She shot a quick glance up at him, her pupils wide and searching.

Finally she said, "John Mark wasn't wrong when he said times were tough. My father used to be a very affluent businessman, before he married my mama. But something...went wrong. He never would say what. They lost most of what they had. She did her best, and kept things fairly on track. But after she died, he just couldn't keep it together anymore. He was sick, and hurting, and grieving, and for a while, he just dropped off the grid. At fifteen years old, I learned just how deep in the hole we were."

Blake's chest ached at the sadness in her voice.

"We were eking out an existence on his disability checks. But he refused to let me sell the house. It was the last place he'd had a home with her. So I did the best I could, supplementing his income by running errands for Trinity, and turning my hand at anything I could find. I discovered I had a knack for refinishing furniture. He would help me sometimes when he was feeling better, and I'd sell the pieces to local antique stores. Sometimes they call and let me know when they have pieces that I can refurbish for them. I've gotten a bit of a reputation for it now."

"That's wonderful, Maddie." Blake had taken so much in his life for granted. He couldn't imagine realizing his family was on the brink of ruin as a teenager and knowing it fell on him to keep them from going over the edge.

"I'm sorry," she whispered.

"Why?" His chest ached at the somber expression in her eyes. They should be happy and smiling, instead of sad all the time.

"I wanted tonight to be special. And it's been nothing but complicated. Everything about us has been complicated."

Blake pushed everything aside in that moment—his own selfishness, shallowness, Abigail, even his own lust for the woman in front of him.

Instead he looked at Madison and really saw her. "No, Maddie. Tonight has really opened my eyes."

She immediately dropped her gaze, but he raised her chin back up with gentle pressure. "I've seen a lot, and I've learned a lot. And it has all told me what an incredibly strong and driven woman you are. That is something to be proud of. And if some guy can't handle it, you kick his ass to the curb."

She gave a huff of laughter. "Yes, sir."

Maddie was a woman to be celebrated. And Blake planned to do just that.

Burying his hands in her hair, he pulled her closer for his kiss. When he came up for air, he whispered, "Don't be sorry, Maddie. You're way more than I ever expected."

This time, he crowded his body close against hers, pressing her into the doorframe. Slowly he rubbed her, up, then down again, imprinting on her just how much he wanted to be with her. Her lips were supple and welcoming, parting in need to invite him in. He dove deep, intent on tasting every inch of her tonight.

In, out and around, he explored her mouth. Nibbled on her lips. Eased his body close to her and away, mimicking the very dance they rushed toward.

He felt her hands roam up his arms, massaging the muscles as she too explored.

She reached his shoulders and dug her fingers in deep, igniting a surge of power that struck hard at the base of his spine. He groaned, needing action. Needing more. He lifted her and almost wept when her legs encircled his waist. "Maddie," he growled. "Please."

"Upstairs," she murmured around kisses that fed the flames.

He took the steps slower than he planned, partly to keep her safe, partly because he couldn't stop kissing her. Maddie's mouth was addictive. Her response egged him on.

She pressed against him, spreading heat through his body in waves, ramping his urgency sky high. He wanted to take his time, wanted to care for her, but he knew the moment was fast approaching when he wouldn't be able to control himself anymore. First, he had to make it good for her.

Maddie deserved more than he could ever give her.

At the top of the stairs, she pointed to an open door down the shadowy hallway. Blake had the barest impression of pale blue walls before he laid her out across the bed. Her face fell into the darkness, but her body was illuminated by the beam of light coming from a lamp left on in the hallway. The green dress she was wearing teased him, leaving him aching for the womanly soft skin it concealed.

With extra care he unbuckled her wedge sandals,

and kissed each ankle bone, celebrating its delicacy. His body screamed at him to hurry, but he clamped down tight and focused on the woman before him.

Maddie.

Lifting one of her leanly muscled legs, he watched as the skirt fell to her waist. He caught a brief glimpse of glittery black material between her legs that had him opening his mouth and brushing his teeth against her calf. Very soon he would taste more of her. She gasped, her muscles twitching beneath his mouth. He repeated the movement closer to her knee, then her thigh, then her inner thigh. Each time she jerked harder, her fingers fisting the pale blanket beneath her. The sound of her gasps in the air was almost as intoxicating as her singing.

Then he buried his face in the heat between her thighs, listening to her cry out as he dragged in her scent with a deep inhale. His brain lit up, sending urgent directives to his body that he struggled to ignore. But his impatient hands grasped the edge of the flimsy material that covered her, ripping it from her hips. He wasn't moving away from her for a single second, not even to remove her panties.

The flesh now laid bare for him was crowned by soft auburn curls. They smelled of musk and some floral scent he couldn't place at the moment. With extra care he parted her lower lips, which were slick with a moisture that had his mouth watering. He opened his lips and pressed against her. Her knees jerked up as if to close off his access, but her hands clenching in his hair sent a different message. Her gasps grew louder, echoing in his ears. Her body throbbed against his tongue. Blake felt himself slipping into a world that was all about Maddie, that revolved around her reactions and his utter need to pull the ultimate high from her.

Her hips lifted against him. He rode her motions out, licking and sucking, instinct taking over. His body throbbed in sympathy to her cries of need.

When her moans reached a fever pitch, he pressed hard, growling his command that she come. Maddie broke against his mouth, one long scream echoing off the walls. It had to be the most satisfying sound Blake had ever heard.

Seven

Maddie lay for long moments, unaware of anything but the pounding of her heart in her ears and the excited throb that dominated her body in this moment. She clutched at the soft blanket beneath her, needing something solid to ground her.

Her very limited experience before hadn't prepared her for the havoc a very focused, very determined man could wreak upon her body. But as satisfied as she was right now, underneath she could feel the return of the urgency. The need to experience the same thing *with* Blake. To return the favor he'd so graciously given her.

He pulled back a little, causing a protest within. He couldn't leave. Not now. Maybe never.

Opening her eyes, she could see him crouched

between her legs. He made no further move away, just silently watched her in the darkness. Slowly she sat up, connecting with his gaze in the dim light. Then she rolled around until she too crouched on her knees. With shaking fingers, she grasped the hem of her dress, lifting it and tossing it to the side. The stream of light from the doorway illuminated her bare body. Only a simple lace bralette covered her breasts. Blake's groan was one of the most gratifying things she'd ever heard. Reaching out, she unbuttoned his shirt, taking her time, letting her fingers brush against his skin. He gasped as she pulled the shirttails loose from his slacks, then ran her fingernails over his chest and belly.

"Please, Madison," he said, breathing as hard as a racehorse.

He made quick work of his belt and zipper, then eased her back against the pillows. To her surprise, he didn't jump right in. Instead he slipped the bralette over her head. Burying his face between her breasts, he squeezed them and played with the pink tips until the fire burned high between her thighs once more. Only then did he take one nipple between his lips and worry the flesh until she squirmed and raised her hips in a plea for more. She cried, clutching at his back through the fine cotton of his shirt. With a growl, Blake tore it from his body and tossed it aside, then pressed down against her.

Flesh to flesh. Heat to heat.

With an urgency that signaled he'd reached the end of his control, Blake used his thighs to press hers even farther apart. She felt him fumble on the condom. Then the blunt tip of him searched and found her core, easing slightly inside. He braced his arms above her shoulders, breathing so hard his chest rubbed against her with every huff. He played for long moments, easing in and out until she thought she would scream in need. He was trying to make it good for her, she knew. But if he didn't enter her soon, she might explode.

Madison needed this to be about them.

Sliding her hands down beneath the edge of his pants, which were miraculously still on, she grasped his clenching muscles and dug deep. At the same time she lifted her hips to him. The feel of him sliding inside her took her breath away. He let himself go all the way to the hilt, then froze. She could feel her body ripple around him, on the cusp of something incredible, something she wouldn't be able to control.

Blake eased his upper body down, letting their skin touch. Then he tucked his mouth against one of her ears. "Hold on, Maddie," he groaned.

Then he started to thrust.

Madison only thought she'd been breathless before. Now every movement forced the air from her lungs. Her body lit up like fireworks. Blake grunted every time their hips met. They strained against each other for that ultimate high. Snapshot sensations imprinted themselves on Madison's mind: the slickness of his skin beneath her fingers; the sound of his voice in her ear; the exquisite pressure of him filling her full. Then he twisted against her and her world exploded.

In the quiet aftermath, listening to the sound of their breathing, it seemed cliché to say she would never be the same again. But Madison knew it to be true.

After long moments, Blake rolled to the side, pulling her with him. In those moments, she had no defense against him. No way to close herself off from the incredible fullness in her heart. Just as she drifted into sleep, she felt the warm pressure of lips against her temple. Blake's words floated around her. "I'll make sure everything is okay, Madison."

Consciousness came slowly to Blake. Normally, he awoke with a start and was out of bed in seconds. Today, the dim light of dawn peeked through the windows as he blinked once, then twice. It took him a moment to realize that Maddie still lay in his embrace.

A first for him.

Usually, as soon as the sex was over, Blake was putting the boundaries back into place. Even if he had to manhandle them back into the grooves. But last night he'd barely slid off Madison, unwilling to get too far from the unbelievably silky skin and the delicate scent of her. He'd pulled her close enough to get the blanket out from under them, covered them with it, then hugged her against his chest in a way he didn't want to acknowledge.

"One Minute" Survey

You get **TWO books** <u>and</u> TWO Mystery Gifts...

ABSOLUTELY FREE!

YOU pick your books – WE pay for everything!

See inside for details.

YOU pick your books –
WE pay for everything.
You get TWO new books and TWO Mystery Gifts…
absolutely FREE!
Total retail value: Over $20!

Dear Reader,

Your opinions are important to us. So if you'll participate in our fast and free "One Minute" Survey, **YOU** can pick two wonderful books that **WE** pay for!

As a leading publisher of women's fiction, we'd love to hear from you. That's why we promise to reward you for completing our survey.

IMPORTANT: Please complete the survey and return it. We'll send your Free Books and Free Mystery Gifts right away. **And we pay for shipping and handling too!**

Thank you again for participating in our ↖ *We pay for* "One Minute" Survey. It really takes just a minute *EVERYTHIN'* (or less) to complete the survey… and your free books and gifts will be well worth it!

Sincerely,

Pam Powers

Pam Powers
for Reader Service

"One Minute" Survey

GET YOUR FREE BOOKS AND FREE GIFTS!

✓ Complete this Survey   ✓ Return this survey

▶ DETACH AND MAIL CARD TODAY!

1 Do you try to find time to read every day?
☐ YES ☐ NO

2 Do you prefer stories with happy endings?
☐ YES ☐ NO

3 Do you enjoy having books delivered to your home?
☐ YES ☐ NO

4 Do you share your favorite books with friends?
☐ YES ☐ NO

YES! I have completed the above "One Minute" Survey. Please send me my Two Free Books and Two Free Mystery Gifts (worth over $20 retail). I understand that I am under no obligation to buy anything, as explained on the back of this card.

225/326 HDL GNNS

FIRST NAME	LAST NAME

ADDRESS

APT.#	CITY

STATE/PROV.	ZIP/POSTAL CODE

READER SERVICE—Here's how it works:

Accepting your 2 free Harlequin Desire® books and 2 free gifts (gifts valued at approximately $10.00 retail) places you under no obligation to buy anything. You may keep the books and gifts and return the shipping statement marked "cancel." If you do not cancel, about a month later we'll send you 6 additional books and bill you just $4.55 each in the U.S. or $5.24 each in Canada. That is a savings of at least 13% off the cover price. It's quite a bargain! Shipping and handling is just 50¢ per book in the U.S. and $1.25 per book in Canada*. You may cancel at any time, but if you choose to continue, every month we'll send you 6 more books, which you may either purchase at the discount price plus shipping and handling or return to us and cancel your subscription. *Terms and prices subject to change without notice. Prices do not include sales taxes which will be charged (if applicable) based on your state or country of residence. Canadian residents will be charged applicable taxes. Offer not valid in Quebec. Books received may not be as shown. All orders subject to approval. Credit or debit balances in a customer's account(s) may be offset by any other outstanding balance owed by or to the customer. Please allow 3 to 4 weeks for delivery. Offer available while quantities last.

▲ If offer card is missing write to: Reader Service, P.O. Box 1341, Buffalo, NY 14240-8531 or visit www.ReaderService.com ▲

BUSINESS REPLY MAIL
FIRST-CLASS MAIL   PERMIT NO. 717   BUFFALO, NY

POSTAGE WILL BE PAID BY ADDRESSEE

READER SERVICE
PO BOX 1341
BUFFALO NY 14240-8571

NO POSTAGE
NECESSARY
IF MAILED
IN THE
UNITED STATES

He could tell himself it didn't mean anything, but that didn't change the truth. He was royally screwed.

She still slept deeply. He smoothed back the jumble of her auburn hair so he could see her face, long lashes resting against freckle-sprinkled cheeks. Her lips seemed redder, swollen from their kisses the night before.

He wondered what other evidence he'd left behind. He sure as hell wouldn't be showing any of that to his father.

The memory of his old man left a bitter taste in his mouth. He could go for a cup of coffee…or three…or more. Maybe just the task of fixing it in an unfamiliar kitchen would help him to obliterate the thought of his father demanding proof of his progress?

He might need something stronger, he was afraid.

On his way downstairs, more things than he wanted to think about grabbed his attention. The cracked mirror behind the lamp on the little table in the upper hallway. The closed doors along the hall. Even though he didn't want to, Blake forced himself to open one. All of the furniture had been pushed into the middle of the room and draped. The back wall, which should correspond to the back of the house, had old water stains running down the flowery wallpaper.

He closed the door with a quiet snick and continued downstairs.

A quick glance into a living area opposite the refurbishing room stopped him in his tracks. A worn sofa, rug and coffee table were pushed to one side of the admittedly large room. The other end was occupied by a hospital bed. Bile rose in the back of his throat as Blake took in the area that had been stripped of linens and personal effects, but still bore all the markings of an end-of-life experience. There was a stripped-down bed, a pole to hang fluids on, and what looked like a heart monitor machine on an otherwise plain end table.

While she'd gone to the trouble of cleaning up, Madison hadn't dealt with the bare bones of her father's last days. The thought of her having to deal with this with no support, no helping hands, devastated him. Granted, he hadn't had a true "loved one" in his life, ever, but how had she continued to push forward, day after day, year after year, knowing that she would lose her father?

How devastating.

He forced himself on to the kitchen. Here the true extent of neglect showed in the daylight. Paint was peeling from the walls and windowsill. There was rust on the faucet and inside the sink. Cracks formed a latticework on tile countertop. Blake wasn't an expert in such matters, but he would guess that the house hadn't been properly maintained for a long time and had once been in impeccable quality.

That tile was Italian. The chandeliers were Toso. The kitchen faucet was originally an Axel. No one let that stuff go unless they had to…or strippers came in to take it.

Which could only mean one thing: Madison's family had never sold the Belarus diamond.

Blake crossed over to the budget-brand coffee maker, contemplating the evidence literally before him. Why? Why in the world would her mother keep that diamond and not sell it when they obviously needed the money so badly? Selling that thing on the open market would have set them for life, even if her father's illness had lasted thirty years. Why would she do this?

And what was he supposed to do about it?

This was the last thing he wanted to deal with after last night. As juvenile as it sounded, he wished he could spend his morning sipping coffee and thinking about how good last night had been. Especially if he wasn't going to be allowed to repeat it this morning. But he couldn't.

He had to think about Abigail, about what she was going through, about the fact that she needed him. How did he do that, rather than obsessing about where he went from here?

He hadn't meant for whatever this was between him and Maddie to go this far. He'd planned to get what he needed with as little collateral damage as possible. It was the least risky way of saving Abigail. Despite that, he would never use Madison's body against her.

He wandered back down the hallway to the living room, staring at the large expanse of empty floor between the pieces of furniture.

But now all he could think about was whether she would believe that was exactly what he had done, when the whole story came out. Because he had no doubt it would. He might hope that his father would keep his mouth shut, but that wasn't likely to happen. Especially not if he couldn't have his way.

"What are you doing?"

Blake whirled around to find Madison standing at the foot of the stairs. She had on a thin robe, thin enough for him to tell that she hadn't put on her underclothes. Did that mean she was still open to being vulnerable to him? That was a precious gift Blake wasn't sure he would ever get over.

"I was going to make coffee, then I got distracted."

He knew it sounded lame but it was all he could come up with at the moment. The last thing he wanted to do was make her feel uncomfortable by talking about the empty hospital bed in the room behind him.

She looked so small and frail with her arms wrapped around her ribs like that. He wanted to touch her, to hug her, but her posture was like one big Keep Away sign. She held herself stiffly, her body wound tight. Angled slightly toward him. He noticed she looked everywhere but at the bed.

He wasn't sure how she could even stand to have it in the house, except she probably had no way of moving it. Madison was strong and capable, but not that strong...not strong enough to move that single-handedly...or without a truck.

And he found that he cared, he wanted to help her. Man, he was fully invested.

"Are you ready to go?" she asked.

"Not...really." Blake didn't understood where the

odd question came from. Yes, he'd put on his clothes from last night. He simply wasn't comfortable walking around her house in his birthday suit. He hadn't come prepared for anything else.

She turned and started down the hall, her voice echoing behind her. "I'm sure you're ready to get on the road," she threw over her shoulder. "Clean clothes, a hot shower."

Blake trailed down the hall behind her. What was up with all the questions about leaving? Was she really that eager to see him go?

He stepped through the doorway into the kitchen, where she had turned to face him, her arms crossed tighter than ever across her chest. He struggled not to look down at the effect that had on her breasts, instead focusing on her face.

"Is something wrong?" he asked.

"No." The word was more emphatic than it needed to be.

"You're not going to offer me coffee?" Not that he cared, but he might as well test the waters.

"My father always said my coffee was horrible. You'd probably do better to stop somewhere on your way home."

He was not buying this. He took a step closer to her. Then another. A broken tile shifted beneath his shoe. Madison glanced down, and her lips tightened.

So was it the house that was her problem? Or *him* in her house?

Blake took another step. Only this time, Madison stepped back.

He crossed his arms over his chest, mimicking her position. "What's going on, Madison?"

Outwardly he projected calm, seeming in control of this entire situation. But inside, his temperature rose and his heartbeat sped up. He clenched his teeth on a jittery burst of panic. But he wasn't about to walk away. Instead he moved closer.

He should walk away. He knew it. Without a doubt, he should obey the Keep Away sign and leave Madison to herself. He should walk out of this house and never think about her again, and never think about that stupid diamond. But he couldn't.

So he locked away all thoughts of that beautiful jewel and focused on the beauty in front of him. He could divorce himself from his feelings, but then he wouldn't know the pleasure that came with her touch, the comfort that came from her listening ear.

Selfish bastard that he was, he couldn't leave her alone. "Madison, what is it, hon?"

As he came within arm's reach, Blake couldn't resist touching her. He smoothed his thumb across one high cheekbone. Excitement ratcheted up inside him, rapidly overtaking the panic.

Yes, he was definitely a bastard.

She turned her head to look away, only to flinch at whatever she saw. He followed her gaze to see the door to the pantry hanging crooked in its frame. As they stared in silence, the refrigerator struggled, its mechanical hum sounding strained. Blake let his eyelids drift closed for just a moment, wondering if somewhere in his shallow soul he had the words to make her feel better.

He used his hand to turn her head, guide her eyes back around to his. "Madison, it's okay."

She bit her lip, worrying it for minute before releasing the plump flesh. "No, it's not." She glanced up at him through her long, thick lashes. "You're the first person to be in this house since the day my father died."

"You know, if you don't let anyone in, then no one can help you."

"My father always told me we had to help ourselves. We couldn't expect someone else to come in and bail us out."

"But you're only capable of so much, Madison."

"It's amazing what you can be capable of when you're desperate."

He cupped her cheeks between his hands. "You don't have to be desperate anymore."

Her eyes went wide for a moment with a flash of surprise that cut through his shallow soul like a hot knife through butter. If he lived to be hundred, he hoped he never saw that pain in her expression ever again.

But he knew only one way to erase it right now. Holding her still, he bent to capture her lips with his. How could Madison taste so sweet? Last thing at night, or first thing in the morning, she was sweeter than pie. And he was desperate for dessert.

He sampled her lips, their breaths mingling as they gave themselves over to the sensations. He felt

Madison's hands against his back, pulling him closer. To know she wanted him as much as he wanted her sent his spirit soaring. He let his own hands wander down, feeling the heat of her through the thin robe she wore. He groaned against her lips. He needed her. Right now. Not after a walk down the hall to the couch. Not after a walk upstairs to the bed.

Right. Now.

With what little brain he had left, Blake pictured the room in his head. Then he lifted Madison off her feet with his hands around her ribs. Her squeal echoed in his ears. He sat her down on the nearby empty space on the countertop.

He didn't think about where they were. He only thought about her, and the urgency driving him to take her once more.

To his infinite gratitude, she spread her knees wide, making space for him. Blake fumbled in his pocket for a condom, then reached around to lower his zipper. His glance down revealed the shadowed valley between her breasts, visible where her robe had slid open.

Blake drew in a hard, deep breath, easing off the brakes on his drive to be inside her once more. He trailed his fingers along the edges of her robe, sampling the plumpness, feeling her gasp, seeing her nipples tighten beneath the sheer fabric. Slowly he slid one panel to the side, revealing her firm, round breast with its pink-tipped nipple. His mouth watered as he leaned over and licked the turgid tip. Madison arched her back, her breath releasing in a hiss. He licked again. And again. Loving the reaction of her body. Knowing that she'd be wet and ready for him.

He dropped his pants and covered himself for their protection. His fingers found her slick and needy. His heart pounded in his throat as he eased himself through her tightness.

"Oh, Maddie," he moaned. "So good."

Then he felt her legs circle around his waist, trapping him close, pulling him closer. He forced his way in to the hilt, both of them shuddering. He ground against her, his entire body tightening with the need to lose control.

"Please, Blake," she begged.

Holding back was no longer an option. That simple request swept aside his hesitation. He dug deep, gathering every ounce of energy he had, desperate to share something special with her, something he'd never felt with anyone but her. He had a need for her response that would send him over the edge.

He smoothed his hand up her body to her breast, palming, then squeezing it. Tweaking the tip in a way that made her body clamp down on him. She gasped with every thrust but refused to let go.

Blake strained, desperate for release. His hand slid around to her bottom, jerking her against him with every thrust. In his need to impress himself on her, to draw out her response, he buried his mouth against her neck, and sucked on her flesh to make the pounding of her heart match his. She cried out, the sound vibrating against his tongue. Her body squeezed around him, sending his need into hyperspace. He ground against her as they both exploded with an intensity that almost knocked Blake out.

He wanted to crawl inside of her arms and never leave, an idea that at once felt overwhelmingly right and oh-so-wrong in a panicky way. The thought of staying just like this, forever, tempted him.

All too soon, Madison began to shift. He stilled her movements with his hands on her hips. Just a minute more…

"Blake," she murmured. "Your phone."

He blinked. Sure enough, a low metallic ringtone came from his phone, not far away on the countertop. On the display, Blake could see that it was his father's housekeeper. Alarm quickly pushed out the euphoria.

"Blake, it's an emergency." He barely recognized Sherry's shaking voice. "I had to take Abigail to the ER."

Eight

Madison could barely comprehend Blake's mad dash for his clothes. Her brain was still swimming in lust and satiation. Then she got a really good look at his face.

"What's going on?" she asked.

"I've got to go," he murmured. He tried to put a button through the hole on his shirt once, then twice. Finally he swore, then ran his fingers through his hair.

Did she hear him right? "What? Why?"

Who had called? Blake was as unattached as anyone she'd come across, seeming to exist in a strange ecosystem that had no one else living inside of it. Yet after one short conversation he was buttoning his shirt crooked in his haste to leave.

"Blake?"

Still he ignored her, as if his mind were already elsewhere. The switch from having his full attention five minutes ago to being completely tossed aside had her reeling. Not that she expected him to ignore an emergency for her, but what on earth had him switching gears faster than a race car? At least his preoccupation covered her awkward dismount from the counter. She might never look at her kitchen the same way again.

After calling his name a few times, she went to stand between him and the phone he had set back down on the counter while zipping up his pants. "Blake? What is happening?"

"I've got to leave right now." His tone didn't indicate he realized he'd already said this to her before.

"Why?"

He blinked, as if no one had ever asked him that. "They've taken my sister to the hospital."

Sister? "Okay. I'll go with you."

"No."

The vehemence encapsulated in that one word took her aback. "Excuse me?"

"No," he said with a hard shake of his head. "I need to leave now."

The hand he waved at her seemed to indicate it was her lack of clothes that was the problem. But was it? "Blake, you shouldn't go alone. Give me three minutes to throw on—"

"No. Just. Not now."

Hurt shot through Madison with the same speed

that lust had earlier. She was a smart girl. It didn't take her too many tries to realize when someone didn't want her around—whatever the reason. But this wasn't something she could let go. Blake did not look like he should be behind the wheel. Besides, if there was one thing she had experience with, it was hospitals.

She doubted Blake could say the same.

This time she placed her hand over the phone as he reached for it. "Blake."

"What?" he asked, the word sounding short and clipped. He never lifted his eyes from the phone.

"Do you know which hospital?"

That had him glancing up. He gave a short shake of his head.

"When you do, do you know how to get there in the quickest way possible?"

"No," he admitted through clenched teeth.

"Then why don't you find out while I get some clothes on?"

She could actually see the gears start to turn before he gave a quick nod. Madison left him to his phone while she ran upstairs. A quick splash of water on the face was all she dared take the time for, then clean clothes and a ponytail holder she would put her hair in on the way. To her surprise, he was still in the kitchen when she ran in with her tennis shoes in her hand.

"She's at Children's Hospital. Her doctor was already there."

Madison paused for a mere second, then forced herself to finish putting on her shoes. "Let's go."

As much as it hurt, she wasn't surprised when he started to argue on the way to the car. "Just tell me the shortcuts. I'll get myself there."

"And get in a wreck because you're upset behind the wheel."

"I'm perfectly capable of driving right now."

Madison glided around the car until she reached the passenger door, then swung around to face him. "But you are upset, right? Shaken, maybe? In need of a friend?" She grimaced, feeling her anger slip the bounds of her control. "If you don't actually consider me as one, I get it. But I still feel some responsibility to fill that role, since ten minutes ago we were still having sex on my countertop."

Without waiting for an answer, she gave the car hood a quick slap, then slid around the door and into the seat. As she buckled her belt, she called herself every kind of fool. Blake still stood beside the car. Had all of this been just about the sex? If she got any more mixed signals, she wouldn't know which way was up.

Maybe he didn't, either.

Madison tried to hold onto that thought while dragging in a deep breath. For a moment, surprise streaked through her. She'd dealt with any number of medical emergencies in her lifetime...none of which had caused her to lose her cool. Of course, she was usually the person in charge. Not simply along for the ride.

Still, she shouldn't have struck out at him like that.

Thirty seconds later, he slid into the driver's seat. "I'm sorry, Madison—" he started.

"Don't be. Let's just go."

Maybe that wasn't the way to handle this. But she just couldn't go through with helping him if he actually said again out loud that he didn't want her.

She wanted to be a good person who would help him regardless. But she couldn't. Better to just do her part, then deal with the fallout later. After she'd had time to process her own emotions over sleeping with him, then discovering he had a whole family she wasn't aware of. And what man his age had siblings young enough to be treated at Children's Hospital? Was this child really a sister? Or something else?

Madison quickly cut off that line of thinking. She was here. She needed to focus on the job at hand. Speculation would get her nothing but upset.

Madison directed him toward the least busy streets she could think of at this time of the morning. The only saving grace was the absence of school traffic. She watched him closely for any signs that he wasn't in control, but those few moments by himself outside of the car seemed to have calmed him.

She only wished she could get all of her suspicions under control just as easily.

Blake locked down his emotions as tightly as he could, just as tightly as he held the steering wheel. He executed the turns with precision, utilizing every ounce of experience he'd gotten on the autobahn, to maneuver the vehicle without slowing down.

"Call Father's housekeeper," he said, not daring to take his eyes off the road. His phone automatically rang the number, which went straight to voice mail.

Blake wanted to hit something, but he refused to slow down long enough to do so. To his surprise, Madison didn't complain. No gasps, no quick grabs for the door handle. She was just a solid, quiet presence in the car who gave the occasional direction to turn.

"Call Father's housekeeper."

When this call also went to voice mail, he let out a string of expletives that would've had a sailor blushing. Still, Madison remained silent.

"Where is she?" he growled.

Madison pointed out the entryway for the parking deck, and Blake pulled squarely into the valet spot.

Madison waved him through to the ER entrance while she paused next to the valet podium.

Blake felt a flash of gratitude, tossed her the keys, then stepped up his pace to get to the ER desk.

"I need to see my sister. Abigail Boudreaux," he told the nurse at the desk.

A part of him was surprised by the shaky, out-of-breath quality of his voice. This wasn't a Blake that he knew. But he didn't have time to think about that right now. The nurse nodded and calmly asked to see his ID. Her entire demeanor was a counterpoint to his.

Madison arrived as the nurse clicked away on the computer.

"Blake?" she asked. "Isn't there a parent you can call?"

"Good luck getting through to him," Blake murmured. Luckily the nurse looked up before he had to explain his words.

"Sir, I'm afraid I can't help you."

Blake froze. "What do you mean you can't help me? I know my sister was brought here."

Madison tugged at his shirtsleeve, but he ignored her. He focused entirely on the nurse, the person who would get him to his sister the fastest. "I want to see my sister. Abigail Boudreaux."

"I'm afraid I can't help you, sir."

For a moment, Blake was almost certain he was going to climb across the counter. What the hell was going on with him? All he knew was he had to make sure his sister was okay.

Just as Blake opened his mouth to start yelling, Madison intervened. "Blake." Her tone was firm and hard enough to catch his attention. He turned her way.

"Blake," she said in a softer voice. "Let me speak to you for a moment, please."

He gave the nurse a hard stare before following Madison over to the side. "I don't have time for this. I need to see my sister."

"I realize that," Madison said. "The thing is, if you're not listed specifically as someone who should be told she's here, they can't tell you her information. They can't let you up to see her."

"What?"

"It's considered an invasion of privacy and it's against federal regulations. Why don't you try the housekeeper again? Or maybe your father? Your mother?"

He ignored the question implied in her words, and tried to dial Sherry again. The call went straight to voice mail.

Blake felt scattered, like his racing heartbeat was pulling him away from information that was very important but he couldn't focus on. Instead he did the only other thing he knew: he dialed his father again.

"Yes?"

The calm sound of his father's voice only raised his irritation even higher. "Where is Abigail? Are you here at the hospital?"

"Hospital? I don't know what you're talking about."

"The housekeeper called me. Abigail had to be taken to the emergency room but they won't let me see her."

"Well, why would we list you as family? Until recently, I hadn't seen you in nearly twenty years. But I guess that's what the message on my phone is for. I haven't had a chance to listen to it yet."

"She called me almost two hours ago. How come you're not down here?"

"I'm in New York. Besides, it's probably just a fake episode to get attention."

"Abigail's epilepsy is not fake."

Blake knew he was yelling at this point but couldn't control himself. Beside him he sensed Madison shift on her feet. Then a warm weight settled at the small of his back. In all the chaos that raced through his mind and his body, that warm contact became a focal point. Her touch sent a wave of peace over him.

His father was in New York. He wasn't here—not that he would care if he was. Instead of trying to understand that, Blake just hung up the phone. He stared at it in his hand for a moment, wondering if throwing it across the room would make him feel any better. Except it was the only way he could find out any information about Abigail.

"What do I do?" he moaned, bending over to press his palms against his knees. How did he find his baby sister?

"Blake."

The softly spoken word brought his attention back to his surroundings. Blake straightened up, drew in a hard breath, then looked at her. "I need to find her, Madison."

"I know. Let me help you."

Just as she had been since they'd gotten in the car. Her words centered him, just like her touch had. "I don't know what to do."

"What kind of episode did your sister have?"

"She has epilepsy. All the housekeeper said was that she was unresponsive this morning. Maybe some kind of seizure?"

Maddie nodded. Her hand ran down his arm, only

stopping when she reached his hand and curled her fingers around his. "Come with me."

As she headed out the door of the emergency room, he glanced back at the nurse at the desk who watched them walk away. "Wait a minute," he said. "Where are we going?"

Madison paused once they reached the other side of the automatic doors. Then she looked up at him. "I know of another waiting room for pediatrics that might be helpful. Let's go in the front of the hospital and see if we can possibly find the housekeeper there. That'll be the quickest way," she said, "even though it doesn't seem like it. Badgering the nurse will get us nowhere. I know—I have plenty of experience."

He walked with her along the sidewalks outside the huge buildings. Impatience bubbled up inside of him, but there were no other options for him at this moment. "How do you know this?" he asked.

"The staff at Maison de Jardin sometimes has to come to the hospital to help residents who've been injured, whose spouses have abused them. And their children." She tossed him a quick glance. "I've been here quite a few times."

She maintained a quick pace, not letting her shorter stature keep her from matching his longer strides. "Plus some of our residents actually come to work here."

Blake paused a step. "Can't you ask one of them to help us?"

"Unfortunately no. I can't ask them to risk their

jobs when they've worked so hard to get into a better place."

As much as the logic made sense, Blake could only see as far as his needs in this moment.

Madison led him in the front door proper and took him around to a large bank of elevators. No sooner were they in one than she hit the button for the third floor.

"Has your...sister...always had epilepsy?"

There it was, the guilt that he couldn't figure out how to shake. "I don't know. I know this particular diagnosis is recent, but I'm not sure how long her symptoms have been occurring."

He shifted on his feet, uncomfortable with the knowledge that he had no idea what was happening, he had no control over the situation, and if he ever found that blasted diamond, he would find himself completely responsible for a child with an illness that could land her in the hospital. What the hell was he even doing here?

They came out of the elevator to a long hallway. Madison rushed down until it opened into a nurses station. "Tamika," she exclaimed. "I wasn't sure if you were working today."

Blake paused behind her as the young black woman in scrubs gave him a good eyeing.

He simply stared back.

"What are you doing here, Madison?" she asked.

"We're looking for... Blake's sister. I was just going to take him across to the waiting room."

Hearing her words, Blake turned abruptly and

saw a waiting room behind them. He strode across the hall into the doorway.

"Mr. Boudreaux!"

Blake was so relieved to see Sherry rising from one of the chairs that he thought he might melt into a puddle. "Where is she?" he asked, rushing over to help her. "Is she okay?"

"Oh, Mr. Boudreaux. They haven't come to tell me anything." Tears overflowed the woman's eyes to trickle down her cheeks. "I can't imagine that little poppet all alone."

So he was one step closer but still knew nothing. Soon Blake found himself with an armful of weeping housekeeper, and his fear for his sister was even higher than ever.

Nine

"Is that really him?" Tamika asked, straining her neck to see behind Madison into the waiting room.

"Stop it." Madison wasn't sure how she felt about Blake in this moment, but she certainly didn't feel comfortable with her friend ogling him. She drew in a calming breath, only to wince at the antiseptic scent of the hospital halls. "We're just trying to find out where the little girl is. The housekeeper brought her in. All I know is that it has something to do with her epilepsy."

"Why would a housekeeper bring her in? Where are the parents?" Tamika asked, bracing her hands on her hips. Tamika's passion lay in caring for the children on this floor—and making sure none of them were mistreated.

Madison shook her head. "Blake tried to call someone while we were downstairs. I guess his father? I'm really not sure. It sounded like he might be out of town."

"How could he not have any information about his child? Are you sure this little girl is his sister?"

Madison did not want to go there. "I've been told very little."

Tamika looked sideways at her for a moment, confirming Madison's own fears.

"That's all I know. He tried to call the housekeeper and couldn't get her on the phone."

"Cell reception up here is terrible," Tamika said. "Her phone probably wouldn't work in that waiting room."

"That's what it sounds like." Madison glanced over her shoulder to see Blake holding a woman wearing a maid's uniform in his arms. "But I'm guessing he's found her now."

Her friend grumbled beneath her breath as she watched them. Then Madison and Tamika shared a glance. Madison felt awkward. She'd done what she told Blake she would. Should she join him now? The housekeeper appeared to be crying, definitely distraught. Should she offer some kind of help?

"I don't know what to do," Madison said. *About any of it*, but she didn't say that part out loud. She guessed maybe she could have gone online and looked into his family, but the excruciating effect of the gossip surrounding her friend Trinity had left a bad taste in her mouth. Besides, she hadn't wanted anything else to mess with her self-esteem. Guess she'd shot herself in the foot there?

"Should I go in there? Should I ask if I can help?"

"Girl, I'd help him all day long," Tamika teased with a saucy wink. "He's very pretty. Even prettier in person than he was online."

"Tamika!"

"Well, he is." She offered her typical shrug when she was misbehaving, then glanced over her monitors for a moment.

"Don't you have a job to do?"

"Not at the moment. All's quiet."

"We need to find you a boyfriend," Madison grumbled. Then maybe she would stay out of Madison's love life.

"Well, if Blake has any friends…"

She'd walked right into that one. She gave her friend a quelling look. "I'm serious, Tamika. I had no idea he even had a sister. He hasn't spoken much about his family."

"What do you talk about?"

At first Madison thought she was being facetious again, but then realized her friend was serious. "We've talked about my family, the house, my job."

"But he's giving no information about himself?" She shook her head. "Girl, you'd better be careful."

Madison knew that. She just didn't know if she was in a position to be careful anymore. Blake's possession of her body had sealed what her spirit already knew. But was he on the same page?

He'd said he wanted to be with her. But he hadn't

really shared himself with her, had he? Other than his art, and hints that his childhood had been quite bad, he hadn't really shared much. It was all about the present...and her. Looking back, that didn't seem right.

"I recognize that expression," Tamika said. "I see more cookies in our future."

Madison arched an eyebrow at her friend but was afraid Tamika wasn't far from right. "Any requests?"

"You know I'm good with any chocolate, and I've got finals coming up."

"I'm glad my pain can feed your success." Madison could already feel the depression sinking in. She should have known that last night was too good to be true.

"I hope not," Tamika said, a frown between her brows. "I know I tease you a lot, but you're the last person who deserves any more grief."

Madison wished she could hug her friend, but the nurses station desk between them prevented that. "Thank you, Tamika."

"My pleasure."

Then a patient pressed a call button in one of the rooms and Tamika went to answer it. Madison stared after her friend for long moments. She'd been so blessed in her life. Yes, she'd lost both her parents. But they'd been a blessing to her while they'd been alive. And her friends, they helped keep her going. She drew in a deep, long breath. She could only do what she knew, which was to help people, including Blake. That was what she would do for now. The rest could be worried about later. She turned back toward the waiting room, only to find it empty.

She glanced up and down the hallway, but it too was empty. The faces at the nurses station were now unfamiliar, as Tamika had left to answer the call.

Madison stood in confusion for long moments. Where had Blake gone? Why didn't he let her know?

Of course, he hadn't wanted her here in the first place. Maybe taking her with him was more information than he wanted to let her in on. This was definitely a new one, and only magnified her impression from earlier that he'd been holding parts of himself back. Possibly hiding his true self on purpose.

What reason could he have for doing that? No good ones that she could think of.

She'd never heard of being dumped at the hospital. Then again, she'd served her purpose, hadn't she? She glanced at her phone. Sure enough, no reception.

So calling him was out. She could stand around and wait for him to get back, but did he want her here? Somehow the thought of sitting here for hours on end while Tamika was working and knew she'd been dumped was just more than she could handle. She'd be more productive at home, where she knew her place and had things to do.

So she headed downstairs. As she stood in the lobby, she called for a cab.

The debate raged within her as she waited. Should she tell him? Should she not tell him? Should she let him make the next move? In the end, she couldn't not say something. Just disappearing without a word wasn't a responsible action on her part. So she typed out a text letting him know she'd gone home.

By the time she'd pulled into the driveway, the screen of her phone was still empty. Just as empty as she was.

Madison put a little extra effort behind her sandpapering. Normally she would have used an electric sander, but she'd chosen to do the manual work on the details simply to keep herself from thinking. It had been twenty-four hours since she'd walked out of the hospital, and Blake had still not contacted her.

She'd gone to work and kept herself busy with files, calls and orders. No one had been hanging around, so she didn't see the point in baking. She'd be tempted to just eat all the cookie dough herself. So by midafternoon, she'd come home and tried to keep herself busy on a new antique dresser that she'd gotten from one of the specialty stores in town. Unfortunately, it wasn't wearing her out as much as she'd like.

But she was too wound up to settle into reading her mother's journals, and nothing on TV interested her. So she'd rather get her hands roughed up and be productive at the same time, instead of spending her time pining over someone who couldn't care less about her.

She did recognize the selfishness in her thoughts. Blake was really concerned about his sister, and she hoped that the little girl was okay. She hoped that his not contacting her didn't mean that something terrible had happened to the child. But how long did it take to send a simple text?

Caring about someone meant you let them know you were okay. She could take the hint.

So she scratched and scraped, going with the grain to preserve the wood underneath the tacky finish and layer of old paint. She knew in the end she would create something that was really beautiful, and that kept her going.

She just wished she could shut off her brain for a few minutes.

Just then her phone dinged. Madison glanced over at it for a moment, not sure if she really wanted to see what was on it. All this time she'd been mentally complaining that he hadn't contacted her, and now she wasn't even sure she wanted to see if it was him, or what he had to say.

Finally, she dropped the piece of sandpaper, and wiped the dust from her arms. Then she took the few steps to pick up her phone and read the screen.

I'm at the gate.

Well, at least Blake was being considerate. The lock on the gate was so old he probably could've pushed it open without even worrying about letting her know. Instead he'd at least given her a heads-up.

Madison wasn't sure what she wanted. This whole relationship had been like a roller coaster. Did she want to let him in? She knew she cared, or else she wouldn't have spent the last twenty-four hours obsessing over him not contacting her. But was this a matter of too little too late?

Curiosity finally got the better of her, and she stepped outside to unlock the gate. They'd never been able to afford a fancy electronic version, so she had to manually pop the lock to let him in.

By the time he drove through, parked the car and got out, she'd closed the gate behind him and was standing at the entrance to the kitchen. The heat outside caused sweat to bead along her hairline. But she wasn't about to let him in this house without a really good reason.

"Hey, Maddie. How's it going?"

For a moment she simply stared at him. Did he really think he could leave her hanging for twenty-four hours and just waltz back in with a hearty how-you-doin'?

"You don't get to call me Maddie anymore."

That wasn't what she'd expected to come out of her mouth, and apparently he hadn't, either. The surprise on his face was clear, and for a moment she felt ashamed. What she'd said hadn't been polite, but then she realized at least it was true. Maddie was a nickname that came with intimacy. Intimacy meant relationship. Relationship meant including someone in your life.

"I'm sorry," he said, and it actually seemed true. "I didn't mean to upset you."

"Then why would you completely blank me out for twenty-four hours? Why wouldn't you at least send a text letting me know if you were okay, if your sister was okay?"

For a moment, his entire expression shut down. His body stiffened as if he would pull away from her. *This is it. We're done.*

Then he took a deep breath and said, "Maddie, um Madison." He shook his head. "You're right. I'm going to go out on a limb and be honest here and say it didn't occur to me that you would want me to hear from me with an update."

"Why?"

Blake wiped the sweat off his forehead. "I know this doesn't reflect well on me but frankly, I've never been in a relationship before. I've never been involved with a woman who would want to know those things. And even if she did, I wouldn't have a clue how to give them to her." He took a step back. "And I also haven't been involved with my family in many years. Dealing with a crisis like this is out of my realm of experience, and it never occurred to me that you would want to be involved, either."

Well, at least he'd been honest. As the seconds ticked by, Maddie just stood there, numb as she tried to understand what living like that could possibly be like. How could you go through life with no one around who cared anything about you? How could you not have contact with your family? Blake seemed to care a lot about his little sister. How had that happened?

One thing at a time. "Blake, it wouldn't matter if we weren't involved. I would still want to help you.

I would still care about what happened to your sister. I would still want to help support you. I thought I'd made that clear."

"That's because you're a much better person than me."

"I'm not an angel. I'm just human."

"Then we'll agree to disagree."

"So I don't know what to do here. What is it that you want me to do? Back off?"

Because that really was not in her wheelhouse. Thankfully, he was already shaking his head.

"Do you want me to not ask questions?"

"I'm guessing that might be impossible for you." His grin had a touch of smirk.

Time to bring her fears to the fore. "Well, I don't really think it's fair that you get to pry into my life and I don't get to pry into yours."

The widening of his eyes told her she'd hit a nerve. Then he gave a short nod. "I'm gonna try, Madison."

"Would you rather walk away now?" Because he obviously wasn't comfortable with this.

As if something inside him was unleashed, Blake sprung forward to wrap her in his arms. He buried his face into her neck. "No. No. No," he murmured against her skin.

Madison's resistance melted away. Blake was different than anyone she'd known, and she just had to work with that. Not accept it. But figure out what that meant for both of them.

She pulled him into the semi-cool house, which was a bit of a relief after the heat of the Louisiana sun outside. He closed the door behind him, then sank to his knees in front of her. He buried his face against her belly. Madison wrapped her arms around his shoulders, the weight of her heart telling her she was seeing him in this moment like no one else ever had.

"I thought I was going to lose her," he said. He didn't look up. He didn't say anything more. And she knew he was admitting something he might not have to anyone else.

"Is she going to be okay?"

He nodded against her. "I never thought I'd get this attached to a child. But she's so small, so fragile. Seeing her in that hospital bed…"

She felt the tremor that shook him and rubbed his back. "How long has she been sick?"

"From what I understand, she was diagnosed several months ago with the epilepsy. Her mother never said anything about it before."

So she had a mother and father, but the housekeeper took her to the hospital? "Where were her parents?"

"My father was in New York. He and my mother divorced long ago. Abigail's mother is who knows where in Europe. How she could leave a seven-year-old like that is beyond even me."

Madison clutched him a little closer, disbelief sweeping over her. How in the world could they do that? Blake's horror made a little more sense now. Wait—

"Blake, is this the family business that brought you home?"

He nodded but didn't say more. Madison imagined this little conversation was the most Blake had shared with anyone, ever. While she should probably be nervous about that, she couldn't help but be grateful that she was someone he felt comfortable sharing this burden with.

After a few long moments, Blake stood and pressed a soft kiss against her lips. "Madison?" he murmured.

She knew what he was asking, without him having to say the words. And she knew what she wanted, without needing any promises.

So she once more took his hand in hers and led him up the stairs to her room. There she pulled her dusty T-shirt over her head and unsnapped her bra so it could fall away. She peeled off her khaki work pants and the plain pair of panties underneath. The whole time Blake watched her, his gaze ravenously devouring every new inch of bare skin she revealed. His fingers played over her, as if using his fingertips to memorize every curve and valley. Her breath caught as he lingered at the tips of her breasts, at the curve of her hips, at the apex of her thighs.

He tore his own clothes off with more haste than decorum, slid on protection and covered her body with his. As he slipped inside her, Madison squeezed her eyes shut, hoping to hide the sheen of tears caused by the emotions welling inside her. Somehow she knew she'd made a choice tonight. There were no guarantees for how it would turn out. But with every thrust he made her his. There was no turning back, only going forward. She didn't know how to do that. But she guessed she'd take it one day at a time.

As he took them both over the edge, she squeezed her arms around him, hugging him close, and silently accepted that despite all the craziness, this was the man for her.

Still she couldn't stop herself from asking, as they lay entwined on her bed, "Blake, is there anything else I need to know?"

Why didn't the shake of his head make her feel any better?

Ten

Blake was surprised when Abigail let him lift her from the car and into his arms. Sherry stood nearby as he carried her to the door. It was amazing how light she felt against him, how fragile. The doctor had said that she wasn't in any more danger, but that didn't take away the fear.

Blake knew the minute they stepped through the front door that his father was home. Yes, it could've just been the cold feel of the house after decades of being possessed by his father, but somehow he knew the concentration of his father's essence when he was around. It was an awareness he'd never get rid of.

Blake ignored the movement in his peripheral vision as he crossed the foyer, and continued toward the stairs. Abigail deserved to be at home, in her own bed, happy and safe. At least he could provide that.

He settled her into her bed and covered her with a comforter. The trusting expression in her brown eyes reached into his chest and squeezed. "It's going to be okay, Abigail." He hoped he sounded more confident than he was. Either way, Abigail got the short end of the stick.

"Thank you, Blake."

"Sleep well, sweetheart." Blake tucked the blanket in around her again, not sure if that was actually how this was done. Then he left the housekeeper to supervise bedtime.

He came back down the stairs with a feeling of dread. But this time it wasn't just about seeing his father. It was the knowledge that he couldn't keep either of the girls in his life safe from Armand. And he had no idea what to do about that.

"Blake, I see you found your way home again."

For a split second, Blake considered walking straight out the door. Not pausing. Not acknowledging his father in any way. But the memory of that little girl in his arms stayed his steps.

"Well, for now I don't have any choice, do I?"

His father inclined his head as he stepped farther into the foyer. "So how much did this hospital visit cost me?"

Even for his father, that seemed like a crass question. So Blake didn't bother to suppress his sarcasm. "Don't worry, Dad. I took care of it for you."

"I'm amazed they let you, considering they didn't want to give you access to her at all."

That gave Blake a little jolt but he said, "They'll take money under any circumstances."

His father nodded; obviously Blake had finally learned to speak his language. He took a few steps toward the front door.

"At least it wasn't an inconvenience to you," Blake said, looking back over his shoulder at his father.

"That's right."

That smirk made Blake want to wipe it off his face. But his father was ready to move on to new sport.

"So you finally bagged her, did you?"

Blake stopped dead in his tracks, struggling to keep his face completely blank as rage swept over him. To hear Madison spoken about in the same way teenagers would talk about a girl in a locker room was infuriating. What they had shared had nothing to do with bagging and everything to do with discovering who they each were. Blake couldn't even believe he thought about it in those terms, but it was true.

Then he realized the implications of what his father had just said, and swung around to face him head on. "What do you mean? What have you heard?"

Blake knew that his father had no friends who were close to Madison or her family or the charity. So who would be gossiping about them with him? Especially since his father had been in New York. "What did you do, Father?"

"The same thing any father does when his son cuts him out of his life. I hired a private detective."

"What the hell? Who spies on their child? What happened to 'show me proof'? Like my last visit."

Armand shook his head. "Your proof is not very reliable. And I know the closer you get to the girl, it will be even less so. Or the closer you get to Abigail. So I went with an unbiased source."

"Hell, if you're going to go to those lengths, why don't you just have someone break into her house and steal the diamond?"

Blake quickly bit his tongue, even though it had to have been an idea that his father thought of long ago. But the thought of Maddie being subjected to someone breaking into her house freaked him out.

"Stealing is illegal," his father said matter-of-factly, as if every machination he'd imposed since Blake had returned home wasn't in some way evil. But it was legal, and thus acceptable. Then Armand went on, "If the diamond is obtained through illegal means that can be tracked back to me, it will be difficult to sell."

"So you want me to steal it instead?"

"Actually, I figure she'll just hand it over to you. Or, if you take something she never knew she had, then is it really stealing?"

Blake shoved the completely insane reasoning behind his father's words away, and focused on the most pressing issue. "I can't believe you had someone spying on me."

And that person had been spying on Madison,

too. The sheer weight of that understanding hit him hard. The things he was bringing into Maddie's life weren't just unfair to her. This was an invasion of massive proportions. He just hoped he could live with the results.

"You will stay away from Maddie," he insisted. "Do you understand me?"

His father only answered with another smirk. In that moment, a large part of the old Blake reappeared. The urgent need to run, to escape, just as he had when he was seventeen, was overwhelming. The only thing that kept his feet planted right where he was was a little girl upstairs and a woman across town, neither of whom he could abandon. When he'd walked out of here as a teenager, he couldn't give a rat's ass about anybody else. There was no one to care about. Every person in his life had disappeared, just like they had out of Abigail's life. But now he refused to run out on her like others had.

But he just wasn't sure how to help her.

"Don't worry, you bastard. You'll get what you want."

But as he walked out, Blake knew he was biding time. He had to find a way out of the situation and quick. And that way out couldn't involve stealing a diamond, even one Madison didn't know she had.

I had options. When I chose to be with my husband, I knew what I was giving up. But not the pain that would follow.

I knew the man I was leaving behind would be

vindictive, and I knew I would be punished, but I had no idea he would take it out on my family like this.

Madison read the lines once more. Many times her mother had mentioned making choices, but for the most part her words were about routine decisions. This was the first Madison had read about a vindictive *man*. What did that mean?

A quick glance over at the clock told her that Blake would be here any moment. He had offered to take her to an event at the ASTRA Museum that Trinity hadn't been able to attend. Madison wanted to make a good impression. To represent the charity in the best way possible. Hopefully, with Blake by her side, things would go smoothly. They'd be no embarrassment or fumbling.

She needed to get her shoes on before he arrived. She set the journal on her bedside table and crossed to her closet. Just as she reached it, she heard the book tumble to the floor. Crossing back, she picked it up to return it to the table, only to have something fall from the back.

It looked like several pieces of paper folded together. Madison could see her mother's handwriting on the back of the outside sheet. That was odd. She'd never found anything more than bookmarks stuck into her mother's journals. Only she didn't have time to look at it right now. She laid the packet on top of the journal and returned to the closet for her shoes.

When she went outside a few minutes later, Blake's wolf whistle made her smile as she crossed over to the car. She slid into her seat and was surprised when he leaned across for a quick kiss. This felt more like a real date. So far she and Blake seemed to only have out-of-the-ordinary times together. But this felt real and good. Madison would be more than happy to have a quiet, normal date.

"So," he said as he got them on the road, "I was wondering how you would feel about meeting my little sister."

For a moment, Madison felt like a bomb had exploded in the car. She glanced over at him as if to say, *Did you feel that?* The only indication that his request was unusual even for him was his super tight grip on the steering wheel.

So he knew what he was doing, and the fact that he was willing to still do it filled her with excitement. She also felt a touch of nervousness, because what did she know about spending time with a seven-year-old? Granted, she'd spent plenty of time with children at Maison de Jardin. But she had a feeling that, like Blake, his little sister would be a whole different breed of people.

"What did you have in mind?"

Blake chuckled. "I was hoping you could tell me. I've rarely spent time with her except overseas and then we weren't really doing kid stuff. She seemed fascinated by me probably because everything else about being in Europe bored her."

Madison laughed. "I doubt that. I find you fascinating all the time."

Her heart sped up when he reached over and

squeezed her hand. It felt so normal, so right. Madison wondered if she had a right to be this happy.

"What does your sister like to do?"

"I have no idea. I think she likes animals? She seems pretty girlie. Likes dresses and the color pink."

"Maybe we could take her to City Park? It's not too hot if we go in the morning. They have some animals, playgrounds and lots of shade there." Was that too mundane for this child? It was going to be a long day if Madison worried herself over everything. She just had to stop and treat Abigail like any other kid she was taking on an adventure.

"Sure. Then maybe lunch out?"

"Good." Madison tried not to sound out of breath. This would be good.

She was really starting to relax and enjoy their time together after checking in at the museum and talking with a few people she already knew. Blake's ability to carry a conversation in a social setting really helped her relax. She knew she shouldn't be dependent on having a wing man, but it wouldn't hurt for these first few events, right?

She reminded herself of that as he excused himself to go make a call to check on Abigail. Sherry had been scared enough by the events the other day that she now gave him regular updates, despite whatever her boss might say. Madison's mind was just boggled by the thought. Blake hadn't come right out and said it, but Madison could tell that his father had to be emotionally abusive or highly manipulative. She had too much experience with these types of situations to not have a strong suspicion about what was going on.

She strolled around the rotunda in the museum, studying the various paintings highlighted here. It was a gorgeous space, one that she enjoyed standing in for a while whenever she visited the ASTRA. As she stood in front of one particular painting, a voice interrupted her thoughts.

"I never realized how much you look like your mother."

Startled, Madison whirled around to find herself facing a man of average height, looking slick in a black suit and blue tie that matched his vividly hued eyes. She was startled, because his eyes were exactly like Blake's, except cold where Blake's were heated.

The man studied her a moment more, then said, "Remarkable." He held out his hand. "My name is Armand."

"Madison, Madison Landry." She sounded out of breath to her own ears, and quickly tried to regain her poise.

"I am aware. Your mother was a beautiful woman, in a class by herself."

Madison shifted on her heels. Though the man was smiling, she felt uneasy. "How did you know her?"

All that Madison knew about her mother's life, outside of her own interactions with her, was from her journals. Which didn't touch on anything before her marriage, except her relationship with her elderly parents. Curiosity swept through her despite her nerves. After all, no one that she'd met at these events had mentioned knowing her mother, despite their pretty strong resemblance.

"Your mother was well known in my social circles," he said, his slight Cajun accent making the words sound exotic. "Before she…removed herself."

Again the man's intense gaze gave her a slight sense of déjà vu. Where was Blake? Suddenly she wanted him with her right now.

"Her beauty would have lit up any social setting, her grace a complement to any household."

Why did it sound like he was talking about Jacqueline as if she were an object? "My mother was a very gracious, caring woman."

With one elegant brow arched, his expression turned almost cold. "That I wouldn't know."

"Then you must not have met her in person." So many people's lives had been touched by her mother's authentic nature. But she also knew that those types of interactions didn't really make themselves known in this kind of social setting.

As if he read her mind, he said, "Circumstances often dictate what we learn about a person."

True, but that was kind of a strange thing for him to say to her. Madison found herself unconsciously taking a step back and forced herself to be still.

She'd been curious about her mother's life before her marriage for so long that she wanted to ask questions. She'd never met someone who knew her mother then. But something about the man's demeanor, the cold way he spoke, kept those questions locked inside.

Out of the corner of her eye, she saw Blake pass through the doorway into the arch. Relief swept over her.

Blake's eyes widened as he approached. She hadn't been mistaken. His blue eyes matched the colder ones of the man in front of her, who was staring her down as if she were a subject to be studied rather than a person to be known.

"Father!"

The steel behind Blake's voice startled her.

Armand turned slowly to face his son. Madison was surprised to see Blake's expression go from anger to almost a total blank. As if he completely locked himself down in his father's presence.

"Son, how could you leave such a beautiful woman unattended and vulnerable?"

There it was. That sense that though the words were innocuous, the meaning behind them was almost a threat. Why was that?

As Blake approached, he stepped right up to Madison's side, closer than he had all afternoon, and placed his hand squarely at the small of her back. The connection helped steady her skyrocketing emotions.

Given her knowledge of Blake's family, she had no doubts that Armand was an abuser. Whether he'd physically attacked the children, she wasn't sure. But the rise of the hair at the nape of her neck meant she sensed danger in his presence. Instinctively she braced her legs and straightened her back, as if she expected him to fly at her at any moment.

"I was checking with Sherry on Abigail. Remember her?"

It was hard to imagine this man as the father of a seven-year-old. It explained a lot about Blake. And made her heart ache for Abigail.

"Oh, yes. She's been most…helpful."

Madison felt like she was listening to a conversation where half the dialogue was missing. As if father and son were communicating telepathically. She could feel her hackles rise despite the innocuous words. What was happening here? It almost seemed as if they were silently challenging each other in a quest for dominance she didn't understand.

Alarms were going off in her head despite how calm everyone was. She knew without a doubt this man should not be left alone with the child.

She wasn't sure why, but that was why she had instincts. Something they taught the tenants at Maison de Jardin to never discount. Her heart raced. She wanted to be anywhere but under this man's gaze.

Blake didn't even look in her direction. He kept his eyes trained on his father, as if one look away might allow him to strike. Somehow Blake's watchfulness kept his father in check.

"She is indeed beautiful," his father said.

Suddenly Madison realized he was talking about her, but as if she weren't really here.

"I can understand your fascination with her. Just

remember your duty. And that bloodlines tell a much bigger story," the older man continued.

Then Armand turned abruptly away and walked back down the gallery to disappear out the doorway. Madison shivered. As her instincts continued to ping and prod, she knew one thing for certain: she hoped she never ran into that man again.

"Family is something, huh?" Blake said.

"A little strange." That was the nicest way Madison knew how to put it. But she couldn't just go around insulting his father.

"Oh, he's an odd bird all right."

But she couldn't shake the feeling that Blake had been trying to protect her somehow. Especially when he'd put his hand against the small of her back. It could've just been a polite gesture, but the firm pressure of the contact seemed to have a different meaning. He wasn't trying to direct her somewhere. Instead, it was almost as if he were trying to reassure himself that she were okay.

It echoed her own uneasy intuition around his father. A high adrenaline rush, as if she'd had a face-to-face with one of the abusers Maison's tenants sought shelter from.

"Abigail isn't safe with him," she said, murmuring almost as if to herself.

Blake jerked to a halt, turning to her and stepping close. "What did you say?"

She looked up into his eyes and wondered if he would accept the truth. A lot of people who had abusers in their lives didn't. But she didn't do what she did every day to make friends. "Blake, I know he's your father, but there's something not right about him."

"You're not telling me anything I didn't already know."

Relief slipped through her. "So you know Abigail isn't safe there. Especially without her mother."

She felt his hand go tense on her back, the fingers digging in on either side of her spine. Not in a painful way, but almost as if he were having a reaction he couldn't control. "I'm working on that."

As she stared up at him, and realized he was a thirtysomething playboy with no experience of children trying to do what he could to help his seven-year-old half sister, pride swelled within her. He didn't have to help. He wasn't Abigail's primary caregiver. She had parents. He could've just walked away and ignored it.

"I'm proud of you," she said.

The breath seemed to almost whoosh from his body. He swallowed hard, and his eyes darkened with emotion. The frown that appeared was sad in and of itself. How few people had said thank-you to him that it would upset him?

"I'm just trying to do my best," he said.

Just then they were interrupted by the waiter asking if they wanted a drink.

Madison kept her gaze on Blake, letting a small smile play at her lips. Her protector. She couldn't be in better hands, could she?

Eleven

Blake eased back into Madison's bed, pulling her close up against his chest when she shifted in her sleep. Dawn was just lightening the sky behind the window shades, but he'd been up for hours.

He'd done his best to do a thorough search of the house. Every step felt like a betrayal, after Madison had asked him to stay the night following their trip to the museum.

He felt like his entire conversation with Madison after his father left had been a big huge lie. He was worried about Abigail; he was trying to find a way to help her, but he couldn't come right out and tell Madison that after his father had been sending him a warning earlier.

Don't get too close to Madison. Because I will

take her out one way or another. All over what her mother did to me. Or maybe his father was just being like this to prove that Blake could not control him in any way. Madison would never be safe. So he'd done the very thing he didn't want to do, and searched her house during the night.

Of course, he hadn't found anything. No secret cubbies, no safes. Nothing that would indicate a multimillion-dollar diamond was hiding somewhere on the premises. He'd searched every room, looked into every crevice. All the while his heart pounding, afraid Madison would walk in and he'd have to explain himself.

He was already sick at the thought that someday soon she'd know why he was here. Or rather she would assume she knew the real reason, though it had changed for him. Because if the last couple of hours had taught him something, it was that he didn't want to hurt Madison. He loved her. And that knowledge had sent him straight back to her arms. He didn't know what else to do, just like he didn't know what else to do with Abigail.

He'd searched his mind for ways out of the situation. Hell, he'd even made a phone call in the middle of the night to Abigail's mother. To no avail, because the woman wasn't answering…just like she hadn't any time in the last week as he'd tried to contact her. She probably figured he would deride her for walking out on her child. But he just needed a solution.

One that didn't involve the Belarus diamond. Because time was running out. And Blake had no more leads.

So instead he buried his head in the sand. Or rather, in Madison's fragrant hair. He breathed her in, and even though his body stirred, he was content to lie there with her in his arms. Right now he had no way to delay the inevitable, but by God he'd find a way to leave her with something good.

By the time the sun had fully risen, and Madison began to stir in his arms, he knew exactly what he wanted to do with his day. He gave her a chance to wake up, and felt his whole body react when she blinked at him with sleepy eyes.

"Good morning," she murmured.

"Yes. Yes it is," he replied. And he planned to make the most of it. "Want me to make you some coffee?"

She nodded, and he slid from the bed. The glance over his shoulder as he walked to the door revealed a warm, sleepy woman stretching beneath a light sheet. He almost turned back, so that he could explore the soft curves and erect nipples beneath the thin covering. But he knew then he might never get back out. So Blake headed down the stairs with a chuckle.

He waited until she had a whole cup of the chicory brew in her before he broached the subject. "So what are the plans for today?" he asked.

"Oh, I don't have to be over at the charity today. I figured I'd putter around with the furniture."

"I have something a little different in mind."

She lifted a brow as she stared at him over the

rim of her newly refreshed cup. She took a sip before asking, "And what would that be?"

"What exactly do you want to do with that hospital bed?"

He knew the question was unexpected but didn't realize how much until she set her mug down on the counter with a hard *thunk*. Coffee sloshed over the side and unto the marble tile countertop. Her voice was huskier than usual when she asked, "Why do you ask?"

Blake knew he had to tread very carefully here. "I'm just wondering. Has it not been moved because you need it for some reason? Or because you need help with it?"

She turned her gaze over his shoulder to stare out the kitchen window. The way her lips tightened for a moment he thought she wouldn't answer, but then she said, "I certainly have no need for it anymore. I know what I want to do with it, but I just…"

Her voice trailed off in a way that made him sad for her. He knew she didn't want to admit that she wasn't capable of something, but they both knew the truth.

It was right there in her sad smile when she returned her gaze to meet his. "So I just cleaned it up as best I could, and I'll get around to it when I get around to it," she said with a shrug.

"Well, how about we get around to it today? What is it you want to do?"

She quickly let her lashes fall, covering the expression in her eyes. "I don't understand. Why would you want to do this today? Or at all? We could do anything. Take your sister to the park today. I could bake. Any number of things that wouldn't be—"

"Hard?"

She glanced back up at him, her teeth worrying her lower lip.

"I know it's hard, Madison. And I just want to help." He held up hands that had no callouses or signs of manual labor. "I can't paint. I could get up on the roof, but I wouldn't know what to do when I got there."

He was encouraged by her small smile.

"But this, I can help with. I just want to lighten the load a little bit."

To his surprise, she covered her face with her hands. Panic whittled its way through him as her shoulders shook. *No. Not crying.* That was the last thing he knew how to handle.

He stood awkwardly for a couple of seconds, unsure what to do as her sobs got louder. Was he totally out of line?

In the end, he just couldn't bear to see her standing there, sobbing and holding herself upright on her own. It seemed to be the epitome of Madison's life. That she handle every emotion, every circumstance *alone*. So he stepped forward and put his arms around her shoulders. He didn't know if it was the right move, he only knew he had to do it.

She leaned into him, her body seeking him out. Her hands dropped from her face and encircled his back. She buried her face against his chest, and the noise slowly subsided. With no other direction, Blake simply rested his hand on the back of her neck and held her. All too soon she pulled away, keeping her face averted as she walked over to grab a paper towel and blow her nose.

"Well, that was attractive," she said.

Blake appreciated her desire to brush off the whole emotional episode. But he felt he had to say, "I'm sorry."

"Don't be."

She turned back around to face him, revealing red-rimmed eyes. "No one has offered to help me with anything in this house. Even my friends. I don't know if they just don't feel like I would want them here, which I probably wouldn't. Or if they just don't want to be involved in such a morbid task. But I've done it all on my own."

She cleared her throat, then went on. "I can't tell you how much it means to me that you would offer, especially since you probably expected me to refuse."

"I had a feeling it might go that way."

"That's because you're a smart man."

Yeah…not. "I don't know about that, but I am persistent."

The laughter they shared broke the tension for a moment, but Blake wasn't about to let this go. "So you might as well tell me, what do you want to do with it?"

She swallowed. "I want to donate it. There's a nearby resident facility that assists elderly, end-of-life patients. I've wanted to donate it to them since my father died, but I have no way of moving it."

"I do believe I can handle that."

"*Then* maybe you can climb up on the roof for me," she teased.

"Only if there's an ambulance nearby."

It made Blake feel really good that he could help her smile through this task. He did his best clown impression while they packed everything up, and the two guys he called showed up with a truck to move it all. Madison only tensed up when they had to come into the house, but he was proud to say that she pushed through. She really wanted this to happen, and he felt sad that it had taken all this time for her to find a solution to this problem. That even though she had friends to help her, she didn't feel like she could call on them for that help.

The director of the facility knew her well, and was grateful beyond measure for her donation. They had a recently renovated room but hadn't managed to afford the furniture for it yet. Before he left, Blake slipped the director a check for a couple of thousand dollars to cover the rest of the furnishings. Now they could open the room for a new patient.

The fact that Madison thought to help someone during this time of grief humbled him beyond measure.

"You're my hero," she murmured against his lips as the truck pulled out of the driveway.

But Blake wasn't a hero. He was a wolf in sheep's clothing. She just didn't know it yet.

* * *

I love my husband so much. I would do anything for him, and even though I know his decision is stubborn and hurtful, I don't understand where he's coming from. He wants no part of my past. He wants to give no more power to a man who valued me only for my face and social graces. But I look at how much we need, how much we're hurting, and I know that selling that ring would make it all better. Why are men so stubborn?

Out of respect for him I've never mentioned this. Never so much as thought about it. Never wrote about my previous engagement in my journals and never talked about it with my daughter. I wish I could sometimes. Talk to her about the hard choices I made, how I knew my husband was the right one for me, how I chose love instead of money.

But I'd hate for her to know that my choice left our family ruined.

Madison reread the passage in confusion, burrowing down against the cushions of the chair in her bedroom. At first, it didn't even register what her mother was talking about. What previous engagement? But as she read through the passage once more, she realized the important part. Her mother had never spoken to her about this. Never spoken to anyone. The reason Madison couldn't find any hint of her previous life in these journals was because her mother chose not to talk about it out of respect for her husband.

Something had happened. Something that made

her mother have to choose, and while she knew that her father had been over the moon for his wife, that choice must have caused this traumatic thing that he'd never wanted to remember.

Selling her ring? What ring was she talking about? Madison couldn't remember her mother having any kind of ring except her wedding band set. It was the only thing of value that Madison had refused to sell. Despite how hard times became, she'd never sold them, even though it would've brought a modest amount. But it was her mother's wedding and tenth anniversary bands. Money could never replace that.

Had her mother kept a ring from a previous engagement? It had to be pretty substantial to be worth agonizing over the selling of it. Why had her mother not just given it back?

She scanned the entries right before that and found nothing relating to the ring. In the entry for the day before she mentioned it, she had lamented over the struggle to pay her husband's never-ending medical bills. Her father had recently been diagnosed with MS, she believed. At least the date looked close.

Then farther down in the entry for the same day, her mother wrote, *My husband says it will get better, but I fear the damage is permanent. He told me he would have his revenge, and he did. My husband's business will never be the same. My husband will never be the same. I hope the sacrifice was worth it for him, now and always. It would kill me to have my husband resent me in the end.*

So yeah, whatever happened was really bad. Madison felt a burning curiosity to know what it was. All this time her mother had written about daily life, the joys of motherhood, her love for her husband, and some of her deepest thoughts. But she'd never written or spoken of this matter and it was obviously a huge deal for her.

For them all.

Madison stood up and paced around her room. She wanted to talk about this, to tell someone. Her normal go-to would be her girlfriends. But Trinity's life is upside down enough already right now. She didn't need anyone butting in. And a glance at the clock told her that Tamika was still at work.

So who could she... How much would this kind of speculation annoy Blake?

She felt like they'd grown much closer, and his help the day before had touched her on a level that nothing else ever had. No one had ever helped her like that. Who else would see beyond a superficial need for food or companionship and go out of their way to help with something that she hadn't asked for? Frankly, she'd been floored.

Heck, he could have simply focused on the attraction between them and Madison would have been none the wiser.

But she'd done her best not to cry over him again, because he'd been obviously uncomfortable with her appreciation. She smiled. Her father had always been the same way. Tears made him panic. So she'd kept a stoic facade the entire time she'd known she was losing him.

Madison glanced back at the journal. But this was something fun, something mysterious. Something that intrigued her.

What could be the hurt in calling?

"Hey there," Blake said when he answered the phone.

The sound of that huskiness in his voice, so similar to the way he sounded when they were together, sent shivers down her spine. "Hey to you, too."

"What's up? You having a quiet day today?"

"Too quiet. I had to find ways to occupy myself, since you weren't coming over today."

"Well, if you're that desperate…"

She laughed at his teasing. "I got tired of sanding, so I've been reading my mother's journals, and you won't believe what I found out."

"Wait a minute. Your mother's *journals*?"

"Yes. She kept them for as long as I can remember. Although the oldest one I can find dates back to the first year of her and Dad's marriage."

The connection between them went oddly silent: no words and no breathing. Madison just figured it was a technical glitch and continued on.

"Anyway, today I was reading a passage from right after my dad got sick, and my mom talked about being engaged before."

Blake cleared his throat. "Engaged?"

"Yes! She said she was engaged and something terrible happened and my dad forbade her to ever talk about it."

"So that would mean…"

Again one of those weird silences, so she asked, "Are you there?"

"Hold on just a moment." She waited, until he finally said, "So do you think she left this guy for your dad? Do you know who he is?"

"She never says his name. She just says that she could sell the ring to help pay their medical bills, but my dad wanted nothing to do with it. Mysterious, right?"

Madison got excited just thinking about it. Who had the man been? What kind of ring was it? She started asking all these questions out loud to Blake, then realized after a few minutes that he hadn't responded. She paused.

"Blake?"

"Listen, Maddie, I need to go. Can I call you back in a little while?"

Disappointment had her dropping back into the chair in her bedroom. "Sure. Just whenever you're ready."

"I'll call you soon." *Click.*

Madison stared at her phone in consternation. That had been strange, and a tingling feeling of unease rippled through her once more. Even though Blake had said he wasn't keeping anything else to himself, she still felt like there were a lot of things about him that she had no clue about. Was this one of them? She didn't know what it could be... He could be conducting business. Seeing someone about his art. He never told her how that worked. But New

Orleans was filled with some very prestigious art galleries.

Was Abby okay? Madison bit her lip. It could have just been he was in a place that didn't have good reception. There was no sense worrying about this. And she knew she shouldn't, but that didn't stop her mind from running down the rabbit hole.

He would call her back. She just had to remember that.

Still, she was disappointed that he hadn't seemed too interested in what she found out about her mother. Maybe to other people it wasn't interesting, and Blake had never had strong familial connections. So it wasn't surprising.

But Madison had loved her mother to death, and been old enough to be really close to her before she passed away in a car accident. It was so unexpected, and Madison had grieved at night in private, but by day she had to continue on the work that she helped her mother with. She was still going to school, because her father had been functional enough that he could be left alone at that point. But the rest of her waking hours had been spent taking care of him or finding ways to financially support their family.

The ring sparked her curiosity. It seemed so tangible, this link to her mother's past. But she'd never seen one. Would her mother have hidden it? Gotten rid of it some other way? Sold it and just not told her dad where the money came from?

Madison's curiosity got the better of her, and she walked down the hall to her mother's room. Though her parents had shared a bed for a long time, the need for extra equipment and furniture for her dad, to accommodate his disability, had necessitated her mother moving her stuff into a separate room. In this big house there were plenty to choose from. They had gotten rid of a lot of things over the years after her mother passed away. That included most of her casual clothes, a few odds and ends other than those Madison had appropriated through the years, like her brush. All that had been left of her jewelry was costume pieces and her wedding set. Other than a few quilts her mother had made, the only things Madison had left were contained inside her mother's old chifforobe. She opened the doors, and was immediately met with the smell of lavender. It had been her mother's favorite scent. She'd often kept lavender sachets around the house.

Oddly, even after ten years, the scent still lingered on her clothes. Madison had chosen to keep some of her mother's more elaborate formal clothes. Dresses made from expensive materials. Her mother's favorite dressing gown—she would never call the beautiful piece of lace and satin a robe. A few pairs of heels that now fit Madison, but she'd never had occasion to wear them until recently. Madison searched through the clothes, though very few of them had pockets. Then she pressed against the back of the chifforobe, checking for any drawers or hidden compartments she might not have been aware of.

Finally she sat down in front of it and pulled out her mother's jewelry box. It was a gorgeous piece that her father had actually made, using beautiful cured maple and mother-of-pearl inlay. She could remember the Mother's Day he had given it to her. Madison was maybe ten or eleven? Her mother had been so happy. And genuinely shocked because he'd managed to keep the secret so well.

Her father had been a builder. He'd come from a modestly wealthy family himself, and he'd multiplied his fortune doing custom builds for the rich and famous of Louisiana. Madison had seen pictures of some of his houses, but he hadn't been able to keep it up and then he got sick. Losing his ability to work had eventually muted her father's love for life.

What had her mother meant about revenge and her husband's business? Madison had so many questions and so few answers.

But the beautiful box held nothing more than what Madison had seen over and over. A few costume pieces that her mother had let Madison try on through the years. But no true jewels. This used to surprise Madison, but now that she was an adult and knew just how much her father's illness had cost them, it didn't surprise her as much. She just assumed that whatever true jewels her mother's parents had given her had been sold through the years. Her mother had always been way more attached to people than things.

She set the jewelry box back into the bottom of the chifforobe and closed the doors.

As much as the mystery intrigued her, she would probably have to face the fact that her mother's secret had gone with her to her grave. Unless there was something later on in her journals. Madison thought she only had about six more months' worth to read.

She raced back down the hallway to pull the next journal from the box in her room. Money didn't matter. But her mother did. She might not find anything, but it was exciting to think the mystery could be solved.

Twelve

Blake watched nervously as the housekeeper settled the booster seat into the back of his car. Then she strapped Abigail in and turned to him.

"All ready," she said with a smile. "I know Abigail was looking forward to this. Thank you for taking her."

Blake just smiled and walked around to the passenger side. The smile masked a pool of unease in his gut. His father hadn't blinked when Blake had mentioned taking Abigail out with Madison. Instead he'd given simple consent.

Blake didn't trust that for one minute, but he couldn't divine any hidden motives and he didn't want to disappoint Abigail by going back on his word.

He hoped she would have a good time, because

he had absolutely no clue what he was doing. Which was why he'd broken down and asked Madison to help him. He felt guilty about terminating their call the day before, but he simply hadn't known what to say. He let her think that he had something else going on, because knowing that she'd been in the dark about her mother's previous engagement, and had no clue what kind of ring she was looking for, made him sick to his stomach.

He had no idea what to do and no idea what to say. Which was becoming a theme in his life right now. But he'd promised Abigail when he brought her home from the hospital that he would take her to do something fun. Why he had done that he wasn't sure, but he wasn't going to let her down. He refused to make her beg like her father did. He remembered what it was like to live the life that she had, where promises had been few and far between, and often broken.

He wasn't going to do that to her.

In the meantime, he hoped he could sidetrack any conversations about Madison's mother. His current plan was to just nod and say *uh-huh*. And offer absolutely no information whatsoever.

He could do that, right?

"Ready, kiddio?" he asked as he pulled out onto the highway.

He caught Abigail's nod in the rearview mirror, her grin infectious, her excitement palpable in the way she swung her little legs.

They stopped by to pick up Madison on their way

to City Park. "Are you excited, Abigail?" she asked as she buckled herself in.

Abigail nodded enthusiastically.

"I think you'll have fun. There's lots of stuff to do at City Park."

"But only until lunch," Blake cautioned. If it was one complaint he'd heard about kids, it was that they expected to do something forever. He didn't think he was up to a marathon on his first outing with her. Nor was she after her recent hospital stay...especially in the summer heat.

Madison grinned at him, sharing a little secret. "Definitely lunch."

Blake had to admit that City Park was an excellent choice. Abigail especially liked Storyland Castle and the Puff the Magic Dragon slide. Madison chased the little girl around the play area, so that her giggles filled the air.

Then they headed back to see the frogs and birds and turtles in the conservatory before strolling under the live oaks with their hanging moss. Having met her mother once after she had taken Abigail to a zoo, Blake had known this would be a big hit. Abigail enjoyed watching the animals for a long time, and getting to take pictures of them with Blake's phone. The only heartbreaking moment was when she asked, "Can I send these pictures to my mommy?"

Madison turned away. Blake wished he had the opportunity to do the same. "Absolutely, kiddio."

They didn't stop for lunch until Blake had taken them on a bike ride and paddled Abigail around the lake in a kayak. The whole time, Blake thought he must be incredibly lucky. Abigail was laid-back and easygoing, and he didn't have a single issue with her. He did suspect that she was on her best behavior. He'd had more than enough of those moments when he was a kid.

By the time they headed to lunch, he was feeling much more comfortable. Maybe he didn't know how to relate to Abigail as a child. But he related to her the only way he knew how. He talked to her the same way he would to anyone else. He didn't baby-talk her or cater to her every whim. He simply urged her to do things that looked fun, and when it was time to move on to something else he was firm but polite. It seemed to work well with this particular child.

They had lunch at a little kid-friendly café, where Abigail got a grilled cheese and chips, eyeing the cakes for later.

Madison talked about wanting to try one of the recipes, and Abigail got all excited.

"Can I help? Sometimes Miss Sherry lets me help her stir things. She says I do a good job."

Madison glanced his way before she said anything and he gave a quick nod. He appreciated her checking in with him before offering anything, but how could he say no to such a sweet little face?

Abigail was occupied talking about the different type of cakes she would like to make for quite a while before she started to run out of steam. Her eyelids got heavy, and she leaned against Madison despite still having part of her sandwich left.

Blake sat in silence for quite a while, just enjoying the shade and the slight breeze in the courtyard.

Madison plucked a thread from the little girl's shirt as she finally said, "So I went through all of my mom's stuff yesterday."

Blake should've known it was coming, but still it was a stock. Even in his surprise he was able to murmur, "Yes?"

"I didn't find any kind of ring. Of course, I got rid of most of her stuff ten years ago. But you never know when there might be a hidden drawer, or a locked box somewhere."

Blake returned her smile, even though inside he felt slightly ill. It was only a few days ago that he himself had spent the night going through her entire house looking for just such a thing.

"I just wish I knew more about what happened. My mom's life at that time is such a blank for me. I think it would just be interesting to know."

And if she knew, she would be entitled to what she could find. But Blake had searched all over that house and found nothing. What the hell had happened to the Belarus diamond?

"For all I know, my mom could've sold an old engagement ring a long time ago. The only rings I could find were her wedding band set."

"So you kept them?"

Madison looked slightly surprised. "Of course. Granted, she could've sold them for a little bit of money. The diamond inside *was* worth something. But my mother was always more interested in people than things. She wouldn't have wanted to get rid of something my father gave her."

Abigail stirred slightly against her and Blake glanced down to see her lift sleepy eyelids. "Is she talking about Father's ring?"

Only years of having to hide himself from his father and present himself as someone he wasn't in society kept Blake's expression neutral. But inside, he was cursing up a storm.

Madison looked down at the little girl in question, but Blake quickly intervened. "No, sweetie. You just rest."

Who would've guessed that a seven-year-old listening from the top of the stairs could have absorbed so much? She was too smart for him to completely brush it off. Otherwise she would start asking more questions, he just knew it. "That was about something else, sweetheart."

Luckily, Madison kept right on, not really paying Abigail's question any mind. "I know it's a silly mystery, but I'm just curious."

Of course, she had no idea of the significance of what Abigail had asked. And her curiosity was something Blake couldn't relate to. After all, neither of his parents had ever been real people to him. Just evil dictators who should be avoided at all cost.

He'd thought that was all behind him, but look at him now.

Any minute, that very dictatorship was going to crush the most precious thing Blake had ever found in his life, if he didn't find a way to stop it.

Tonight he'd try to reach Abigail's mother one more time—and hope his luck held out for an alternative ending.

Madison took Abigail's hand in hers and led her away from the table with a smile at Blake. He'd really done well and handled way more things than she'd thought he would, but taking a little girl to the little girls' room might be asking a bit much.

The restrooms were in the far back of the little café. They paraded past the sandwich counter and the goody counter on their way. "I think I might have to ask Blake for one of those big Rice Krispies treats," Madison said. "Doesn't that look good?"

Abigail paused to look at the huge confection. "He won't want me to have that. My father says sweets rot your teeth."

Not an uncommon belief among older people. "Well, maybe if you only eat sweets and never brush your teeth. But you take good care of your teeth, right?"

"Sure do. See?" Abigail gave her an overly wide smile.

Madison dutifully inspected her teeth and pronounced them perfect. "I think we're safe to ask Blake anyway."

Abigail looked up at her, then asked, "Do you think my brother likes me?"

Madison glanced down with a frown. "Of course he does. Why wouldn't he?" She ruffled one pigtail. "After all, look how cute you are."

Abigail giggled but quickly sobered. "My father said that if I don't behave myself, Blake will leave and never come back. Just like my mommy."

Just the thought of anyone telling that to a small child took Madison's breath away. *Bastard.*

She led the little girl through the door to the restroom, and let it slide closed behind them. She knelt down next to Abigail. "Honey, I don't know what your father told you. But Blake is not going to leave if you misbehave. All children misbehave at some time or another. It's just a moment for them to have a learning experience."

Abigail's doe-brown eyes widened. "Really?"

"Really. It's just part of growing up. You'll get in trouble, but that doesn't mean that the people in your life don't still love you."

"Like you love Blake?"

No way was she going to admit that out loud to a child who might repeat it. "Blake is a very special man. And I think you'll find, if you give him a chance, that he will love you lots."

Abigail smiled, seeming satisfied, then went on to do her business. Madison knew her words were true. Blake might not have felt himself capable of it, but this last week had proved he had more than enough love to give. He'd just never known how to access it before.

Abigail took her time washing her hands, as she had plenty more questions for Madison. It seemed that her little nap had revived her energies quite well.

Some were as innocuous as, "Did you like the

tree frogs, too?" and "Can you bring me to the park again?" Then the uber serious, "Are you going to marry Blake?"

"Give it time, kid. Your brother and I haven't known each other that long."

Besides, the time they had been together had been quite tumultuous. Madison knew how she felt about him, but she was used to loss. Used to people leaving. And Blake had made no mention of emotions, though his actions spoke pretty loud. Still, she wasn't in any hurry to tell him her own feelings.

Abigail continued to chatter, which stopped the sweat from breaking out on Madison's brow. Hopefully she'd dodged a bullet there. She seemed to be handling the girl talk situation pretty well.

An unusually high number of the children who came through Maison de Jardin were boys. That was who Madison had the most experience with. She knew nothing about fixing hair or playing with dolls. A couple of teenage girls had come with their mothers to the shelter, but they weren't nearly as easy to befriend as the smaller kids.

"What is your mother's name?" Abigail asked.

Madison was a bit taken aback, and paused for a moment before answering. "It was Jacqueline."

"Was?"

Madison wasn't quite sure how much experience Abigail had with death, but she didn't believe in lying. "My mother died when I was younger."

"Were you a little girl like me?" Abigail asked,

standing at the sink while the water ran over her hands.

Madison wasn't sure how much she should tell a child this age. "She was in a car accident when I was sixteen."

"So she didn't leave you like my mommy?"

"No," Madison couldn't believe how horrible that must be for Abigail. She waited a moment before saying anything else to see what the little girl was thinking.

"My mommy left because I was too much trouble."

Damn. "Oh, Abigail, that's not true."

"Oh, it was. My mommy told me so a lot of times. I tried to be good, but I guess I wasn't good enough."

Pure rage swept over Maddie. How dare someone tell a child that. She was sure Abigail had been on her best behavior during this trip, but she still couldn't imagine a child being so bad that you would outright tell them you were going to leave because of them. She was sure many parents thought it during the course of a stressful day, but they would never say it out loud, because they honestly loved their children.

"I'm really sorry, Abigail."

"Father said Mommy is fragile." She tilted her head so she could look at Madison in the mirror. "What does fragile mean?"

Selfish was what Madison wanted to say, but instead she said, "It just means that someone might crack easily, like a glass."

"I knocked a glass off the table once and it shattered on the floor."

"Yes, that is fragile."

"Do you think I broke my mommy?"

Man, talking to kids was a minefield. "Absolutely not. That is not what I meant at all." She knelt down beside Abigail. "Your mommy being fragile has nothing to do with you. It has everything to do with your mommy. And I hope that she can find something while she's gone to make her stronger."

"You can become stronger?"

"Of course. You just have to exercise and eat your veggies." Madison pumped her arm to make a muscle, which caused Abigail to giggle.

Abigail finally finished with her handwashing, or what Madison would consider playing in the water, and got herself a couple of paper towels. As she dried off, she said, "I like you, but I do wish your ring had been Father's ring."

"How come?" Madison asked.

"It's what Blake needs. Father told him to get it."

"I don't think I understand," Madison said with a frown.

"I was listening on the stairs. Father didn't know, but I think Blake did. He and Father were arguing. Blake was mad because Father wouldn't take care of me."

She brushed her hands down over her little dress in an imitation of an adult. "Father said Blake could take me home with him, if he got the ring back. Otherwise Father would ignore me, or maybe send me away."

Madison could not wrap her mind around the horror of what she was hearing. Surely Abigail had to be mistaken.

"Your father told him to get the ring, from me?"

"I don't know." Abby scrunched her brows together. "That's what I thought he said. But he wasn't sure where it was."

"Maybe he was talking about someone else." *Please let him be talking about someone else.*

"Maybe so." Abigail looked up at Madison. "But I really want to go live with Blake. I can be really good and he won't want to send me away."

Since she wasn't sure what had been promised, Madison heard this hope with a touch of alarm. "Abigail, you realize Blake hasn't ever had children."

"I know." She shook her head vigorously. "But I can teach him how to have a little girl. I won't misbehave…much. Do you think he will help me learn?"

Madison blinked, desperate to not show tears in front of this girl who had been through so much in such a short amount of time. "I think you and Blake could teach each other a lot."

She gave Abigail a quick hug, then took her hand to lead her back to the table. Along the way, she had to wonder about the ring the little girl had mentioned. There was no way that could have anything to do with her.

But as she thought about those first days together, and her confusion over why Blake would want to be with her at all, the question wouldn't leave her. What ring had he and Armand been talking about?

Thirteen

"Quit blowing up my phone!"

For a moment Blake just looked at his cell phone, shocked. He'd called Abigail's mother, Marisa, over a dozen times, to no avail. Apparently she'd finally gotten tired enough of the noise to answer.

"Well, since I've run out of other options, I didn't know who else to call."

"Why are you calling me at all?"

Um, your child might need you?

That didn't seem to occur to her, as she went on, "The last thing I need to hear is how I have to come home. I am not coming home to that psychopath, and I can't find a new husband with a kid in tow."

Blake kept his mouth closed for just a moment. He wanted to lay into her about parental responsibility and how scared Abigail was and that she was really behaving like a child herself, but he couldn't. He had to help Abigail. He couldn't find the diamond. *Marisa* had to help him.

"Look, I'm just trying to figure out what's the best course of action. You left a very sick child in the hands of a man who couldn't care less about her."

"He doesn't need to care about her. That's what nannies are for."

Wow. How cavalier could she get? "He got rid of the nanny."

"Why?"

"You didn't see that coming? He let the nanny go. He said there was no reason to pay someone to watch out for her, because he doesn't believe that Abigail is really sick."

"Well, when he gets tired of dealing with her as much as I did, he'll get someone else. Doctor appointment after doctor appointment..."

"He's not going to take her to a doctor. He doesn't believe there's anything wrong. Your daughter is being neglected."

"She'll be fine," Marisa insisted. "He'll eventually hire a new nanny, and he'll take care of her. He's in a much better place to take care of her than I am. I'm broke."

"You just emptied your bank account. How can you be broke?"

Blake knew that wasn't the right question to ask. He just needed some answers.

"Look, I don't care. I don't care why you left. I

don't care that you're not coming back." Although he did care for Abigail, he just didn't want to get into that with Marisa now. "I just need to find out anything you can tell me so that I can take over Abigail's care."

"Don't bother. He's got more money than God. She's going to be much better off in his hands than her other options."

Blake had firsthand experience that said otherwise. The volcano of the emotions inside him erupted. "Really? An old man with a narcissistic personality disorder about to go broke is the best parent for a sick seven-year-old child?"

"What do you mean, *broke*?"

"Broke. No money. So if you think you're going to get a very nice settlement in the divorce, you can forget it."

Marisa was quiet for so long, Blake thought she might be reconsidering her actions. But no...

"I'm not supposed to get anything based on the prenup. Why do you think I'm out here trying to find somebody new? But Abigail is supposed to be taken care of."

There was no getting through to this woman. Blake insisted, "Well, there's nothing to take care of her with. He's basically housing her and that's it. She's already had one episode that landed her in the hospital."

"Well, if that's how it's going to be, she'd be better off with her real dad."

Blake held very, very still. It took him a minute to

absorb what she had just said. "Are you telling me…
that Abigail is not his?"

"Well, she should be. I mean, we were married."

So? "Is she biologically his daughter?"

"Well, no."

Blake couldn't believe it. Of all the things he'd
thought she might tell him, this was not one of them.
He sat for a moment in stunned disbelief. He wasn't
sure exactly how this would fix everything, but he
knew it would. And he would make sure that it did.

"Why didn't you tell him?" he finally asked.

"I needed him to keep her. Besides, you know how
he is. The minute he found out that I slept with somebody else, we'd both be out the door. He wouldn't put
up for that kind of humiliation. And I'm too good to
be a chauffeur's wife."

What should I do? What should I do? Blake
racked his brain for an answer.

"Look, Marisa. Will you fill out paperwork that
lets me take care of her?"

"Well, she's not gonna be in a good place with
me. I just can't deal with that stuff. As a matter of
fact, the first time I get the chance I'm closing this
baby factory."

Nice. "But Abigail? Will you let me take care of
her if I can find a way to make it happen? And before
you ask, there's nothing in it for you. I'm all about
Abigail right now."

"I guessed. Better double down over here if I'm
gonna find a new man before Armand cuts me off.
Take her."

Blake wanted to rail at the harshness of the conversation he just had as she clicked to disconnect. But he couldn't. He couldn't get lost over what Abigail did or did not have. He had to look to the future. He had to figure out how to use this new information to get what he needed. Without the diamond, this was his only option.

If he lost Maddie in the process, so be it. But at least she wouldn't have to know that he got involved with her under false pretenses. He didn't want to hurt her like that, even though walking away from her would leave him out in the cold for the rest of his life. He'd never found anyone like her before, and he doubted he ever would again. But he couldn't worry about that right now, or he'd be paralyzed with indecision.

Instead he needed to figure out what he had to do to take over parental rights. He had a feeling his father wouldn't want to be humiliated by having Abigail's true paternity made public. Not to mention his lack of funds for a lawyer to fight for custody once her mother handed her rights over to Blake.

He just had to hope in the end Abigail would have him. He wasn't that much of a catch as a father, but he'd at least try. Which was more than his own father had done.

Madison strode back and forth across her bedroom, the sound of the squeaking floorboards more than a little satisfying. She wasn't sure why; she wasn't accomplishing anything. And she wished she could. She wished that she could stomp her way right over to Blake's apartment and demand the truth. Even if her only source was a seven-year-old child.

She just wanted to know: Was Abigail right? Had Blake and Armand been talking about her? Had Blake honestly met and dated her to try to get something out of her? And if they wanted something from her mother, why had they waited all these years? She wanted answers, not more questions.

But she was also afraid to get those answers.

Madison paced furiously, anxiety sending her energy into hyperdrive.

Why had her mother told her none of this? She may have felt she owed her husband something, but what about her daughter? What about the life she left her to? And even though she knew her mom hadn't left willingly, she had chosen to delay the inevitable until it was too late, leaving Madison with an adult-size responsibility and very few resources.

How could she find the answers? She hadn't missed a journal. Out of desperation, she walked over to the box and glanced over the half dozen, leather-bound journals. As she ran her hand over the spines, she suddenly remembered the pieces of paper that had been stuck in her mother's journal the other day.

Shifting the books to the side, she found the papers in the bottom of the box where she'd dropped them before leaving last week. Excitement caused her to breathe hard as she unfolded them. There was more of her mother's handwriting on the pages, but this was different than the journal entries. This was addressed directly to her.

Dearest Madison,
I'm hoping you never have to read this. I'm
hoping that the lawyer never has to give you
this in the event of my death.

What lawyer? Had her mother planned to take this to the lawyer to go with her will, and never made it?

But I need to tell you a story. One that I
should tell you in person, but I would do any-
thing to not hurt your father. If I'm gone, you
need to know this.
When I was young, before I knew my own
mind, I went along with what my parents told
me to do. That was the acceptable thing in that
time, for girls of my class. That you obey your
parents, learn how to talk and act, not be too
smart, or too sassy. Marry well and be an asset
to your spouse.
And I tried. I tried to make my parents
happy. They were elderly, as I was a late-in-
life baby, one that they never really expected
to have. They always seemed frail in my mind
and they didn't live very long past my mar-
riage to your father. Anyway, when I was fi-
nally of marriageable age, I was pursued by a
man named Armand Boudreaux. He was well
known in our social circles, and his family was

very wealthy. He was slightly older than me, and well on his way to making his own fortune.

Armand was mostly charming, but I quickly learned that he hid an often subtle cruelty. He wasn't in love with me but seemed to want to acquire me because I exceeded his qualifications for a wife. And I think, on some level, that he thought I would counterbalance what he knew he was lacking in himself: compassion and a genuine interest in other people. Which would help cement his social status.

At the same time, my parents were building a house, and I met a new young man. He was a very well-known architect and builder, rising quickly in fame and wealth. Handsome and articulate. I'll admit, I became obsessed. Your father was smart and charming, and he understood me in a way that neither my parents nor Armand ever had. He brought out the best in me, and didn't ridicule me for wanting to do things that didn't seem to fit with my social status. He taught me to refinish furniture, build things. He encouraged me to paint and take pictures—lots of things that my parents didn't understand.

It didn't take long before I was completely in love and stuck in a place I didn't know how to get out of. Though my parents loved me, they were quite old-fashioned. I'd made a promise to Armand, and they expected me to fulfill it.

There was also the social pressure of know-

ing that their peers would be there to judge the decision that their daughter made, and thus it would reflect on them. Every generation has peer pressure; it just comes in different forms. But in the end I couldn't walk away from your father, so we eloped. On the eve of my wedding to Armand, I ran away with your father and left my parents and Armand letters telling them that I was sorry, but I could not go through with the wedding.

I had every intention of returning the ring. The engagement ring that Armand gave me was more than special. The diamond was a rare oval blue diamond called the Belarus diamond. Quite famous, and quite expensive. But upon my return, I found that Armand had embarked on his own form of revenge. I'd known he would be upset, and I suspected he would lash out. But I never anticipated what actually happened.

Armand went out of his way to ruin your father's business. The one time I approached him, he called me some quite inappropriate names, and honestly I was afraid of him, so I never approached him again. As time went on it became clear that your father might have to relocate to save his business, so I decided to hold onto the diamond as insurance for my family to hopefully save us from the ruination that I brought upon them.

Only we never had the chance to leave. Your

father became ill and I thought the diamond would be the only thing to save us. But your father refused to allow me to sell it. He wanted no part of Armand and refused to listen to me.

I could not go against his wishes, but I kept the diamond and hid it, so that you, my daughter, would have it should you need it. It is yours to do with as you wish. After all, it was a gift, and it would be my wish that you should never be so destitute that you feel like you cannot sustain yourself or your loved ones. I know that feeling well. And never ever want that for you.

I'm sorry that I couldn't make things easier. I love you and your father more than I can ever tell you. Be well, my child.

Love, Jacqueline

Madison flipped to the next page to find directions on where the diamond had been hidden. She stared for a moment, uncomprehending, then blinked. Her mother had put the diamond in a place no one would ever have looked for it. *Genius.*

Without hesitation, she grabbed her shoes and ran out the door. Her jog across the back trail to Maison de Jardin was familiar and yet felt longer than she could have imagined. Her heart pumped from the run and in anticipation of what she might find. Would the diamond still be there?

The house was quiet during the day, with everyone gone to various jobs or school. Madison made her way to the conservatory without running into anyone who might still be home, and quickly found the statue that her mother had indicated.

Madison stared at it. She had always seen the statue as a representation of this place's purpose. It was a little girl and her mother with their hands clasped and arms raised in dance. The purpose of this home had always been to bring happiness and joy to women and children who had been mistreated. To help them get back on their feet and find their dance again.

Finally Madison moved around to the back of the statue and started to dig at the mound of dirt around the base.

It took a couple of inches before she found the little compartment. Her smile felt like it lit up her whole body. Who knew there'd been a secret compartment all her life in the base of this statue?

Unfortunately she couldn't get it open, and had to go get a screwdriver to pry the edges apart. Finally it popped open, and Madison was able to work the little drawer out. Inside was a metal box, which she opened to find multiple layers of protective wrapping.

But as she pulled away layer after layer, Madison could not believe her eyes.

The fact that the diamond had an actual name should have been her first clue that it was something extraordinary. But that had kind of flown under Madison's radar. The oval-shaped jewel was a brilliant blue color, so brilliant it made her gasp. It shone against her dirt-stained fingers. The size would have made it very uncomfortable to wear, in her opinion, but she could see why someone like Armand would give it to his future wife. By doing so, he could prove he was the best husband in the world.

Only he didn't realize money wasn't everything.

Suddenly she understood what her mother meant. Selling this particular ring, this particular diamond, would have taken care of them for life, no matter how many medical bills her father had. Madison wouldn't have a house falling down around her ears. She wouldn't have had creditors banging on her front gate.

She wouldn't have had to spend her high school years working after school, or taking on other jobs while caring for her father.

Suddenly her elation faded. She could also now understand why someone might falsely portray himself, pretending to like or love her in order to get his hands on this.

Was Blake really capable of that? Was every moment they'd been together a lie? Madison had to know.

I know what you did. Meet me at ASTRA.

Blake clenched his fingers around his phone as he remembered the text he'd received from Madison last night. So he'd had an entire night to agonize over what had happened, wondering and worrying until he'd been sick to his stomach. She refused to answer her phone, which made him suspect she had turned it off after telling him when and where to be.

That wasn't like Madison at all, so he knew this was bad. Very bad. Which meant she'd found out something about the ring…and its connection to his family.

Had it been Abigail's innocent remarks over lunch that had alerted her? Had she found something in her mother's journals that made the connection with his family? Had she put two and two together and come up with the original plan his father had put into place?

Blake knew he couldn't change what had happened before, but if she'd found out part of the truth, would she listen to him when he told her what he was trying to do *now*? His true role in this entire mess? What he hoped worked—for both her sake and Abigail's?

He stepped into the rotunda to find her staring at a painting across from him, her arms wrapped tightly around herself. If he needed any evidence of her defensiveness, that would've been it. It wasn't a position he'd ever wanted to see her in again. It reminded him that too much had been thrown Madison's way.

She deserved the best—much more than life had dished out to her.

He approached cautiously, giving her a chance to see him out of the corner of her eye before he reached her.

"Madison, what's going on?" he asked.

He expected tears or a defeated attitude. Instead

she seemed to almost closed down. Only her eyes seemed sad. "I know what happened. Abby told me."

"Abby told you what?"

Blake wished they weren't in the rotunda. All of a sudden he desperately needed something to lean on, to support his shaky legs, but even touching the walls in here would set off an alarm.

"When we went to the restroom, Abigail told me more about the ring. She recounted the conversation between you and your dad." She waved her hand in the air as if to erase her words. "In a roundabout kind of way. She didn't really know that it was about me. But it made me curious, so I went looking."

She reached into her purse and pulled out a box. A very expensive jewelry box. Blake held his breath as she opened it. Inside was the ring.

Of all the things Blake had expected to see today, that was not one of them. He stared for a moment, almost bemused. It was incredible, just like all the reports had said.

But he quickly moved his gaze back up to hers. There was no point in pretending anymore. "How did you find it?"

Madison sucked air into her lungs, blinking away tears at his implied admission. "My mother left me a letter. One that she never got a chance to give to the lawyer. I found it in one of her journals. She explained all about Armand. And quite frankly, after hearing that, I'm not surprised that she kept the ring."

"She was well within her rights to keep the ring," Blake insisted. "My father is...not an easy man."

"If he had just left them alone, she would've given it back."

"But he feels like he should have his cake and eat it, too. Which means being a major league asshole, and still getting his way."

Madison looked away, and he could see her bracing herself. She took a deep breath and straightened her back. "Why?" She glanced back at Blake and he could see the crack in the calm facade. The grief he'd never wanted her to experience again. She'd had enough loss. "Why would you do this? Why would you take it this far?"

He wished he could give an answer that left him looking squeaky clean. But he didn't have one of those tucked into his back pocket. "Maddie... Madison," he stumbled over the nickname after remembering her assertion that it should only be used by those who'd earned the privilege. "I just want you to understand that I never meant to hurt you."

"And you think finding out that you met me and dated me under false pretenses wouldn't hurt?" She stared at him for a moment. "Unless you never intended for me to find out?"

"There's really no way for me to defend myself against that," he said, utter defeat a physical weight on his chest. Because if he'd had his way, she would never have found out about any of this. He searched for a way to tell her the story that would not make him look like an insensitive jerk, but there really wasn't one.

"There's no point in me lying anymore," he conceded with a grimace. "I went into this knowing that I had to hide my motives from you. I thought it would be a date, maybe two, and then I'd be out of your life. It would all be over. No harm done, and no lasting repercussions for anyone but Abigail, who would have a better life. But that's not how it played out." He stared at her, aching to take away the hurt that bowed the lines of her body. "I knew with every move, every choice, that this wasn't right. But I simply could not stay away."

"And how I felt didn't play into it?"

"It did. But by that time I was in too deep and desperately searching for a way not to hurt you."

He didn't want to offer excuses, but she deserved more of an explanation. "It was obvious that you did not have the ring yourself and didn't know anything about it. I kept searching to keep my father at bay while I desperately tried to find some way to help Abigail."

"So what she said was true? Her father is going to...what? Trade his child for this?" She lifted the box once more.

He knew it was unbelievable. But having Armand as a father convinced Blake his father spoke the truth. "I told you he was a bastard. That's exactly what's happening. He wanted me to find the ring and get it back for him, and in exchange I will get full parental rights to Abigail."

She stepped closer as a couple of women walked into the rotunda and began discussing the paintings. "Why would a parent do that?"

"Madison, I've spent a lot of time with my father. And I've finally figured out that if you try to understand his motives, you're just going to spend a lot of time banging your head against a wall." He sighed. "No one can understand that, because we're not like him. He is his own selfish, narcissistic self. That's not going to change and the only option is to stop him at whatever cost. That's what I've been trying to do. Why I tried to keep him away from you before." But Blake feared he was fighting a losing battle. "Right now, I have to keep Abigail safe. Regardless of what I want, and regardless of the fact that I love you."

Madison's whole body jerked. Her eyes squeezed shut for a moment. "Please don't say things you can't mean."

Well, he hadn't meant to say it but... "I did mean it, Maddie, and I will always mean it. But I fully accept why that would mean nothing to you."

He reached out to grasp her arms in an effort to get her to look at him. The touch was bittersweet, as he knew it would be his last. "I'm more sorry than I can tell you. I didn't intend to get involved, I didn't intend to fall in love, and I had no idea what an incredible person you really are. But I have to save Abigail. I've lived that childhood, and I will not allow her to live it, too."

Madison nodded, though whether his words made sense to her, he wasn't sure. Then she explained. "I love you, too. But that's not why I am doing this. I'm doing it for Abigail, too, because no child deserves to live neglected and unloved. I've fought against that my entire life, and it's more important to me than anything."

She raised her hand between them. "That's why I want you to take this."

Blake blinked. He glanced down at the box, then back at her face. "I...don't...understand..."

"I want you to have this, so that Abigail will be taken care of."

Blake was already shaking his head. "Maddie, this was your mother's. It should take care of you for the rest of your life. Especially after you've given your life to take care of others."

She stared down at the box for a moment. "Taking care of others is not something that requires a reward. I did it out of love," she said, then pressed her lips together hard. As her eyelids drifted down, a single tear rolled over her cheek. "Just take it."

"I believe that belongs to me."

Heated fear washed over him as Blake turned to see his father walking across the rotunda, which was otherwise empty now.

"Thank you for finding it for me, Madison," Armand said. "That seems to be more than my son was capable of."

Madison began to extend her arm, and Blake quickly stepped in front of her to face his father. "Absolutely not. You are not taking this from her."

"But I thought you said Abby could live with you if I give this back?" Madison said.

"No, he said I can have her parental rights, if I *stole* this from you."

"I believe I have a claim," Armand insisted.

"It was a gift to Madison's mother. It doesn't belong to you anymore. If it did, your lawyer would have been able to get it back for you long ago."

Armand's practiced smile grew wider. "But I'm the one who would benefit most. Unless you count Abigail."

Madison gasped.

"I will fix this, Madison," Blake insisted.

His father studied him for a moment. For once, Blake felt no urge to shift in his shoes. This wasn't about meeting his father's expectations. This was about two different scales, and the fact that Blake was looking out for more than just himself.

"I never thought you would defend a woman," his father said.

Blake was a little taken aback. Why wouldn't he defend another person? He just didn't know a lot of people who needed defending. But then again, his father's measurements were based on his own warped standards, and Armand had never gone out of his way to defend anyone but himself.

"Some people grow up, Armand, and learn to deal with the consequences of their actions. That's what's happening here. As a consequence of my actions, I'm going to lose Madison. She's fully justified in walking away from me. And I'll let her because I betrayed her. You, on the other hand, have just lost your free ride."

"I have no idea what you're talking about."

"Madison doesn't need to give you that diamond.

It will have no effect on Abigail. Because you have no claim to her."

"That doesn't even make sense. I'm her father."

"You *thought* you were her father, biologically at least. But you're not. She's not even yours. I can get a DNA test to prove this and have her taken away. Or you can sign over your rights."

He should've been satisfied that his father looked stunned, but it didn't make him feel good to take the old man down. It only felt good to know that Abigail would be safe. "If you sign over your rights, I'll pay you enough to get back on your feet, and you can dissolve your marriage with no contest." He straightened, hoping his height advantage would convince his father he wasn't to be messed with.

"If you refuse, I'll make sure everyone in your social circle knows that your wife cheated on you with the chauffeur. That you've raised a child who wasn't yours all these years, and blackmailed your son into stealing from another woman for your benefit."

Behind him Madison gasped, but Blake couldn't stop now. "I have nothing to lose," he said. And that was true. Without Madison, he would never be truly happy again. "You do. So are you going to take the easy way out, or lose your reputation along with your fortune?"

Only someone who'd lived with Armand all these years would know just how much his reputation meant to him. Not to mention the fact that it was his only way of getting his business back on its feet.

His connections within Louisiana society, and the country as a whole, were his only source of revenue.

"Do you really expect me to give up a fortune to the daughter of my enemy?" he asked, his genteel facade slipping even further with his sneer.

"He wasn't your enemy," Madison said from behind him. "He was just a man who actually loved my mother. Not one who wanted her to enhance his reputation and social status."

"And that, Father, is the problem with your life in a nutshell. You just want to keep up appearances. Not to mention the fact, if you walk away now, Madison won't have to take out a restraining order against you."

For a moment, Blake thought his father might burst an artery. His entire face flushed and he practically shook with anger.

"So what will it be, Father?" Blake prodded. "Should I contact your lawyer?"

Armand visibly pulled himself together. "Of course," he said in a clipped, controlled tone. No yelling would be allowed in public today, Blake guessed. Then Armand turned on his heel and walked away, ever displaying the calm veneer of a wealthy gentleman, hiding the snake lurking beneath.

"How much is that going to cost you?" Madison whispered.

"It doesn't matter. As long as I can support Abigail, we'll be good." He turned back to face her. "I'm so sorry, Madison. You didn't deserve that. Any of it."

Reaching out, he wrapped her fingers around the

jewelry box. "Take this to Trinity, and ask her to find you someone reputable to sell it." He swallowed hard. "I need to know that you're taken care of in the way you deserve."

Madison stared down at the box for several moments before she glanced back up with tears in her eyes. "What makes you think I deserve the money from this?"

"Life. You've had a raw deal, Madison. You deserve far more than life has given you."

"And yours wasn't just as bad? At least my parents loved me. I didn't have to live under that guy's thumb my entire life. That was a close call, I'd say."

Blake cocked his head to the side. Was she actually joking? "Um, yes. I'd agree."

"Blake." She drew in a deep, hard breath. "I believe I've come to a decision."

This is it. Here comes the goodbye.

She held up the jewelry box, staring at it. "I believe that I'm going to need help taking care of this incredible piece."

"Yes?"

"I think you and Abigail would be perfect for the job."

What? "I don't understand."

"Well, I can't ask just anyone. I need someone who really knows me, knows what I believe in. It has to be someone I can trust."

"That would not be me." *It couldn't be me.*

"Are you sure?"

Blake swore as he broke out in a cold sweat. "What are you saying?"

"Yes, you lied to me. You met me under false pretenses and kept secrets from me."

"Yes, I did, Madison. I'm sorry."

"And I know you really are. Do you know how I know that?"

Blake shook his head, not trusting his voice.

"Because you just volunteered to give up a fortune to take care of a child who isn't even yours."

Her dark green gaze made his head swim. Was she really saying this?

"I know better than to think that your father will let you off cheap. And I know better than to think that raising a young girl alone doesn't scare the pants off you." She stepped in closer, bringing her heat to mix with his. "Those are the things that are important to me. That's the Blake I fell in love with—the man who isn't perfect but is trying his best…" She brushed her lips over his, pulling a heartfelt sigh from him. "And his best feels pretty darn good."

Blake struggled to keep his wits about him. "How do you know I wasn't lying? That I'm not lying now?" Maybe he was a fool to ask, but he'd rather know for sure before he fell too deep to dig himself out.

"It's quite simple, really," she said. "All I need is your response to my plan."

"You have a plan?"

"I do. And only the best of men would go along with it."

Blake wouldn't consider himself the best of men, but somehow he knew he'd support Madison in anything she wanted to do. He couldn't hold back. He wrapped his arms tightly around her and buried his face in her neck. "I love you, Madison."

"I love you, too," she whispered.

Then he pulled back. "You know we come as a package deal now—Abby and me?"

"Absolutely…" She waited for a moment, then asked, "So, don't you want to know the plan?"

"It doesn't matter. I got the girl…girls. That's all I need."

Epilogue

Madison watched as Abigail charmed an older couple who had come to the exhibit. This might be the
little girl's "debut," but without a doubt, in her frilly
dress and hair ribbons and curls, she was stealing
the show from the main attraction.

Blake stood at the entrance to the rotunda at the
ASTRA, ready to answer any questions people might
have. In the past year, he'd become an expert on the
Belarus diamond and its caretaker of sorts. Madison
couldn't believe that he'd gone along with her plan.
But he'd not only supported her, he'd embraced the
purpose behind it and spent every day helping her
fulfill her goal.

To use the Belarus diamond to create funding for
those in need.

To that end, they'd arranged with the museum to exhibit it here for special functions. Part of the ticket proceeds would go to fund Maison de Jardin and charities like it. Ownership had been officially established with the charity. Madison didn't need or want the jewel. She had all she needed with her fiancé and the half sister who was now legally his child.

Trinity stepped up to her, resting her arm around Madison's shoulders as she took a sip of her sparkling water. No champagne for the mom-to-be.

Trinity's happy-ever-after had come around the same time as Madison's. The chaos and suspicions surrounding her first marriage and husband's death had been tough, but she'd been rewarded with a new husband…and a family of her own. Michael Hyatt's estates were in good hands, Trinity's hands, and Maison de Jardin was protected from vultures like Michael's relatives.

But even more important, the business consultant they'd hired was now Trinity's new husband. He'd rocked the Secrets and Scandals blog with his revelations, and come out on the other side as Trinity's biggest supporter and the father of her unborn baby. Their story was still a source of extreme interest from New Orleans' society.

"How's the second attraction of this little charity exhibit doing?" Madison asked with a chuckle.

Trinity grimaced. "Who knew so many nosy people would want to stare at a pregnant lady?"

"Only if said pregnant lady was the most talked about heiress in all of Louisiana…"

Trinity arched a brow in her direction. "You haven't done so bad yourself. I thought the phone would never stop ringing once your story broke."

"We both ended up with some pretty spectacular legacies, didn't we?"

Trinity smiled. "Funny how they weren't as important as the people that came with them, huh?"

Even if they weren't still here. They'd dedicated tonight's event to Madison's parents and Trinity's late husband, Michael, who had helped found Maison de Jardin.

But those legacies had brought other people into their lives: for Trinity, her new husband and the baby she was expecting, and for Madison, Blake and Abigail. For the first time in a long time, Madison's life felt full. Full to overflowing.

Blake's gaze caught hers from across the room. The intensity of his feelings reached her even though they weren't speaking. Not a day went by with him that wasn't her best. But tonight...tonight was special.

Somehow they both knew it.

Tamika sidled up to the girls, smiling over her champagne flute. "Ladies, I'm getting lucky tonight."

Madison and Trinity exchanged a glance. Tamika ignored them. "I figure all of this good luck has to rub off sometime. Trinity is married. Madison is getting close. We think. Surely it's my turn next."

"Go stand next to Blake."

"Why?"

"He's the lucky one."

"I didn't need to know that," Tamika said with a laugh.

"No, really. Today's the day."

Tamika and Trinity leaned in close. Madison smiled, unable to resist letting them in on the secret. She wiggled her fingers. "Because tonight, I think I'll let him put a ring on it."

* * * * *

*Scandal and seduction
go hand in hand
in the
Louisiana Legacies
duet:*

Entangled with the Heiress
Reclaiming His Legacy
by Dani Wade

*Available exclusively
from Harlequin Desire!*

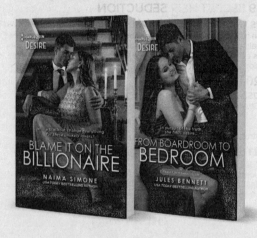

"So, as you can see, my father will stop at nothing to get what he
wants. He doesn't care who he hurts or maligns in the process. I
refuse to let your family become involved."

A frown settled on his face. "That's not your decision to make."

"What do you mean it's not my decision to make?"

"The Steeles can take care of ourselves."

"But you don't know my father."

"Wrong. Your father doesn't know us."

Mercury wondered if anyone had ever told Sloan how cute
she looked when she became angry. How her brows slashed
together over her forehead and how the pupils of her eyes became
a turbulent dark gray. Then there was the way her chin lifted and
her lips formed into a decadent pout. Observing her lips made him
remember their taste and how the memory had kept him up most
of the night.

"I don't need you to take care of me."

Her words were snapped out in a vicious tone. He drew in a
deep breath. He didn't need this. Especially from her and definitely
not this morning. He'd forgotten to cancel his date last night with

Raquel and she had called first thing this morning letting him know she hadn't appreciated it. It had put him in a bad mood, but, unfortunately, Raquel was the least of his worries.

"You don't?" he asked, trying to maintain a calm voice when more than anything he wanted to snap back. "Was it not my stolen car you were driving?"

"Yes, but—"

"Were you not with me when you discovered you were being evicted?" he quickly asked, determined not to let her get a word in, other than the one he wanted to hear.

"Yes, but—"

"Did I not take you to my parents' home? Did you not spend the night there?"

Her frown deepened. "Has anyone ever told you how rude you are? You're cutting me off deliberately, Mercury."

"Just answer, please."

She didn't say anything and then she lifted her chin a little higher, letting him know just how upset she was when she said, "Yes, but that doesn't give you the right to think you can control me."

Control her? Was that what she thought? Was that what her rotten attitude was about? Well, she could certainly wipe that notion from her mind. He bedded women, not controlled them.

"Let me assure you, Sloan Donahue, controlling you is the last thing I want to do to you." There was no need to tell her that what he wouldn't mind doing was kissing some sense into her again.

Don't miss what happens next in
Seduced by a Steele
by Brenda Jackson, part of her Forged of Steele series!

Available April 2020 wherever
Harlequin Desire books and ebooks are sold.

Harlequin.com

HDEXP0320

SPECIAL EXCERPT FROM

HQN

When India Robidoux needs help with her brother's high-profile political campaign, she has no choice but to face the one man she's been running away from for years—Travis, her sister's ex-husband. One hot summer night when Travis was still free, they celebrated her birthday with whiskey and an unforgettable kiss. The memory is as strong as ever—and so are the feelings she's tried so hard to forget...

Read on for a sneak peek of
Forbidden Promises *by Synithia Williams*

"We need everyone else in the family to demonstrate that family and friendships are still strong despite the divorce. I'm pairing Travis up with Byron and India."

India's jaw dropped. Everyone turned to her. Everyone except Elaina, who stood even more rigid next to the window.

"Me? Why me?" The words came out in a weird croak and she cleared her throat.

"Because you make sense," Roy explained.

Travis crossed the room to the food. India quickly stepped out of his way. Her hip bumped the table, rattling the platters set on the surface. Travis raised an eyebrow. She forced herself to relax and nod congenially. She wasn't supposed to react when he was near. They were cool now. They'd cleared the air. Deemed what had happened years ago a mistake. She couldn't run and hide when he came near.

She focused on Roy. "What do I have to do?"

"There will be a few times when we'll need family members to campaign for Byron if he can't be there personally. We've got a lot of ground to cover, and if we can show a united front, I'd recommend having at least two family members together in those cases. I'll partner you with Travis for those appearances. The two of you can play up how great he is as a brother and friend."

Roy made it all sound so easy. Sure, everything seemed simple to everyone else. They didn't realize the easy friendship she'd once shared with Travis was gone. No one knew she could barely look at him without thinking about how she'd loved him. How she'd dreamed about his kiss even after he'd married Elaina. Fought to forget the feel of his hands on her body as she'd stood next to her sister at their wedding.

"Now that that's settled," Roy said, obviously taking India's silence as agreement, "we can get to our next point."

"Are you okay with spending time with me?" Travis asked in a low voice.

India's heart did a triple beat. He'd slid close to her as Roy moved on. His proximity was like an electric current vibrating against her skin.

"Of course," she said quickly. "Why wouldn't I be?"

"You wouldn't be the only person not wanting my company lately."

The disappointment in his voice made her look up. He wasn't looking at her. He frowned at the floor. His lips were pressed into a tight line. She wanted to reach out and touch him. To attempt to erase the sadness from his features. "I'll always want your company."

His head snapped up and he studied her face. She really shouldn't have said that. The words were too close to how she really felt.

"We'll need to pick out a suitable fiancée for him."

Roy's voice and the randomness of his words broke India from the captivating hold of Travis's eyes. She tuned back into the conversation. "Fiancée? Who needs a fiancée?"

Byron chuckled and placed a hand on his chest. "I do."

India looked from her father to Byron. Were they serious? "You didn't mention you were getting married."

Byron shrugged as if not mentioning a possible fiancée wasn't a huge deal. "I didn't decide to ask her until recently. We've been dating for a few months."

Dating for a few months? Wasn't he the same guy Travis had teased about three women calling him just yesterday? Her brother was a ladies' man, but he wasn't a dog. He wouldn't be considering marriage to someone if he still had multiple women calling his phone. Would he? Had he changed that much while she'd been gone?

She spun toward Travis. "You aren't letting him do this, are you?" She pointed over her shoulder at her brother.

Travis stilled with a chocolate croissant halfway to his mouth. "Do what?"

She stepped closer and lowered her voice. "Marry this Yolanda person. Who is she? Are they really dating?"

Travis sighed. "They've gone back and forth for a while."

Which really meant that her brother had been sleeping with her for a few months, but there was no commitment. Her hands balled into fists. She couldn't believe this!

"Don't spout off the campaign bullshit with me," she said in a low voice that wouldn't carry to her plotting relatives still in the room. "Not with me. This is a campaign maneuver."

"Roy has a point." Travis said the words slowly, as if he couldn't believe he was agreeing with Roy. "Your brother can't be a senator if he's out there picking up women in bars. He's got to settle down. Yolanda is who he chose."

"Did he choose her?" She wouldn't doubt that Roy, or their dad, picked the perfect woman for him.

"He said he chose her."

"Do you believe him?"

Travis glanced at the group huddled together. "I want to believe him. Giving up what you want for an unhappy marriage isn't worth the price of a senate seat." He turned a heavy gaze on her. "Not when it ruins a true chance at happiness."

India leaned back. She was stunned into silence. Her throat was dry and her stomach fell to her feet. The regret in his eyes created a deep ache in her chest. Had he given up something for an unhappy marriage? Before the words could spill from her lips, he took a bite of the croissant and strolled over to join the strategizing team, leaving India with another unanswered question to taunt her at night.

Don't miss what happens next in
Forbidden Promises by Synithia Williams!
Available February 2020 wherever
HQN books and ebooks are sold.

HQNBooks.com

PHSWEXP0320